The Beaufort Woman

Book Two

of

The Beaufort Chronicle

Judith Arnopp

Copyright © JudithArnopp2019
Second Edition

The author has asserted their moral right under the Copyright, Designs and Patents Act 1988, to be identified as the author of this work.
All Rights reserved. No part of this publication may be reproduced, copied, stored in a retrieval system, or transmitted, in any form or by any means, without the prior written consent of the copyright holder, nor be otherwise circulated in any form of binding or cover other than that in which it is published and without a similar condition being imposed on the subsequent purchaser.

A CIP catalogue record for this title is available from the British Library.
Cover design by Covergirl

Edited by Cas Peace
www.caspeace.com

Dedication

The Beaufort Chronicle is dedicated to my parents, Doreen Lily Robson, 1923 - 2015, and Victor Ronald Robson 1920 - 2016. Thank you for showing me the way.

Other books by Judith Arnopp:
The Beaufort Bride: Book one of The Beaufort Chronicle
The King's Mother: Book Three of The Beaufort Chronicle
The Heretic Wind: The life of Mary Tudor
Sisters of Arden
A Song of Sixpence: The story of Elizabeth of York and Perkin Warbeck
Intractable Heart: The story of Kathryn Parr
The Kiss of the Concubine: A story of Anne Boleyn
The Winchester Goose: at the court of Henry VIII
The Song of Heledd
The Forest Dwellers
Peaceweaver

Part One

Lady Stafford

<u>Bourne, Lincolnshire - June 1460</u>

The ground passes swiftly beneath me. I cling to the reins, my eyes half closed, avoiding low branches as I thunder through murky brown puddles. At my side, a sudden splash of colour; a red cloak, a blur of chestnut flank, and with the wind in my ears, I turn my head and smile at Harry.

With a grin of determination, he drives his horse harder, pulling ahead of me, throwing up clods of mud that spatter my face and skirts. I laugh aloud and dig my heels in harder; my mount lifts his head and surges forward, his nose drawing level with our opponent's tail.

Harry turns in the saddle, waves an arm and shouts something, but his voice is quickly swallowed by the speed of the chase. We thunder on and before I know it, a ditch appears from nowhere and my horse and I take flight. As we soar through the air, the wood falls silent and time seems suspended. I cling to the reins, hold my breath, out of control, afraid I will fall.

With a jolt, his forefeet touch solid ground and I am forced forward onto his neck. To my relief, he pulls up sharp and stands head down, his sides heaving, his mouth foaming. I sit up and raise my hand to straighten my veil but it is gone, lost somewhere on the wild ride, leaving my hair in a tangle down my back. I have a brief vision of Mother's face were she to see me now, muddy and dishevelled in full view of our attendants.

"Margaret!" Harry wheels his horse about, slides from the saddle to grasp my bridle, and places a hand on my boot. "Are you all right? I was afraid that last ditch would see you on the ground."

I grope for composure, try to still my beating heart and cool my burning cheeks. Managing to laugh, I look down at my husband and feign a jaunty smile.

"I was determined not to fall, Harry. You need not have worried; but I appear to have mislaid my cap and veil."

The hind will be far into the thicket by now. Harry and I turn and look back into the soft green wood to see one of our squires leaping puddles as he hurries in my wake to return my cap.

"Thank you."

I take it from him and, without the aid of my women, do my best to put it on straight, arrange the veil to hide my ruined hair before we begin a leisurely ride home.

"The quarry is long gone." Harry wipes his brow and gathers his reins, ready to mount again. On this occasion, the deer escaped unscathed, but we will not go hungry for our larders are well stocked, our cellar replete with wine. It is not need that calls us from our fireside to hunt, but the longing for fresh air. I feel vital and alive. I run a gloved hand down my horse's neck and turn again to smile at Harry.

So far, he has proved a good husband. He lacks the noble looks of Edmund, but I am learning there is more to a man than a fine physique. My life with Edmund was spent waiting and worrying but, as

Harry's wife, most of my days are spent with him, and hunting is not the only pleasure we share. Harry is a quiet, studious man whose interests lie in books rather than war; he prefers to be home, running his estates and caring for his tenants than careering around the country in the service of the king.

He is loyal to King Henry, of course, but he takes little part in the disputes that continue to beset the throne. The feud between the two royal houses endures; they fight, cousin against cousin, their households forced to take sides and no one allowed to remain impartial.

At the end of last year, the Duke of York fled to Ireland, and his cousin and ally, the Duke of Warwick, took refuge in France. Now, there is an uneasy peace as the country waits to see what will happen next. For a while at least, Harry and I are free to relax.

Letting our mounts cool and catch their breath, we ride with long, loose reins toward home, and soon the timbers of the house come into view. We pause at the top of the hill to allow our attendants to catch up, and the servants at the castle, noticing our approach, scurry about in preparation for our arrival. I glance at Harry, catch his eye and issue an unspoken challenge.

Without a word, we simultaneously dig in our spurs, surprising our horses into life again as we compete to see who shall be the first to reach home. At the sound of our speeding hooves a cry goes up and, just in time, they throw open the gates. As we clatter over the drawbridge and into the bailey, Harry is just ahead. He leaps from his horse and hurries to assist me from mine. We are both breathless.

"I beat you squarely, Margaret. Admit it, you are defeated. I am the better horseman."

"Perhaps I allowed you to win; had you thought of that?"

He throws back his head with a snort of derision and, as we ascend the steps, I try to take his elbow. But instead, he throws an easy arm around my shoulders and plants a kiss on my forehead.

"Of course you did, sweetheart. Of course you did."

After the brightness of the day, the hall is dark. Slowly pulling off my gloves, I blink while my eyes readjust. Harry pours a cup of wine, continuing to crow of his prowess in the saddle until a boy comes forward and hands him a message. I toss my cloak at a hovering servant.

"Bring us some more refreshment, this wine is rancid," Harry says, unrolling the parchment and carrying it to the window where the light is better. "Damn!"

I turn, surprised at his profanity.

"What is it, Harry? Not Henry; it isn't bad news of my son?"

I hurry forward, my heart suddenly sick, and reach for the letter.

"No, no," he says, his brow furrowed as he scrunches the parchment into my palm. "It isn't from Pembroke. It is from my father. Salisbury and Warwick have landed in Kent and are marching on London, and he rides to defend the capital. I am summoned to join him."

Without reading it, I let the letter drop, and pull a face.

"Must you?"

"I have to go; there is no way I can refuse."

A thousand reasons why he shouldn't leave rush through my mind; silly things like an appointment with the tailor, the regime of care we have embarked upon for his skin complaint, the sick horse in the stable that he has been tending. I open my mouth to speak but he is already turning way, bellowing for his squire.

"How long will you be gone?"

He does not heed me; my voice is lost in the hubbub. Silently cursing York and his persistent dissent, I follow in Harry's wake, waiting for my chance to speak, but he is soon lost among a crowd of retainers.

I fall back, barely able to see the top of his head in the clamour, but I can hear his voice. His scribe hovers at the back of the crowd, quill in hand, straining to hear so he may list Harry's instructions.

I am forgotten.

Reaching for a cup of wine, I slump into a chair. I realise the futility of trying to prevent him from leaving. The friction at court has become untenable, and late last summer violence broke out again with a heavy humiliating defeat for the king at Blore Heath, which was quickly followed by victory for Lancaster at Ludford two weeks later.

The conflict between the two houses is like a great seesaw; one moment the king is winning, the next he is cast down. When York's army scattered and he and Warwick fled to exile overseas, I had hoped it was all over. Since then, things have been quiet; I cannot believe it is to begin again.

As painful as it is to see Harry go, I know it is his duty to answer his father's call yet I cannot help but remember when Edmund rode away from Lamphey on that last day. Despite everything that has happened to me since, I cannot forget that.

During the two years Harry and I have been married, I have become fond of him. It is an easy relationship, much easier than the one I had with Edmund. He treats me as an equal, appreciative of my skills in the still-room, gently encouraging my studies, and tolerant of my devotion to God, which inwardly I fear he does not share.

Harry has a gentle humour, a compassion for those less fortunate, and a wry and sometimes cynical opinion of his betters. As a younger son, he has come to accept his lot in life, his ill health, and his political obscurity. We are rich but not so prominent that we are constantly at the beck and call of court, but the quiet, country life we live suits us, and he is a good stepfather to my son.

The one thorn in my shoe is my separation from little Henry, but we have made several visits to Wales and I am touched by and grateful for my husband's obvious affection for my boy. I can never give Harry a child of his own but I have bequeathed him mine, and it warms my heart to see their flourishing relationship.

Ours is a good match, a good choice. I have benefitted from his gentleness and he has benefitted from my knowledge of herbs and medicine. His sore skin is soothed now; the nightly creams and poultices I take so long to prepare have brought him ease and, with the constant itching soothed, he can now sleep at night. Without me to ensure he keeps up the regime, however, he will soon become uncomfortable again, and all my work will be undone. I want to remind him of this but I do not speak of it, for I know he would scorn my concern.

It seems our honeymoon is over, the long period of peace is ended; our days of placid domesticity may seem dull to some, but I don't want them to end. I do not complain. I stay calm and quiet as I watch his preparations for battle, and never once do I let my smile drop.

"Farewell, sweetheart." He kisses my brow. "I will be back soon."

He moves away, and before I can stop myself, I grab the sleeve of his coat. He turns, a questioning frown on his forehead, his eyes silently beseeching me not to make a fuss.

"Take this," I say, pressing a small glass phial into his palm. "Apply it each evening before you retire."

He laughs. "My squire will think less of me but, for you, Margaret, I will do as you ask."

One more kiss and he is hurrying away, calling for his horse, setting the dogs barking. With a flourish of banners and a clash of armour, the troop ride beneath the gate and a sorry peace descends with the dust.

It seems I am destined to be left behind, alone.

In the solitude, with little to distract me, my thoughts turn to my son. I know he has a comfortable home at Pembroke and is as safe as a boy can be, but I cannot shake off the nagging worry that he might be ailing. Deciding a visit is overdue, I summon Harry's steward.

"Oh, Master Bray. Your step is so soft it startled me."

"I apologise, Madam. I will endeavour to tread more heavily next time I approach."

"I want to travel to Pembroke to visit my son. Please make the arrangements for my journey."

He hesitates, clears his throat.

"I don't believe that is wise, my lady. The armies are mustering and the roads will be full of men, and besides ... my lord of Pembroke will not be at home. He will surely be fighting for the king."

I had forgotten that but it makes me no less determined to go. With just the household staff for company, Henry will be alone – vulnerable, and perhaps in need of me.

"But my son will be there. It is he I wish to see."

"I fear …. If you will pardon me, my lady, my Lord Stafford would not forgive me should I allow you to travel. Wait a few days and he is sure to escort you there on his return. There is much unrest in the countryside…" He clears his throat again, plainly embarrassed at having to deny me. I take pity on him. He is a good man.

"Very well."

I press my lips together firmly, suppressing sudden disappointed tears. They build in my chest. I want to sob, cry like an infant and demand he do as I say, but I am too well schooled to give in to a display of pique. Instead, I raise my chin and look him squarely in the eye. "I shall write to my son instead. Ask a page to fetch me pen and parchment."

"I will fetch it myself, my lady."

He leaves as quietly as he came, and while I await his return, I stare moodily into the flames. My arms ache for want of Henry. It has been almost six weeks since I saw him last; he is growing up quickly and I am afraid he holds more affection for his nursemaid than for me. A self-pitying tear pricks at the corner of my eye, but I blink it away.

I have no time for weeping.

When Master Bray brings my pen, I quickly scrawl a letter to Myfanwy, hoping and praying she is still in residence at the castle. Shortly after I left Pembroke, she retired to one of Jasper's estates in the north and there gave birth to his illegitimate daughter, but the last letter I received from her suggested she would be returning to the south as soon as she was churched. She has not yet written to confirm her arrival.

My husband considers my friendship with Myfanwy a great scandal, and so would my mother if she knew of it, but in my short life, I have made few lasting friends and I cling to this one, despite her scandalous ways.

Pray, send me word of my son, (I write.) *I fear for him in these tumultuous times. My husband is riding with his father in defence of the king, and I expect Jasper has been summoned too. It is hard for us women at such times and I constantly pray for the king's deliverance and a return to peace.*
Perhaps when Warwick and York are quelled, you can bring Henry here to us at Bourne for the summer. It seems so long since we were together, so long since there was real peace in the realm.

My pen scratches on, but it is a sorry substitute for dandling my child on my knee. I imagine rocking his sturdy body in my arms, resting my chin on his head, closing my eyes and inhaling his baby scent. For a while, lost in my dream, I am happy, but when I finally open my eyes, loneliness erupts from my throat in an ugly sob. My maid looks up from her place by the window, her startlement forcing me to control myself. I will not cry, not in front of her. Turning my head slightly away, I dab inconspicuously at my eye with the edge of my sleeve. I force my mind to other things but one thought is never far away. It constantly bobs to the surface, like a cork in the river.
If only Henry could be with me; if only I could bring him home for good.

For the next few weeks, when I am not on my knees in the chilly stone chapel, I meander about the house. I strum half-heartedly on my lute; I count the jars in the still-room, or prise emerging weeds from the crumbly soil in the garden. When I am not pretending to be busy, I spend far too long scanning the horizon in hopes of a message, either from Harry, or from Pembroke.

During a break in the rain, I venture outside; tread the wet gravel path where, despite carefully dodging puddles, the moisture soon seeps into my slippers. Weeds are already encroaching upon the young plants I put in a month ago. I stoop and dig my fingers into the earth, grasp a root and enjoy the small triumph of pulling it free.

While I am looking about for a basket to deposit it in, the rain begins again. Cursing beneath my breath, I wipe the sticky soil on my apron, and head for the shelter of the hall. As I draw near, I hear the sound of a horse galloping fast along the castle road.

I pick up my skirts and hurry toward the bailey, arriving just as the messenger dismounts from his lathered horse. I grab for his bridle, backing off as the beast snorts a mouthful of green foam across my bodice.

"Are you sent by my husband? What news have you? Is he safe? Is he wounded?"

The messenger pulls his forelock, fumbles in his bag, and brings forth a damp, crumpled message.

"The battle is lost, my lady, but your husband lives, as far as I know. He escaped by the skin of his teeth. My Lord Buckingham was eager to fight, win the battle and get back to London to reclaim the Tower from York, but it was hard going. This damn ... begging your pardon, the rain turned the field into a quagmire. We would have had the victory had Lord Grey and some others not turned their coats. They stood by, my lady, and let Edward of March right through their ranks. There was nothing we could do against him. The whole thing was over in half an hour or less. It was a rout, my lady. I daresay Sir Harry's message contains the detail …"

He hands me a muddy note and I tear it open, frown at my husband's handwriting, scrawled in such haste it is barely legible. I tilt back my head, feel the rain spotting my face, and address the sky.

"Oh, my God, not Harry's father? Not Buckingham?"

The messenger pulls off his cap and hangs his head.

"I am afraid it is true, my lady. The Duke of Buckingham and several of our best men: Beaumont, Egremont, Shrewsbury and Sir William Lucy were slain in defence of the king, but … the king himself … the king has been taken …"

"Taken? York has dared to lay hands on the king? Where has he been taken to?"

"I do not know, but you should take some comfort from the news that the queen and the prince rode north to safety before the battle commenced. We will fight another day, my lady. It is not over yet."

My mind darts hither and thither, one thought falling quickly on the heels of another. The queen may be safe, but how can we fight on when the king is in enemy hands? Without our king, we are disempowered.

I wish Harry were here so I could comfort him. Poor bereaved Harry! What will we do without his father's support? I try to calm myself, imagine Harry's measured voice reasoning that, although the losses are grievous and we are faced with a greater challenge than ever before, of course, Lancaster will never be vanquished.

Rather than putting my mind at rest, the message has thrown me into deep turmoil. The days drag by so slowly, yet I can settle at nothing. I tug half-heartedly at the weeds, deal with the household matters as perfunctorily as I can before taking myself off to pray in the cool, dark chapel. It is my only comfort. The only action I can take.

On my knees for many hours, I pray for my late father-in-law, I pray for Harry, I pray for the king in the hands of his enemy, and I pray for the queen and her infant son, exiled in the north.

The future is a bleak blank wall. Here, in the relative safety of Bourne Castle, I cannot see beyond my next meal, my next prayer, so how much worse must Queen Margaret feel with her husband taken and his country in the hands of the foe?

The world has gone mad; all that I have been bred to take for granted is overturned.

Bourne, Lincolnshire – August 1460

The summer I had so longed for drags on. I walk the garden path alone; the sun casts shadows through palmate leaves, the spring flowers wither and die, replaced by lush, green foliage, thick stalked daisies, and dark nettles that clamour against the fence.

With just the household for company, I feel like an exile, cast adrift from the rest of the world with only letters from my mother and my sister Edith to break the monotony.

Mother, blinkered to the troubled world around her, is full of advice on how to conceive a child. She has never quite accepted the fact that Henry's birth left me barren, and fails to see that, even if I were fertile, the absence of my husband would make conception impossible.

With a stifled snarl of impatience, I toss her letter aside and turn to Edith's but soon let it fall into my lap. It is full of gossipy, housewifely tips, and questions about Henry's constitution that I have no hope of answering. For while I am here, breaking my heart over our separation, my son remains in Wales, bonding with whichever woman has the luxury of caring for him.

Why have I heard nothing?

Why has Myfanwy not written?

It is my nature to fear the worst and, as the weeks of silence stretch into months, I cannot rid myself of the idea that Henry is ailing, so sick and malnourished that they are too afraid to tell me of it. When night falls, I can find no peace. I pace the floor of my chamber, growing hotter and more distressed with every turn of the room. In the end, I snatch up my pen and write; just nine words scrawled across the page.

For the love of God, Myfanwy, send me news.

Without wasting another minute, I call for a messenger who, when he appears, is yawning, his hair looking as if he has been out in a high wind.

"This message is of vital importance, and is to reach Pembroke Castle as quickly as you can get it there. Do not spare your horse."

"Yes, my lady."

He bows awkwardly and repeatedly, as if I am the queen herself, and I realise he is new here. I have not seen his face before. I hope he can be relied upon. As he rides away into the gathering dusk, I bite my lip, willing him to reach Pembroke unscathed.

He has been gone just one hour when I hear the sound of a horse returning, and realise he must have run into trouble on the road. I stretch my neck, peering from the window into the ill-lit yard. His horse is grey and dusty, foaming with sweat and, with a twist of my stomach, I realise it is not my messenger returned at all. This is a different man, and he bears the livery of Jasper Tudor.

With a cry of relief, I dart across the room, throw open the chamber door. My shawl catches on the latch and, in my haste, I trip over my skirts, almost falling, but I manage to save myself, skittering down the stairs and arriving dishevelled and breathless in the bailey below.

The messenger has just dismounted. He reaches for his saddlebag, delves into it and retrieves a rolled parchment before turning, his eyes scanning the walls of the castle and the numerous windows of the lord's apartments.

Barely containing my impatience, I wait while he makes his slow approach. There is something familiar about the set of his head on his shoulders, the way his hair falls across his brow.

"Ned?"

I step from the shadow of the keep, put up a hand to shield my eyes from the glaring torches. "Ned? It is you? Oh, I am so glad to see you! You have grown so tall!"

I grab his hand, preventing myself from kissing him just in time. It has been three, nay, almost four years since I saw him last and he has grown from a gangling lad into a young man. His grin is as crooked and wide as ever.

"My lady." He sweeps off his cap and bows as he has been taught.

"You have news, Ned? From Jasper? How is Henry? Have you seen him? Is he well?"

"Very well, my lady. I have the marks to prove it." He draws back his sleeve to reveal a yellowing bruise on his bony wrist."

"Henry did that?" I open my eyes wide, relieved when he answers my query with a laugh.

"Your son plays rough, my lady. Before he left for the fight, my Lord Pembroke gave him a wooden sword and young Henry has elected that I should be his enemy. You can imagine who the victor might be."

The parchment is in my hand but I am so enrapt in the picture Ned is painting that I do not open it at once.

"And how are you, Ned? You look well. You will soon be joining Jasper's troop?"

He looks downhearted.

"Nay, Lady. My chest ... I, I am short of breath and have not the stamina for a fight although I do not lack the heart."

"I am sure you do not. Come, come inside. I will order refreshments brought to my chambers, and you can tell me more about my son. He thrives, you say?"

I spend the next hour reconciling this tall fellow with the boy I had last seen at Pembroke. He had been wounded in Edmund's service, receiving an arrow in the chest after a skirmish with our old enemy, ap Nicholas. I had seen to his injuries and, to facilitate a full recovery, taken him into my household until he healed enough to re-join my husband's troop. On the day Edmund rode to his death, Ned stayed behind with me.

He proved a more than loyal servant, supporting me in my early widowhood, aiding me when I was all alone and my birth pangs began, but somehow, when I left Pembroke to begin my marriage to Harry, he was left behind. His sudden reappearance in my life, the familiar grin, the quirk of his brow, brings those days rushing back. I had been so young, and so afraid. It now all seems ... well, a long time ago.

"And Myfanwy; has she returned to Pembroke?"

Poor Ned has just taken a bite of pie. He struggles to chew and swallow before replying, wipes his mouth on his sleeve.

"Yes, my lady. She is well." He takes another bite, licks crumbs from his lips, and speaks with his mouth half-full. "Why don't you read the letter?"

I get up and move away, leaving him in peace with his pie and ale. The parchment is smooth beneath my fingers; I shiver, anxious of what lies within. With a deep breath, I move closer to the window and roll it out, squinting at Myfanwy's spidery scrawl.

Do forgive me for not writing sooner. Every day I had hoped for some word from Jasper so that my news to you might be more positive. I know you must be worried, about Henry, about your husband, and about Jasper and the king and queen too. I shall do my best to relate all I know, which I am sorry to say, is not much.

Henry is thriving. That is good news to your ears, I know. Of Jasper I am not so sure. I have had messages but the news in them is so extraordinary I am not sure I have understood it correctly. It seems that Queen Margaret has been in dire straits. Half her retinue has deserted her and one of her own servants took her prisoner, threatening to kill her and the prince. While he was in the process of stealing all her jewels, she had the wit to escape and fled to Jasper at Harlech. The messenger who brought the news claimed she rode pillion with some young commoner. I have it on good authority that Jasper plans to move her to Denbigh as soon as he can arrange it.

The times we live in are so extraordinary, Margaret. I do hope there is an end to it soon. I long for stability but we must be strong like the queen who, although she lives in daily fear of assassination, is already mustering another army. Jasper says her one aim is to regain custody of the king and send York and his cronies packing, back where they belong. Lancaster is not beaten yet.

As for Henry, all these troubles pass over his head. He practices daily with a little wooden sword, attacking the legs of the servants and lording it over his playmates. God-willing, peace will come soon and you can visit us here, or perhaps we can travel to England to spend some time with you. I speak of you every day so that he will keep you in his memory and he sends his blessings and love.

Oh, one last thing, Margaret. I am concerned about Ned and wonder if you know a tonic that will aid him. He droops every time Jasper rides off without him and his chest shows no improvement. He has a dry, nasty cough that no amount of remedies will cure; perhaps you have more knowledge than I. Do you think you can make him well enough to return to soldiery, or should he seek another path?

And so Ned stays with me. At first, he resists the cup of medicine I bid him drink each night at bedtime. I tell him he must nurture his cough if he wants to ever be fit enough to fight or to win his spurs. I can see by his scathing look that he recognises my lie and, with a twist of guilt at misleading him, I try to convince him there are other paths he could follow.

"Life isn't all about war, Ned," I tell him, but even to my own ears, my words do not ring true. All my brothers were raised to be knights; it is the way of the world. Young boys are sent to the households of great lords to be trained in the skills of warfare. What else is there?

"What else is there?" Ned asks, as if reading my mind.

"Oh ... lots of things. You could be a politician, a statesman, a scholar."

He looks at me darkly. "No, I couldn't. I don't have the mind for that, but I have the heart for battle. I should ride in defence of my king. I should cut York down and put another in his place."

My laugh is tinged with bitterness. If only that were possible, but Ned is as useless as I am. I also long to put right the wrongs of this sorry world. I pour the brew into his cup.

"Drink it and go to bed now. We will think more of your future in the morning."

He looks ruefully at the thick brown liquid.

"If this doesn't kill me," he says with a grimace before tipping it down his throat.

When I was a child, I pictured myself in charge of a great household as I am now but, in my dreams, there was feasting, music and dancing, fine clothes and regular trips to court. I never imagined endless days of solitude and anxiety for an absent husband. I am tired of my workaday gown, the monotony of my household duties, and resent my exclusion from the events surrounding the crown.

The summer drags on. Slowly, the fields begin to turn colour, the wheat in the meadows waves softly in the wind like a warm yellow sea. At the end of the month of October, the crops are harvested and stored in the vast barns in readiness for winter. The apple store smells of summer, the fruit bulging with goodness, and in the dairy the shelves are lined with round cheeses, all neatly wrapped in cloth. The surplus livestock has been slaughtered, cut and salted, great hams hang from the ceiling of the kitchen storeroom, and barrels of herring are ranked along the walls. Winter may do its worst and we will not starve. We are ready.

I begin to plan projects for the long cold nights; an altar cloth for the chapel, new covers for the chairs in the hall. Knowing the weather will soon turn for the worse, I have taken to spending an hour or so each evening on the parapet walk of the outer wall. I drink in the last dregs of the dying sun and dream rich warm dreams of the day when civil unrest will cease, Harry will come home, and I can be reunited with my son.

Far below me, our tenants are collecting the last vestiges of wheat from the field. They have been there since supper time, their figures nothing more than shadows on the bright landscape. I close my mind against worry, rest my cheek against sun-warmed stone, and watch them at their toil.

There are six men and three women, their aprons swollen with their gleanings. Every so often, the light evening wind wafts their voices toward me, high, sing-song sounds of the day's end.

As I watch, one man stands, puts a hand to his aching back and the other to his brow. Then he points into the distance and calls to his companions, who straighten up, their gaze following the line of his finger. I also turn and squint into the setting sun and discover a cloud of dust betokening the approach of a small party of horse.

Placing both hands on the parapet, I strain my neck forward and narrow my eyes, trying to discover whose badge the horsemen wear. Is it a message from Harry, or from Myfanwy?

As the tiny dots on the horizon gain shape and become discernible figures, I catch my breath and look again, wishing I were blessed with long sight.

The rider at the fore is mounted on a bay horse but they are as common as sparrows, it could be anybody. As I watch, my heart begins to beat just a little faster. I keep my eye on the man in front and, as he draws nearer, I see he has taken off his helm, his balding head glinting in the dying light.

My breath catches in my throat. I lean perilously forward over the battlement, hardly daring to believe it is truly Harry come home at last.

Soon, he is close enough to return my wave. Unheeding of the tears that have leached unnoticed from my eyes, I climb down the winding stair. I have to force myself to tread carefully. I take deep breaths, grip the hand rail with shaking fingers, taking one step at a time, unwilling that my husband should be greeted by a frantic, dishevelled wife.

By the time Harry's small troop rides beneath the gate, I am waiting calmly at the door, my hands decorously clasped before me, my heart thumping so wildly in my chest, I fear I may be sick. As he swings from the saddle and turns to face me, I take mental note of the weight he has lost, the dark circles that ring his eyes, the new creases above his nose.

"Harry," I say, taking one step closer, waiting impatiently while he frees himself from his gauntlets and tosses them to his squire.

"Margaret!"

He holds out his arms and, although he is filthy from the road, stinks of sweat, horse and wood smoke, and his skin is as red and sore as a leper's, I move into the circle of his embrace.

Two hours later, Harry has been fed and is sitting in a tub while the filth of the road leaches into warm, scented water. He has sent his man away and gladly I play the part of a servant, pouring jugs of water over his head and kneeling to scrub his nails with a stiff brush.

"You don't need to do this, Margaret."

I look up at him, smile because it is so good that he is here with me again.

"I know, but it pleases me."

I plunge his hand back into the water, watch the suds dissipate. "I am so sorry about your father. He was very good to both of us ... he never once reproached me for not giving him a grandson."

A surge of water slops onto the floor as Harry hauls himself up, splashing me as he reaches for a towel. He steps from the tub, leaving large wet puddles as he hurries to sit naked at the hearth. He rubs his hair, emerging red-faced.

"He had a grandson already. The vacant dukedom will now be filled by a six year old ..."

"Yes, I know little Henry – he is my cousin Margaret's son, although I have not met him. My mother makes certain I am kept abreast of family matters. Poor little mite, his wardship will no doubt now be in the hands of the king."

"No doubt; or that of York - in all but name."

I fetch another towel and begin to rub his back, noting the red wheals left by his scratching. When he is dry, I hold out a loose gown.

"Put this on and wait a while. I will send a girl to fetch some salve from the still-room. You really shouldn't scratch so."

"It itches like the devil."

"I know, but scratching will only make it worse." I let out a sigh. "We had gone so far in treating it, and now we are back where we started."

I pour a cup of wine and hand it to him. "If you are not too tired, perhaps you can tell me all you know of what is happening. Where is the queen? And the king, is he well cared for? Is York allowing his physicians access? I should imagine it suits them for the king to remain in madness."

Harry stretches and lies back in his chair, flicks the ends of the cloak over his legs.

"The last I heard, the king was quite well; just over-eager for peace and too obliging to those he should know by now are his enemies. They have only to swear fealty to him and he forgives their sins against him."

"He is a good man. It should not be seen as a failing."

"Kings have no business being so virtuous. Especially when the country is on its knees."

A girl hands me a trio of small jars. I pull out the stopper and signal for Harry to slip from his robe. Drawing a candle closer, I apply the salve in small dots over the worst of his lesions. I pray he is not on the verge of another attack; sometimes when his skin becomes too inflamed, fever consumes him.

I have discovered that his condition is called St Anthony's Fire, and among the numerous remedies, none of which have proved very successful, is the recommendation to offer up prayer to St Anthony. I have lately made it my daily habit to do so.

When he tires of my ministrations, he pulls away and wraps himself up in his robe again. He stares gloomily into the fire. Since his return, I have done all I can to cheer him, offering comfort and sustenance. During his absence, it was his light-hearted banter I missed, his cynical humour and gentle teasing, but the man who has returned home to me is morose. I am unsure if I should probe the reasons why, or go to bed and leave him to his musing. He sighs lustily, and draws his eyes from the flames.

"I am sorry, Margaret. I am poor company tonight."

"You are tired. Why not go to bed now? Things will look better in the morning."

He sits up.

"You might as well know it, my dear. York has persuaded the king to sign an agreement; the act of accord, they are calling it. It allows the king to rule for the remainder of his life time, but names York as his heir. King Henry is disinheriting his own son."

My mouth drops open.

"Disinheriting Edward? The queen will be furious! Oh, Harry, you don't think he has listened to the rumours York is spreading about the prince not being the king's son? Surely he would not heed such a lie!"

"I don't know, I don't know. None of us can reach the king; many have sought audience, only to be turned away with the excuse that his health will not allow it. Only York has the king's ear."

I sink to my knees, place a hand on Harry's arm, and drop my voice to a whisper.

"You ... Harry, you don't think York is so greedy for the crown that he would harm him?"

"How can I know the answer to that? Sometimes I think there are no limits to that man's ambition. We must await news from the queen; have you received word from Jasper? He was with her lately in Wales."

"Nothing, not for ages."

"Things should quieten down now, for a while at least. Perhaps it is a good time to travel to Pembroke to visit your son. I can ride from there to seek out Jasper and discover how the land lies."

"To Pembroke! Oh, Harry, when? When can we leave?"

Later, when we are tucked snug within our bed and have enjoyed gentle pleasure, he falls quickly asleep, leaving me wide awake, imagining little Henry's surprise when we arrive so unexpectedly.

I plan what gift to take with me. He is growing so fast, I have no idea what will please him. As the night wears on and daylight begins to peek between the shutters, my eyes at last grow heavy. The last thing I hear before I sleep is the cry of a cockerel heralding the morning.

<u>Pembroke Castle, Wales – late October 1460</u>

As soon as I can, I detach myself from our host, leaving him and Harry to masculine discussions of war and politics. Myfanwy puts down her needle as if to join me, but I hold up a hand.

"Please, I'd rather go alone."

I try to keep my step slow and steady, but as I move along the familiar passages, my feet move faster and faster of their own accord. With a shiver of remembrance, I pass the chamber where Henry was born, go up a few steps, down a few more, and reach the nursery. A servant comes forward from the gloom and, keeping his eye on the floor, bows before opening the door.

I pass into the antechamber, hold my finger to my lips to silence the nurse who is about to call out to my son. I do not want to alert him to my presence. Rather than meet the formal, polite child to whom I was introduced earlier, I want to observe him as he really is.

It is a cosy scene. A fire burns in the hearth, there are thick tapestries on the walls, the shutters are closed, and shadows from the flickering torches leap on the walls. Henry is sitting on his bed, his back toward me, his head bent, intent on something in his lap. A strip of pale white skin shows between his collar and his hair, a roll of fragrant flesh that I long to kiss. Beside him on the bed, a small brindle dog is slumbering. I watch for some time. My son is peaceful, content, not missing me at all.

This is his normality; the world he has grown up in. He will be fonder of his grubby-faced nurse than he is of me; he knows nothing of the raw, tearing pain that I suffer in his absence. I am glad of that, of course, but oh, how glorious it would be were he to turn and see me, his face lighting up with joy at our reunion. I long for him to rush into my arms but I know when he turns, he will show only indifference to my unprecedented appearance in his nursery.

The moments turn into minutes. Soon, his nurse will come to put him to bed, snuff out his candles. I should speak now, for the longer I watch, the shorter our time together will be but, suddenly, I am shy, uncertain what to say to this infant who is more stranger than son.

I draw in my breath, teetering on the edge of indecision, until the dog lifts his head, fixes me with a defensive stare and growls, low in his throat.

A ball tumbles to the floor, bounces twice as Henry twists round on the bed. He recognises me at once, and a red flush rises from his throat as he slides from the mattress and stands staring at me, uncertain what to do.

"Hello, Henry."

"Hello," he says, uncertainly.

I move into the room, forcing myself not to approach him directly. Instead, I pause to examine a collection of 'treasures' on his shelf; a small wooden sword, a few feathers, a handful of large broken seashells, a rather grubby red velvet ball.

"How lovely," I say, raising my head and smiling at him. He smiles in return.

"I used to collect things when I was a girl."

When I was a girl? I sound like an old woman, yet I am not yet eighteen. He steps a little closer, keeping one hand on the bedpost. I decide to keep talking, retain his interest, and prove I am a friend, an ally in his world of grown-ups. "I had a red ball too, and my brother made me a wooden doll, and my sister, your aunt Edith, fashioned it some clothes from the same fabric as my best gown. That doll became my best friend."

"Boys don't have dolls."

"No, no; of course not."

His dog grunts as it leaps from the bed and we both turn to watch him waddling toward me on gross short legs. I do hope he doesn't bite. I stand warily while he sniffs at the hem of my gown and, pretending to love dogs, I bend down to let him smell my hand. "What is his name?"

"Key."

"Key?" I wrinkle my brow. "What an odd name."

"Not key; *Ci*." He emphasises the last. At first, I think he is repeating the same word, and I am puzzled for a moment before realisation dawns. I remember that Henry is being raised in Wales.

"Oh, yes, of course. 'Ci' is the Welsh word for dog. How clever."

Hearing his name, the dog begins to bark, high ear-splitting shrieks. I stoop to ruffle the fur about his ears, more to silence him than anything else, but he bounces away, barking even louder than before.

"Quiet." Henry swipes his arm downward, and Ci desists, skulks away toward the hearth. "Silly dog! He gives my nurse a headache." Henry beams, his face lit with humour, and my heart lifts.

"Oh, poor nurse, we can't have that."

I fumble in my head for something engaging to say, something that will make him smile again. I am enraptured with his smile. "Your father had a dog, did you know that?"

He shakes his head, his wide eyes fastened on my face.

"When your father and Uncle Jasper were boys, Edmund, your – your father – he named his dog Jasper, for a joke – only your Uncle Jasper didn't think it very funny."

He is too young. The humour is lost on him, and my heart begins to sink. "It was all right, though, because your father, out of pity, shortened his dog's name to Jay. He was a fine old fellow. We lost him a few years ago, just before ..."

The conversation lapses. Henry smiles politely and our burgeoning friendship begins to founder until, suddenly inspired, I find a way to penetrate his infantile armour.

"I saw your friend, Ned, the other day. He was telling me of your prowess with the sword."

Henry, unsure if my words are genuine, yet certain his mother would never speak a mistruth, looks doubtful, his eyes sliding toward his wooden sword on the shelf. I give a light laugh, wishing I could lift him onto my lap and inhale the scent of his hair. "It is true. Poor Ned is quite black and blue; I gave him some special balm for his bruised wrist. He tells me you will make a fine knight."

"Like Uncle Jasper?"

"Yes, yes, Henry; just like him, and like your father too."

His face flushes, and with great daring I reach out and with one finger gently smooth his hair from his eyes. Like a nervous, shy puppy, he tolerates it, and it is all I can do not to sweep him into my arms and smother him in kisses.

"Perhaps tomorrow, Henry, you could show me round the castle? I spent a long time here but for most of it I was confined to my chambers, waiting for you to be born."

He opens his mouth to answer, but at that moment his nurse arrives. She hovers uncertainly at the door, bobs a curtsey when I turn my head.

"Pardon, my lady, but it is past Master Henry's bed time, and he will be so tired tomorrow; there are always ructions when he is tired."

My happiness drains away. Of course, as his mother I should know how tiredness affects my own child; I shouldn't need instruction on the matter. But I stand up, hold out my hand to Henry, and my heart lurches when he takes it in his hot, chubby fingers and kisses it.

"I will see you in the morning, Henry. Sleep well."

He bows his head, knuckles his eye and follows his nurse to the fireside, where she is shaking out his night rail.

I am not required here.

I turn and leave, meander back to the hall, my emotions in turmoil. I am glad, so very glad to be with him but oh, so heartsick at the gulf between us; a gulf so wide I have no idea how to cross it.

I rejoin the men in the hall. Myfanwy is still there, hovering in the background but taking no part in the conversation. Harry and Jasper rise when I enter, Harry looking at me questioningly.

"Henry is well," I say as I take my seat beside him and accept a cup of wine from Jasper. "He is growing so fast. I hope we can spend more time together over the coming week, I have a lot to make up for."

Harry clears his throat.

"We, Jasper and I, were discussing the situation at court. Jasper feels the queen will not rest until she has the king back under her control. Her hatred for York is in the open now; she isn't even pretending she wants to come to terms."

I swallow a mouthful of wine, and wait while it runs thick and warm to my belly.

"I am not entirely surprised. What woman wouldn't fight for the rights of her son? Whatever York's feelings on the matter may be, Edward of Lancaster is the rightful heir."

Myfanwy leans forward in her seat, her hands clasped as if to contain her excitement.

"You have, of course, heard the rumours?"

I turn sharply in her direction, noting with envy how her skin glows in the firelight, her eyes shining like warm jewels. Myfanwy forgets my blood ties with the queen's champion.

"The slurs against Somerset, you mean? It is nothing but vicious gossip."

Myfanwy sits up. "Yes, I know that, but ... perhaps York believes it."

"The slander is of his own making! No such calumny comes from our camp."

"Well, it is of little matter what his reasons are, the situation remains the same." Harry interjects some peace into the simmering quarrel. "With the king under York's control, we are rendered impotent. If we take action against York, he will waste no time in screaming 'treason'."

"But we would not be riding against the king, just his gaoler!"

Jasper gives a harsh snort of derision.

"He would not see it like that. With the king in his hands, York holds all the cards. If we move at all, we have to be very sure of victory or be prepared to suffer the consequences. I fear we won't have to wait very long before our queen begins mustering support. I just hope our armies are ready."

All eyes are on Jasper as the significance of his words sink in. Every man I know is prepared to die on the battlefield for the king, but to suffer the punishment for perceived treason against him is something else again.

Suddenly, Death, ignominious Death is in the room with us, our loyal words for the king tainted by York's treachery, our duty distorted into treason. As the silence stretches, Jasper becomes aware of our scrutiny. He sits up, his skin flushing a deeper shade of red. He slaps his knee, forces his face into confident lines.

"Anyway, this is dismal talk. Let us drink to the health of the king, and damnation to York and all his adherents."

He raises his cup and we all do likewise.

"To the king!" we repeat and drink deeply. No one names the Duke of York aloud, but I know that every one of us is silently calling down ill-fortune upon him.

December 1460

Christmas is quiet this year, the uncertainty at court reverberating across the country, even as far as Wales. We make an intimate party at the high table, looking down on the household as they devour the feast laid before them.

I am seated between Harry and Henry, enjoying my son's presence, noting what pleases and displeases him. His delight is contagious. He laughs aloud at the tumblers but grows restive during the course of a long dreary poem about a boy on a knight's quest.

The food is definitely to his liking. He insists on sampling every dish, and consumes spoonful after spoonful, even when he has clearly eaten his fill. Next to him, his grandfather, Owain, ruffles Henry's hair and looks over the boy's head into my eyes.

"He is the living image of his father, Margaret," he tells me. To save an argument, I agree, but it is not true. Henry is not at all like Edmund, or any of the Tudors. He has my eyes, sometimes a likeness to my uncle. Henry is Beaufort, through and through.

From Jasper's side, farther down the table, Myfanwy leans forward and points at Henry's drooping head.

"He has had enough, Margaret. You should send him to bed."

Myfanwy, of course, having birthed two of Jasper's illegitimate daughters, is an expert on raising children. I bite my lips against a tart reply, and take a closer look at Henry. His face is flushed, his eyes heavy and ringed with shadows, but he is valiantly fighting defeat. I should have realised and sent him away sooner, instead of selfishly keeping him at my side.

"I am not tired, Mother," he protests, as I summon his nurse.

"If you go to bed now, you will be fresh for tomorrow. I am not planning to join the hunt in the morning, but you and I could climb up to the top of the tower and watch them leave. We will have a good view from there, you can see for miles."

Usually nothing could keep me from the hunt, but Henry's pull is greater than that of the chase. He scrambles from his seat.

"Very well, Mother. Goodnight." As he has been taught, he takes my hand and stoops to kiss it but, weakened by the wine and the levity of the evening, I swoop down and take him in my arms, clamp him to my breast.

I feel the breath rush from his little body, and to my joy, his hands slide up about my neck. The feather in his cap tickles my nose as I close my eyes and inhale the sweet young scent of him.

"Goodnight, Henry," I say, as I release him so suddenly that he staggers, grabs at his nurse to steady himself. He tugs at the bottom of his jerkin, straightens his cap, and gives a small bow before allowing himself to be led away. At the door, he turns again and rewards me with a shy smile, raises his hand.

Once he has left the company, I grow bored. I have eaten more than enough, and since I have no interest in wine or dancing, and the topic of war is forbidden at Christmas, I begin to count the minutes until it is time to retire.

Another tray of wine is brought to the table, and a woman takes her position before the dais. She places a low stool on the floor, and runs her fingers across the strings of her harp. Instantly, the sound relaxes me, the music making my eyes sting as it flows like water about the hall. I rest my chin on my hand, begin to drift happily ...

Bang! Bang! Bang! A great rumpus at the door, and abruptly the music stops. I open my eyes, sit up straight and twist my head toward the disturbance.

"My lord!"

A messenger pushes his way through the huddle of servants who had gathered to listen to the singing. A little way from the dais, he pauses. His clothes are sodden, his legs muddied to the knee, and it is evident he has ridden hard.

The hall falls silent as Owain and Jasper stand to receive the message. Myfanwy reaches out to clasp the hem of Jasper's robe. Harry and I exchange glances. His face has turned quite pale.

Everyone knows the significance of the messenger at the Christmas feast; even in stories, they seldom bring good tidings. Jasper clears his throat and reads out the contents of the letter.

It is a call to arms, summoning the men to muster beneath the royal banner. The time has come. The queen has called all loyal Lancastrians to the fight, and the celebration is spoiled.

Jasper, shaking off the somnolence of too much wine, begins to issues orders in harsh tones. Owain shakes his grey head, drains his glass, and turns to me.

"So, unfortunately, our visit is to be cut short, Margaret. A pity, I was just getting to know little Henry."

His hand, large, warm and dry, swamps mine. He doesn't kiss it but instead draws me closer to place a kiss on my brow. I flush scarlet and bob a curtsey.

"When it is all over," I hear myself saying, "you must come to us in Lincolnshire."

He raises one eyebrow, his forehead furrowing doubtfully.

"What, all that way to the other side of England? By Christ, if I stray that far from Wales, I might wither and die."

Dutifully, I join him in laughter, but both of us know this is a poor time for joking. He sobers, lightly places a finger on my cheek. "But, do you know, Margaret, you and that boy of yours might be worth the trouble."

He lets go of my hand, spins on his heel and marches toward the door, calling on his squire and manservant to make ready his horse and belongings.

It is all over; the table is a vanquished battlefield of scattered bones and half eaten pastries. An upturned wine cup has tumbled onto a platter of apple tarts, flooding them with ruby wine that overflows, dribbling onto the cloth. A servant girl approaches with a tray, hesitates when she realises my presence. I wave a hand, instructing her to continue, and she begins to collect the plates, piling them onto her tray.

She is totally unconcerned with the events taking place around her. She thinks only of her task, cares nothing for war, whatever the outcome of the battle. No matter who sits on the throne or governs the country, her life will continue unchanged. Whether Jasper is in command or not, she will always be a servant at Pembroke. I, on the other hand, should York have victory over the queen, have very much to lose.

If Lancaster loses this fight, our actions will be seen as treason – as the wife of a traitor, I could forfeit everything, and Henry could be placed in danger, too.

"Margaret." Harry is coming toward me. He has exchanged his festive velvet for travelling clothes; his sword is strapped to his hip. He is pulling on thick gauntlets, ready to ride.

"What are you doing?" I cry. "Surely you will not ride out straight away? At least, wait until first light."

He places a hand on each of my shoulders and looks affectionately into my eyes.

"There is no time. I have to travel fast and light, Margaret. There is much to do, things to arrange. You are to stay here until it is safe to travel. Then, make straight for Bourne. I will send word to you as soon as I can."

A thousand questions and protests burst into my mind before exploding and dying like shooting stars. "Henry," I manage to stutter. "What about my son, shall I take him with me?"

"No, no, he is out of the thick of it here. It is safer at Pembroke than on the road."

"So, should I not stay here, if there is peril on the road? Why don't I wait with Henry to ensure his safety?"

He takes hold of my head, a hand over each ear, and kisses my brow.

"Because, if the worst comes to the worst, I may have need of you at Bourne. Be on the alert, Margaret. Expect the unexpected."

He kisses me again and hurries away, calling to his servants.

I raise a hand in farewell but he does not turn again. As I watch him go, Myfanwy's warm hand slides into mine. The servants continue to clear away the remnants of the feast, the hall empties until just we two remain, still in our festive finery, but quite alone.

Bourne, Lincolnshire - Spring 1461

Waiting for news of the outcome of the battle is like sitting in the dark. I am blind and can see not a step into the future. A thousand possible scenarios rage in my imagination. Lancaster vanquished, the queen taken, the royal family fallen into York's merciless hands, no one left to fight on.

For many hours, I kneel on hard cold stone until my knees are numb, and a screaming pain stabs in the small of my back. Lit only by candles, the frigid chapel becomes a place of hope, the beads of my rosary small round bargaining counters as I make a deal with God.

"Send Harry home safe, make us victorious, and I will be your servant."

Silently, I pledge my devotion. No matter where the future takes me, if He will only send us victory, I shall give my life unto Him. I bow my head, the beads press into my forehead as the chill seeps into my bony knees, and encroaches into my soul.

The candles gutter from a colder blast at my back, and I hear a footstep behind me. Torn rudely from God's presence, I turn my head, try to rise, but I have lost all feeling in my lower limbs. I stumble forward, but an arm reaches out and saves me from the fall.

"Ned?"

I cling to his sleeve and allow him to lead me on legs I cannot feel to the welcome sanctuary of a chair. "What news is there? Is there a message from my husband?"

He nods vigorously.

"I should say there is, my lady. A messenger is taking sustenance in the hall. The battle is won. Your lord is safe and ... York and his son are dead!"

"York is dead?"

For a moment I feel nothing, the news is like a blow to the stomach, but then feeling returns. I should not feel such joy, but suddenly it is as if a leaden weight has fallen from my shoulders. My prayers are answered! The brutal elation of victory surges through me. "The battle is won? And Harry, he is well? He is not wounded."

"I am sure the messenger would have mentioned that, my lady. Come, come with me, and you can question him yourself."

Still hobbling on numb feet, I make as fast a progress to the hall as I can.

Harry is not wounded. Lancaster has victory. York is dead.

The news circulates in my head, a smile stretches across my face and my heart beats fast in anticipation of further good news. God has blessed us, and I will not forget my promise.

I burst into the hall and the room falls quiet. The messenger tries to rise from his seat, but I wave him back down.

"No, remain seated," I tell him, taking note of his soiled clothes, his haggard, filthy face. The sleeve of his jerkin is missing and something that looks a lot like blood soaks his linen at the elbow. "Were you in the fight?" I ask him. He shakes his head.

"Nay lady, but I was set upon by deserters on the road. It is nothing." He waggles his arm around to assure me his wound is light.

"You'd better give me the message, and tell me everything."

A servant steps forward.

"I have it here, my lady."

I snatch the parchment, unroll it and frown in the ill-light to decipher three short lines of Harry's scrawl.

We have the victory, my love, and I will return home soon. York is no more and we are in ascendance. My messenger will tell you all. I will be with you as soon as I may.

Clutching the letter in my fist, I turn back to the messenger.
"Did you see the battle? How did it go? Were many lost?"
"There are always losses, my lady. I saw the battle only from a distance. Your lord is tired but he seemed unharmed."
"And York, how did he die?"
"In the battle, I do believe, my lady, and the Earl of Salisbury has been taken prisoner. Afterwards ..." He hesitates, licks his lips and turns a little pale.
"Go on with your tale."
I try not to interrupt him further, but beneath the cover of my gown my knees are quaking, my toe tapping with anticipation.
"During the battle there were many losses, and York was among them. His son, Rutland, was taken afterward, trying to escape north toward the town. After the battle, they ... his ... my Lord Clifford ordered that York's head, and that of his son, be taken and placed on the Micklegate Bar; they, erm ... they gave the duke a paper crown and made much mockery of him."
I try to make sense of his garbled tale.
"Salisbury is dead, and Rutland too? And they mocked them, you say?"
My elation diminishes.

"Salisbury still lives and they have taken him to Pontefract, my lady, but Rutland is dead. The victory took us all by surprise. York was outnumbered. His other son, Edward of March, was still on the road, not yet arrived at Sandal Castle. We expected the duke to stay inside, but, instead of waiting for his son, York suddenly broke his cover and met us on the field. None can fathom why."

"No."

I am struggling to accept his grisly tale. If York took such action against us, I would condemn them for it, but I cannot disparage my own queen. As queen consort, anointed by God, she is unassailable. I can only believe there were circumstances I know nothing of. I force a smile and turn back to the messenger.

"Thank you. Now, there is food and a bed waiting, and perhaps you would care for a bowl of warm water." I snap my fingers at a lurking maid servant. "See to it."

Turning on my heel, I hurry back to my apartment, take sanctuary again in my private chapel, and send my thanks to God along with a prayer for the souls of our departed enemies.

I feel no sorrow. York and his family are my cousins in blood but I cannot regret their deaths, not when it means so much to our cause. This victory at Wakefield means life will once more return to an even keel. Surely, nothing can stand in our way now. We will regain possession of the king and I can go to court again. I will order new gowns, some new shoes, and Harry and I will dance beneath the gaze of our restored monarchs.

But soon, terrible stories filter to me of the queen's ire, and our glory is dimmed. The gossips are saying that after the battle, when the heads of York and Salisbury were taken to her, she mocked them. I try to reconcile the woman I met all those years ago with the harridan who reputedly slapped the face of her dead enemy before ordering his head crowned in paper and stuck upon the highest tower.

These stories must surely be slander. The queen I knew could never stoop so low. It must be a slur, spread by York's adherents to darken her name. If, God forbid, they are true, then Queen Margaret has indeed been tarnished by war.

I can barely wait for Harry's homecoming, and for the first time in months I start to make plans for the future. It doesn't take long for the small lingering guilt at the fate of our enemies to dissipate, and life seems to open up into endless sunshine.

On the day I receive a letter from Harry to say he is riding home, I am in high spirits. I can settle to nothing. I cast aside my needlework, leaf half-heartedly through my book of hours, change my sleeves a number of times. Even the arrival of a parcel of several pairs of new shoes does nothing to relieve my agitation. From now on, life will be very different.

With the threat of war lifted, we can look at making improvements to our home, build the viewing point in the garden I have always desired, and best of all, we can have Henry and Jasper to stay.

In my mind, I picture spending every summer season with my son; we can hunt and practice his archery. Harry and I can teach him how to govern his estate. As Earl of Richmond, he must move between two worlds. He must show compassion for the common people and deal fairly with his tenants yet, at the same time, perfect a courtly manner. He will learn how to address the king, the proper garb to wear at court. The future beckons, and for the first time since I left my mother's house so many years ago, I feel free and blissfully happy.

A cry goes up from the battlement and I sense the ripple of activity that speaks of an approaching party of horse. I leap from my chair, arrange my sleeves, straighten my bodice and ensure my cap is straight. Then I stride from the hall to stand on the steps, a cup of welcome in my hand, and prepare to greet my lord.

He rides through the gates, pauses with one hand on the pommel while he throws up his visor, and looks down at me with tired, red-rimmed eyes. I take a step forward, wait while he swings stiffly to the ground.

He takes the cup and drains it, passes it to his servant before turning back to me and clasping both my hands.

"I would kiss you, sweetheart, but I am filthy. I hope you have ordered a bath made ready."

"I have, my lord, and fresh clothes are laid in your chamber."

"Come with me, wife," he says. "I have some news you must hear."

I follow behind him, noticing the tautness of his shoulders, the way his hands are clenched into fists. Increasing my pace, I draw parallel, a worried frown tempering my joy.

"What news, Harry? Can you not tell me now?"

He stands aside as a trio of chamber boys hurry past with vast jugs of water.

"Let me get my things off first, Margaret. I am exhausted. It was a hard ride."

"At least tell me whether it is good or bad news."

I follow, one step behind, into his chamber. He throws off his cloak, sits down on the bed and begins to struggle with his boots. Sinking to my knees, I take his boot and draw it off for him, trying not to recoil from the stench of his unwashed feet. We repeat the exercise with the other foot, and then I help him unbutton his tunic and slip it from his shoulders. His linen is soiled with sweat and dirt.

"HARRY!" I am beginning to nag. "Please, good or bad?"

He sighs, lets his head fall forward, his stringy hair covering his face. I notice a patch of angry red skin on his neck. He pulls his shirt over his head, revealing more sore patches that are crying out for my ointment. He dips his hand into the water, flicks his wrist twice, splattering water on my gown.

"Bad, I'm afraid."

"What? Harry, please." I cannot resist the urge to stamp my foot and he raises an eyebrow, surprised at my show of temper.

"Calm down, Margaret. Come, sit here."

"I don't want to sit."

"Very well, stand then."

He looks tired, worn out with troubles, and I am sorry for adding to his strife, but I have to know.

"My stay here will be necessarily short. The dreams of peace you spoke of in your letters are just that, Margaret. Dreams. York may be dead, and Salisbury too, but their cause is very much alive in the form of their sons, Edward of March and Richard of Warwick. The cousins have reunited and even now they march, fully armed, on London. It will be a race to see who gets there first; the queen or Warwick."

"But if we can just recapture the king ..."

"The king will be no use to us if Warwick gains control of London."

My hopes of a return to normality were short lived indeed.

March 1461

The letter looks harmless. Expecting the usual news of Henry's progress, I break the seal, unroll the parchment and frown at Myfanwy's unruly handwriting.
Oh Margaret, she begins and my heart contracts, my eyes moving quickly across the paper.

I am sorry my letter is so tardy, but I have only just had news of it myself. Owain Tudor is dead. As far as I can gather, on Candlemas last, Jasper and his father were attempting to link up with the main part of our forces on the border but were intercepted by Edward of March and there was a short skirmish.

Our army was scattered. Jasper fled, I know not where, but his message assures me he is safe and unharmed. But when Owain's men put to flight, March pursued and captured them. They do say that four thousand men were slaughtered that day. Afterwards, they took Owain, Throckmorton, and Scudamore captive and imprisoned them in Hereford.

Oh, Margaret, Sir William Vaughan who, as you know hated Owain, wasted no time in condemning him to a traitor's death. They say he died well, with Queen Katherine's name upon his lips ... but that is little comfort to us. I wish I could be with Jasper; it is hard to lose a father when he still mourns the loss of his brother ...

I let the letter drop, my mind reliving memories of Edmund's father. I recall his stories; his ascent from the strongholds of north Wales to the royal court of England, and the bed of the dowager queen. I had always loved the way his face softened when he spoke of his dead wife, Katherine.

Owain, although of common stock, was a knight of the old school, valiant, brave and chivalrous. Now, my Henry, already bereft of a father, will never know his grandfather either. A tear drops onto my lap. Owain's grizzled face swims in my mind's eye.

One day, we will have vengeance upon Vaughan. Jasper will see to that. He is Henry's one surviving champion. I thank God that he is safe. Jasper is not one to give up and will already be rallying new support. I pick up the letter again, my eyes darting across the page.

I have told Henry nothing of this. He is too young to understand, but I now include stories of his grandfather in the tales I tell him at bedtime. Rest assured, Owain Tudor will never be forgotten in this household; not as long as I am here to keep his name alive.

"Nor will he be forgotten in all Wales."

I speak aloud, and the resilience of my own words brings a watery smile to my face. I know that, just like everything else, I will find the strength to overcome this.

*

The angry tide encroaches, destroying everything in its path. As Warwick marches north toward London, Jasper approaches from the west, and the royal Lancastrian army, made up of mercenaries from the north, travels south, scorching a swathe of terror across the land.

While the common folk shiver beneath a mantle of snow and ice, their plight is worsened by the queen's supporters, who steal and pillage, and murder. Unable to control them, the queen can do nothing but watch as the marauding Scots devastate Grantham, Stamford and Northampton.

When battle is joined, the warring nobles of England fight for the second time up and down the cramped streets of St Albans' town. Warwick, taken by surprise, is defeated and flees. He rides away fast, forgetting the prisoner in his care, and when our men take possession of the town, they find the bewildered king sitting beneath a tree.

At least he is safe in our care again.

But our victory is stained, our triumph tainted as whispers reach me of the common people's detestation for the queen. Her recent sacking of St Albans fills them with fear that she means to destroy London too.

As her army draws closer to the capital, in the minds of the populace she becomes the 'vengeful queen,' and their hearts overspill with terror. Behind the stout defences of the city walls, the townsfolk take refuge, barring the gates against her, and refusing her entry.

Furious but futile against such determined hate, the queen and her army reluctantly retreat. They traverse the devastated roads back to Yorkshire, scattering chaos and misery in their wake. Darker days have never been known in England.

Almost a week later, news comes that Warwick and Edward of March have arrived in London. This time when an army arrives at the gates, the people throw them open, and give hearty welcome to Warwick and his new-made king, Edward IV.

"You cannot go, Harry. You are too sick."

"I have to go. There is no ..."

He sways on his feet, closes his eyes and grips the bedpost.

"There, you see. Just as I said. Now, lie back down and let me tend you. A sick man will only be a hindrance to the cause, not a help."

As easily as if he were a child, I push him down and try to tug the blankets to his chin. He pushes my hand away. His face is as white as the linen he lies upon, but he hauls himself up again.

"Bring me something to stop the dizziness."

"No, I won't; and the king wouldn't ask me to."

By all accounts, the king is too far gone in madness to care one way or the other who rides with him into battle. It is the queen we heed now.

Despite London and most of England having turned against her in support of the Yorkist king, she refuses to surrender her cause. It is for her son, of course, and if I were in her position, I would do the same. But by all accounts, many of my fellow Lancastrian supporters are wary of young Edward of Lancaster. They whisper of cruelty and the mistreatment and bullying of his servants. He is also accused of hiding behind his mother's skirts, manipulating her love for him.

After the battle at St Albans, when his father the king was discovered in the company of two Yorkist knights, Margaret let Edward decide how the men, who had done no more than follow York's orders, should die. The boy could have chosen to show them mercy, yet instead, he chose beheading. I suppose battle hardens the best of us, and in his short life, Edward of Lancaster has known nothing but war. Yet I would hope that in similar circumstances, my own son would show mercy.

Now, refusing to give up the fight, the queen is summoning supporters for yet another battle. Everyone is sick of war. Our men are depleted and sickening, our women have been tested to the utmost. We live on a knife's edge, afraid that each day will bring new disasters. More than anything, England needs peace. Sometimes, I think, for the sake of peace, perhaps it might be better if York wore the crown. But I do not speak that thought aloud; it is a brief and fleeting thing.

I close my eyes, send up an earnest prayer to atone for even contemplating such treason, and turn back to my husband, who is trying to struggle out of his nightshirt.

"No, no, no! Harry, you are sick. Let me at least fetch you a remedy to bring down the fever. Perhaps you will be fit to ride out by morning."

"It will be too late by then."

"Then you will have to ride harder and faster to make up for it. You will not set one foot from this house until you are fit enough to do so."

His capitulation illustrates just how ill he really feels. He crawls back into bed.

"Very well, Margaret. I am beaten. Do your worst."

I spin on my heel and hurry to the still-room to prepare a posset. Sending my serving girl away, I take down an old book of recipes, drawing the candle closer so that I can read the close-written text. I run my index finger down the page, carefully noting the correct ingredient. It will not do to give him too much.

With great care, I pour an infusion of cherry bark and coriander to treat his recurrent fevers, but after some hesitation and soul searching, I add three drops of poppy juice. I stare for a long moment at the innocuous looking cup before hastily crossing myself and hurrying back with it to his chamber.

He tips it back, drains the cup and hands it to me. I kiss his brow.
He slides down the bed, turns onto his side and hauls the covers over his shoulder.
"See they make my horse ready. I will leave at dawn. Tell them to ... wake me ..."
Harry will not wake at dawn. If my calculations are correct, he will not wake until the battle is done and the fate of York and Lancaster decided.

"Harry, NO!" I break out of the daydream. He pauses, the cup half way to his mouth. I snatch it away.

"I am sorry. I made a mistake. I will mix you another."

"Margaret." He struggles from the bed, his voice halting me in my tracks. I pause and wait for him to confront me at the hearth. He narrows his eyes, twitches his head, silently questioning.

"What do you mean ... a mistake? You never make mistakes. I have seen you myself, double checking, making sure before you even dose the dogs for worms. What are you up to?"

"Nothing." I make to move away, but his hand snakes out and pinions me. He takes the cup, waves it beneath his nose.

"What is in it?"

I swallow, turn my face away.

"Cherry bark, coriander, and something to sweeten it."

"What else? Have you tried to poison me?"

"Don't be ridiculous. As if I would ever dream of doing such a thing."

I am facing him now, hating the suspicion, the disappointment in his eye.

"What then? Tell me."

He forces me back to the bed, grabs my wrists and makes me sit.

In my mind, I invent a hundred reasons for wanting to prevent him leaving. To me, each one is a viable excuse but I know he will hate me for it. I have spoiled our perfect marriage, possibly forever. A sob is bottled up in my chest; suddenly it releases, an ugly noise marking an ugly deed.

The mattress dips as he sits beside me. Gentle now, he picks up my hand.

"What was in it?"

I sniff and wipe a tear away.

"A little poppy juice to make you sleep."

The hammer of his condemnation hovers just above my head. His voice when it comes is thick with suppressed anger.

"So I would be spared the battle? You think I am not man enough?"

Shame floods me. I let my head fall backward and look upon the smoke-blackened timbers of the roof. They are stark and threatening, hanging over us like a curse.

"No, don't be silly. You are ill, Harry. My instinct was to protect you."

"At whatever cost?"

"At whatever cost."

A long silence. Only the rapid sound of my breath, the rasp of Harry's congested chest. I feel I am waiting on God's judgement. I probably am. At last, Harry emits a long breath.

"You are headstrong and ... and ... *devious*, Margaret. I feel I hardly know you, as if I have lived these last years with a stranger. How could you do that to me? Have you no care for the king, for the country?"

I sit ramrod straight, enveloped in shame, my hands clenched in my lap. I know my expression is mulish. I know I have done a terrible thing. I wish I could say I am sorry, but I am not. I am only sorry I lacked the courage to carry it through. I will never make him understand.

How can I describe the terror of my last weeks with Edmund, my fear of reliving them? His face blurs beneath my tears. He gets up and strides about the room. I have never seen him lose his temper before. He has always been calm and mild – mistakenly, I also thought him meek ... and manageable. Perhaps he is right and we have never really known each other.

"Well? Explain yourself. Why did you do it?"

"You were sick, Harry. I was afraid ..."

"Afraid I would die? What of all the men, our friends, our allies, who also risk their lives for our king? Did you think of them?"

I shake my head, remorse and misery washing over me.

"I am sorry, Harry. I thought only of you ... of myself. I cannot bear the thought of losing you. I didn't think, until the last moment. Can you not forgive an action I did not carry through?"

"What hour is it?"

"It must be a little after three."

"Call for my horse to be made ready."

"Yes, Harry."

Miserably, I get up and cross the room to do my husband's bidding. This battle will be a test. If Harry comes safely home and Lancaster has the victory, I will know God forgives me, but if we lose, I will know that I am by Heaven condemned.

*

When the news comes, I cannot quite believe it is all over. I cannot comprehend that God has given victory to York's son while our own rightful king is vanquished, and bundled for safety over the border into Scotland.

We have suffered heavy losses and my first thought is for the queen and her son, now exiled. Already, people are referring to the battlefield as *The Bloody Meadow*. Messengers bring news of a mass slaughter, the river known as the Cock Beck running red with blood. Ned, carrying a message from Harry, weeps when he tells me how, after the battle and the slaughter that followed, the exhausted survivors slept where they fell, among the corpses of their comrades.

He describes the devastation caused by Warwick and his king, and tells me that a few Lancastrians managed to flee into exile. Only Jasper, the guardian of my son, is left at large, alone and unsupported in Wales.

So many of our friends have fallen, or faced execution at the hands of the victorious new king. His vengeance knows no bounds. It is with great fear that I remember our queen's lack of mercy in her short-lived days of victory, and I understand that York's son is playing the old game of tit for tat.

I can only hope this son of York, *King* Edward, will never lay hands on the king he deposed. Momentarily, I am swamped with anxiety for my cousin, King Henry, but it is quickly replaced by a greater terror for my son.

"Bring me a pen and parchment," I call, and sit down to scrawl a hasty note to Myfanwy, urging her to send all the news she has. Her reply is many anguished days in coming.

I am forbidden to write of Jasper's whereabouts but I know he is safe. We, at Pembroke, are in grave danger. Herbert has been given jurisdiction over south Wales, and even now the custodian here is under orders from Jasper to prepare for siege. The steward assures me we can hold out for many months. There is time yet for the queen and Jasper to turn this war around. Jasper refuses to submit to York or relinquish his title and lay down the banner of Lancaster; he says he must fight to the bitter end.
I am afraid, Margaret. How far are we from the end? How long can we resist them? I don't know whether it is safer to attempt to send Henry to you, or keep him here with me. If you decide he is better with you, send for him and I will try to get him away, but the roads are perilous ...

I don't know what to do. Even in peaceful times, the roads are fraught with danger. Travel is always risky, even in a large group with an armed guard. I know Pembroke can withstand anything, I have seen it myself. The walls are impenetrable, the storehouses and armoury stocked high. Surely it will be merely a matter of waiting for Herbert to grow bored; once he realises the futility, he will ride away. If they can only hold firm against him, Henry may well be safer under siege.

Bourne Castle – Summer 1461

Harry and I share a private supper in his chamber. I toy with my food, picking it up and putting it back on the plate untasted. My innards are churning with suppressed panic and I can barely wait for the meal to be over so I may return to the chapel to pray for Henry's safety.

I fear I am being punished, perhaps for my attempt to keep Harry from the battle, or perhaps for my wavering support of the queen. Slowly, tales filter from Scotland of her penury, her charitable status at the Scottish court. She has my pity but I find it so difficult now to support her, even in my heart, for I fear she has now become as mad as the king.

At least, Henry's malady renders him harmless but Queen Margaret has become a bitter and vicious enemy to King Edward, and her reckless pursuit of victory endangers us all. With most of her supporters scattered and only Jasper continuing to harry the Herberts in Wales, she still refuses to acknowledge her cause is lost. All I can do is pray for her, but most of my pleas to God have to be for my son.

"Margaret." Harry breaks the silence. He pulls a piece of bread apart, uses it as a sop for his gravy and pokes it into his mouth, chewing quickly before swallowing. "You know I must make peace with the king?"

"Edward, you mean?"

He puts down his knife, wags a finger.

"You must face it, Margaret, Lancaster is lost. All we can do is come to terms with the new regime, preserve ourselves ... and your son."

"My son!" A morsel of bread spits from my lips. "My son, who is even now besieged by the servants of this man you expect me to embrace as king."

"He does not make war on children. Even Herbert wouldn't dare to harm Henry. Had Jasper not ordered the castle into a state of siege, he would probably be living here with us, right now."

"No." I shake my head violently. "I do not believe that. Hasn't this *king* of yours given Henry's lands and titles to his brother, George?"

"He has bestowed Henry's lands on Clarence, yes, but not his title. Your son is still the Earl of Richmond."

"For how long?"

I push my plate away, lean back in my chair, fold my arms and stare moodily into the flames.

Harry sighs. "Why do you judge him without giving him a chance? He may make a fair king. Face it, Margaret, King Henry was hardly viable; he was ruled by his power-hungry advisors."

"My uncle, you mean? Or do you refer to York, your king's father?"

Reaching for his wine cup, Harry takes a long draught, bangs it on the table.

"Just lately, Margaret, you make everything a war. I know you are worried for your son …"

"Of course I am worried. Even now, while you try to court me with intimate dinners, my son is imprisoned in a castle where Herbert's men prowl like wolves outside the walls."

I glance at Harry's face and find it set and hard, not at all like the Harry I used to know. My heart sinks. I strongly desire a return to our former good fellowship, but there is so much between us. He sits on one side of the gorge and I on the other, the gulf between us wide and deep. Both of us lack the means to cross it.

He picks up his knife and stabs a chunk of cheese.

"In a few days I am travelling to Eltham, where I will pledge my allegiance to King Edward. Will you come with me?"

We stare at one another across the table. My jaw is clenched so hard I feel my teeth will break.

"No."

His eyes are sorrowful, as if he has lost something dear to him. He swallows, turns his face away.

"I had hoped for a different answer. You disappoint me, Margaret. I thought you would see the sense of self-preservation."

"What about loyalty, sir? Have you forgotten that?"

"No."

He relaxes. Keeping his eye on the spoon he toys with, he presses his finger on the tip of the handle, making the bowl bounce on the cloth. "I have much time for loyalty, but not when it is misplaced."

"Misplaced ...? "

He leans forward, suddenly angry again, suddenly intense.

"You say you want your son to be safe, Madam. Perhaps he will be better placed with a strong leader on the throne."

He waves an arm in the air; I follow his index finger as it punctuates his words. "Edward of March, KING Edward is not so bad. He is not evil. YORK was not evil. They are driven by politics and trade, and want what is best for their country. They are no different to us; or different only in the fact that they can provide a solid, dependable ruler, when all we have is a loose cannon; the choice between a bemused king and a-a-a-an evil child."

For a moment I think he means Henry, but then I remember Edward of Lancaster, a boy described unvaryingly as arrogant and cruel.

"How can you be sure he would keep my son safe?"

Our eyes meet, a long moment of contemplation in which I can almost see half-formed sentences entering his mind before being dismissed. In the end, he puffs out his cheeks.

"I can't be sure, but I am convinced Edward can make the crown secure. England is sick of war, all of us, rich and poor alike, are suffering. All the reasonable men I know crave a united front. When I meet with the king, I promise I will plead your son's innocence. He knows as much as anyone the vulnerability of children in time of war."

I raise my eyebrows.

"How? Why? He has no sons …"

"He has brothers. His mother took George and the younger one, Richard, into exile, fleeing the path of our queen when she marched into war. For months, he would not have known if they lived or died. We are all equal in war, Margaret. We all hate it, no matter whose badge we wear. Give the man a chance."

He stares at me, waiting for my capitulation but, although my banner is flagging, I cannot relinquish the sulky stand I have taken.

"You can go speak to your king, give him your allegiance if you will, but do not ask me to do so until my son is here, safe and sound, with me."

Harry gets up so suddenly his chair falls backwards, skidding across the floor.

"Very well," he says formally. "I bid you goodnight, Madam."

I miss him. I had not realised how much I had come to value his warm presence in my bed, his gentle lovemaking, his humour and affection. I roll over and bury my head beneath the covers. Perhaps I am a fool.

The queen would not make self-sacrifice for my benefit, and King Henry, God bless him, is so far gone in madness as to have forgotten my existence, let alone which banner I follow. Perhaps for the sake of marital harmony, I should do as my husband bids. It is my duty, after all.

But in the morning, when the sun is high in the sky and Harry stands coldly and bids me goodbye, I have forgotten the lonely hours of the night. I keep my face blank, offer him my frigid cheek. When he ignores it and takes my hand instead, it is as if he has punched me, low in the stomach.

September 1461

For months, I hear nothing. My days and nights are spent worrying and praying. All I know is that the king has lost patience with the insurrection across the border and has shared the administrative power of Wales among his own men. Only a few Lancastrians remain at large; Jasper among them. Herbert, now to be known as Lord Herbert of Raglan, is like the leader of a pack of dogs, determined to sniff him out, and King Edward himself has left his capital and is camped in the Welsh Marches.

"We should help Jasper, Harry," I mutter, keeping my voice dipped so the servants do not hear. "I owe him my life, and that of Henry."

"What can I do? I have my pardon now and am sworn to the king."

"You know the king has sent in his fleet to Pembroke to support the siege? What chance do they have?"

"Very little, my dear, but I have faith that Henry will not be harmed. The king is not a vengeful man."

But how can he be sure? I have never set eyes upon King Edward, and most of the stories I have heard are the sort that are always told of rulers. None would dare describe a warrior monarch as squat or bald or ugly so, as in the legends of old, Edward is described as invincible, tall and golden-haired – like a young god. I scoff at such tales.

At the end of September, the news I have been dreading comes. Pembroke has fallen, surrendered into the hands of William Herbert by the lack-hearted Sir John Scudamore. I leave my chamber, run to find Harry in the stables where he is tending the welfare of his horse.

"Go to your king, Harry. Ask him for Henry's wardship."

But we are too late. Those who have supported the queen who mocked and murdered the king's father are shown no favour. Instead, when Pembroke Castle is taken, my son is given into the keeping of William Herbert.

Harry quietly tells me of it. I bury my face in my hands, rake my skull with desperate fingers.

"Margaret." Harry pulls my hands away, lifts me to my feet. "Do not worry; he will be safe. Edward does not make war on children. Besides, he is too valuable to be harmed."

I raise my head. Our eyes meet. My passionate storm passes. My Henry is second in line to the Lancastrian throne. We know that, and so does the king. He will always be a dangerous lure, a banner of insurrection. My head spins with the realisation that, for the security of Edward IV's crown, my Henry may never regain his freedom.

The country is bruised. All of us, regardless of our status or politics, have lost someone, or something. An all-consuming fear for my son overrides everything as I struggle to pick up the life I led before our cause was lost. In desperation, and unbeknown to Harry, I send Ned across the war-torn country in search of news of him.

"Find Myfanwy," I tell him. "Discover what information she has."

As he rides away, I hang tightly to the door frame to prevent myself from giving chase and demanding to go with him.

Another span of lengthy days follows; I spend the hours pacing, praying, biting my nails. Jasper has escaped, fled the country; we know that much, and we know that Henry is with Herbert, but of the state of his health, his happiness, or his whereabouts, I can only guess. Myfanwy will know. I cannot imagine why she has not written.

Waiting, I am always waiting. Ned should have returned by now. I try not to think of the misfortunes that could have befallen him on the road. I climb the twisting stairway and take a position behind the battlement, squinting across the countryside to the road that will bring Ned home with news.

On the day I spy a lone rider, I pick up my skirts and hurry, too fast for safety, down the narrow twisting stairs. By the time the weary horse limps through the gates, I am pacing the bailey.

"Ned ..." I start forward but pull up abruptly when I realise it is not him. This messenger is a stranger, but the badge he wears on his tunic is not. I sigh with impatience when I realise he brings a message from my mother.

My body deflates, the expectation draining away. I take the rolled parchment, jerk my head in the direction of the kitchens and tell him to ask for refreshment. He will stay until tomorrow and carry back any answer I may have for my mother.

I have not seen her since the day I left for Wales with Edmund. As a woman, I can now see that I was nothing more than a means for her to increase her standing with the king. What other reason could she have had for selling my virginity so young?

I carry the letter to the garden, not unrolling it until I am perched on the edge of the stone fountain. The words I read there sting my eyes. My vision blurs. John Welles; as good and as kind a stepfather as a man could be, lately perished at Towton Field, along with thousands of others. Mother is widowed again and in need of me.

Please come, Margaret, she writes. *I have need of my family about me and I have not seen you for such a long time. Edith is here, but she is great with child and will soon be entering her confinement. It would warm my heart to see you again.*

My little brother John will be Lord Welles now. I still think of him as being in long coats, his hair a mass of tawny curls, but he must be almost eleven. How long before Mother begins to arrange an advantageous marriage for him?

With a sigh, I put the letter down. I do not even consider responding to her summons. I will not go; not now. I have other, more important things to worry about but I hurry off a quick reply, giving my condolences, and a long list of reasons why I cannot leave.

It is almost a month later when Ned returns, and I do not miss the irony that, having spent all my days on the battlement watching for his approach, he arrives as night is falling and I have retired to bed.

"Bring him to me," I order when they tell me he has come at last.

"What here, Madam, to your chamber?"

"Yes, yes."

I leap from bed and wrap a loose gown about me. They do not realise he has seen me in worse straights than this. On the night I gave birth to Henry, Ned was a welcome friend in an hour of need.

He comes in, cap in hand, his eye strategically lowered to the floor, and I speak before he can even greet me.

"What news, Ned? Did you find her?"

"Eventually, my lady. She has taken refuge at the priory at St Nicholas. She ... she is ..."

"What? Is she unwell, is she harmed?"

"... with child again, my lady."

A sigh of relief. It could be worse.

"And what of Henry?"

"Taken to Raglan, as I understand it, my lady."

"Raglan? As a prisoner?"

He shrugs, helplessness in his eyes.

"I don't know for sure, but Myfanwy said he was treated with honour when they were discovered. She wept as she spoke of their parting and begs me to tell you there was nothing she could have done to prevent it."

Had I been with him I would have stopped it. I would have laid down my life to stop my poor child being taken into the hands of those villains.

"Myfanwy is travelling back to the north, to be with her daughters for the birth."

"She didn't want to come here?"

He shrugs again. "I think she wants to be where the Earl can reach her, if he needs to."

Of course; as long as Jasper is in Wales she will wish to be as close to him as possible, but that doesn't help me.

I sag, the strain of the last months suddenly overwhelming. If I thought it would help, I would give into the grief that is constricted in my heart, pressing on my throat, making me choke. A tentative hand falls on my shoulder.

"Are you all right, my lady? Let me help you to a chair."

Not for the first time in our acquaintance, Ned aids me bodily. I remember to whisper my thanks.

"You are a good fellow, Ned. You will be well rewarded for your trouble."

"I need no reward, my lady. Shall I summon your woman?"

I nod and he moves toward the door, where he hesitates.

"I am certain young Henry will be fine, my lady, so I beg you not to worry."

Not to worry. Yes. I must remember not to worry. I wave him away with a flutter of my hand.

By the time Harry comes to find me, I have been put to bed. By the light of one candle, all conflict between us forgotten, he climbs in beside me and grasps my hands.

"Ned told you?"

He nods, a restorative smile on his face.

"The boy will be safe at Raglan. Herbert may be a violent man but he has ambition too. The price of

Henry's wardship will be too much for him to forfeit lightly. You remember his wife, Anne Deveraux?"

I narrow my eyes, trying to picture her.

"I think so ..."

"She is a good woman; she will cherish Henry and ensure he lacks nothing."

Only a mother can know the pain of another woman nurturing the child from whom she is separated, but I seek and find some comfort in his words.

His fingers play with my hair. I turn my face into his shoulder, hoping he will not expect me to lie with him tonight. I love him dearly and am glad of our reconciliation, but just now my heart and head are full of other matters.

My body relaxes, and, more comforted and warm than I have been in many weeks, I slowly edge toward sleep. Just when I reach the floaty stage between waking and dreaming, Harry speaks again.

"Perhaps we can bypass Herbert and write to Anne herself. I will ask permission for you to visit Henry at Raglan. That would put your mind at rest, wouldn't it?"

I am instantly awake again, my mind alert and calculating. I struggle from his arms, turn to his shadowy face on the pillow.

"Oh yes, Harry. It would indeed. Come; let us compose a letter now!"

Bourne Castle - 1465

After four years of Edward's rule, I look back on my early optimism with scorn. How could I have ever thought it would be so easy to win the favour of the new king? We write letter after letter, but although

Anne Deveraux's replies are courteous and full of news of Henry, she makes no mention of our request to visit him.

I try to picture him, but can only visualise the baby I left behind, the toddler I visited at Pembroke. I cannot visualise my Henry as an eight-year-old boy. And how will he remember me? Without Myfanwy to remind him of me, I will be forgotten. He will grow up as part of the Herbert family, with no notion of his own bloodline, his own worth.

News from Myfanwy arrives intermittently, but reading between her words, I discern that Jasper is no longer in Scotland with the queen but in Brittany, seeking support to raise an army to bring back to Wales.

The queen and those who have followed her into Scotland never cease harrying the borders, creating as much trouble as they can for the man now styling himself king of England.

I am unsure of my own loyalty. Although I love and honour the old king, Harry's consistent argument that he was never an effective ruler is wearing me down. Perhaps he is right. Perhaps this Edward will prove the better man. If he would only allow me access to my son, I would swear fealty to the devil.

I cross myself at the thought, send up a repentant prayer, for, of course, I would never do such a thing. But Edward of York is not the devil and oh, how I wish I could spend just an hour in the company of my son.

Harry assures me the only way to achieve that is to gain the favour of the king, and I swear I will try, but my family and connections make it difficult. Their behaviour constantly throws my own loyalty into doubt.

A few years ago, after several failed skirmishes in the north, my uncle Somerset made his peace with King Edward. For months, we were astounded by reports from court that he and the king were the best of friends; drinking together, whoring together, sharing the same bed. His actions were regarded with suspicion by the Yorkists, while those of us loyal to the old king, labelled him a turncoat. Things became so bad that he was attacked by a mob in Northampton.

For a little while, it seemed my uncle had changed his colours completely. The Beaufort family was in favour again; my mother pardoned and all her lands restored. Harry and I were sure I would soon find favour too, and I would be allowed to see my son. But then Somerset defected again, and early last year joined his forces with the queen's at Hexham against the king, where they suffered a humiliating defeat.

King Edward, furious at the betrayal of a man he had cultivated as a friend, ordered Somerset's immediate execution. His death was a stunning blow for Lancaster, and meant real disgrace for the Beauforts. Now, with my chances of pacifying the king in ashes, my only hope is to do as Harry suggests and sever my ties with my own family, for the sake of my son.

The setting sun tinges the blue sky pink, soft-hued like the petals of a flower. I wait in the garden until the last of the light has faded and the bushes become unidentifiable humps of deeper darkness. My book falls from my lap as I stand and when I stoop to retrieve it, I hear someone entering the garden.

"Margaret, are you never coming in?"

I turn and smile at the sound of his voice. Harry's face is shrouded in darkness.

"It has been so pleasant, so warm. I was reluctant to say farewell to such a lovely day. Tomorrow it will rain again."

He takes my elbow, and I walk with him toward the hall.

"You can't know that." I hear amusement in his voice.

"Yes I can. Can't you smell it in the air; a sort of damp, fresh tang?"

"No, and neither should you claim to, or they will take you as a witch."

We laugh together, as is our habit. We could spend our days in maudlin gloom, but we refuse to allow that to happen. Our cause may be lost but I try to be optimistic. I try to look to the future. If a sorrowful tear leaks from my eye, I cuff it away, lift my chin and tell myself that tomorrow the king will relent. He will welcome Harry and I to his court, and the longed-for letter will arrive from Anne Deveraux, inviting me to Raglan.

"Supper will be cold by now."

Harry opens the door, and as I sneak past him, I steal a kiss before hurrying away. He darts after me, his arm sliding about my waist.

It is an intimate supper of capon and pickles, and venison pie. I have just shaken out my napkin and am taking stock of what lies before me when a servant scratches at the door and hands Harry a message. I put down my knife again.

"It is late in the day for a messenger. Is everything all right?"

"It is from my brother, John." He looks up, his forehead furrowed, his mouth falling open in surprise. "The king is married!"

"Married? I thought you said Warwick was negotiating a marriage with the Duke of Savoy's daughter? ... I misremember her name." I frown, trying to recall it.

"No, this is something else. Warwick will be furious. It seems our hot-blooded young king has married a commoner, and one of us, too ..."

"Who? What do you mean 'one of us?'"

I snatch the letter away and frown at it before looking up at Harry.

"Oh my, Harry, what I wouldn't give to be a fly on the wall when Warwick learns of this."

"I am not sure I've even met her. I know her parents, of course, but not well."

"Elizabeth Grey; her husband John was killed at St Albans, I believe."

"There have been so many deaths, Margaret. I don't know how you remember them all. It says here he left her with two sons to raise."

Two sons.

Silence falls, both of us deep in thought.

"So, she is fertile, and she must be a remarkable woman to rise from the spouse of a renegade knight to the wife of a king."

"A beautiful one, by all accounts."

"Well, I hope for her sake her looks do not fade too soon. I have heard King Edward is a fickle man."

I link my fingers primly in my lap and watch Harry reach for a slice of pie. He sinks his teeth into it. He will grow a paunch if he is not careful. He chews quickly, speaks before his mouth is properly empty.

"He is a young man, and his blood is hot. Perhaps he will stick to his fireside more now that he has a wife to warm him."

"Perhaps."

My mind is racing, imagining this beautiful queen filling the royal nursery with heirs. With each child she births, my son will slide farther down the ladder, farther from the throne. I can only pray she is suddenly barren, or produces only girls.

"John suggests that while the king's new wife lulls the king into good humour, I should petition again for the reinstatement of your lands."

"Do that, Harry. There should be no delay, for there is no telling how long his good mood will last."

"If we can regain some of your properties and perhaps purchase a few pockets closer to Windsor, I can be more active at court."

Harry has no real interest in politics; his newfound desire to serve the king can only be due to his interest in my son. I am touched by his thoughtfulness.

"After dinner," I say, turning back to the meal, "we shall write to the king and compliment him on his marriage. He will be glad of our support. I am sure he cannot relish Warwick's displeasure."

"Well, Warwick is not the king."

"Do you think he realises that?"

Harry laughs as he watches me chew daintily on a portion of pie.

"You are incorrigible."

"I beg your pardon?"

"In the nicest possible way, of course."

I rip a slither of meat from the capon and pop it into my mouth. I am not 'incorrigible', I am realistic. I may not have met Warwick, but we have all heard the tales of his vanity and greed, his lust for power. Edward is a young man and by all accounts an indolent one. It wouldn't surprise me in the least if Warwick exploits the king's laziness to ensure his own political agenda.

"We are very far from things here in Lincolnshire. It would be better to be nearer the hub of the country, and a little closer to Wales too."

Harry pours more wine into my cup and I pick it up, salute him before tasting it. The liquid flows, warm and rosy, to my belly.

"You won't be kept away from Henry for much longer, I am certain of that."

I hope he is right. Dear God, I hope he is right.

March 1467

Harry unrolls the parchment, holds it to the light, his eyes scanning the king's message.

"He has granted us Woking ..."

"Woking? Really! Oh, Harry, that is good news."

I try to take the letter from him but he jerks it away and reads to the end.

"Not only has he granted the Manor of Woking but also invites me to a council meeting at Mortlake."

He smiles widely and I find my face stretching to match his pleasure. Of course, in granting us Woking, the king is merely returning what is rightfully Beaufort property. It was the home of my grandparents, the childhood haunt of the father I never met. It is a good day, and I thank God for it.

Harry's inclusion in the forthcoming council meeting can only mean that the king has forgiven him his transgressions and has accepted him as a true supporter of his rule. I dare not believe that the grant of former Beaufort lands means he has forgiven me also.

"When can we go there, Harry? Perhaps we could make a short visit to decide if it will make a suitable permanent home."

"Yes, that is a good idea. You can stay there while I am with the council; it is not so far to Mortlake."

"I will instruct my women to make ready for a journey. Should I take court clothes in case we are summoned by the king?"

Harry shrugs, his eyebrow quirking at my optimism.

"You could if you wish, but I wouldn't wager on a summons. He won't want to appear too eager to show us his favour. We must work slowly and with caution."

I bite my lip. Patience has ever been hard for me, but I reassure myself that at least Woking is in my hands and full royal favour cannot be far off. I may yet be appointed to the service of the queen and, once I am there, I can proceed with getting Henry's lands reinstated as befits the Earl of Richmond.

Woking - May 1467

Sensing my need to be alone, Ned stays three paces behind as I walk in the footsteps of my grandfather. My feet are silenced by a carpet of grass that runs alongside the moat to where the water laps, deep and green. A moorhen emerges from a cluster of reeds near the inner bank; he dips and nods, leaving a trail across the looking glass surface. Soft cool shade to my right while, to the left, the curtain wall rises high.

I place my palm on warm stone and try to remember if I have been here before, but the memory is lost, obscured by all that happened after. Childhood was such a fleeting thing; too many memories have been chased away by its abrupt ending. I turn toward the sun that falls warmly on my face, and smile at Ned. He ducks his head, sweeps his arm wide across the vista. "It is very pretty here, my lady."

"Yes, it was my grandfather's favourite home."

"Do you remember him?"

I shake my head. "No, nor my father. They both died before I was born ..."

"That's sad."

"Yes. But I know no different."

We subside into silence again. I look across the smooth water to the distance where the moat joins the willow-banded river. The wind stirs and a cloud of small birds fly up of one volition. I have the strangest feeling I have been here before. I am the ghost of a forgotten child.

"I have no memory of being here, Ned, yet it is as if I have come home."

"My mam would say it was your ancestors stirring your blood, my lady, welcoming you back."

I turn to him, my eyebrows raised, startled that he should have so precisely interpreted my feelings. With a burst of optimism, I turn full circle and survey the tranquillity again.

"I will bring Henry here. He will enjoy it. It is about time he grew closer to his Beaufort blood."

With renewed purpose, I retrace my path across the springy grass toward the gatehouse to rejoin Harry in the hall where he is conferring with Master Bray. They both look up when I enter. Master Bray bows his head with deference and begins to tidy the desk.

"Don't hurry away on my account," I say as I untie the strings of my cloak. "I've been for a walk along the moat. It is so pretty, Harry. I saw so many small creatures I couldn't name, and the sun is as warm as high summer. You must find the time to walk there with me."

"I thought you'd be in the garden, deciding where to site your medicinal bed."

As soon as we had arrived, I had noticed the garden was in a sorry state yet it was possible to see the skeleton of a once loved plot beneath.

"Yes. I might do that this afternoon. I wish Myfanwy were here, she was always so useful in the garden."

He does not answer; his disapproval of my friend doesn't need to be spoken aloud.

"I am sure I will find someone," I finish lamely.

"Yes," he waves his hand. "Ask the staff, there is bound to be someone in the village with enough knowledge."

I move close behind him, peep over his shoulder at the letter he is reading.

"When do you leave for Mortlake?"

"Tomorrow."

"So soon? I had hoped there would be time to summon your tailor."

"My clothes are fine. The king will not expect me to arrive decked out like a courtier. My visit is for business, not pleasure."

"Yet, he might invite us to court. We should be prepared for that. I expect you will be summoned to pay homage to the baby princess."

I almost succeed in keeping the envy from my voice. In providing Edward with a daughter, the queen has validated the marriage and silenced those who speak against her. Next time, she may produce a son.

Harry, not noticing my bitter tone, puts the letter down, turns toward me and takes me by the shoulders, looking earnestly into my face.

"Don't get your hopes up, Margaret. It is early days yet. We may never be summoned to court. By all accounts, the queen is filling the court with her relatives, conniving to secure all the best offices for them. Many of the nobility are put out about it, and not just the friends of the old king."

I do not remind him that the Lancastrian faction is all but destroyed. All that are left are those who have subjected themselves to Edward. The majority of the rest are exiled overseas. Only Jasper continues to harry the king from the border of Wales before slipping away again, out of reach among the vast mountains.

Of course, I do not listen to Harry's words of caution. As soon as he has left for the council meeting, I summon my seamstress and begin to plan an extravagant new wardrobe.

Every fibre of my being informs me that a summons to court cannot be far away. I call my woman to bring from my coffers the length of embroidered linen I have been working on during the long winter evenings.

By the end of the afternoon I have ordered a fur-trimmed red velvet cothardie; several gowns for day wear; embroidered and jewelled hennins with long sheer veils; partlets, some lightweight and some for colder weather, and sleeves that are slashed at the elbow in the new fashion, to reveal the fine cloth of the chemise beneath.

As well as all this finery, I also replenish my night wear, and order several pairs of new shoes. As an afterthought, I request a suit of court clothes be made for Harry. Not being one for finery, he will complain bitterly, but we must do all in our power to impress the king.

Afterwards I sit back, expecting to feel satisfied, but it is at times like this that I miss a companion with whom to share such pleasures. Although I have women a plenty, I do not seek their company, for none of them match the close sisterhood of a real friend.

As the seamstress leaves, clutching a pattern book and a handful of fabric samples, I sigh and decide to take a turn about the garden. I pick up a pen so I can make notes. There is much that needs to be done there. If I don't get it into order, my supply of medicinal herbs will soon diminish. I walk purposefully to the back of the hall, skim down a short flight of steps, duck beneath the lintel and into the courtyard garden. I come to an abrupt halt.

It is raining. I hadn't realised.

The overgrown pathway is full of puddles, the leaves dripping with water, the emerging flower heads laid low by the burden of rain. As I stand there deciding what to do, a raindrop drips down the back of my neck, making me shudder. I turn on my heel and retrace my steps. It is hours until dinner so, taking refuge in my other joy, I climb the stairs to the library.

Thankfully, a fire has been lit. I select a book and climb onto the window seat, curl my knees to my chest to serve as a table on which to rest my book. The pages are thick, the rich jewelled illuminations bringing warmth to the chilly spring afternoon.

I lose myself there, lingering long over my favourite passages, tracing a finger across the intricately decorated border until, with a pang of sorrow, I turn the final page. I place the heavy book on the seat beside me and reach for another.

The first page reveals the fine flowing hand of the previous owner.

This book is mine, Anne Neville, gifted to me by my mother.

Anne Neville was the name of Harry's mother before she married, a lady whom I have yet to meet. I trace the marks of her pen with my forefinger, remembering that now we are in Suffolk, we are living much closer to her. I put the book down, move to the table in the centre of the room where parchment and quills lay strewn across the board. I light a candle and sit down, pick up a pen.

Three weeks later, Harry comes home. He swings from the saddle and opens his arms, his face relaxed but tired. It tells me all I need to know; the meeting with the king went well.
"I missed you." He kisses my brow and flings his arm about my shoulders.
"I missed you too. How was it with the king? Did he speak to you? Did you broach the subject of ..."
"Margaret! Take a breath. Come, let us go inside. We can talk there."
I stop, forcing him to stop too.
"We have a visitor," I say, suddenly anxious.
"A visitor? Anyone nice?"
I am full of doubt. Perhaps I should have waited. Perhaps I should have spoken to him first. I open my mouth to explain but before I can speak, a figure appears at the top of the steps.
"Harry!"
His head snaps round.
"Mother?" His mouth stretches wide as he races up the steps and takes her in his arms, planting kisses on her cheeks. I duck my head as happiness floods through me.
I have done the right thing.
Keeping hold of Anne, he opens his other arm, inviting me to join them.
"I take it this is the work of my scheming little wife." His smile belies the censure of his words. Anne puts a hand to her mouth and laughs but there are tears balanced on her lashes.

"Had Margaret not invited me I should have come soon anyway. I am so glad to have you both so near."

Anne is not how I expected a mother-in-law to be. The moment I sent my impulsive invitation, I began to regret it, imagining a termagant, a judgemental kill joy who would bring a bitter shadow into our marriage. But I was wrong. She arrived like a breath of warm wind, took me into her heart and, in two short weeks, has become the mother I have lacked.

She wears her widowhood nobly. Instead of mourning his loss and refusing to value the life that God has given her, she thanks God for the time she enjoyed with Harry's father. She is grateful for the children she bore him, the life they had. It is a good attitude and one I hope I can emulate.

Each morning, I am careful to remind myself to be glad for the time I had with Edmund. I put aside the grief that I can never bear another child. Like a mantra, I chant my thankfulness for Henry, for Harry, for Woking, for my health and good fortune. I am determined, with Anne's help, to become a better woman. I increase my charitable donations and begin to visit the poor in the village, ensuring the sick are nursed and the children are nourished. I find joy in this such as I have never found before.

So, for a while, there are three of us, but it is never a crowd. Anne shares our humour; she enjoys the garden, lends me her wonderful books and suggests new editions for my growing library. When she discovers me sketching designs for the refashioning of the great hall, she is full of advice that I eagerly accept.

Even at her age, she knows the latest dances, the way the women at court are styling their clothes, the most flattering way to pluck one's brow. I absorb all this knowledge like a garden that has long been starved of rain. For the first time since I left Wales, I have a female friend, and this time she is one of my own class. My lessons in courtly manners, that ceased when I left my mother's house, now begin again, and I relish them.

Having enjoyed a lengthy supper, Harry and I are nestled in our bed. We speak in whispers, the chamber lit only by the night candle and the embers of the dying fire. I snuggle into his shoulder, his familiar smell comforting, like home.
"Your mother is so nice."
His arm tightens around my shoulder.
"I know."
"Do you think she is lonely?"
"Lonely? She is surrounded by people."
"Yes ... but that isn't the same as being with friends. It isn't the same as having a husband to share your life. Widowhood is hard ..."
A lump gathers in my throat, forcing me into silence as Edmund's handsome face rears in my mind. I love Harry, but I have not forgotten the misery of losing Edmund, the terror of being pregnant and alone in a hostile country. The future was a blank wall then. I had never thought to remarry at all, let alone find such joy in marriage for the second time.
"She is mourning just now. When her grief passes, perhaps she will wed again, she has many years left, I hope."
"How old is she?"
He lets out a gust of breath, his voice rumbling in my ear.
"I am not sure. It isn't something you ask, is it? Fifty, maybe ... she could be more."
"She is still very handsome; she should have no trouble finding a husband."

"She is rich too, probably richer than is good for her."

I laugh gently. "I know all too well how wealth can attract the most reprehensible of suitors."

"So, you find me reprehensible? Surely not? I was never interested in your fortune; it was the lure of your big brown eyes that attracted me."

The laughter grows, it bubbles up inside until I can no longer contain it. We both know I am not blessed with alluring eyes, or anything else, but it doesn't matter, not to us. A happy tear finds its way onto my cheek and he traps it with his finger, wipes it away.

"I would have married you had you come to me in rags, my dear."

His words are soft, turning the humour into something else, something that resonates deep within me and brings swift, sweet sentiment that stings my eyes. His lips are on my face, erasing the tears and blessing me with his love.

August 1467

I can hardly contain my excitement when Harry announces we are to take a tour of our holdings in the West Country.

"Oh, Harry, that will be a welcome change, the country has been in upheaval for so long. How nice it will be to travel safely again."

He makes a non-committal sound, prompting me to look up, and I see at once that he has further news.

"What is it? What are you hiding?"

"Nothing." His eyes are large and round, a sure sign that he is keeping a secret.

"Harry." I get up and prowl toward him, armed with a large cushion. He throws up his arms, raises one knee, and cowers away. Collapsing into giggles, I discard my weapon and fall onto his lap, kissing him on the nose.

"Tell me at once, Harry, or I will put itching powder in your shirt."

"No, you wouldn't," he says, kissing me in return. "But I will tell you anyway. I have a letter from Herbert giving permission for a visit. I thought we could go once our business has been dealt with."

"What? Really? Oh, my, where is the letter?"

He fumbles inside his tunic and draws it out, still teasing, snatching it back as I reach for it. I make a wild lunge and tear it from his grasp, turn my back on him.

"It must be the king's doing, Harry," I exclaim as I scan the carefully worded invitation. "You must have pleased him and persuaded him of our loyalty. I wager he spoke to Herbert and instructed him to make us welcome."

Harry smiles modestly and shrugs his shoulder. "You may be right. I was on my best behaviour ..."

I cut off his words by flinging my arms around his neck to leave a smacking kiss on his cheek.

"You always are. Oh, I must make a list of all the preparations to be made. I will need a new travelling coat and some new shoes, and we must think up a gift to take for Henry ..." I stop suddenly, my heart welling with the realisation that I really will soon be reunited with my son.

It has been a long, long wait. He was such a little thing when last I saw him, I will barely know my son now. I try to imagine him. Is he dark-haired and small like me, or brash and golden-haired like his father? A shrim of delight washes over me, and I turn my wide smiling eyes on my husband. "When do we leave?"

"In a fortnight. I have some business at Martock and in Bristol. We can travel to Raglan from there, perhaps at the end of September?"

"I will write and let Anne know right away, and then I shall begin my list." I signal for Harry's man to bring me parchment and pen. Outwardly calm, I take a seat at the table. Inside, I am tingling with excitement.

The weeks seem to crawl by until it is time for our travels to begin, but at last we are on our way. To avoid the dust thrown up by the long cavalcade that accompanies us, Harry and me ride ahead. The sky is blue and cloudless, the sun warm on our faces, and I am in high spirits. A week at Martock, a few jaunts for Harry into the busy streets of Bristol, and then we will be on our way to Raglan, and Henry. If it were as easy to spur on time as it is to urge my horse to go faster, I would gallop all the way to next week.

Raglan Castle - September 1467

Raglan is firmly embedded in the landscape, lording it over the humbler dwellings that cluster at its foot. I smile at Harry, both nervous and excited and, obligingly, he urges his mount to a faster gait. I do likewise.

It takes longer than I imagined to travel the road leading to the castle. The way is circuitous, forcing us to circumnavigate the massive walls, the soaring crenelations. I need have no worries for Henry's safety for no one could creep in to steal him away. The place is impregnable.

The newly constructed gatehouse is decorated with colourful badges; Herbert is not shy of boasting of his newfound status. We pass beneath the vast walls into an inner court, and are swallowed into the hubbub of castle life.

I look about the milling courtyard, the grooms, the labourers hauling stone up wooden scaffolding to further raise the half-built walls. I refuse to appear impressed at the finely dressed stone, or openly admire the way the walls are set with many windows. The building may not yet be complete and, as yet, few of the windows are glazed, but it is clear to see that when they are finished the new family apartments will be ablaze with light.

A boy appears to take my bridle and as I prepare to dismount, Harry leaps from his saddle and assists me to the ground. My knees, suddenly weak, give a little and I clutch at his sleeve while the feeling returns. My belly churns with a mixture of excitement and dread. Will Henry remember me? Will his welcome be warm?

"My Lord Stafford, Lady Margaret! How was your journey?"

I turn to find a diminutive woman with a kind face and welcoming hands. I incline my head, unwilling to respond too much to the greeting of she who has stolen my role as Henry's mother.

"You must be Lady Herbert."

"But you must call me Anne." She swings an arm wide and invites us to follow her.

"The children are in the meadow, I expect. It is their usual haunt this time of day."

I am surprised. I would not have thought a visit from an estranged mother was an ordinary day for anyone. It certainly isn't for me. It is not easy to dislike her gentle face, her constant chatter. She links her arm through mine.

"Let us seek refreshment and I will send a servant to fetch the children. I told them to keep themselves clean but ..." She raises her hands and lets them fall again, in mock despair, "... well, you know what children are."

But I, being separated from my son, don't know, do I? I want to point this out, stress how much I resent her easy conversation about the child who is life and breath to me. The son she has stolen.

She leads us up a flight of steps. As we move into a passage it turns suddenly dark, and then light again as we cross into a long hall with a multitude of windows. We have been in splendid rooms before, of course we have, but none as new and grand as this. I make a note to have plans drawn up for Woking as soon as we return.

I am determined not to react, or to act as if I am unaccustomed to so much light and luxury. I flick a glance at Harry who, to my extreme annoyance, is craning his head, taking in the grandeur as if he is a ditch-dweller suddenly waking in a palace.

Anne moves to the window, and beckons me to join her. She points to two figures near the fish ponds. "There they are, always together. I am glad they've become such friends."

I hungrily follow the line of her finger and my heart lurches. My son is an infant no longer; he is a boy with gangly limbs and thick brown hair. My Henry. My eyes mist over, my throat grows tight.

"Who is that with him?"

Anne is close beside me. I can feel her breath on my cheek, she leans so close.

"My daughter, Maud. They are of an age."

Henry and Maud are walking slowly toward the castle, lifting their feet high in the long grass, deep in conversation. She carries a posy of late summer flowers, and he has removed his tunic, his shirt sleeves gleaming white in the sunshine. They look ... comfortable.

I am glad he has found a friend, but cannot help a stab of envy. I wonder what they speak of, what secrets they share. Will he resent being torn from the idyll of his morning to endure conversation with a mother he hardly knows?

As the children disappear into the shadow of the keep, we turn back into the room. A servant enters with refreshments. Too nervous with anticipation to drink, I clutch my cup of wine as if my life depends upon it, and wait with a labouring heart for them to climb the stairs. The latch on the door rattles, and a lifetime of waiting ensues as they pause, lingering too long with muffled giggles outside, and then it rattles again, and slowly opens.

I raise my chin, my face burning with emotion as a boy sidles into the room. Two steps in, he pauses to bow. I note the elegance and poise he has gained – the last time I saw him he still wore the plumpness of babyhood; now he is all skin and bone. I briefly wonder if they are feeding him properly.

As if under enchantment, I find I cannot move. I watch in a daze as my husband goes forward to greet Henry first.

"Henry." He clasps the boy's shoulder. "It has been a long time."

As Anne and her daughter quietly leave us, Harry and Henry turn toward me. He is smiling. I dare not blink for fear he will melt away.

"Hello, Mother."

I stare at his outstretched hand for several moments before I remember I must offer him mine. Harry relieves me of my cup, and Henry takes hold of my fingers. His palm is warm.

As he leans forward to place his lips on my knuckles, I notice his nails still bear the signs of his playtime in the meadow.

"Henry ..." My face feels as if it will split; there are tears on my cheek but I smile so widely that my jaw aches, and my heart leaps and bounces. "You have grown so tall."

"I am almost as tall as you, Mother."

I do not tell him I am pitifully short. I would not damage his pride, not for anything. All the worries I had for his well-being melt away. I can see he is well cared for, educated, and given the deference due to him. And, more importantly, he is happy. For the first time in his short life, he can enjoy the company of children of his own status, instead of consorting with servants.

An awkward silence settles while I search for something to say, something casual, something winning but not overly emotional. I do not want to smother him. I step closer to the window, and open my hands to the view. "I saw you walking in the meadow. It is very lovely here."

"Yes. The parkland is big. I sometimes ride to the hunt with ...with ..."

"Sir William?" I prompt as his voice trails away.

"I was going to say the Earl."

The word smacks me in the face. Herbert has been given the Earldom of Pembroke, and control over lands that rightly belong to Jasper. I glance at my son, notice that his lashes are short and sandy. I wonder if he realises that Herbert now controls the estates that once belonged to his family, people who loved and protected him. I cannot remind him, he is yet too young, but, oh, what will I do if Herbert turns Henry's head and his loyalty shifts to York?

"I am glad you enjoy outdoor pursuits, your father did too. He and your uncle Jasper often rode out together, hunting and hawking. I do myself, when I am able."

"I thought he was a soldier."

"Who? Your father? Oh, he was, but that wasn't all he was. Before the trouble came, he was young and as carefree as anyone else. He often spoke to me of his youth; his upbringing in the north of Wales, his mother and father."

His head turns, his brow crinkled in thought. "Wasn't his mother a queen? I think I remember Myfanwy telling me ... Queen Katherine?"

"Yes, that's right." I resist the urge to feel the texture of his hair, test the softness of his cheek. The bridge of his nose is sprayed with small reddish freckles.

"Then, why was he not a prince?"

I suppress a laugh.

"His father was ... sprung from the Welsh nobility, but he was not a king."

"Tom - that is one of the earl's other wards - he says Owen Tudor was the bastard son of an alehouse keeper, and that my father was a bastard too, begot while the queen was in her cups."

I cannot hide my shock. I grow hot as blood swamps my cheeks. I open my mouth and close it again as I try to stammer a few words before lapsing into confounded silence. I cast a helpless glance at Harry, who steps forward and takes Henry's shoulder.

"You mustn't listen to nonsense like that, lad. It is nought but wicked talk from jealous tongues. I knew both your father and your grandfather, and they were fine, upstanding men. Owen was devoted to his wife, fell in love with her on sight, and died with her name on his lips, so they say. You couldn't come from finer stock."

I blink moisture from my eye, swallow the lump in my throat, evoked by Harry's kindness.

"That's right, Henry, pay no mind to tittle-tattle. You can be proud of both your Tudor and your Beaufort blood."

"I am." He looks down at the toe of his shoe that is mired by mud, and then back up at me, gives an uncertain smile. "Lady Anne was telling me about your family ... my *Beaufort* family ... it is hard to follow."

I wonder what he has been told. Of my father dying by his own hand, accused of disloyalty to his king? Of the taint of bastardy handed down from my great-grandfather's day? I wager there has been no mention of loyalty to our deposed king, our political achievements, our noble bearing, our right to the throne stolen by a single act of Henry IV.

And the Beauforts would have made such great kings.

A voice outside gives warning of the approach of our hostess. The door opens and Anne Herbert enters with a huddle of children in tow: a child of perhaps two or three sits on her hip and another, a boy I think, clings to her skirts. Her daughter, Maud, holds the hand of another girl, slightly younger than herself. Anne Herbert has been more fortunate than I – I try not to feel barren as the room erupts with noisy introductions.

Henry is swamped by tow-headed Herberts; they treat him as if he is one of their own. Anne orders him to carry over a tray of drinks and dainties, and he does so without demur, as if long accustomed to doing her bidding.

We sit close to the window, the sun warm through the thick, green glass, and while the children exchange pleasantries, we sample the fayre until Anne breaks the silence.

"I am so glad you came, Lady Margaret. I have wanted to invite you for so long. I think Henry is happy with us."

I continue to chew, swallow as soon as I am able. I dab a crumb from my lips.

"I am sure he is. I can see he is very well, and he seems settled."

"He is one of the family." She smiles at Henry who returns it before ducking his head to take another bite of his pastry.

"Yes."

Doesn't she have enough children of her own? Can she not see the pain of having to sit by while my child is taken from me? Can she not imagine the torture of our separation?

"I know how you feel." She leans forward, puts her cup on the table. "When my elder sons left here to be trained in the art of war, I thought I should die without them. If I were unable to visit them regularly, I don't think I could bear it, so please, Margaret, do come often, won't you?"

Her own sons? I hadn't realised she had more, but surely a large number of offspring must offset some of the pain of losing one or two of them. She will never know the misery of having just one son who is her only font of love, her only hope of the future. But I smile, and promise to come.

"Perhaps you could visit us in turn. I should like to show Henry our home at Woking, where his grandfather lived."

She smiles widely, and Henry does too.

"As soon as the country is more settled, we will arrange it. We have every hope of a long lingering peace now that King Edward has restored order."

Is it a direct taunt, I wonder, or is she just oblivious to my past, my family connections? Perhaps she is just stupid.

I watch her wrap an arm about one of her daughters, pick a few crumbs from the child's skirts and flick them from her fingers into a dish. She is motherly, I have no doubt of that, and I am glad that such a woman has care of Henry. She will watch him, make sure he is happy. I decide to make a friend of Anne Herbert, and ensure that she keeps her promise to me.

"May I show you the gardens? I have heard you are very skilled, perhaps you can offer me some advice ..." At her suggestion, the children, too long constrained indoors, leap from their seats and skip toward the stairway. While Harry helps me with my cloak, and Anne fusses about the cleanliness of her daughters' skirts, Henry stands and waits for me, warming me with his wish for my company.

A glorious week follows, filled with hawking, feasting, and quiet walks in the gardens. Never has time passed so swiftly, and I wake on our last day with great regret. I have taken to rising early so as to be ready by the time Henry is released from his lessons. Leaving Harry snoring, I slide from bed and into the antechamber where my woman has laid out my clothes for the day. I wait impatiently as she sponges my body, anoints me with fragrance and helps me into my clothes; then I am forced to sit while she teases the knots from my hair before binding it tightly and hiding it beneath a fresh, crisp coif.

At last, I am free to venture to the hall to discover if anyone else is abroad. I push open a low door and step into an empty room. The fire has been set, the flames not yet properly taken hold, and smoke belches up the vast chimney. I move toward it but am prevented from drawing too close because of the dogs sprawled on the hearth. Over the past few days they have become accustomed to my presence, and most of them pay me no heed. But this morning, one I have not seen before raises his head and growls menacingly.

My body freezes, certain he is going to attack. I dare not move, *cannot* move as he lumbers to his feet, his head low, the fur on his neck bristling. My breath stops, my eye mesmerized by his yellow teeth, the thick strings of drool hanging from his mouth.

"Down, Demon!"

At the harsh voice, the beast subsides to the hearth, and begins to lick his paw as if he had never contemplated killing me. Almost swooning, I turn toward my saviour as he steps from the shadow, a sheaf of letters in his fist. "Lady Margaret, I presume. I hope you weren't alarmed by my dog."

A tall, thick-set man, unshaven and, judging by his mired clothes only recently dismounted from his horse. He looks tired, unkempt, his eyes red from lack of sleep. Belatedly, I notice a helmet and gauntlets on the table, a pile of saddlebags on a chair that speak of a new arrival. I can tell who he is by the stolen crest upon his coat.

"You have me at a disadvantage, Sir," I lie, clasping my hands behind me and raising my chin as imperiously as I can manage. He views me down his long nose, hawks unpleasantly and spits into the fire.

"The Earl of Pembroke, Madam ... at your service. You can call me Herbert, everybody else does."

"Then, I must thank you for your hospitality, Sir. Our stay here has been most enjoyable. Your wife cares for my son as if he is one of her own."

"Hmm. Anne mothers everyone, she would take in every waif and stray that passes the castle if I allowed it."

I bite my tongue, refusing to respond to his deliberate goad. His comparison of my son to a vagrant is clearly intended as an insult. The wardship of Henry can only be to his benefit. It certainly isn't to mine.

"And you have done so well with the improvements to the castle." *One would almost think you were born to such grandeur,* I add silently but, for Henry's sake, I do not speak aloud. "You are a lucky man."

His eyes do not flicker but remain fastened on my face. I hope my expression does not betray my rapidly beating heart.

"I chose to follow the true king, if that is what you mean by luck."

"Yes, my husband was in the company of the king a short time ago, and agrees he has all the makings of a good ruler."

If he notices I do not share the sentiment, he does not say so. He yawns rudely without covering his mouth. His tongue is vast and coated with something yellow and gruesome. I try not to flinch.

"And you have not yet been summoned to court, Lady Margaret?"

"Not yet, no." I close my lips tightly over my teeth, contain my annoyance within my clasped hands.

"Well, you can't blame the king for being choosy as to whom he invites. Now that Stafford has his foot in the door, it won't be long before you wiggle your way in."

I cannot believe his discourtesy, his lack of finesse. He has no care for my thoughts or feelings, and displays not the slightest hint of fear that his foot will ever slip from the high rung of the ladder he is balanced upon.

His ill-manner breaks my resolve. I open my mouth to fling the insults right back into his ugly, crude face. My voice emerges in a squeak, my tirade halted by quick footsteps coming helter-skelter down the stair. Herbert and I both turn as Henry tumbles into the room.

My son bows quickly and, without properly regaining his breath, gasps a good morning.

"Mother; my Lord. How are you both today?"

My son is staring at me intently, his eyes boring into mine, and I realise he is warning me to keep a rein on my temper. I let my anger go, and instead revel in the pleasure of his company.

"I am well, Henry," I say, regaining my equilibrium and moving toward him to receive his kiss. "Are you going to show me your hawk again this morning?"

"Yes. Shall we go now, before we break our fast?" With an elegant bow to Herbert, he grabs my hand and all but drags me from the hall.

We pass quickly through the inner court, already teeming with life, and hurry toward the gatehouse. Thankfully, the drawbridge is lowered. We step aside to make room for a cart; its wheels make a rumbling sound as it crosses over and passes into the keep.

On the other side, Henry slows his pace, drops my hand and allows me to catch my breath. He squats at the side of the moat, throws a small stone into the deep dark water and watches the circles that radiate from it. He glances up at me through his fringe. "Sorry, Mother, but I thought you were going to argue with him. You must never do that, not if you are to be allowed to continue to visit me here. I hope I have not made you angry."

"No, no. I could never be angry with you." I move close and crouch at his side, sweep his hair from his eyes with my finger. "You were right. I was about to be unforgivably rude."

"I was listening on the stair; he was trying to goad you. He is not a bad man but is ever vigilant for those who might be an enemy to his king."

"But I am just a woman, Henry. What threat could I ever be?"

"Margaret of Anjou is just a woman, Mother, and they are very wary of her."

"Well, then it is a good job she is safely in exile. Come, we should not let all this spoil our last day. Show me your hawk. Perhaps we could ride out later on and you can demonstrate your skill."

"I am not very skilled yet, but I will be."

There follows a windswept day of laughter in the park. I am proud to note that Henry is a capable horseman, his mount responsive to his command, and the hawk on his wrist on its best behaviour. The fresh air whips colour into Henry's cheeks, his eyes shine with pleasure, and I realise I have not enjoyed myself so much for a great many years.

Afterwards, we dine in the great hall, and I manage to successfully swallow my dislike of Herbert and join in the conversation, sharing jokes and stories as if Anne and her youngsters are long-time acquaintances.

Henry sits beside me. Throughout the meal, he talks of his hawk, his love of dogs, his lessons, and his sword practice. I sense his frustration at not being able as yet to beat the older boys.

Later, with our bellies replete, we play cards, just the two of us, seated a little apart from the others, who gather at the hearth as if recognising my desire to be alone with Henry on our last night. When he beats me for the third time, I reach out and trap his hand. He raises his eyes as if I am about to accuse him of cheating.

We stare at one another while my thumb caresses the back of his fingers. "I have enjoyed my time here with you so much, Henry. I hope it won't be long before we are together again."

He smiles cheerfully. "I hope so too."

"I shall write to you very often and send you presents."

He wrinkles his nose. "Myfanwy said she would write, but she never has. I think she has forgotten all about me."

My breath catches at the stark unhappiness in his voice. His early years were spent far more in Myfanwy's company than my own, and I know she cares for him dearly.

"But I am your mother. I would never forget to write."

He shrugs and bends his head to the cards again, sorting them into pairs. I look across at the hearth, my eye caught by Herbert's. He rubs his nose and looks away, unsmiling, unabashed at having been caught watching us. I know without a shadow of doubt what has become of Myfanwy's letters to Henry.

"Herbert is a great soldier." Henry's voice drags me back to the matter in hand as he deals out the cards and replenishes my pile of coin so we might play again.

"So I have heard. Your father was a great man too. I have no doubt he would have easily matched Herbert ... had he lived."

I watch him fan out the cards he has dealt himself. He bites his lip and narrows his eyes in concentration. Does he know of the role Herbert played in his father's death? Can he be aware of the circumstances? He gives no sign of it, and it is just as well. His life would be impossible if he knew he lived at the mercy of a man instrumental in his father's death.

The room is lit only by the night candle and the ebbing fire. Harry's breath in my ear is regular. Every so often he shifts to a more comfortable position, mutters a few indistinguishable words before snoring again. I envy him such oblivion.

In the morning he will be rested and fresh for the road while I will be shadowy-eyed and irritable. My eyes hardly close all night as I fret about the necessity of leaving Henry again. I dread Herbert's complete authority over my boy's future.

The only comfort I can find is in Lady Anne, who I am sure has taken him to her heart. She has almost become a friend during my stay, and assures me she loves him like her own, and will write to me should any ill befall him.

I pray God it never does.

At dawn, I hear my woman moving stealthily about the antechamber as she lays out my clothes. Sickness churns in my belly at the thought of leaving, but the sound of water trickling into a bowl forces me to rise. I throw back the covers and brace myself for the pain of parting and the long lonely months that will follow.

Woking - Spring 1468

I can scarcely credit six months have passed since we rode away from Raglan. The last memory I have is of

Henry waving from the top of the tallest tower, the one closest to the moat and the gatehouse. His white kerchief flapped like a banner; each time I turned it grew smaller, his wave less energetic. I wept all the way home until Harry grew impatient, stopped trying to cheer me, and kicked his mount forward to ride on ahead.

During these six months, I have not been idle. First, there was the surprise announcement of Harry's mother's betrothal to Walter Blount, and the wedding that followed. She glowed with happiness on the day of their marriage, and it was not until then that I realised how hard widowhood had been for her. As they rode away to their new life with promises to visit soon, I was both glad for her joy and heavy-hearted at parting with another friend.

While I keep myself occupied with charitable works, Harry is busy, riding back and forth, from court to home, to the West Country, to Bristol. Sometimes, when he visits our estates, I accompany him; sometimes, I stay behind to oversee the improvements taking place at Woking. I am most excited about the new solar apartment. Not quite as ostentatious as the rooms at Raglan, but when they are complete they will be bright and spacious, and hopefully allow the sun to warm us and keep our spirits raised even on the darkest days of winter.

There are also preparations to be made for a stay in London in May. My garderobe is full of new clothes suitable for court, for the king has at last agreed that I should accompany Harry on his next visit. When I run my hands through the sumptuous silks, rub my cheek on the fur and count my numerous pairs of shoes, my whole body thrills with anticipation.

I am not in any way keen to meet the king. My opinion of him has not altered at all, but I am very eager to return to court. I have never properly attended as a woman grown; I was just a child when I was introduced to King Henry and Queen Margaret all those years ago. Now, there is a different king, a new set of courtiers, and I wonder who else will be present. Will I be able to learn the new dances in time? Is the queen quite as beautiful as they pretend?

The Mitre Inn, Cheapside - May 1468

Although The Mitre is one of the most renowned establishments in London, it is not the royal court and I chafe at the confinement while Harry goes to London alone. Calling my women, I decide to go shopping, and trying very hard not to envy Harry sampling the delights of Westminster, I soothe myself at the best goldsmiths. When Harry comes home, full of talk of the king's intention to invade France, I pretend indifference, although in truth I am dying to hear it.

"You could come to Westminster," he says in an attempt to appease me, "but I cannot force the king to receive you."

"You expect me to kick my heels waiting in some outer chamber until he sees fit to receive me? I think not. No, I will do some visiting in your absence. I may even write to my sister Edith; her home is not too far away."

I keep my nose tilted toward the ceiling, knowing my pride hurts no one but myself. He gives a deep sigh before he walks away – and I bite my lip. Perhaps I am hurting Harry too; he had such hopes for this trip. How very like this damned Yorkist king to spoil it for us. The teasing invitation to London, and the subsequent lack of royal summons is the king's way of further punishing me, but I refuse to wait outside like some pet dog while Harry is invited to the royal presence.

*

The picture of Edith I have treasured in my mind all these years is quite flawed. She has changed, and is no longer a pink-cheeked maid but a full grown, one might say matronly, woman. But when she opens her arms, the distance between us closes, and I receive her kiss with pleasure. The strangeness is only skin deep.

We seat ourselves in the gardens where she is full of praise for her brood of children, and I see she does not resent the thickening of her body, for she has compensations. As she speaks, her hands perform a dance of their own, in a way I had quite forgotten.

"Tell me about Henry, Margaret. How often do you see him?"

I need no further prompting. Praise for Henry is never far from my tongue. The picture I paint is a glorious one; there is no fairer child this side of Heaven, no one better in the tiltyard, or in the schoolroom.

"I would do anything for him, anything," I end, my eyes misting with tears.

"That is part of being a mother, Margaret. I would do anything for my children too. Have ... have you written to our mother, you know she has been very ill?"

"No, I didn't know, and I haven't written. There is too much ..." I lower my head and she reaches out and grasps my hands.

"What happened between you? I know there is something, but she will never say ..."

I sigh, looking back along the years to the woman I idolised in the nursery, and shrug my shoulders.

"Nothing happened. No harsh words were spoken but I suppose I just grew up and realised certain things that made her become well ... tarnished."

"Tarnished? How?"

"I – I don't know ..."

I stand up and move away along the path. Edith follows, catching my arm.

"You might feel better if you tell me, Margaret. You shouldn't keep things buried inside."

I sigh again, close my eyes and tilt my face up toward the sky.

"I feel as if she sold me, Edith. I was a child. She promised the marriage to Edmund would not be consummated, she promised me I would see her regularly, and then ..." My voice grows louder, tears spout from my eyes, surprising even myself. I almost shout. "And then she let them take me into Wales, far away from all I knew, and Edmund ..."

"Was he so bad, Margaret? Oh, my poor sis..."

"NO! He wasn't bad at all. After a while, I even came to love him, and had he lived, we would have been happy. But I was a *child*, in a strange place with strange customs. Surrounded by adults, every one of them telling me what I should do, what I should say... She *knew*, Edith, she knew he would bed me, and I was not ready. Edmund made the clauses of our marriage quite clear to her before we were betrothed. He told me it was so, and he would not have lied to me."

She stares at me, her double chins gathered in concern, her eyes full of trouble as I continue. "Her haste to marry me off to the highest bidder robbed me of the big brood of children I always wanted."

"It was a very good match." Edith wallows helplessly, trying to comfort me. "And you do have Henry; it could have been so much worse. I think she was just trying to get the best for you, as she has for all of us."

While Edith's words eat into my mind, the world pauses, the birds stop singing. It was not the marriage that hurt me, or the things that took place within it. They are just part of life, nothing to shy away from, nothing to fear. It was the way I was given away, traded, as if I were a sack of corn or a bale of wool. As a grown woman perhaps Mother had forgotten I was just a little girl, and how strange the world would seem to me. I have almost forgotten how young I was myself.

Edith's words force me, for the first time, to see that the position Mother sought for me was not for her benefit. It was for mine. All at once, her ambition for me does not seem so calculated, or so cold. What she did for me, I would do for Henry. I would climb a ladder to the moon to secure a good marriage for my son, and I doubt it would be different had I a daughter.

I watch Edith dab at her tears. She sniffs, licks her lips, and when eye contact is resumed, she gently continues. "She didn't know what would happen; all she could do was hope for the best. She had no control; none of us have control over the fate of our children once they leave our nurseries."

I stare at her without really seeing her. My mind is far away, in another world where I have a daughter about to enter marriage. I would want a powerful match for her, too.

"Yes, perhaps you are right. I have never looked at it that way before."

Mother should not have lied to me, but I can see now that her lie may have been her way of protecting me. I should have spoken with Edith a long time ago.

Woking - 1468

I return to Woking disgruntled, most of my fine new clothes still unworn. Try as I might, I cannot hide my resentment at Harry's acceptance at court and my own exclusion. I know he can sense it, but he avoids any discussion. He rides at my side, trying to distract me into a better humour by pointing out landmarks on the way.

In the end, he succeeds, and by the time we are half way home, I begin to feel better. Harry is right, I am too impatient, and there are so many things I have to be grateful for. I love Harry; when he is absent I miss his silly sense of humour, our camaraderie that is so rare in marriage. He is with me now, and I would be foolish to waste time sulking because of the king's vindictive behaviour.

I have no intention of letting the king's continuing punishment spoil my life. While I wait for his pardon and welcome to court, I turn my attention to improving the accommodation at Woking and attending to the physic garden.

As always in times of stress, Harry's skin is inflamed, the sores on his neck weeping again. The salve I usually administer is becoming ineffective, and I have a new recipe I wish to try. I also intend to force myself to sit down and write to Mother; it will not be an easy letter to write but I have a better understanding of her now and think I can find it within myself to forgive. It is time to move on from the past. As Edith stressed, I would not have Henry had Mother not arranged my union with Edmund.

It is a fine summer. We entertain a lot this year. Edith, her husband and their brood of children spend a week with us in July, and Harry's mother comes in

August with her new husband in tow. A few days later his brother John arrives.

It is a happy time. We shut out all thoughts of the king and the happenings at court to relax with our family, and take joy in them. Only Henry is missing.

At the end of the month, Harry attends the Grand Tournament with his nephew, the Duke of Buckingham. He tentatively suggests I go with him, but I decline, claiming a megrim, and he rides away alone. I spend my time writing letters; to Henry, to Myfanwy, to Mother, to Anne Herbert. When I write to Anne, I enclose a package of new shirts I have embroidered for my son, who I am told is growing fast.

News filters to me of Jasper's continuing harassment of the king's forces on the border, eluding capture and angering the Yorkist leaders. I am torn. In my heart, I applaud Jasper's refusal to submit, and secretly long for his one-man campaign to reinstate Henry VI to succeed. If it was so, with the true king restored, my son could return to our care. But I am conscious that Jasper's actions could also place my son in real peril, for Henry is in their hands, a hostage to our good behaviour.

I always mourn the end of summertime. I look glumly on the lank dead growth in the garden, the yellowing leaves on the trees, soon to be swept away by the vast storms of autumn.

Indoors, at the fireside, although it is many weeks away, I sew New Year presents for the household; fine linen for Harry, a nightshirt for Henry, a partlet to send to Myfanwy, who is still living as Jasper's concubine in the far north of Wales. I also fashion caps for her daughters, Ellen and Joan. I pray more too, asking God's mercy for the needy, for Henry's health and happiness, and for a continuation of peace in England.

As the cold of winter begins to bite, my knees grow bruised, and the small of my back aches from kneeling. With a hand to my side, I rise and make a painful journey back to the newly refurbished solar.

In the daytime, the light pours in through the thick green glass, but this evening the shutters are closed, the chairs pulled up before the hearth with a screen erected to shut out the draughts.

"Harry!" I exclaim when I see him holding his hands to the flames. "When did you get home?"

We meet and embrace in the centre of the room.

"An hour since. You were praying, I suppose? I didn't like to disturb you."

"I wasn't praying for long," I lie, and turn to the table, which is piled high with food. "I am glad I ordered supper here in our rooms."

I take my seat at the table and Harry joins me, signalling to the servers to begin.

Harry often nags me to eat more. He says I fast too much and too often, but I have no great interest in food and eat only until I am satisfied. Because his appetite resembles a donkey's, I appear half-starved in comparison. I watch him take a big bite of pie, wash it down with a slurp of ale. He dabs his mouth with a napkin.

"I have some news." He chews again, swallows, and leans toward me across the table. "From the king."

I raise my brows, my interest piqued, and urge him to continue. "At last, the king has accepted our invitation and promises to hunt with us ... quite soon, in fact."

"Soon?" I throw down my napkin and rise to my feet, as if the king and his company will arrive any moment.

"Well, not that soon, but sooner than I expected. He will arrive in December – just before the Christmas celebrations begin.

"He is coming here ... to Woking?"

"Where else? I know no better hunting ... apart from Windsor. I thought we could ride out to Brockwood, entertain him there."

The hunting lodge at Brockwood will be perfect. I smile with satisfaction and snap my fingers to send a page to fetch Master Bray. Between us, we will make the king's visit something he will never forget.

For the first time since the disappointment of May, I am glad the new clothes I ordered for court still hang pristine in the garderobe. All I need do is decide which gown to wear, and hope and pray they still fit.

*

"It is to be a hunt, Margaret! You cannot wear that." Harry, ignoring the kneeling woman who fiddles with the hem of my gown, examines me from head to toe, taking in the satin and velvet, the newly furred sleeves.

"I won't be hunting all the time. This is for afterwards. I am planning a vast celebration. How do I look?"

I stand erect, posing regally.

"Perfect. Like a queen."

Ignoring his stunned expression, I run my fingers across the fabric and strain to see myself in the looking glass.

"Good. I am determined to prove we are every bit as good as he and his Grey widow."

Harry raises his eyes to Heaven, shakes his head and wanders off on an errand of his own. He will never understand the importance of living up to one's status. Even Master Bray has a better grasp of that than Harry.

I hold out my arms so that my seamstress may ensure that the bodice is snug yet comfortable, and there is no straining at the waist. She sits back on her knees and removes two pins from her mouth.

"I think it needs to be taken in a nip at the waist, my lady."

"Taken in? I have lost weight again?" Harry, who is always saying I don't eat enough to feed a flea, will say 'I told you so.'

"How quickly can it be ready?"

"By tomorrow, my lady, it is only a small task. I shall also sew extra pearls on the bodice, as you requested."

"Thank you."

I smile at her and she bows her head, rises to her feet and begins to unlace me at the back. I pull off my veil and cap, take the pins from my hair and massage my scalp while the woman lets the gown pool around my feet. I step from it, a hand to my brow. I have the beginnings of a headache but it is hardly surprising considering the long lists of tasks I have before the king arrives.

For days now, I have barely sat down, but today I am beaten. I summon my chamber women and ask to be helped to bed.

It is unheard of for me to lie down during the day and the news brings Harry to my chamber. Just as I am dropping off to sleep, the door creaks open. "Margaret?" he whispers loudly and, with a sigh, I turn in the bed and pull back the drape. I can see only his head as he peeks around the door.

"Yes, Harry, what do you want?"

Ludicrously, since I am clearly awake, he tiptoes across the room and perches on the edge of the mattress.

"Are you all right? They said you are ailing. You are never ill. I was worried."

Keeping my hand in his hot palm, I roll on to my back, stare at the canopy.

"I have a head-ache; that is all. I thought a short sleep might chase it away."

"Oh, you have been doing too much again." He strokes my hair from my face, feels my forehead, pulls down my bottom eyelid as my mother used to do. "Bloodshot," he says, his brow wrinkling. "Perhaps I should join you; sleep may come quicker if you lie in my arms."

His ploy is not lost on me, but I allow him to climb onto the bed and gladly rest my head on his shoulder. To the rhythmic rise and fall of his chest, his fingers gentle on my upper arm, I close my eyes and let contentment wash over me. I begin to drift away, the sound of his breathing like an opiate.

"Ahh, this is nice…" His voice rumbles in my ear, but sleep is tugging me. I am safe and warm, there is no need to answer.

It could be a moment, or maybe hours later when I realise his soft caress of my arm has shifted to my breast. His touch is more urgent, his breathing deep and slow.

I open my eyes.

Me and Harry lie nose to nose on the pillow, his pupils dark and wide. Something lurches in my belly as I begin to fall into them. My mouth tilts into a smile and we roll over together. I raise my arms, link my wrists about his neck and pull him closer, mouth on mouth.

December 1468

"It is raining, Harry!" My voice is full of dismay as I open the shutters. "A week of dry weather, yet the day everything hinges on dawns grey and wet."

He throws back the covers and joins me at the window, peering past the opposite tower to the stripe of daylight on the horizon.

"It will not last. I swear, by the time the sun has risen, the rain will have gone with the night. Did you sleep well?"

He kisses my forehead, then opens his mouth in a huge yawn, revealing the gap in his jaw where a couple of teeth were knocked out during horseplay with his cousins when he was a boy.

"I barely closed my eyes. My mind is so busy with the arrangements."

"Do not worry yourself so. The king will still want to hunt no matter what the weather brings, and his appetite is hearty and undemanding as long as the food is edible. He is easily pleased."

"I have ordered only the very best," I answer sharply. "Swan, conger eel, his favourite lamprey pie, and almost a thousand oysters. There are to be at least twenty servers and the banqueting tent has been erected in the prettiest part of the wood."

"Twenty servers, Margaret? Just for the king? I rather imagined he was looking to escape all that for the day ..."

"Nonsense, he is a king. It is what he will expect."

Harry sighs, scratches his flaky scalp and shuffles off in search of his man. He will wait on the king at Guildford, and will escort him to the feast from there. I have ensured his clothes are of the finest cut and fabric available, and I myself will be wearing the furred velvet gown that Harry believes to be unsuitable. It is imperative that we do not waste this opportunity to impress the king. If we are ever to enter his inner circle of trusted friends, nothing must go wrong.

As my women fuss around me, anointing my skin with fragrance, helping me into fresh linen and fine silk petticoats, I allow my mind to wander.

By all accounts, the king is tall and handsome; a knightly figure with a golden tongue and a wayward eye for women. Yet descriptions of kings are ever so. Only a fool would describe the reigning monarch as ugly, squat and simple. I saw his father once and he was a dark-haired man of middling height, so I expect the king to be of a similar stature.

Master Bray answers my summons and we run through a hundred issues. Is it still raining? Is the tent erected and dry? Are the braziers burning bright? Have the cooks got the food in the ovens, the meat on the spits?

As always, he is patient, answering calmly and quietly, appeasing my nerves.

"All is in readiness, my lady. We wait only upon you."

I pause, my mind rapidly running over the arrangements, my heart leaping and bouncing with nerves. I pick up my psalter.

"I have to pray."

The cool, calm quiet of the chapel quickly soothes me. The hard stone is solid beneath my knees, God's love and approval hangs thick in the air, like a comforter. I bow my head, clasp my hands, my lips moving rapidly as I beseech Him to show favour to me this day, and let me find approval with this Yorkist king.

"The rain has stopped, my lady. I think the afternoon will be fine, after all." I glance at my women, Elizabeth Johnson and Jane Atkins, who sit opposite me in the litter. Elizabeth clasps my riding clothes, and my spare fur-lined cloak. Jane's nose is red and moist from the chilly air; I hope mine is not the same. For the umpteenth time, I pull back the leather curtain and peer outside.

"This time of year, the day will be over before it has a chance to warm up, but I ordered the braziers to be kept burning overnight, so it should be warm enough in the pavilion."

"I doubt the men will be cold after the hunt, my lady. They invariably return with their blood up and heed the weather not at all."

"Hmm."

Having no wish to make idle conversation, I answer shortly. I want to contemplate the next few hours. In my mind, I run through likely scenarios in which I delight the king with my ready wit, my great elegance.

"Have you met the king before, my lady?"

"No ..." I turn to look at Elizabeth. "Have you?"

"Oh, I have not met him but I have seen him. He is a giant of a man, tall and golden like a great living statue."

"Really? I always imagined those things were fabrications, born of flattery."

"Oh no, he is ... charming, and with an eye for the ladies."

"Hmm. I doubt he will have an eye for me."

She lapses into silence and I return to my waking dream. In this scenario I am blessed with beauty. I flutter my lashes, laugh at his jokes and the king is besotted and summons my son to court, and shows him the honour he deserves.

We approach the hunting lodge, passing a party of horsemen who have paused at the roadside. One of their dogs runs after the litter, barking, his tongue lolling, his great tail wagging. A rough male voice calls him back. I am reminded of Edmund's dog, Jay, as he would have been in his prime.

When I knew him, he was elderly, his muzzle speckled grey, his hunting days over. Poor dear Jay, he expired just after his master died, as if his reason for existing had passed. I often miss him.

Harry doesn't keep dogs in the house, only in the stable for hunting. Perhaps I should get one for myself. Not one of those ridiculous little things women tend to adore, but a proper dog, with silky ears and a tail like a banner.

Jane leans forward, peers beneath the curtain.

"I think we are here, my lady."

"Are my cap and veil straight?"

"Yes, my lady. We can ensure you are tidy once we are inside."

All is in readiness for the king. I am dressed; the tables are set, the servants all in their places, and the delicious aroma of roast swan wafts about the pavilion. The only thing lacking is the king himself.

I curse beneath my breath as I am beset with the sudden need for the close stool. I have been suffering with nervousness all day and now they are late. If Harry has allowed himself to be distracted on the road, I will never forgive him.

My stomach churns sickeningly, and my palms are clammy. It will never do to greet the king with sticky hands. I summon Jane and she assists me behind the screen, holding my skirts and supporting my arm as I rise, ensuring my petticoats are straight. On my return to the hall, a ewer steps forward with a bowl. I rinse my fingers in cool water, dab them dry on a towel.

Master Bray steps close beside me.

"Sir Harry and the king have been sighted on the road, my lady."

I reach out, grasp his sleeve.

"Thank you, Master Bray. Oh, pray that this day goes well."

His smile is warm and reassuring.

"It will, my lady, if there is any justice in this world."

If there is any justice? So far, in my experience, that has seldom been the case. But I cannot dwell upon that now. The time is almost here.

"Come along," I call to my women, and they cluster around me, checking the folds of my veil, the fall of my skirts. With my chin high, I lead them outside, and we arrange ourselves in a pretty manner to meet the king.

My head feels light and there is a sharp ringing in my ears. It could be nerves, or it could be that I have eaten little since supper last night, and the aroma of the feast is taunting my appetite.

Horse hooves thump in the wood, a rider swerves into view, a boy dismounts, scurries toward us.

"They are coming, my lady. Prepare to greet the king."

"As if we haven't been prepared for hours," I grumble, swatting at some imagined stain on my sleeve.

The day is darkening, the wood misty and moist as I spy a splash of colour among the dank greenery. A host of men ride into the clearing, and I recognise Harry riding beside a stranger. A stranger with bright, golden hair.

They heave their horses to a halt. Harry leaps from his mount, lets go of the reins and hurries to the king's stirrup to help him alight.

The king gestures him away and leaps to the ground, light on his feet, a vibrant, youthful splash of grandeur. His hair is bright as he looks about him; his smile, despite the dullness of the afternoon, is like the sun. My heart plummets.

For once, the gossips spoke the truth. He *is* like a golden god. The tallest, most striking man I have ever met. I feel short and ungainly, like a child, like a dwarf. I stand as tall as I can and hope with all my heart that he does not mistake me for one of the entertainers.

As he strides toward me, I sink to the ground in obeisance. I stare at his well-turned shoes, his strongly formed calf muscles, and think only one thing. *How on God's earth am I ever to impress this man?*

"Lady Margaret, we are delighted to meet you."

I struggle for my voice, find it just in time.

"And I, you, Your Grace."

He looks at the purple sarcenet banqueting tent, the pristine tablecloths, the high table laden with shining pewter dishes, and the throne-like chair calling a welcome.

"You have gone to a lot of trouble."

"It is my pleasure, Your Grace. Nothing is too much. I have waited so long to meet you."

He ignores the veiled rebuke, takes a cup of wine from a server and gulps it down in one draught. A little trickles down his chin and he traps it with his finger before a servant has time to fetch a napkin.

"Shall we take our places, Your Grace?" Harry steps forward, ushers the king to his seat. Once he is settled, we take our places either side of him.

Although I am famished I can eat very little, for my stomach is overtaken with nerves. The king, on the other hand, clearly does not suffer the same complaint. He partakes heartily of everything put before him, nodding and congratulating me before he has even swallowed.

I nibble a slice of lamprey pie.

"Such a shame the queen could not accompany you, Your Grace. I hope she is well, and your daughters too."

"The princesses Elizabeth and Mary are growing apace, and the queen is big with child again, which is why she could not join me. The physicians say we can expect the birth sometime around March. We hope for a son this time."

His eyes focus on my face, as if searching for an ill-wish upon his longed-for son and heir.

"Oh, so do we all," I lie, with a wide indulgent smile. "There is no blessing quite like a son."

He regards me from the corner of his eye, one side of his mouth downturned. He chews thoughtfully for a while.

"Remind me, Lady Margaret, you have a child, don't you? Richmond's son."

"I do, yes, Your Grace. He is called Henry ..." My voice trails away as I recall he was named after the king deposed by this man. He keeps his bright blue eyes on me but says nothing as I continue. "My son is in Wales, with his guardian, William Herbert."

"Ah, yes. That's right. He is in good hands, good loyal hands."

"I should hope so, Your Grace."

I keep my eye on my trencher, taking dainty bites, trying not to let either my nerves or my dislike of the king show. For Henry's sake, I must make a friend of him.

As the plates empty and Edward pushes his away, I clap my hands, summoning the servants and giving the signal for the entertainments to begin.

The minstrels come first. Three players singing of misfortune and lost love. The king, mellowed by wine and replete with food, leans back in his seat. As the last notes die away, he looks at me and wipes away a tear.

I lean a little closer, risk a smile. His head lolls until he drinks again, watching me over the rim of his cup. "You must accompany your husband next time he comes to court," he says. "The queen would be pleased to make your acquaintance. I believe her mother and yours were friends?"

Trapped in his wide, unblinking gaze, I smile and blush, praying he will not see my terror. Moments pass while he assesses me, then he licks his lips, his tongue red and moist.

I try not to think of all the women he has kissed and discarded. And then he speaks, sending a cold spark of fear to the base of my spine.

"Your eyes are very much like those of the doe I shot this morning, Lady Margaret."

Woking - July 1469

We are lately returned from hunting at Windsor. My body is stiff, but it is the sort of tiredness that feels good. After a long restful sleep, I venture into the garden while the dew is still on the ground.

So far, the summer has been all I could wish for; the beds in the garden are abundant, the stores in the still-room flourishing. Every day, as soon as I have prayed and broken my fast, I make my way outside and spend as long as I can dead-heading the spent blooms and pulling up stray weeds.

I prefer to garden alone, so I can let my thoughts wander without disturbance. I pick up my trug basket, brimming with clippings. As I approach the medicinal bed, the gate squeaks and I hear Harry's rapid footfall on the path. I turn to greet him, my smile withering the moment I notice his grim expression.

"There is news, Margaret. Come."

He turns on his heel. I drop my basket and run after him, grabbing at the back of his cloak, but he eludes me. I follow to his private chamber, the place he likes to go over his books and write his letters.

He throws open the door.

"Ned!" He is sprawled in a chair, the mire of the road still upon him. "What has happened? Is Henry ill?"

"Not ill, no, my lady ..."

Harry steps forward, takes my arm, leads me to a seat.

"I want you to stay calm, Margaret. There has been another battle."

"Another battle? When? Why? Who is ...?" His raised hand silences me. I lick my lips, look earnestly from Harry to Ned and back again. It seems an hour before Harry speaks.

"You have heard the rumours of the recent uprising in the north?"

"You mean the one led by Robin of Redesdale? Is that what you mean?"

"It was a lure, a trap, set by Warwick."

"Warwick?"

"Let me finish!"

I shrink back from the reprimand and allow him to explain, although my mind teems with questions.

"We think Warwick instigated the uprising and when King Edward rode north, he – Warwick - rode into London and took possession of the capital."

"But why ...?"

"He has been at odds with the king ever since he married Elizabeth Grey. Warwick has come to hate the queen and her family ... He is not alone in that."

"No ..."

I have heard tales of the queen's family receiving preferment over worthier nobles, but I had not thought it would lead to this. "But Warwick? In rebellion against the king? It makes no sense. Warwick helped Edward to the throne. One might even say he put him there!"

"Exactly, and now that the king has shown he has a mind of his own, and isn't prepared to always agree with Warwick, the earl has taken matters into his own hands."

"Go on."

I clasp my hands tightly in my lap, my eyes fastened on his face. I am ready for anything.

"There was a battle ... at Edgecot Moor ... William Herbert and his brother, Richard, were taken ... and executed."

My head feels light and fuzzy. I spring from my chair, sending it spinning across the room.

"What? Herbert is slain? Where is Henry? Where is Henry?"

My voice cracks. The room spins. I feel hands on my body, pulling me this way and that, trying to force me to sit down. Blackness swirls in from the edges of the room, their faces, white with panic, shouting words I cannot comprehend. I am engulfed.

I struggle through fog, my mind screaming, my stomach rebelling.

"Margaret, Margaret!" Harry shakes me, and my teeth clash together, my head lolling like a ragged doll. "Drink this."

A cup. I cling to it, gulp thick, red wine. I open my eyes and discover dread is all around me.

"Where is Henry?" I repeat, my voice no more than a croak.

"We don't know. It seems Herbert took the boy with him for his first taste of battle. He has not yet been found."

"Oh my God." It is not blasphemy. It is a heart-wrenching prayer. Ned's white face swims into view.

"I searched for him, my lady. As soon as I heard the news, I diverted from the road to Raglan and rode for Banbury instead. I saw many soldiers on the road, many injured, many slaughtered, but no sign of your son."

"No sign of Henry ..."

My lips feel numb, the screeching in my head a banshee of panic. "We must go and search for him. When he is found, we must beg the king for his release into our keeping."

"Margaret." Harry takes my chin and turns my face to his. I refocus my eyes with difficulty. "The king has been taken. Warwick has him captive."

My mouth falls open. Nothing makes sense any more. How did this glorious summer morning turn to this? My world is crumbling, falling apart.

Fighting free of the petticoats tangled about my legs, I scramble to rise.

"Then we must search for Henry ourselves. I will be ten minutes, no more. Have the horses made ready, Ned."

Twenty minutes later, taking only the things we stand up in, we are riding the road to Banbury. Harry has issued orders for the steward to send men and supplies after us. Master Bray will see to it. Harry rides beside me, grim-faced, unspeaking, while Ned, still worn out from his earlier journey, droops in the saddle.

It is difficult to know where to begin searching. Henry could be anywhere. I imagine him hurt, lying in a blood-filled ditch, his eyes wide open, staring unseeing at the sky. I imagine him captured by the enemy, tortured, bullied.

He is just twelve years old! My mind screams – he is just a child; surely, even our enemies will recognise that fact. I try not to acknowledge the horrors our soldiers of Lancaster have heaped upon the young men of York.

Close to Oxford, when it grows too dark to see the way ahead, we stop for the night. I force down some food but I do not sleep. The images of Henry in dire need do not allow me to rest.

I am up at dawn, dressed and ready to move on, but Harry forces me to take a little breakfast, and insists on finding fresh horses for the rest of the journey.

Ned, who has been talking with the stable boys, comes to us just as we are making ready to leave. Straightaway, I notice his expression is more hangdog than before.

"What now?" I ask, dreading his answer. He shuffles his feet, reluctantly opens his mouth and blurts his news.

"I overheard the boys talking in the stable – just gossip, I hope, but there is a rumour that the queen's father and brother have been executed."

Harry emits a strange sound, something between a shout and a gasp. We exchange disbelieving looks, although neither of us doubts the story. He scratches his head, screws up his face.

"There will be no going back for Warwick now. The king will never forgive this ..."

"And neither will the queen."

Warwick is an outcast now; an enemy to both York and Lancaster, but I feel no pity for him. He has ever been a thorn in Lancaster's flesh but I do spare some pity for his wife and daughters. Women are ever the victims in our men's wars.

My sympathy grows when we learn that he has married the elder girl to the king's brother, George, a feckless sot who has ever hankered for his brother's crown. Warwick is in very deep, so deep I do not doubt he will soon founder. Unless, of course, he wins.

I have never before seen a battlefield. The fighting is over, the soldiers have departed, and people have begun to take away the mangled remains of the slaughtered. But it is still a terrible place; it is as if the ghost of the carnage remains, the stench of the hatred is not yet spent. The ground is mired, the mud in places stained red, and churned like a field set for barley.

I cannot believe my Henry was here to witness this. There are great holes in the once-green meadow, dead horses, abandoned wagons, spent shot, and broken blades, pieces of harness. I think the reverberation of battle will linger here forever.

We rein in our mounts and, side by side, survey the field. There is nothing left, nobody to ask direction. I kick my horse into the centre of the ruined meadow, stand up in my stirrups, turning this way and that, desperately searching for a small frightened face, the sight of a lone brown-haired boy concealed somewhere. He must be close.

I wrench the horse's head around and trot smartly back to Harry.

"What now, my lord?"

He shrugs. "Perhaps we should try Anne Herbert; she may have had news of him."

"She would have sent someone to tell me were that so."

"But you are here, Margaret; she will not imagine for one moment you would ride out in search of him."

"She is a mother too. She would know I would not just wait at home."

But that is a woman's lot, is it not? To wait at home while our husbands and sons perish and maim themselves in battle. It has ever been so.

The road to Raglan is long and hard, my nether parts are chafed by the saddle, my head aches from peering into the sun-bleached horizon. With every mile we travel, I wish it were ten more, but at times I feel we are moving backwards.

Harry forces us to stop at an inn for refreshment. He questions the innkeeper who looks at us askance, as if we are not to be trusted. I doubt he even believes us when we tell him who we are and hint at the business that brings us here. In truth, I probably would not believe it either.

Our clothes are mired, our faces grubby, and we lack the vast company that usually attends those of our station. As a result, the ale he serves us is not from his choicest barrel, there are small unidentifiable things floating in it. I throw mine away.

"Come along, Harry. There is no time to waste."

And so we journey on, lacking the energy for conversation. Even Ned's buoyant assurances have ceased. It is almost another full day in the saddle before the highest tower of Raglan castle emerges from the hazy horizon.

As it looms larger, I dig my heels in hard and begin to pray that I will discover it is all a mistake, and Henry is here, working hard at his lessons, oblivious to the violence that has broken out afresh.

I almost fall from the saddle. Anne Herbert emerges from the hall, a different woman entirely from the serene figure I met before. When she sees me, and realises why I have come, we forget the enmity of our now-dead husbands. Her carefully contained grief overflows, and we cling together, our mutual sorrow taking precedence over news.

"I am so sorry, so sorry!" I cry, and she shakes her head, her mouth agape with the tragedy that has befallen her. I hold her while she shakes and moans, but as soon as she begins to calm, I have to ask her. I can hold back no longer.

"Have you news of Henry?"

She shakes her head again, her raw eyes full of pain.

"Why did he take my boy with him? What did it serve?"

She shudders, her mouth turns upside down, and her voice comes angry.

"He thought he would have the best of them. He said it would do Henry good to see what becomes of those who turn against their king."

So, it was a lesson, a lesson to a suspected insurgent who was no more than a child. Henry's Lancastrian blood was suspect and therefore ripe to be risked in the adult game of war.

"Come, Margaret. You will stay with me. Rest here tonight. I will send a rider to make enquiries. There are people I can ask." She halts, takes a sorry look about the courtyard. "We will have to leave Raglan now, and we have been so happy here. William had such wonderful plans. The children and I leave for Weobley tomorrow."

"I know, Anne. I know how it feels to be widowed. I know that your future seems bleak but I urge you to have faith. Believe that happiness will return and you will be glad of it. Although it may not seem that way at this time."

She shakes her head once more in disbelief, and I remember that I once felt I could not go on. Only Henry gave me cause. Anne has a large brood of children. I am confident she will recover soon enough. Time will draw a cloak over her pain; they may have been brought low, but her day will come again.

For now, all I can do is accept her hospitality for the night. I soak in a warm bath; Anne's women wash the dust from my hair, rub moist fragrant salves into my tender bruises, and clothe me in a borrowed nightgown.

As I lie in the same high-canopied bed that cradled me in happier times, I concentrate on the messenger who is riding through the night with a letter to Jasper, to inform him of Henry's disappearance.

I do not sleep at all. Listening to Harry's exhausted snores, I grope for the comfort I once found here. But the joy of my last visit has gone; the warmth has fled. I stare wide-eyed into the darkness and fret about tomorrow, worry about Henry, about England. Damn Warwick for casting us all once more into disarray.

Dawn is breaking when I become aware that Harry is burning hot. I put a hand to his forehead and he pulls away, muttering fretfully as he kicks off the covers. The fever has returned.

It has been months, almost a year, since he was last afflicted. I swing my legs from the bed and fumble in the gloom for a wrap. In my haste to leave Woking, I did not think to bring his salves, let alone a remedy for fever.

In the antechamber, the woman assigned to serve me is sleeping with her head back, her mouth open. I shake her awake and she blinks at me blearily, wipes drool from her chin.

"What is it, my lady? Are you ill?"

"No, it is my husband. He has a fever. Find whoever has the key to the still-room. We will need willow bark tea ..." I search my brain frantically for a likely cure. "St John's Wort ... feverfew ... anything. Just be as quick as you can."

She pulls on a loose gown, her long braids swinging as she hurries from the room. Snatching up a jug of water, a cloth, and a bowl, I return to the bedchamber.

Harry is still sleeping. He has kicked off the covers, his bare limbs unconsciously seeking escape from the heat consuming him. I wring out the cloth in tepid water and hold it to his brow. He startles awake, stares at me unseeing and yells a profanity. My normally mild-mannered husband is often rude during these raving attacks.

"Hush, hush," I murmur, as if he were a child. "You will soon feel better. Hush now, Harry, go back to sleep."

He makes an unintelligible sound and I draw back from the waft of foul breath. He is parched. I reach for the cup on his nightstand, and cradling his head try to ease some water into his mouth. Most of it flows down his chin, drenching his nightshirt, so I take a clean kerchief from my pocket and soak it in water, trickle a few drops onto his lips. His tongue emerges to lick it up. I continue to dribble water into him and after a while, he grows a little calmer, but remains hot. For the rest of the morning I encourage as much liquid down him as he will allow, placing cold cloths on his forehead and wrists in an attempt to cool him.

By noon, I am still in my night clothes, and have not even taken time to pray. When Anne puts her head round the chamber door, I am more grateful than I can express. She is pale and her eyes are ringed with shadows, yet still she thinks of me in my need.

"Margaret, let me take over. Go and get dressed, have some food, take some fresh air. I will see that Harry is properly cared for."

I look from her to Harry, who seems to be resting more peacefully now.

"The fever has broken, I think. He is ... often like this. I do not know why. There is a cup here, if you can try to get him to drink. I will return as quickly as I can."

I try not to show my impatience as the woman helps me dress. I put on borrowed linen and my own gown that has been brushed and sponged during the night. Once my hair is tucked away and my lacings are tight, I feel more like myself, more in control of the ruin my life has become.

"Thank you."

The woman bobs a curtsey and leaves me in peace. I shake my sleeves, arrange my veil, and make haste to the chapel that lies close to the old hall.

As I hurry from one sumptuous chamber to another, I pity Anne afresh. It will be hard for her to relinquish her role as mistress of Raglan. The Herberts have made a splendid home here; the richly carved beds, the tapestries, the plate are all as exquisite as those of a king. Now, they are no use at all.

It is quiet in the chapel. As I move forward into the soft-hued light, a kind of peace descends upon me. My feet pass over golden brown and yellow tiles, toward the altar where I prostrate myself and make obeisance to God.

For an hour I pray for Harry to be released from the fever, for Henry to be safe from our enemies, and for peace to be restored to England. I do not plead victory for one side or the other but leave that in God's hands. All I ask for is guidance. It is a perilous path we tread in this time of uncertainty. The wrong decision now could mean the end of everything.

Time does not remove my anxiety for Henry, but the human mind cannot accommodate constant panic. After a day or so, the terror turns to something very much like despair. I am sure I have lost him, but I can scream and rail against it no more. My imagination leaves me in no doubt as to his possible danger, his fear at being alone in a hostile land, but if I am to retrieve him, I must be rational. I must think clearly and not give in to the hysteria that threatens to overwhelm me. I find solace in action and send messengers to every possible place he may have taken refuge.

I am exhausted and worn by constant prayer and nursing my husband. I need to return home, but Harry's malaise delays our departure by a few days. Even then, he is not fully recovered, and we are forced to travel slowly and make many stops. It is with great relief that I eventually spy the towers of the old hall of Woking through the trees.

When Elizabeth and Jane come hurrying down the steps to meet me, the pity in their eyes undermines my pretended strength and I collapse into their arms. They half-carry me up the steps, past Master Bray who waits, hands clasped, near the door. As I am ushered inside, I pause and pull away from my women.

"Master Bray, Sir Harry has been very ill, please make sure he goes straight to bed. Do not detain him with estate matters. As soon as I am refreshed, I will summon you. There are many matters to attend to."

"There is no hurry, my lady. I am just glad you are returned safely. I believe there is a letter waiting for you in your apartments."

I jerk my head, open my eyes wide. "From whom?"

"From your son, I believe."

For a moment, I am held by the twinkle in his eye. Henry is alive!

I do not wait for refreshment, nor hurry to disrobe from my mired clothes. While maid servants run back and forth with hot water for my bath, I break the seal on Henry's letter, plump down on the bed to read it.

To my lady mother ...

I quickly scan the page then, once I am assured he has come to no harm, I read it again, more slowly, my indignation growing with each carefully spelled word.

Lord Herbert took Henry with him to the battle because it would be '*instructional. A boy needs to learn about warfare.*' When things took a turn for the worse, he cried to Henry to flee, and Henry did just that.

The letter falls to my lap. I stare without seeing, while, in my mind's eye, Henry rides as if chased by the devil, through hostile countryside, hounded by his enemies. It is cold, it is growing dark ... I pick up the letter again.

I rode all day before taking refuge in a small wood where I chanced upon a party of horsemen. One of them was Sir Richard Corbet, a kinsman of Lady Anne, who knew me at once. He took me under his wing and to the house of his brother-in-law at Weobley. They are taking good care of me and you can imagine my surprise when Lady Anne arrived soon afterwards with Maud, and the other children.

I suppose things will be different now, and I will be given another guardian. I would like to stay with Lady Herbert but if that is not possible then my hope is to return to the care of Uncle Jasper…

I close my eyes. Henry is safe and unharmed, he is well. I am still thanking God for it when my eye slides to the postscript.

I left my bow and quiver at Raglan. Could you send me a new one please, if it is not too much trouble?

My mouth tilts into a smile. With a hand to my mouth, I laugh aloud and clasp the letter to my bosom. Thank God, thank God, thank God!

<u>London - October 1469</u>

All afternoon, our people have been in council with those of Anne Herbert, wrangling over my son's future. I have high hopes of Henry being returned to my custody. I am determined, once a resolution has been agreed with the Herberts, to approach George of Clarence to negotiate a return of the lands and properties of Richmond.

Harry is cautious. He urges me to bide my time, wait until things have settled, but I cannot ignore this opportunity to have Henry back in my care. He gives meaning to my life and without him, even on the fairest of days, the sun never shines quite brightly enough.

I pray, as I always do, for success, for a reunion with Henry, for Harry's complete return to health, for this new peace in England to be lasting. It is about time fortune smiled on me.

Since I was eight years old, I have been buffeted by fate, scarce given time to breathe, or know the comfort of real security. This time, however, I am hopeful. This time, I am certain, all will be well.

Over supper, we speak in low voices, neither of us sure how to live beneath this enforced rule of Warwick. Even if the earl allows Edward to resume his role as king, it does not mean he will be allowed to rule. In reality, it is Warwick who will be in control. Edward will be nothing but a puppet.

Harry toys with his supper.

"How can we ever trust anyone? There is not a soul at court who speaks their mind, all of them on the alert, saying only what is expected. Oh, for a world when a man's thoughts were his own."

"I have no care for court. If I can only get Henry back ..."

"He would be better in the household of some great lord. A boy needs a strong guardian; it is the way of the world."

I sigh, fiddle with my wine cup, twirling it so it catches the firelight, and the jewels on the rim send myriad colours to dance on the ceiling.

I have long dreamed of Henry living beneath my roof, taking lessons from me, walking with me in the parks, riding to the hunt. Yet Harry is right. I know he is, although, for the life of me, I cannot see the justice in the separation of a mother from her child.

After everything I went through to give birth to him and keep him safe, it seems only just that I should be allowed his company. Harry coughs, the phlegm thick in his throat, and in response my nursing instincts temporarily overcome the maternal. Without seeming too, I assess his appearance.

He is pale, ringed about the eyes, and seems older than his years. I make a mental note to prepare a restorative for him to take each morning and night. He needs rest and relaxation, nourishment and plenty of sleep, but it seems that is as much to ask as having the care of my only child.

Harry puts down his cup. "I think somebody has arrived." He moves to the door, opens it and cocks his head, listening. "Yes, somebody is coming up the stairs, and they seem to be in haste …"

I stand up, my thoughts, as usual, rushing to Henry. A quick double knock and, without waiting for a reply, the door is thrust open.

"Master Bray?" Our voices merge. Our faces are questioning as Reginald Bray launches into an explanation.

"My lord, my lady, I have news. Edward of … the king, King Edward, has been freed and is returning to London."

My hopes of winning back the Richmond estates for Henry dwindle like water down a rain pipe. Harry turns to look at me; he doesn't say it but I know he is thinking: 'I told you so.'

April 1470

Trouble besets us. While Harry rides with King Edward's army, I pray for my family, for peace, as my kin fall further from the king's graces. My stepbrother Richard and his son Robert have fallen into dispute with Sir Thomas Burgh, and they foolishly attacked Gainsborough Hall. Considerable damage was done to the property; they stole some plate and drove the king's hapless servant from his newly acquired lands.

Sir Thomas is a 'new' man, a favourite of the Yorkist king, who has profited from estates confiscated from Lancastrian lords. My Welles kin now find themselves in considerable trouble.

Summoned by the king, my brother rides to court to plead his case. They forget that honour is sometimes dispensed with in time of war. Despite issuing Richard and his brother-in-law, Sir Thomas Dymoke, with pardons, King Edward, who has sworn to stamp such insurrection from the land of England, declares that if Sir Robert does not lay down his arms, his father and uncle will be executed.

Is there no end to this eternal conflict? Will England ever be consumed by hate?

I think of my stepbrother Richard as I first knew him; a young man. My mother's son. For the first time in years, I feel I should go to my mother, put aside our differences. She is a woman whose son is in peril. I know how that feels.

Harry returns home a few weeks later. He seems to have shrunk; his shoulders are bowed, his eyes reduced to grey holes, sunken and wizened. Sorrow sits heavily upon him, and when he looks at me, I take on the burden too and begin to weep before he can impart his news.

"I am sick of war."

He throws down his gloves, runs his fingers through his hair. When I can breathe again, I clutch his travel stained fingers in my palm, and listen to the news I would rather not hear.

"Surely not, Harry. My brother and nephew were pardoned. What happened? Does the king have no pity?"

"They would have been spared had Robert laid down his weapons when the king ordered it, but …. he had to play the hero. He probably thought he could best the king's army, save his father and restore the throne to King Henry in one move."

"But life isn't a game of chess."

"No, Margaret, and it seems that Warwick and Clarence are behind it all."

I scowl, my mind running over the events of the last months.

"I hoped they had given up their meddling."

"The king is convinced of it. At the battle after … after he ordered the execution, the main cry of our opponents was 'A Warwick, A Clarence', although neither man had the gall to show up on the field."

Harry goes on to tell me of the fiasco that was the fight near Stamford. He tries to make light of the horror of it, but I can see through his words to the gruesome reality. Ten thousand more Englishmen now lie slaughtered and this time the fault is entirely Warwick's.

"Where is Warwick? Surely he cannot survive this second insurrection."

"I rode with the king as he trailed them across country. There is no doubt that both he and Clarence have fled. Only time will tell where. The suspicion is that they have gone to Flanders, or perhaps France."

I stare into the fire, the crackling flames like a marauding army or a pestilence, consuming all in their path. When it is obvious I have no further comment, Harry clears his throat again.

"On my way home, I called in at Maxley to see your mother. I told her the news …"

I look up sharply, and my grip on his hand tightens.

"That was kind of you, Harry. Thank you. How did she take it? What did she say?"

He sighs heavily. "As you would expect. She wept, of course, and cursed the king … She asked for you, Margaret, begged me to take you to visit her. She is growing old. I think her death bed beckons and she has things she wishes to say to you before it is too late."

"Yes."

I turn my face toward the fire again; feel the force of its destructive heat. How must it feel to lose a son, a child you have carried in your body, brought forth in great pain?

I pray to God I never know.

Although she has many children, I am sure my mother's heart is sore. I know from Edith's letters that she and Richard had recently been in dispute over the possession of land. How futile that must now seem. How ridiculous to fall foul of one's own kin over a parcel of barren land. Yet, in these horrid times, when cousin fights cousin, it is a common enough thing. I rouse myself, try to formulate a smile.

"I will go to her soon."

On my knees in the chapel, I pray for the souls of my murdered kin. It is not easy to forgive myself for knuckling down beneath the king they sought to displace. If I were a man I would stand and fight, unite the great lords of England to reinstate the old peace of Lancastrian rule, but I would never fight for Warwick. England is not his to rule.

I end my prayer that has been more of a tirade, and go about my business as if the world outside our door is not disintegrating.

Woking - October 1470

The summer is long and uncertain. King Edward has changed since his return. Harry says he is wary now, less ready to trust and more willing to punish. Where once the king would throw an arm about a man's neck and welcome him as friend on their first meeting, now he is cautious and vigilant for hidden enemies. Those around him tread with greater care.

News of the latest battle seeps back to Woking. People refer to it as Loosecoat Field because the army, wearing the badges of Warwick and Clarence, cast off their coats and fled before King Edward's fury. There was great slaughter, and afterwards, no one, not even those from the discontented north, is prepared to fight beneath Warwick's banner. Now that the earl and his hapless son-in-law have fled, an uneasy peace has resumed.

To add to our apparent joy at Edward's return, we celebrate the news that the queen is pregnant again. This time, everyone is sure it will be a prince. I hope they are wrong.

Today, I move among the flowerbeds beneath trees turning golden in the autumn sunshine. The garden is replete with seeds and berries. I harvest some for medicine, and some to sow again in the spring to raise new plants.

Running a great household is rather like ruling a country; you must look after the lower orders to ensure the nobility thrive. Our tenants are the base upon which we flourish. Our estates prosper under my care. Unlike many other great houses, our people are well nourished and their ailments attended to as soon as they appear. Good health and care makes for prosperity, just as good shoes help a body stand straight and tall.

The only member of the household not to fully benefit from my medicinal skill is its master. Too often he comes home exhausted, and it takes all my skill to nurse him back to health before the king summons him again. Sometimes, it seems like a punishment, as if the king cannot bear to let him be or allow him to stay home and be content. One day his summons will be the last straw.

Harry rides home from court. I watch him hand the reins to a groom and climb wearily up the steps to the hall. He stands before me, grasps my arms and kisses my forehead. Although his eyes are tired, I can see he is happy to be home. I turn in his embrace and we walk slowly into the house, the darkness swallowing us. There is a pile of messages and issues he must deal with, but I distract him with a roaring fire and a cup of warm wine.

"How was court?" I kneel at his feet to help him remove his boots. He crosses his ankles, lies back in the chair.

"A little tense." He sips from his cup. "The king suspects everyone, and you cannot blame him. Rumour is rife that Warwick is in France and has joined forces with Margaret of Anjou. Some say he has wed his youngest daughter to the prince."

I sit back on my heels in astonishment.

"Prince Edward? Warwick has wed his daughter to ... that cannot be!"

This rumour must be false. It is hard enough to believe Warwick is so desperate and determined that he would ally himself with Margaret, but to wed his daughter to the son of the man he has fought so hard to overthrow! What can he be thinking?

"I am surprised Margaret let go of her hatred for him long enough to accept his terms."

"They are laughing about it at court, saying she made him grovel. Kept him on his knees for a full quarter of an hour."

I allow my mind to dwell upon the satisfying image of the great Earl of Warwick brought so low.

"I still don't believe it."

Harry yawns. I see a coating of yellow on his tongue and make mental note to dose him with rhubarb twice a day for a fortnight.

"Edward's spies say that Warwick has abandoned his plan to replace King Edward with Clarence, and now intends to crown Edward of Lancaster and rule through him as his father-in-law."

Suddenly, Margaret's reasons for her alliance with Warwick are clear. She would do anything for her son, just as I would. My eyes meet Harry's. It is so long before I blink again that mine begin to smart. I think rapidly, run through all the possible scenarios.

"He would have to contend with Margaret first. And where would that leave us? I am content for Prince Edward to rule, but I would find it hard to lie down quietly beneath Warwick's jurisdiction."

"He has not succeeded yet ..."

"But he is strong, wily. A few years ago, we would never have thought he would succeed in deposing King Henry and replacing him with King Edward. Yet he did it. The crown is not to be his but he hungers for it anyway, and just as he once thought to rule through Edward of March, he now imagines he can rule through Lancaster. He is taking a second shot at the same target. His ambition knows no bounds."

"The king is raising arms as we speak. That is why I have returned. I am to gather every man I can and ride north with the king by the end of the week."

"But you are not well!"

He wags his hand. "I am well enough. Don't fuss."

A few days later, he rides away again. I watch him go, raise my hand in dutiful farewell, but inside I am fuming. He should be in bed, he should be resting. I can see no reason why he should risk life and limb for a man whose grip on the crown is slipping through his fingers.

If he has to fight, it should be on the other side, although with Warwick now involved, the line between the two sides is blurred, confusing. Even I am not clear where my loyalty should really lie.

I spin on my heel and re-enter the hall, but I can settle to nothing. The autumnal garden holds no fascination; the pages on the books in our vast library contain no mystery. I pick up my sewing, set a few stitches that are too large and uneven. I cast it aside, get up and go to the window, throw open the shutter and look down upon the darkening garden.

This sense of unease continues for almost a week. Each minute of the day, my belly bubbles with unease. I try to write letters. It is an age since I heard from Myfanwy, and Jasper is still in France. I would dearly like to know his opinion of recent events, but I dare not contact him for fear my message will be intercepted and misconstrued as treasonous correspondence.

In the end, I sit down and write to Henry. A brief instructional letter to ensure he is working hard at his lessons and remembering his prayers. I am just warming the wax and preparing to seal it when I hear a great commotion outside. The door is thrown open and Ned stumbles in, waving his arm behind him.

"A messenger, my lady, from Sir Harry."

I know it is bad news before I even leave my chair. I somehow move toward the door, my knees trembling, my legs turned to string. I hold out my hand and a travel-stained messenger places a rolled parchment into my palm.

As I read the first line, my hand flies to my mouth. I let out a cry of rage. I knew he should have made an excuse to stay at home.

"The king has fled." My voice croaks, I cough to clear my throat. "He has taken ship, exiled with his brother, Gloucester. Sir Harry is in the custody of Warwick."

"Warwick?"

Ned is close by my side. Suddenly in need of some solidity, I hang on to his coat. "Come inside, my lady. I will call your women."

I do not cry. I do not rant or rail. Like a sleepwalker, I allow Ned to sit me in my favourite chair. I stare at the floor, my mind teeming with different options.

Jane and Elizabeth come; they fuss about me, fetching drinks and restoratives, urging me to take to my bed. The fog in my mind swirls, like wraiths in a burial ground. I cannot think. I cannot decide what is best, and then Ned steps from the corner where he has taken refuge.

"Shall I ride to discover where he has been taken, my lady? That way we might better know what steps to take to free him."

The fog clears. I stand up too suddenly, sway on my feet and grab the back of a chair.

"Free him. Yes. That is what we must do. I will ride with you, Ned. Fetch Master Bray, call for a few men at arms to escort me. Have them saddle my horse; we will travel faster that way."

"Travel faster, my lady? Where are we going?"

"To see the Earl of Warwick. Once we pledge ourselves to his cause, my husband will be freed."

*

The world has turned upside down again. King Edward is in exile, his pregnant queen has fled with her daughters into sanctuary at Westminster, and our own dear King Henry has been restored to his rightful place.

As soon as I explain to Warwick that my husband and I pledged allegiance to Edward for the sole purpose of protecting the interests of my son, he promises to think about releasing him. I want to grab him by the throat, shake the living breath from him, but he is a giant of a man. I am a gnat beside him.

Instead, I try to smile as I gently remind him that Harry's health is precarious and, as an ardent supporter of King Henry, our contacts may prove valuable in the coming months.

After a few weeks Harry is restored to me. He is ailing but relieved to be free. Thanking God, I insist he return to Woking so I can set about the long healing process. But it is not long before duty calls, and we are summoned back to London for an audience with the restored king.

The court of Lancaster is gay. Even the Earl of Warwick is courteous, although I do detect some lack of ease. Clarence skulks in corners, clearly unhappy to see my wavering cousin, Henry, wearing the crown he expected to claim for himself.

It is satisfying to don my best court clothes and converse with people from whom I have been estranged for years. I meet cousins I have never seen before. The Lancastrian court, so long exiled in France, is glad to be back in England and is not afraid to show it. The celebrations are long and loud; loud enough to drown the punishment of those who dared support the Yorkist king.

At the head of all this gaiety sits King Henry. He looks older than his years, and is clearly bewildered to be back in the glittering court after such a long captivity in the Tower. He smiles vacantly, raises a wavering hand when we applaud his return and drink to his health.

At least he is unharmed. I hope his bewilderment does not last. He taps his right foot in time with the music, claps belatedly when prompted by Warwick, who stands sentinel at his side.

Clarence, keeping his distance from his father-in-law, sprawls in a chair and partakes of too much wine. At his side, a white-faced Isabel Neville fiddles with her jewelled girdle. Cousins or not, the company is mismatched and disaccord sits heavily upon us all, but each one of us maintains the pretence that nothing is amiss.

I watch Harry from across the room, pleased at his recovery. There is vigour in his movements now, a gleam returning to his eye. As his wife, however, I know he is unhappy. As he speaks, he nods his head, but I can see his smile is false, his body tense and ill at ease. He is dissatisfied with the turn of events, and I wonder …

A soft touch falls upon my elbow, and a familiar voice rumbles in my ear. I turn and almost drop my cup.

"Jasper!" I move into his arms, feel the roughness of his beard on my cheek. "I hoped you would come. Oh, you look so well. It is as if the years have melted away."

I cannot conceal my delight and cling to his sleeves, afraid that if I let go, he will dissipate like a waking dream. With Jasper's presence all the memories of my time in Wales return. My eyes grow moist but, realising I have breached the formality of court, I take a breath and offer him my hand. His lips brush the back of my fingers. His eyes are warm and friendly. I can trust this man with my life. Suddenly, I realise how vulnerable and isolated I have been.

"You look well, Margaret, and I believe you have grown. You almost reach my shoulder now."

I laugh delightedly, drawing Harry's attention. When he recognises my companion, he excuses himself from his company and moves toward us, his smile wide.

"Jasper. It is good to see you." The men slap each other's shoulders, smiles and laughter all round. My mouth stretches so wide, my jaw begins to ache.

Jasper draws back a little.

"There is someone else you might like to speak to." He crooks his finger, beckons someone forward, and my heart leaps like a hind in the forest.

"Henry!" It is almost a shriek. People turn to smile as I behold my son emerging from the crowd. I laugh as though my heart will burst with happiness. I plant my lips on his brow, close my eyes, inhaling his scent, my hands tight on his shoulders, revelling in his solidity. Even when he pulls away, his face scarlet with embarrassment, I cannot contain my joy.

"I had no idea you would be here. Oh, I am so happy we are together again – all of us."

I reach out, clasp Harry and Jasper's sleeves, my smile embracing my three favourite men in the whole world.

Recovering from his embarrassment, Henry regains his usual colouring. He has grown so tall but, belatedly recalling how discomforting parental attention can be, I refrain from mentioning it. I ask gentle, harmless questions and he responds with tales of his progress with the sword and in the tilt-yard. I listen, entranced by the way his hair falls across his forehead, his large shy eyes moving to encompass all three of us in his gaze. I can see little likeness to his father, but he reminds me of someone I cannot quite place. I note the quickness of his speech, the birdlike tilt of his head, the wide narrow mouth that draws upward like a bow when he smiles. He is familiar, he is handsome, he is here, and everything in my world is now perfect.

"We are invited to meet privately with the king," Jasper says, brightening my existence further. "He wishes to make Henry's acquaintance; after all, he is kin."

He smiles at Henry, who flushes with pleasure and bows slightly. "It will be an honour, sir."

I can scarcely believe all this is true. The king restored, the Yorkist exiled, Henry back in my company and set to stay in my care for at least a week or two before returning to Jasper's household. It is everything I have dreamed of, and a little more besides.

The only shadow at court is Warwick; his constant presence at the king's side, his eyes ever watching, ever assessing us all. Ostensibly, he is one of us now, yet he remains apart. It is unnerving, disturbing.

Men at arms guard the door to the king's chamber, but when we are allowed to enter, we find him alone. He has taken off his cap, his scalp showing pink through greying hair. He does not turn when we approach but remains staring into the flames.

"Your Grace."

We bow before him but he does not move. Harry and I exchange glances as Jasper clears his throat and speaks a little louder.

"Your grace, Harry; it is your brother, Jasper. I have travelled far to see you."

The sorry head turns slowly towards us, and bleak, grey eyes confront us. The king blinks rapidly, his lips working as he fumbles for lost words.

"Jasper ...?" The king shuffles forward, hands outstretched. He plucks at Jasper's tunic before staring up into his brother's face. "By God, is it you? Where is Edmund?"

With a gasp, I close my eyes against the sadness that name evokes. Poor King Henry, so much has happened to him, and so quickly have his fortunes changed that he has lost his grasp on the present. He looks about the room, examining each one of us.

"Where is Richmond?" he repeats. I swallow pain, and taking Henry by the hand, step forward.

"Edmund is not here, Your Grace, but his son, Henry, is here ... by the grace of God."

The king squints at me, his brow furrowed. I can almost see the mechanics of his mind as he works out who I am.

"Is it little Margaret?" His face stretches in joy, his arms open, and I am engulfed in the noxious fumes of an ailing man. "Little Margaret, little Margaret." He touches my face, his hands fall on my shoulders. Hands that I wish had a firmer grip.

"I am so pleased to see you, Your Grace. I have brought my son, Henry, to meet you." I drag Henry forward and watch him execute a perfect bow.

"Henry ... Margaret ..." The king looks from my son to me as he tries to understand the length of years dividing our last meeting. "But you have grown so fast. I expected a babe ... just a small infant, but look at you!"

My son flushes. I can see he is tongue-tied, so I speak for him. "Henry is fourteen, Your Grace. Almost a man grown."

The king looks him up and down. "I thought you would be taller."

Criticism of my son always raises my hackles, but I force them down, run a hand down Henry's sleeve and look up at him.

"There is time for him to grow, Your Grace. By the time he is twenty, he will be as tall as ... as you."

I almost said 'as a king', but that could be misconstrued. King Henry is nodding, a smile playing on his lips.

"He would make a fine king, little Margaret, a fine king."

Jasper, who has been lounging on the back of a chair, straightens up and raises his brows eloquently in my direction, but I make no response, although I agree wholeheartedly with the king.

Afterwards, we dine with the king's chamberlain, Sir Richard Tunstall. Sir Richard has been a long-time supporter of our cause, fighting at Wakefield and Towton, personally escorting the king to safety after the failed battle at Hexham. When Harlech Castle fell, he was taken and imprisoned by Edward, but pardoned soon after. Like many others, he pretended allegiance, but did not hesitate to switch his loyalty back to Henry as soon as the opportunity arose.

Jasper raises his cup. "To friends reunited."

We all drink deeply before talk reverts to the old topic of war and allegiance. I remain silent. Women are not supposed to discuss strategy and warfare, but I can listen. I can learn.

I pick at the food on my plate. Jasper, having sated his hunger, pushes his away and leans back in his seat.

"What do you make of Warwick? Do you trust him?"

Tunstall puts down his knife and dabs his lips with a napkin, the candlelight reflected in his eyes as they slide from face to face.

"I trust he will remain loyal to the king for as long as it pays him to do so. It is power he craves. Edward has severed Warwick's influence over the rule of the country, and as long as that continues and Warwick believes he is best served by Lancaster, he will be our man. But should that change ..."

He shrugs and takes another draught of wine.

"And what are the queen's thoughts on it?" Jasper does not ask of the king's thoughts. We all know Henry's opinions are worthless. He is nothing but a puppet, a means to an end. Just as York sought to rule him, now his wife and Warwick do the same. Tunstall tilts his head back and looks down the length of his nose before letting it fall forward again.

"The queen trusts no one; not even those closest to her. She holds everything to her chest. She has been betrayed too often. She tolerates Warwick ... and his daughters ... but only for the assets they bring."

I lean forward into the candle's glow.

"Warwick's daughters. Anne, is it not? And Isabel? What do they make of this abrupt reversal of loyalties?"

"I know not. Isabel and George seem content with each other, but I understand they have both had enough of the situation. Warwick may have made a mistake there; promising Clarence much, yet delivering nothing."

"And the prince. What does he think of his wife? I'll warrant he had not bargained on her."

"The queen hasn't taken me into her confidence and neither has the prince, but I have seen the lady Anne – and for a newly-wed bride she weeps a great deal."

"So, it is not a happy match."

"At my guess, my lady, it is not one made in Heaven."

Jasper takes a handful of nuts, pops two in his mouth. "She will come round. She is a Neville. The reward of a crown will soon salve any dislike she has for her spouse."

A ripple of laughter runs around the table. I feel a sudden joy to be here with my family, my son. I reach for Henry's hand and, as if infected by my mood, he looks up and smiles. I tilt my head to one side.

"What do you think, Henry? Will the match between them thrive?"

"I cannot say for sure, Madam. I am unversed in such things, but it seems to me that if enemies are matched for the sake of peace then each should do their duty. Beget some heirs quickly, and to the devil with enmity."

Jasper throws back his head.

"In other words, they should shut up and rut."

Another laugh; louder this time. I am shocked at their coarseness, but at the same time flattered that they are unhampered by my female presence. I feel like one of the men, party to their troop.

Woking - March 1471

For a brief spell, gaiety returns to England. We dance at court, we feast and make merry. Even in November, when we hear that Elizabeth Woodville has birthed a son in the sanctuary at Westminster, we are not concerned. What possible threat can the mewling infant son of an exiled usurping king be to us now?

Edward is in Holland, so my sources say. He and his brother, Gloucester, and his close companion in crime, William Hastings, are no doubt plotting revenge in some meagre tavern. I care not. My spirits are high and indomitable.

Christmas is the best for years. Harry's megrim seems to be passing, and Henry and Jasper join us at Woking. Anne and Harry's brother arrive in time for the exchange of New Year's gifts. I sit back in my chair after the feast, feeling as fat and complacent as a farm cat. When it is time for them to leave, parting will not be so hard, for I know they will soon return.

"Bring Myfanwy with you next time, Jasper," I whisper as he takes his leave of me. He doubtfully raises one eyebrow.

"I will try," he promises, and I have to make the best of that. It is many years since I saw Myfanwy, and so much has changed. I wonder if our bond will be as strong.

I hold my son close, whisper my blessing, but I do not weep. Before the spring arrives, I will see him again. We have planned a visit to Wales in February if the roads are passable; that is not long to wait. Harry and I stand on the hall steps and watch them ride away. After a while, he drops his hand and returns to the hall, but I wave until even the dust on the road has settled.

When February blows in cold, and snow defeats all my plans, I am disappointed but not unduly so. I know the winter cannot last forever; there will be other visits, more good times. The years stretch ahead in an unspoiled vista. I envisage Henry grown and married, raising children of his own. All that is far away in the future, but it is a hope I cling to. Grandchildren will compensate for my lack of daughters, and all the years I missed with Henry.

As February melts into a windy March, I turn my attention to the garden once more, organising my men to see the borders are cleared. Like a miser in a strong room, I check over my store of seed, consider the things that failed to thrive last season, where to plant them that they might do better this year.

I am surprised when Ned comes to tell me my cousin, Somerset, has called to see Harry. I wipe my hands, remove my apron and hurry to the parlour where he has been asked to wait.

"Edmund, how nice to see you."

I hold out my hand for his salute, look down on his dark hair as his lips graze my wrist. In truth, I am not as pleased to see him as my words imply; his presence stirs a feeling of unease deep in my belly.

"You look well, Margaret," he says in his rough way. I smile, barely preventing myself from refuting the compliment.

"Harry is out on the estate, but he should not be long. I hope you are able to stay. It is long since we saw you last."

He tosses his riding gloves onto the table.

"You heard the Woodville woman spawned another brat for Edward? A boy this time."

He looks at me, his expression grim.

"Yes, we heard some time ago, before Christmas. It is of little matter, I think."

"Edward plainly thinks otherwise. I have had word he is preparing to take ship to England to claim back his crown."

I cannot prevent my eyes from opening wide. Will strife in England never be over?

"I had hoped he would realise he was beaten. England can stand little more of this interminable war."

To hide my annoyance, I move to a table by the window and pour wine into two cups. I hand one to Edmund. As I do so, the door opens and Harry comes in, his lips parted in mid-conversation with someone behind him. He comes farther into the room, Reginald Bray a step behind. Harry stops when he sees I have company, his face darkening a little.

"Edmund. I did not realise you were here."

Harry is dressed in his favourite clothes. His tunic bears the aroma of horse, a smear of green froth on his sleeve. I hand him a cup of wine, which he takes with a nod of thanks. Edmund wastes no time in coming to the point of his visit.

"You heard Edward is on the move?"

Harry is immediately wary. He lowers his cup.

"No, I had not heard; and you, I suppose, are mustering men to ensure he does not set foot on our shores."

"Something like that. We need to know you are with us."

Harry pales and licks his lips. I hope Edmund does not notice his lack of ease.

"Harry has been ill," I interject before my husband can reply. "He is only recently recovered enough to leave his bed."

Edmund looks Harry up and down, taking in his casual clothes, the healthy hue the March wind has left on his cheek.

"You look well enough to me."

Harry opens his hands, palm up.

"I am fine. Margaret fusses." He drains his cup. "The problem will be determining where Edward of March is likely to land."

I hope Somerset marks the fact that Harry has given Edward his old title of the Earl of March instead of king.

"We have men on the alert, up and down the country. If he lands we need to be ready to deal with him swiftly."

"Of course; of course."

Harry frowns at the hearth. I can see thoughts running through his mind as he quickly assesses his situation, deciding how he should act. Edmund, ever an impatient soul, grows tired of waiting.

"So, we can rely on you?"

"I should think so, if his crossing is successful."

Even to my ears Harry sounds distant, unconvinced of the looming crisis. I break the tension.

"You will stay to supper, of course, Edmund. I have ordered salmon and eel." I stretch my mouth wide in what I hope is a winning smile, and he relaxes.

"How can I resist such an offer?"

All through supper, my eyes keep straying to my husband, who is pensive, his thoughts elsewhere. I wonder if he frets over some matter of business, or if his promise to ride against Edward was given lightly.

Later, in the privacy of our chamber when our servants have left us, he can avoid the question no longer.

"Tell me, Harry, what is on your mind? Did you mean it when you said you would ride with Somerset?"

He sighs, his shoulders drooping.

"I think so. I am not convinced the k... Edward will make a successful landing. The north sea is treacherous."

I climb on to the bed and cover my legs with the blanket.

"But if he is successful, what will you do?"

He looks up at me, his brow furrowed.

"Why are you so persistent? Why is my answer so necessary just now when I am ready for sleep?"

"I want to know if you are with us, or against us."

Our eyes meet. His look injured and, sensing we are on opposing sides, I feel my jaw tighten. If he supports Edward, he will be denying Henry any hope of ever having his rights restored. With my cousin Henry on the throne, my son's hopes are raised.

Harry makes no reply.

"I would have your support, Harry. If not for the king's sake, then for my son's."

"Perhaps I have more care for the country. King Henry is old and ineffectual. In fighting for him, we are really fighting for Margaret, and do we really want her son on the throne? A boy like that would be little better than his father – others would rule through him. King Edward has at least proven by his treatment of Warwick that he will be ruled by no one. England needs a king, Margaret, a man who will rule, not a puppet who will be led. Now, let us have no more of this. Go to sleep, I am tired."

He turns on his side, pulls the sheet over his shoulder, leaving me with barely anything to cover myself. I slide down the bed, angry and sore of heart, and frown into the darkness.

Woking - Late March

Harry is taciturn for days. He spends as much time as he can outside the hall. At meal times, he picks at his food; drinks deeply of his wine and excuses himself as soon as he may. I cannot read his face, which he purposely keeps empty; his thoughts are closed. When news filters in that Edward has landed successfully in the north, I know another battle looms. I am fearful as to the path he plans to take.

Somerset and a retinue of forty men call again. This time, he stays for four days. On the last day, I hear raised voices issuing from Harry's sanctum but I dare not enter. He has made it clear the decision is to be his alone. I lurk in the hall until the door is thrown open and Edmund strides across the room, hollering for his horse. His servant scuttles behind him, bearing his master's helmet and gauntlets.

Edmund pays me no heed but brushes rudely past, hurrying from my house, riding out through the gates a few moments later. A brisk wind whips about my skirts as I watch him go, then I spin on my heel and return to the hall.

Harry waits, head down, by the fire. He does not look up when I go to stand before him. I clasp my hands, trying to contain my anger, my over-spilling anxiety.

"Harry, why have you quarrelled with my cousin? I have to know what is going on."

He looks up; his eyes are red-rimmed, his face white, the blue veins showing on his temples, a pulse throbbing in his jaw.

"I told him I cannot ride with him today."

I gesture to the pile of papers on his desk.

"Well, surely he understands you have some business to attend to and can meet -"

"No. You misunderstand me, Margaret. I will not ride out for King Henry; not now, not ever."

"You cannot ride with York! Harry, King Henry is my cousin!"

He cuts me dead, his head swinging sadly from side to side.

"Your cousin is a feeble king. I would fight and die for him were he able-minded, but I will not die for a French woman. I will not ride with Margaret of Anjou ... or her son."

I move closer, poke my face close to his, keeping my voice low, anger spitting like sparks between us.

"My Henry is but two steps from the throne. In supporting York, you condemn him to a life of obscurity."

"Such lives are better, Margaret. I warrant you cannot name more than a handful of kings who died peaceably in their beds."

He watches me while I scour my mind for a merry monarch given the grace to die in his sleep. I shake my head to dispel the thoughts as Harry continues, persuasively. "You could teach your son to accept that Lancaster's days are done. Let him make peace with York, marry, raise a host of grandchildren for your pleasure. Teach him that, Margaret. Such a life is all I have ever longed for."

I cup my cheeks with my hands, tears stinging my eyes. I hate to argue with Harry, who is my dearest love. I regard him sorrowfully.

"So you will ride with York, Harry, and once more break the ties of kinship with my family. I pray you are not making a grave error."

"I pray that also."

We are quiet now. I cannot stop him. He is a man and will do as he must. I am a woman who should do as she is bid.

"I have letters to write." I turn away, but as I reach the door, he calls after me.

"Do not meddle, Margaret. Politics is not for women."

April 1471

How can I keep from meddling? With Harry gone and the future uncertain, I do what I can to protect our position. If Harry must ride at the side of King Edward, then I must try to appease both my Beaufort kin ... and Lancaster's queen.

I write to Jasper, begging to know his whereabouts and the position of my son. I write to my cousin, Somerset, temporizing over Harry's position, pretending he will join with him as soon as he may. I send letters to Myfanwy, to Queen Margaret, to my mother-in-law, and even to my own mother. All seem precious to me in these days of uncertainty.

Although I know not how to, or whom to pray for, I take up residence in the chapel. In begging for success for Lancaster, I must condemn my husband and his king to defeat. In praying for Harry's safety, I condemn the rightful king. Unsteady and afraid, I make do with the middle ground and pray for all mankind, for an end to war, an end to dissent.

I pray for peace.

When I leave the chapel, I pace the floors until my ankles ache, and my lower back screams for respite. I walk back and forth, take a seat by the window for a few moments and then I am on my feet again, back and forth, back and forth.

My servants whisper tales of foreboding. I do not want to hear, but I cannot help but strain my ears as they prepare my bed, where I know I shall find no rest at all.

Just as the day is over, and I have dismissed all but one of my women, a knock comes upon the chamber door. Ned is outside, twisting his cap in his hands, his face anxious.

"Master Davy is here, my lady, with a missive from your husband."

I climb from bed and wrap a shawl about my shoulders. Descending to the hall, I take the message from Harry's man.

"How is he?" I ask before I break the seal.

John Davy's long pause before he replies tells me more than his words.

"My lord is well, and preparing for the morrow. I left him with the king, in a meadow near Barnet where they plan to do battle in the morning."

"Dear God, have mercy ..." I murmur as I unfold his letter and quickly scan the page. Harry, in his present health, has little hope of surviving the fray. I look down at the letter, the words dissolving in my tears.

He has enclosed his will, bequeathing his soul to the lady Mary and the blessed company of Heaven, and leaving most of his land and possessions to 'my most entire beloved wife, Margaret.'

My hand flies to my mouth. I have been a poor wife to Harry, making his life difficult, plaguing him to act against his better judgement. He has ever been a good and loving husband to me; all he wishes for is peace, and I have given him nought but conflict. I do not deserve him.

Leaving the document amid the remains of my supper on the table, I make haste to the stone cold chapel and fall upon my knees again. This time, I beg for forgiveness, repenting of my former headstrong ways and asking for time to make reparation. Harry's life is suddenly more important to me than any other matter in this world.

If I had been born a boy, I would be fighting on the opposite side, facing death or victory, but since I am a woman, the only weapon I possess is the power of prayer. My cold lips brush my entwined fingers, my whitened knuckles press hard against my mouth, my pleading words flying as thick and fast as arrows.

At first, the news is garbled. Messages come that the battle has gone badly for Edward, and his men are fleeing in disarray. Frantically, I pray for Harry's survival. Beseech God to give him the sense to keep from the thick of the fight. Do not play the hero, Harry ...

"I do not care in what state you send him home, but please God, send him back to me."

Then a message comes that states the opposite. York has victory, but now the lines between factions are blurred. Montagu and Warwick, lately of York, have been slain by their former allies. Oxford's army has been routed by Montagu, who now ... I am confused, reality has flown, exploded into a maelstrom of uncertainty and doubt.

I fly about the palace, ordering messengers to ride out to secure more solid information. I must have clarification. I have to know the hand that fate has dealt us. I have to know if Harry is still among the living, or if he ... I cannot frame the words.

I climb to the highest tower and watch the messengers ride out, fanning in different directions, taking separate roads to discover what they can. But, as I stand there, with fear churning in my belly, I realise I can wait no longer. The only way to ascertain the truth is to ride out and discover it for myself.

I lift my skirts and make haste down the twisting stair, calling for Ned as I go. He meets me at the bottom.

"Ned." Breathlessly, I hang on to his arm, a hand to the pain in my side. "Make ready my horse. You must ride with me to London. Only there can I ascertain the truth."

London - 16th April 1471

The capital is very different from the last time I saw it. Just a few weeks ago, the city celebrated the return of King Henry. Now, the Yorkist king is back and the people rejoice again, each man hoping his previous welcome for Henry has gone unnoticed.

The air rings with uncertainty, with suspicion. Neighbours are wary of one another, brother mistrusts brother, cousin suspects cousin. Our horses push a way through the crowd toward Westminster, where men are hastening to offer allegiance to Edward, fearful of punishment for their wavering loyalty.

A crush of people fills the courtyard; some coming, some going, a crowd of supplicants at the door. Not one of us is sure of what is happening, or what will happen next.

Ned dismounts, and helps me from my horse. I look around in growing panic.

"Wait here, my lady," he says as he leads both animals to the stables, but I dismiss his advice and wend a path through the throng toward the steps of the great hall.

Usually, a crowd would part to make way for me, but today I am unrecognised. I push through the crush, fighting my way to the entrance, but the way is blocked.

Foolishly, I elbow and shove until I find myself wedged between a stout lady and a middle-aged man whose stench suggests he has not bathed in a month.

I realise the danger too late. They tower above me, as my nose is crushed too close to the man's armpit, I try to turn. I fight for footing but my legs are taken from beneath me. I cry out, grab at the man's coat. My veil is pulled from my head, lost beneath our feet, and my knees weaken, begin to give way. I am falling, soon to be trampled, but then a strong hand takes hold of my elbow, hoisting me up so my feet no longer touch ground. I cannot breathe. I open my mouth to gulp in stale air. Blackness rushes in. I am going to faint.

"Lady Margaret? It is Lady Stafford!" someone calls from far away. "Make way there, make way!"

Everyone is shouting. I hear my name, coupled with curses and obscenities as I am lifted bodily from the fray, carried through the outer door and past the men at arms who guard the inner sanctum of the newly restored king.

Someone puts me in a seat. I sprawl like a drunkard, my skirts in disarray, my cap slipping sideways, revealing my hair. My head sinks into my hands, my body judders, and tears drip down between my fingers, to run along my wrist.

"Lady Margaret?"

A cultured voice pulls me from the brink of oblivion, and I look up to find the king leaning over me. His brow is creased, his eyes concerned. "Are you quite recovered? Here, take a sip of this."

He holds out a cup and I take it gratefully, drinking deeply, the wine fruity and revitalising. As my composure returns, I remember where I am, realise the state of my attire and try to straighten my skirts. When I attempt to rise, his hand falls, large and warm, on my shoulder, pushing me back down.

"Sit still," he says, "until you are mended. I understand you wished to see me."

"Yes." I look up into clear blue eyes. "I wanted to know the outcome of the battle, the whereabouts of Harry ..."

"Ah, we were victorious, but Harry ... Harry was wounded, I think ..."

His face seems to waver, one minute close, the next far away, his voice fluctuating like the sound of rushing water in my ears.

"Edward, have a heart. Lady Margaret, come closer to the fire. We cannot discuss such a matter on the door step."

She comes upon me unaware, a breath of sweet scent, a gentle touch on my arm, her voice soft as a baby's. I look up into wide eyes, an upturned mouth. My fogged mind acknowledges that the stories were right; she is very fair. "Come," she says, "let me help you."

Her hand is firm beneath my elbow as the queen and I cross the floor, where she settles me in a seat close to hers.

"Now, Lady Margaret. As I understand it, the news of your husband is not good. But remember, neither is it the worst. Edward, tell the lady of her husband's fate."

The king clears his throat.

"Stafford was wounded, but not seriously so. We left him at an inn near Barnet. I am sure he has sent word to you by now."

He is right. Harry would have sent word to Woking, expecting me to be there. Once again I have acted rashly, making a difficult situation worse. I stand up too quickly, my head swimming again; I clasp the back of a chair and force my vision to comply. The room settles. I blink at the king.

"I must go to him. Thank you, thank you so much, Your Grace."

Belatedly remembering I am in the presence of my monarch, I curtsey as deeply as my unsteady head will allow.

"We will order up a carriage," the queen announces. "You are not well enough to ride."

"I will be well enough, Your Grace, now that I can breathe again. I thank you for your concern but ... a horse will be faster. I must make haste ..."

I sink to the floor in an extravagant curtsey, and the queen offers her hand, her laugh like a set of tiny bells. As I rise again and turn to leave, a door at the end of the hall opens and a weary-looking woman enters, followed by a posy of little girls.

They run into the room, chattering like sparrows, and the king hurries forward, sweeps his son from the nurse's arms and thrusts him beneath my nose.

Dutifully, I peep at the red face amid the swaddling, and make the appropriate sounds of admiration.

"A handsome child, Your Grace, and such pretty daughters too."

Their time in sanctuary seems to have done them no harm. I try to squash the pang of envy as I watch the girls cluster about their mother's skirts. Her gentle hand runs across a small girl's hair; a girl with the upright stance and direct stare of her father.

The king perches on the arm of the queen's chair, and she leans forward to inspect her son before turning her beaming face toward me.

"You are among the first to see our son, Lady Margaret, our little Edward, Prince of Wales."

Her voice is doting. She has everything. I must live apart from my son while she enjoys the company of hers. They present the perfect picture of unity – just the sort of royal family the country needs. They are young, strong and fertile, and suddenly I have a vision of England years from now, ruled over by this infant's grandchildren, their names written in stone, their as yet untold stories becoming history while my son's name fades into obscurity. Envy, one of the deadliest of sins, weighs heavily on my soul.

I shake myself.

"I should make haste, Your Grace, if you will allow."

Edward stands up, offers me his hand.

"Of course, Lady Margaret, we must not keep you."

"But come to court again soon," the queen calls after me. "We welcome your friendship, Lady Margaret."

I turn and bow my head, and when I rise, her smile has slipped a little. Behind the royal welcome I sense wariness, their shared mistrust of me, and all my ilk.

Just outside the town of Barnet, I duck beneath the inn's low lintel and blink, adjusting my eyes to the dark interior. The inn-keeper bows and scrapes, offering mead, offering food, offering the comfort of a private parlour. I brush his gratuities aside.

"Where is my husband? Where is Sir Henry Stafford?"

"He will be above, my lady. I laid my best room at his disposal."

For a fee, I think, as I hurry toward the stairs. The rickety rail moves at the touch of my hand, the treads creak beneath my feet. I open the first chamber door I come to and a couple leaps in their bed; a young girl hastily covering her nakedness. Red-faced, I retreat and, more cautiously this time, try the next room.

The shutters are closed, the room as dark as night. I can just detect the outline of a figure upon the bed, recognise the discarded mail, the bloodstained doublet on the floor.

Carmarthen castle and the last moments of Edmund's life loom from the past; the stench of the squalid tower room in which he died, assaults my nose. For a moment it seems history does repeat itself.

I will not allow it.

Gathering all my strength, I step into the room, drop my basket and hurry to the bed where Harry sweats and groans. The hand that grasps mine is hot; when I draw my fingers across his brow, I find it fevered. Dread gathers like a handful of stones in my belly. Without relinquishing my husband's hand, I yell over my shoulder for Ned to bring my basket.

"There is a package of herbs," I tell him. "Angelica, chamomile and coriander for the fever, and yarrow salve for the wound."

My eyes flinch from the bloodstained bindings on the injury I have not yet examined.

He groans aloud as I draw back the covers and lift the filthy bandage. A deep, dark gash, mud and debris mixed with blood all congealing into a scab. I stare at it, transfixed by its dreadfulness, and know that we will need to tarry here at Barnet for some time.

I lean over and sniff the wound, breathe a little easier when I find it is as yet free of taint. I bite my lip, considering how to treat it. If I probe it, try to clean it, I might just make things worse.

After a long moment while Harry mutters and curses on the bed, I decide not to disturb the wound too much. With as little interference as I can manage, I daub some salve on a fresh bandage and dress it. Then I dose him with the fever remedy, wash some of the battle filth from his torso, cover him with clean blankets and sit down to wait for him to wake ... or die, as the Lord directs.

The longest night follows. I do not sleep but grow so tired that my tormented mind confuses me. Sometimes, I fancy I am with Edmund, my fingers entwined in Jay's wiry coat, watching again as the plague and battle wounds take him.

Other times I am here, in the present, which is no improvement on the past. Reality stabs, a sharp reminder that I am losing my husband, my Harry who has become my dearest love.

For hours, I watch. I bathe his forehead, I pour fever remedy between his parched lips, moisten his tongue with water. And all the while, I pray to the good Lord to spare him.

It is a little after dawn when the fire slumps suddenly in the grate and I waken. My neck is stiff where my head has lolled forward. I wipe a trickle of drool from my chin and lean closer to the bed. Harry is sleeping, peacefully it seems, and my dread lessens, just a little.

I cool his brow, moisten his tongue again. The medicine is all but depleted, and I have a dire need to use the chamber pot. I rise quietly and tiptoe from the room.

When I return, for want of something to distract me, I begin to tidy up. I throw the filthy bandage onto the fire, add more wood and agitate the dying embers into flame. Then I gather the pots and phials and pile them anyhow into my basket. I am gently straightening Harry's blankets when I become aware of his eyes upon me, eyes that are calm and clear.

"Harry!"

He fumbles for my fingers, clamps them hard in his palm.

"Where did you go? I thought ..." Sickness has reduced his voice to a croak, and his head lolls against his pillow. His eyes close again.

Stroking back his thin hair, I watch him relapse into sleep, but his breath is regular now, his colour returning to normal.

I shut my eyes and send up a silent whisper of gratitude, for my prayers have been answered.

Early May 1471

Early in May, Harry is drawn home to Woking on a litter. The skin on his face is sore, peeling off like flakes of ancient whitewash, his pallor like parchment, the tremor in his hands that of an old man. I ride beside him, trying to distract him from the pain of travel with light merry conversation. It is a strain I gladly relinquish when he falls into a swoon-like slumber. Thereafter we travel in silence, only Ned breaking the peace from time to time to point out a pothole in the road, or to alert me to a fallen branch.

While my life with Harry teeters on the brink of tragedy, the battle for the crown continues. I play no part in it now; I no longer favour either side. My only concern is for Harry.

Thankfully, the journey is not a long one and we arrive home on the fifth day of May. My first thought is one of surprise to find the fruit trees are blossoming in the garden. I had not noticed the season turn; for once, I have not waited and watched for the first green leaf of spring.

I order that Harry be taken straight to his chamber where his bed has been made ready. Then, as soon as I have refreshed myself, I go to the still-room to prepare fresh remedies. I find comfort in the order there. The shelves are replete with jars and bottles, and the hanging racks are full of drying flowers that still bear the hint of last summer's fragrance.

Selecting an array of jars, I hurry back to Harry's chamber. I am contemplating another peep beneath his bandages when Ned appears. He hesitates at the door, shifting from one foot to the other. I know he has news to impart, and by his face I can tell it will not necessarily be welcome.

As I draw close, I notice a letter in his hand. He holds it out and, with dread looming, I wipe my hand on my apron and take it from him.

Close by the fire where the light is better, I force myself to understand the words that seem to float about the page. I frown, bite my lip as phrases like 'report the death', 'ultimate defeat' and 'Lancaster vanquished' rise up in a tide of despair.

I plump suddenly into a chair.

As the news seeps into my mind, the world around me turns black. I stare into the hearth. There is darkness in the depths of the flames, darkness and ice that burns like the devil in my heart.

I will never again speak the word 'Tewkesbury' in anything louder than a whisper. My hand shakes as I re-read the slaughter that is written there. The scribe's pen describes an army in disarray; men fleeing for their lives, some drowning as they fought to cross the river. Two thousand Lancastrians slaughtered, our leaders dragged from sanctuary on the king's orders to be cut down in the marketplace.

The abbey and churchyard at Tewkesbury Abbey are forever tainted with the sins of York – that vain and glorious golden prince. My heart sickens; the taste of vomit is on my tongue. Somerset is dead; our prince of Lancaster has been butchered, our queen taken prisoner, and derision heaped upon her grieving head.

Tears fall upon my hands and my shoulders shake, my heart is as hard and heavy as a leaden ball. Something touches my shoulder and I look up into Ned's stricken face. My heart leaps as he slowly offers me a second letter.

The seal is already broken but I do not question it. I close my eyes and hold my breath as I seek the strength to read. I know without being told that the news is bad.

Sickness consumes me. I turn away and retch into the hearth. Ned's hand is upon my back, gently rubbing. I stand up, and his hand falls away. Our eyes meet, his own horror echoing mine.

"Not the king ... not that poor harmless man ... oh Ned, this world is too cruel ..."

He offers me a cup but I shake my head, close my eyes as the image of my good cousin, the lonely, bewildered king – the rightful king of England – faces his enemies alone in the Tower.

"They are saying he died of melancholy ..."

"Melancholy!" I spit the word, the taste of hatred bitter on my tongue. "Our king died of York's voracity, York's lust for power. By Christ, I hope I live to witness the day God wreaks His revenge upon that man ... King Henry was a saintly soul ... untouched by sin ... how could they?"

I sit down suddenly onto the settle. My face falls into my hands as grief takes me. The only sound in the room is the sorrow that rakes my soul.

Ned's comforting hand remains on my shoulder. I turn my head slightly and notice how grimy his fingernails are.

"Take heart, lady," he says. "At least Jasper is safe. We can fight again ..."

"Fight for whom? We have no leader now ..." But then something shifts in my mind and realisation dawns. Lancaster still has a leader. My despair lightens, just a little. We are not vanquished yet ... not until the last day, when the last man falls.

October 1471

It is the darkest summer I can remember. Although the sun shines, the flowers bloom, the birds procreate and sing their gayest song, my heart is bleak, and the future bleaker still.

In just one year, everything has changed, and our security has plummeted. Our king has been murdered, my Beaufort cousins are dead, our cause lost. Any thought of coming to terms with the Yorkist king has flown. In the gloomy days after Tewkesbury, Jasper, who failed to reach the battle in time, turns tail and flees back to Wales, collecting my son and taking the boy into exile in France, out of the reach of the vengeful king of York.

I feel as if my heart has been torn from my body, my lungs perforated. Only grief remains. When word comes that they have been blown off course and arrive instead on the shores of Brittany, I bid them stay there.

Trust no one (I write) especially Edward of York. Never be tempted to return, my son, never try to make terms with that man, never agree to a betrothal with his daughter. He will stoop to any level to trap you into returning to these shores but pay no heed. Our day will come again ...

Thereafter, I walk in shadow. With no hope of seeing Henry, my future without him is as bleak as the emptiest wasteland. At dusk, I stand atop the highest tower, looking without seeing, into the darkness.

"I don't believe a woman has ever been more desolate," I murmur to myself, taking some comfort that my situation cannot become any worse.

Then I hear a hesitant step behind me and I turn to find my woman, Elizabeth Denham there. She hesitates, afraid to come forward but the look on her face gives the lie to my last thought.

"My lady," she says at last, "I think you should come ... it is Sir Harry ..."

As soon as I see him, I know there is nothing to be done. I can only ease his passing. He holds my hand as he slips away. I stroke his limp white fingers and watch as his breath slows, and the rattle in his throat obliterates every other sound.

I am destined to be left behind, to mourn, to lose or be parted from the people I love. Perhaps I am cursed; perhaps I should love no more. Perhaps my future lies in a nunnery – I could make my vow to God and retire from this dreadful world, surrounding myself with prayer.

The sound of Harry's breathing halts. Slowly, I raise my head and see that he has gone. My throat closes with pain and a tear drops from the end of my nose. As I look upon his beloved face, the burning spear of grief plunges deep into my chest ... and remains there.

There is no more Margaret.

Life has beaten me.

Part Two

Lady Stanley

<u>Le Ryall, London - May 1472</u>

For a little while, I am quite mad with grief. Unable to take control of the simplest of matters, I leave all arrangements to Reginald Bray, whose silent capability provides me with the luxury of total despair.

I pray all day and all night, but God is slow to send relief. Why? Why does he take everyone I love? My husbands, my son, my king?

I am alone. My marriage bed is empty once again, and Harry is no more. How can so much warmth and love become nothing but a corpse in a winding sheet? Where does all that vitality go? His death defeats me. I feel betrayed, routed.

*

I cannot be sure what instinct draws me to my mother's house but within a few weeks of Harry's death, I find myself here. Mother has changed, grown older, less preoccupied, more inclined to listen until I have reached the end of my sentence.

She does not judge my long absence, does not question my unannounced visit. Calmly, she orders her servants to make ready the guest apartments, and does not bat an eyelid at the extensive household staff I bring with me. I have been cared for by Reginald Bray, Ned, and my chief women, Jane and the two Elizabeths, for too long to do without them now.

Mother's parlour is dimly lit and stifling hot, yet she clutches a shawl about her chest as if the day is freezing. I can feel my cheeks glowing in the heat of the flames, and discreetly move to a chair a little farther from the hearth.

"What will you do with yourself now, Margaret ... once you have had time to grieve?"

I have been here for less than a week; her words suggest she has already had enough of my dismal company.

"It is not yet six months since I lost Harry. I have not given it much thought, Mother."

She plucks a handful of nuts from a bowl and pops a few into her mouth, chewing carefully before speaking.

"Well, you should think about it. A woman in your position will not be left in peace for long. Your fortune and title will soon bring the wolves down from the hills."

The shadows lighten a little as the sun peeks from beneath the white blanket of cloud. I can see her face, drawn and lined, her eyes watching in anticipation of my reply. She is right, of course. In this world of power hungry men, my fortune will outweigh my barren state and allow me little respite from suitors. If I am not careful, the king will sell my hand to his nearest and dearest.

I have no desire to be wed into the Woodville family – not that there are many left unwed. As soon as she was made queen, Elizabeth Woodville secured the most profitable alliances available for her relatives. Many eyebrows were raised when the marriage was announced between her twenty-year-old brother John and the elderly Dowager Duchess of Norfolk. No doubt the old lady was happy enough to trade her social standing for the pleasure of a handsome young man at her board. Despite the horrified gossip of my mother's friends, I cannot image they also share a marriage bed.

So, whom should I marry? Marriage is not something I relish. I have been lucky twice – such fortune is not likely to fall on me again. I will never replace Harry, I know that, but even so, there are few to choose from. I have been so long away from court that I am acquainted with few eligible men, and so many have perished in the wars. The thought of an alliance with a brute or a bully shrinks my courage. I push the idea away, yet it might be best to appear to contemplate it. I raise my eyes from my lap.

"It is too soon to even contemplate marriage yet, Mother, but ... if I were to remarry, where would you advise me to cast my eye?"

She straightens in her chair, clutching her shawl tighter. Mother is good at match-making; she studies the marriage market as I study herb lore and Latin. I am confident she will suggest only a good, lucrative match.

If I must link my life to a man, then I fancy a widower, an old fellow who might endow a large legacy; an ageing soul long past any hopes of an heir. Since a child is out of the question, I will never again go willingly into a man's bed – and I will never love again.

Mother taps her chin with her forefinger as she consults a mental list of eligible men.

"You need someone powerful in his own right; someone with influence at court. You have been away for too long; it is time you stopped pining over your lost son and made your mark on the world. No more second born sons for you ..."

"Henry isn't lost, Mother; he will never be lost. I will fight to my last breath to make it safe for him to come home."

"Then you need a man who will assist you, a man with the king's trust ..."

"Or someone strong enough to overthrow him ..."

Silence pulses in my ears. My hand falls like a clamp across my mouth. My last words are astounding, even to me. Until I spoke the words, I had not realised such a thing was in my mind.

Mother clears her throat, breaking the silence.

"Yes, well, as I said, I will give it some thought."

"Very well, but please, Mother, if I have to share my life with a stranger, at least let him be tolerable. Do not saddle me with a monster."

"Do not be too squeamish, daughter," she laughs, and with a wry smile I rise from my chair, her gentle chuckles following me to the door.

Any thoughts of loving the Yorkist king or his low-born wife died a violent death when King Henry was murdered. During the days that follow, treasonous thoughts continue to dance in the wings of my mind.

England is run by murderous traitors; if only there was a way to depose them. Why should a Beaufort not take his turn at wearing the crown? At least my son would not sully himself with rascals and strumpets as Edward does.

But since Elizabeth produced a son, Edward walks with more confidence. He sits securely on the throne now, he is unshakeable. The people love him, and the old king is all but forgotten, by everyone but me.

As I go about my duties, helping mother's women in the still-room, receiving guests, consulting with Reginald Bray as to the drawing of my will, my inner thoughts linger on Edward's right to the throne he has stolen. I flirt precariously with treason.

I have had much time for reflection lately. Hard as it is to think of it, I keep returning to my widowed state. I am not yet thirty yet have married three times; one annulment and twice being widowed. I wonder if I am cursed, or if God is punishing me for some long-forgotten sin. I pray almost constantly. Even when I am not in the chapel, a prayer for guidance chants in my head. If ever I needed direction, it is now.

I know I must consider another match, but I do not want another husband. I had not relished the idea of marriage to Harry before I met him, but as luck would have it, he was a worthy man, and it was a good and happy match. I pray it might be so again, although in truth I hold little hope of it.

Master Bray helps me draw up a will. With some defiance against this unknown man I am to marry, I make my wish clear that I am to be buried with Edmund, the father of my son. I arrange for his body be brought from Grey Friars to Bourne Abbey, so that, when the far off day comes, I may be interred with him. I also bid Master Bray to speak to my trustees, to arrange a sum of monies from my own estates be set aside for Henry.

With so much death around me, who knows what would become of him were he to be left motherless. Should he ever wish to return to England, he will need the funds to do so and I cannot forever guarantee that I will be here. With a shiver of foreboding, I sign the papers providing him with independence; it is all I can do.

These maudlin thoughts of my own death send me to the chapel even more frequently than is my usual habit. Mother complains that I am growing pale and wan.

"You will never catch a man if you don't get a little colour in your cheeks," she says. To appease her, I pray early, take a long walk in the garden before dinner, and another before bed. The long hours of exercise bring the required roses to my face, but also leave me exhausted.

One afternoon when I return from a walk, I find mother entertaining a gentleman in her private parlour. This in itself is unusual, since guests are usually greeted in the great hall. I pause on the threshold, and they both turn, their faces opening in greeting. I curtsey before moving forward to join them at the solar. Mother bustles to meet me, places a hand on my arm.

"Sir Thomas, you know my daughter, Margaret?"

He bows elegantly, takes my hand and leaves his greeting upon my wrist.

"Sir Thomas," I murmur, and as the first stirrings of suspicion bubble in my belly, I wish I had thought to wear a better gown. As we take our seats, I tuck my workaday shoes out of sight beneath my skirts.

"Lady Margaret, I have heard so much about you. You are a scholar, and something of a healer, so I've heard."

His eyebrows are raised, waiting for my reply. I am aware of mother watching us. She is tense, expectant. I catch her eye and her expression of innocence informs me that Sir Thomas Stanley has indeed come here today as a suitor.

I put on my best smile and, trying to forget that I am small and plain, I adopt the air of a graceful lady.

"I would not go so far as to name myself a healer, Sir Thomas, but I confess I do have some skill with herbs. I attend personally to the health of my household. As to being a scholar, well … I can read and make sense of the philosophers, and I have some Greek and Latin, of course."

I ensure my smile hovers on my lips as he makes reply.

"Then, you know more than I, Madam, but what good is philosophy to a soldier? I have no need of it on the battleground."

From what I have heard, the skills of both Stanley brothers lie more in evading battle than valour on the field. I link my fingers in my lap.

"Some would say that life itself is a battle, and the rules apply equally. One must know one's friends ... and one's enemies, of course ..."

"Ha! I sense a ready wit, Madam, but it is lost on me. Battle is about strategy, cunning ..." He turns to my mother. "Very fine malmsey, Lady Margaret, you must give me the name of your vintner."

I keep my eyes lowered, realising I have displeased him already. Mother turns all her charm on Sir Thomas and, casting a warning frown in my direction, suggests a stroll about the garden.

As we meander through the straggling flowers, I resist the urge to untangle the roses from the passionate embrace of bindweed, pluck ragwort from beneath the hedge. My mother is unconcerned about her gardens and allows her gardeners to grow lazy; to her, it is a place to exercise the dog, or send the grandchildren when they grow too rowdy for the parlour.

Sir Thomas monopolises the conversation, which consists mostly of self-praise. He rambles on about his inherited Barony, and titular title of the King of Mann, an honour that nowadays is as empty as a drunkard's flagon.

He boasts of his vast estates, his fine string of horses; his wine cellar, his recent appointment as steward of the king's household. I perceive him to be a windbag, an empty, vain cockerel crowing of his assets. In terms of manliness, compared to Edmund he is nothing. In terms of honour, next to Harry he is a villain. I like him not, but ... he does have the ear of the king. He is strong, he commands a great army. He is in ascendance at court, and could protect me ... but is he manageable? Would his bullish ways crush me, and force me into compliance? Or could I persuade him, tease him round to my way of thinking?

It is clear he will not be ruled by feminine wiles, but since I lack those accomplishments, this bothers me little. I must look for other ways; find a chink within his armour that will allow me to quietly rule him. I need him to help me bring Henry home ... the other matter can wait.

He continues to dominate the conversation until a cloud hurries in to cover the sun. He looks anxiously at the sky.

"Looks like rain," he says. "I must take my leave before you ladies suffer a soaking."

With promises to visit again soon, he bends over my hand, his lips this time touching the skin on my wrist. When he straightens up, he fixes me with his eye and deep within them, I detect approval. Somehow, I have managed to please him; it can only be that he has mistaken my silence for interest. While I have been inwardly yawning, he has believed me spellbound. Perhaps his vanity will provide the way forward. Is it possible to guide him with flattery?

June 1472

The wedding takes place at his holding, Knowsley Hall, in Lancashire. The gossips mutter at the haste, complaining that poor Harry has not yet been dead a year. They do not consider my vulnerability. If I do not act quickly and make my own choice of husband, I could find myself married off to a fortune-hunter on some whim of the king.

I may not greatly like Thomas, and there is little chance of us discovering love within our marriage, but our mutual need binds us. In exchange for the prestige of my name, and a lifetime's interest in my properties, he offers me protection, and a boost to my annual income. Most of all, I hope against hope, he will secure me a position at court.

King Edward places his trust in Thomas, but I am increasingly hopeful that my husband's loyalties are not set in stone. It is only two years since he welcomed back my cousin, King Henry, during his brief readeption. Now, in word and action, Thomas declares wholeheartedly for York, but I cannot help but wonder where his loyalties, if he has any, really lie.

Time will tell.

Since Edward's victorious return, Thomas has done all in his power to win back his trust and the Stanleys' strong northern power base is essential to any king. Without their support, Edward knows he cannot survive. I watch and I listen, and the longer I am in my husband's company, the better I come to know him.

We spend our first summer quietly at his holding at Lathom in Lancashire. While my personal staff organise the chambers set aside for me, Thomas guides me around the warren of rooms, apologising for the draughts, the damp, and the lack of facilities.

"I have great plans for this place," he says, looking around dispiritedly at the chamber we are to share. "It will be done some day, probably when I am in my dotage."

"It is very nice," I lie, "very comfortable."

His roar of laughter surprises me.

"How will I ever believe a word you say now?" he splutters. I feel my face grow pink, unsure how to respond at being caught out in a mistruth.

"I was only trying to be polite."

"Relax, Margaret." His hand falls heavy on my shoulder. "I am not going to eat you. You may do as you please, think as you please, as long as it brings no trouble on my head. You need not fear that I will bother you for the delights of your body either. I have heirs enough to please a king, and I fancy you not at all."

My face grows hotter as fury gathers in my heart. My fists clench, and I close my lips tight against a rude tirade. I have no desire to lie with him, but ... to be told ... so directly, that I hold no attraction for him is like a blow to the face. I am offended that he does not wish to share my bed.

For a few moments I am paralysed by his insult. Frozen with indecision, I stare at him until his smirking, coarse face clarifies the matter, and I remember how much I dislike him. I am far, far better than he is.

"Good," I say, looking him squarely in the eye. "I have no wish to lie with you either. I am tired now. Ask my women to come and help me disrobe. I am in need of a long sleep."

I sit on the bed, bouncing on the mattress to test the softness. My shoes are tight. I kick them off, lift my skirts and begin to roll down my stockings to let him see what he can never have. His eyes linger on my naked legs as I flex my feet and wiggle my toes.

"Ooh, I need new shoes; these ones have been made too small."

He hesitates, looks at me sideways. For a moment I think he is about to speak, but he thinks better of it and stomps away. He throws open the door, bellowing for my women and, when he is gone, I clench my fist and vent my fury on his musty pillows.

I learn afterwards that he spends the night, and every night thereafter, in a guest chamber, and good riddance to him. In the morning, I dress my best and greet him cordially before embarking as I mean to go on – as mistress of his household.

As he promised, my husband gives me a free hand to organise the domestic matters, and from his manner I glean that he approves of the new furnishings I bring in, and the changes I propose to the gardens.

I have no idea how my husband occupies his days. Reginald Bray assists with the care of my own estates, and together we keep check that the alterations taking place at Woking are progressing well.

I seldom meet Thomas during the day-to-day running of the household, and when we do meet, our conversation is polite and cold. Before the summer is out, we have come to an understanding – we both share a common cause, the desire for mutual promotion beneath the rule of York, but there are boundaries and we both know where they lie.

In September, we plan to travel to his holdings at Chester and Harwarden, and thereafter to London and the royal court. I waste no time in ordering velvet, some gorgeous tawny-coloured chamlet for a new kirtle, and fur to trim my winter gowns. I also purchase new harness for my favourite horse, so I may travel in style and comfort.

My excitement at finally being welcomed at court is so great I can scarcely conceal it, but I am determined not to appear gauche before my husband. When Thomas discusses it, I pretend indifference; on one occasion, I even yawn behind my hand. Only my women, Elizabeth and Jane, know the fever with which I plan my wardrobe.

This is my chance to make an impression on the king and queen, and secure a position in the royal household. I practice my deportment, which is already perfect. I work on my curtsey until, to the amusement of my women, I can manage to show deference with a cup of wine balanced on my head.

Mother always said that the condition of one's petticoats reflects in one's deportment. "It is a matter of confidence," she said and it is a lesson I have never forgotten. One should strive to be as flawless as possible, like a precious jewel. From the skin out, I must be perfect.

Each afternoon, my women and I embroider embellishments on my shifts, even though nobody but myself and the laundry maids will ever set eyes upon them. My kirtle and petticoats are new, and my shift and stockings of the finest silk. I am ready; as perfect as it is possible for me to be.

It has been dry for weeks, but now the spell of summer weather has broken. On the morning that we ride to Westminster, a steady rain falls, blanketing the world in a veil of light mist. In the court apartments allocated to us, my ladies tut as they flick moisture from my hair, and offer me a soft cloth to dry my face. I stand before the hearth and take refreshment with my clothes steaming.

My skirts are damp, my fingers chilled from holding the reins. I wish now I had agreed to travel by litter, for it will take an age for my clothes to dry. Thomas removes his dripping cloak and pours himself a cup of wine.

"You look fine, Margaret. How can you bear them fussing you like that?"

I wave my women away, and take the cup he offers.

"I just want to look my best."

Thomas is a man. He is tall and imposing to look at. He will never understand the insecurities of being only five feet tall. Everyone, even juvenile boys, looks down upon me, even though I am their superior in age, status and intellect. I live in the constant fear of being told to go and stand with the children. I refuse to let this make me feel inferior, constantly reminding myself of who I am, where I came from ... and where I am going.

The wine is thick and fruity on my tongue. Unlike my husband, I drink sparingly, unwilling to greet the king and queen with a light head. I frown as he pours another glass and tips it down his throat. He smacks his lips, sets the cup on the table and grins at me defiantly.

"Come then, Madam, are you ready?"

Stifling my annoyance, I take his arm, loop my train about my wrist, and allow him to lead me through the halls of the palace to the presence chamber. Guards snap to attention as we draw near, someone throws open the doors, and our names are called.

On the dais, the king of York waits with his queen, their children prominently displayed around them. Their heads are high, their eyes welcoming yet wary; the perfect portrait of a royal family.

A victorious king and his fertile queen, together with three perfect golden princesses, political pawns in the marriage game, and the jewel in their crown; little Edward, Prince of Wales. Another child, a girl of just a few months old, remains in the nursery. With a deep breath I bury my envy, and greet them with a deferent smile.

Prince Edward is only two years old, but he will soon be sent from the comfort of the royal nursery and the doting company of his sisters to his own establishment at Ludlow on the Welsh border. The queen will then learn what it means to be parted from a beloved son.

At least she has the compensation of other boys; two sons from her first marriage, Richard and Thomas Grey. She also has a riot of little girls.

In Wales, the prince will be cared for by the queen's brother Anthony, Earl Rivers, and he, together with my husband's brother, William, will head the prince's royal council. It is a great honour for William to be chosen and, since Thomas and his brother are close, the honour of one reflects well upon the other.

We draw closer to the dais, prostrate ourselves before them. My damp skirts spread around me, the weight of my headdress resisting as I strive to bend my head. Beside me, Thomas's breath labours as he forces his large frame into submission. He suppresses a belch.

"Lady Margaret, My Lord Stanley, we are glad to welcome you to our court on such a dismal day." The king snaps his fingers for wine and a page goes running.

We straighten up, my eyes meeting those of the queen. Her lips tilt into a smile, increasing her already radiant beauty. She murmurs a greeting and holds out her hand so that I might kiss it. While I do so, I strain my ears to hear Thomas's conversation with the king. The queen's voice intrudes, her questions falling thick and fast.

"My brother tells me it is a beastly day, Lady Margaret. I hope you didn't get too wet."

"Only my cloak, Your Grace. I came properly prepared."

Why can I not admit to a soaking? It is no dishonour. I begin to worry she will notice the hem of my gown is damp, and catch me out in my futile lie. I must do all in my power to appear honest.

"Well," I add, before she can speak again, "perhaps my skirts did get a little damp."

"Our English rain respects no one, no matter our rank. Tell me, Lady Margaret, I have heard you are very learned in healing, give me your judgement on my Cecily's rash. The royal physician says it is nothing; do you agree?"

She beckons a child forward and the girl daws back her sleeve to show me a cluster of red spots on her inner elbow, some of them raw and weepy.

"Have you been scratching them?" I ask.

She pulls a face. "They are itchy."

"I agree with the physician, Your Grace, and suspect it is nothing serious but I can make up a salve that should soothe it as well as preventing her from scratching and making it sore."

"That is good of you. My mother said you would know."

Jacquetta, Duchess of Bedford, hovers behind the queen's chair. We bow our heads in cool acknowledgement.

"I knew your mother, Lady Margaret. We were very good friends at one time. I hope she is well."

That was before the feuding. Before the wars came, when Lancaster was in control, and she and my mother were prominent members in the household of Margaret of Anjou.

I smile warmly.

"I am glad to see you here, Your Grace." I bow my head and when I raise it again, I notice her eyes are soft with friendship.

Of the three of the women gathered here, Jacquetta has perhaps suffered the most. When Warwick fell foul of the king and fled overseas, the queen took sanctuary with her children at Westminster. I was exiled in Wales, where I lost a husband and came close to losing my son. But Jacquetta bore the brunt of Warwick's hatred for the entire Woodville family.

After he ordered the execution of her husband and son, he accused Jacquetta of witchcraft. The thought of such a thing strikes terror into every woman's heart. During the French wars, it was Jacquetta's first husband who ordered the burning of the Maid of Orleans. The experience touched all women deeply, for every one of us knew the Maid was no witch. And later, well – none of us can forget Eleanor of Cobham ...

When it was Jacquetta's turn to be accused, all minds turned to the Maid and Eleanor, and the roaring of the hungry flames grew loud in all ears.

Jacquetta was taken from her home, kept in chains, away from the world. Her daughter, the fallen queen, was unable to countermand it. Specious evidence was raised against her, her trial set to follow. How she must have trembled in those dark, forsaken days. How she must have despaired.

Looking at her now, I detect the shadow of that time, lurking deep within her eyes. Every one of us gathered here is marked by the trials of our past, but the stain of Warwick's accusation will never leave her – no matter how hard she scrubs at it.

Elizabeth is secure again. She has borne an heir, York will never fall now, and even I can see a way forward beginning to emerge. But Jacquetta is marked, the accusation against her indelible; witchcraft is a slur that sticks, and she of all people cannot forget the consequences.

The queen rises suddenly from her chair, pulling me from reverie.

"Come, Lady Margaret, walk with me. I have been sitting too long. You can tell me what herbs make up this soothing ointment of yours. I am sure we will have it in the physic garden."

She takes my arm and, her tall elegant frame dwarfing mine, we parade around the hall as if we are the best of friends. Her conversation consists largely of gossip, sometimes she even speaks behind her hand so that those nearby may not hear. I answer yay or nay as required, aware that Thomas and the king are watching every step we take.

She is fragrant and amusing. I am almost charmed, and certainly jealous of the way fortune smiles upon her. What I wouldn't give to be her. She is pretty, queen of all England, married to a powerful man whose royal nursery she has filled with children. Her future is assured, her destiny unblemished.

Who would not want to be her?

Yet, although she is surrounded by women, she seems lonely - isolated. The noble women of England despise her for her common blood; they are waiting for her to trip up, to reveal a dirty petticoat. I feel the stirring of pity, remembering my early days in Wales when I was a foreigner in a strange land.

Elizabeth is no foreigner, but she is set apart from the noble women of England who form a faction of contempt against her. Even so, I am suspicious of her friendship. She is warm where I had expected hostility; she is candid where I had expected deceit.

Her reception has unbalanced me. I came here prepared as to how to behave, but now ... I am unsure. I can hardly refuse her company, and she does not seem so bad. All I can do is follow her lead.

*

Within weeks, I am firmly ensconced in the royal court. The queen includes me in every event, invites me to the nursery to admire her son, and consults me on everything from which shade of silk suits her best to the suitability of the royal nursemaid. I can detect no rancour, no duplicity, just a genuine need to be liked.

She is not openly shunned by the other women at court, for who would dare snub the queen? But they do resent her. Elizabeth, despite her mother's good breeding, is inferior to the very women who now have to defer to her. She takes precedence over everyone, even the king's mother and sisters, and it goes hard with them, their rancour obvious in their sour expressions.

In-laws are never easy, but I wonder why Elizabeth does not set out to woo their good opinion, as she has mine. Instead, she seems to rub her status in their faces and delights in getting her way with the king, especially when it goes against the desires of his mother. Cecily Neville can scarcely disguise her distaste, and neither can his sisters.

The king needs little excuse to declare a night of celebration and the wedding of his youngest, favourite brother is no exception. Richard of Gloucester has made a wise choice in the widowed daughter of the traitor, Warwick. Given her experiences, I expected Anne Neville to be hardened, but she is a small, self-effacing girl who flushes each time the king addresses her.

During his defection from York, Warwick made good use of both his daughters, using Isabel to lure George of Clarence from the king's side, and marrying Anne to his former enemy, Edward of Lancaster, as part of his alliance with Margaret of Anjou.

Even at the time, I thought the arrangement hard on Anne, despite Lancaster having my full support. It was difficult enough for me, when I was sent into Wales to marry a stranger, but at least Edmund was on the same side. Anne was bred, almost from birth, to mistrust and detest Lancaster – it must have been unimaginably hard for her.

Perhaps her meekness is the result of her experiences. Perhaps she was once bright and bonny, but she certainly is not now. Although she has known Richard of Gloucester since her youth, she makes a silent bride. I wonder if she welcomes the union. While she and her spouse sit mutely in a place of honour at the top table, the court around them descends into depravity.

Led by his favourite, William Hastings, King Edward drinks deeply, vying with Hastings for the favours of a serving maid. The queen sits with her head high, ignoring the insult but I can sense her concealed fury. She laughs a lot, claps her hands delightedly at the tumblers, her voice high and happy as she pours golden pennies into the hands of the players. All is delightful. All is bright, yet I, a newcomer to court, can smell the rancour beneath the show.

Gloucester takes no part in the revels. I have heard he is a modest, pious man, and it seems the report is true. Usually, after a wedding, the couple are escorted to bed with bawdy jokes and a rumpus of obscenity, but tonight, when it is time for the bride and groom to retire, Gloucester curtly defies anyone to see them off to bed. Anne is glad of it, her relief written clear on her face.

They are an odd couple. Gloucester, quiet and deep; Anne, shy and closed. It is impossible to tell what either of them are thinking; whether it will be a night of passion, or a curt goodnight. My mind drifts back to the night of my wedding to Edmund, the terror of what was to come, my relief when nothing happened. I was young and Edmund allowed me time, and in the end, we were happy. I hope Anne Neville is as fortunate in her husband as I was in mine.

A great laugh issues across the hall; a laugh I recognise. I turn my head to see my husband with a servant wench balanced on his knee, his hand high up on her thigh, her head thrown back in merriment. My throat closes, not with jealousy, but with shame, both for him and for myself. Tears of humiliation stab at the back of my eye.

The queen stands. "I am tired, Lady Margaret. Come; let us leave the men to their celebrations." I stumble after her, overwhelmed with gratitude.

Her apartment is warm and comfortable with the fire burning high, the shutters closed against the night; a haven of peace after the excesses of the hall. While I remove her headdress and begin to comb her hair, a musician strums a lute. She closes her eyes, tilts back her head.

"Your touch is so soft, Margaret, I could fall asleep."

"I am almost done, Your Grace, if you desire to go to bed."

"No. No, I expect the king will be some time yet."

My face goes hot at the implication of her words but I do not let my hand falter.

"You must not let it bother you, Margaret. If I were to be upset by every slut who puts herself in the king's way ..."

"It is not that, Your Grace. I am not upset. I am ... dishonoured."

She turns suddenly on her stool, and the comb falls from my fingers.

"No; you are quite wrong. *We* are never dishonoured by their behaviour. They dishonour themselves. We must rise above it. Men are like ... small children chasing butterflies. Once they catch them, they no longer desire them and let them fly again, tainted and spoiled. Then they come humbly back to us. It is wives that matter, not whores. Wives are never dishonoured."

She is right. I allow myself a moment to view men from this new perspective she has shown me, and I realise how ridiculous they are.

Amusement tickles the side of my mouth. She meets my eyes in the looking glass, reads my thoughts and a tinkle of laughter floats around the chamber. The musician stumbles in his playing and looks up in surprise.

We sober slowly. I wipe a tear from my eye, suddenly serious again.

"Sir Thomas and me – we – ours is a convenient arrangement. I do not mind him taking his pleasure where he can, but I dislike seeing your royal court so sullied."

Elizabeth shrugs. "It is the king who leads them ... or, perhaps I should say, it is the king who allows Hastings to take the lead."

"Perhaps he should be found a post far from court, where his behaviour will not matter."

She taps her fingertip to her chin.

"Perhaps, Lady Margaret; you may be right, but I doubt my influence on the king extends to severing his ties with Hastings."

I open my mouth to speak again but the door opens and one of the women from the prince's nursery enters. She hesitates when she sees me, dips a clumsy curtsey to the queen.

"What is it?" Elizabeth's face is tense, paler. I pretend to fold a wrap and put it away in the clothespress, but all the time I watch curiously.

"It is little Margaret, Your Grace. She won't settle and I was told to ask you to come."

Elizabeth stands up, her hair falling free to her hip. As she hurries past, I am bathed in her sweet fragrance. She pauses at the door.

"Lady Margaret, come with me."

It is not a request. I smooth my skirts and follow her. Her legs are longer than mine, and her haste such that she soon outstrips me. She travels so quickly up the winding stairs that I am panting slightly when we reach the nursery door.

The fire is roaring, providing the main light in the room. A woman with a patch of white puke on her shoulder paces back and forth, back and forth with a bawling infant in her arms. Two small girls watch from the doorway, thumbs in their mouths. The woman turns to the queen, forgetting to curtsey, her brow creased with worry.

"I can't make her stop, Your Grace. I have tried everything."

"Have the physicians been summoned?"

The woman shifts the child to one arm, drags her forearm across her sweating forehead.

"They have, Your Grace, but they offered no advice I did not already know."

The queen places a finger on her daughter's cheek, but the child continues to scream, her face red and creased, real tears spouting.

"She's been fed, I suppose?" the queen asks, and the nurse manages to conceal her irritation at such an inane question.

"Yes, Your Grace, and we tried her again just now."

"Lady Margaret, what do you think? Can you help?"

I step forward reluctantly.

"I have only borne one child, Your Grace. My knowledge is not great ..."

"But you know herb lore ... you told me yourself."

"I have never healed any babies, but I shall do my best."

I feel the child's forehead. It is hot, damp with sweat. It might be colic, or the beginnings of a fever. "Can I take her?"

Reluctantly, the nurse passes Princess Margaret into my arms. She is tiny, almost skeletal. I tuck her into my arm and bite back the tearful memory of Henry at such an age. His infancy was such a short pleasure before he was taken from me, but I thank God he was healthy.

Margaret continues to yell. I look around for a bed, lie her down upon it and begin to loosen her swaddling.

"What are you doing?"

The queen is beside me, peering over my shoulder at her tear-drenched, snotty daughter.

"She has worked herself into a pet, Your Grace. I think she is too hot. If we loosen her bands for a while she might quieten down. It is very hot in the chamber."

"It is." Elizabeth signals for someone to quench the fire while I slowly untangle the child, her thrashing limbs making my task more difficult.

Unclothed, she is even smaller, her blue veins visible through transparent skin, her arms and legs like sticks.

"How old is she, Your Grace?"

"Erm. I was churched at the end of May; she must be six weeks or more."

"Yet she has gained no fat? She feeds well?"

I address this last question to the wet nurse, who nods frantically.

"When it pleases her, but ... frequently she brings back up what she has taken."

"And does she sleep?"

"Not as much as you'd expect; she dozes in fits and starts. She cries almost every waking hour. We are at our wits end."

I look down at the baby on the bed, and put out my hand. She grasps my finger tightly, quietens a little. She blinks and squints as her crying ceases. For many minutes, her tiny chest continues to judder with distress. Finally, she stops, and her breathing regulates. I look up at the queen.

"I think she was hot, perhaps she could be wrapped less tightly?"

Elizabeth meets my eyes. "But won't her limbs grow misshapen?"

"I do not believe so, and if anyone is to get some rest, I think Lady Margaret's sleep will be beneficial for all of us."

Everyone stares down at the child as with a few whimpering sobs, she lapses into a sleep of exhaustion. I am afraid to move her now in case the wild cries begin again.

"Cover her and leave her there to sleep. Get some rest while you can and, in future, I suggest lighter wrapping, smaller but regular feeds, and maybe administer a little honey beforehand to stimulate her appetite."

The nurse nods. The queen takes one last look at her daughter, strokes her downy hair and, beckoning me to follow, tiptoes from the room.

"Thank you, Lady Margaret," she says as soon as we are outside the door. "You have such a way with her, such confidence. I am in your debt."

I bow my head. "No, Your Grace. I am pleased to offer my help, although I have but little skill."

We turn and begin to walk back toward her apartment.

"Little Margaret has had the physicians called out to her more than any of my other children. I fear for her."

She bites her lower lip, her face quite bleak. Without thinking, I place my hand on her wrist and squeeze gently.

"I shall pray for her, Your Grace."

December 1472

I sit in the royal nursery, where baby Margaret still clings miserably to life. I have been summoned here regularly since the day in June when I managed to soothe her.

The children are bored from being cooped up in the palace due to the heavy rain. The girls sit on the floor, threading beads onto a string, but the Prince of Wales, indifferent to his baby sister's malady, throws a ball about the chamber, bounding after it like a puppy.

The Princess Elizabeth abandons her task and comes to watch me, as if fearful I might drop her sister. I smile, but she does not return it. Mary, who is never far from Elizabeth, follows, with Cecily close beside her, her thumb in her mouth.

"Your thumb will drop off if you keep sucking it," I tell her and she whips it out, hides it behind her back, her eyes wide.

"No, it won't, Cecily. That is just a tale to make you stop sucking it."

Young Elizabeth is old for her years; she is as golden as her father, and promises to be just as tall. I am never sure whether she regards me as friend or foe, although I strive to be the former.

"But you can never be sure of that," I tease. "Suppose Cecily dismisses my warning and wakes one day to find it has dropped onto her pillow, then you will both wish you had listened."

A shadow falls between us and we look up to find the king has entered unawares.

"Besides," he says, sweeping his daughter into his arms, "even if your thumb doesn't drop off, sucking it will spoil the shape of your mouth. You would not want buck teeth – like a rabbit."

He makes a face like a rabbit and waggles two fingers like ears behind his head. The girls collapse into giggles, Cecily wrapping her short arms around her father's neck and planting a kiss on his nose.

"I like wabbits."

"So do I;" the king exclaims, "but I'd not want to be one!"

He lets the child slide from his arms and turns to me.

"How is our royal babe this morning, Lady Margaret?"

I bow my head, dip my knees and look down into the child's face.

"I wish I could say she is well, Your Grace, but she is sickly again. There always seems to be something."

He touches her head, runs his finger across her downy hair.

"The physicians are useless. We have had the best in the land, yet she makes no improvement. One suggested it is something to do with her heart ... not strong enough to ..." His voice breaks, his eyes filling with tears as he clears his throat. "But please, Lady Margaret, do not mention that to the queen, I am not sure she would be able to bear it."

His words make her infinitely more precious. I hold the child closer, place a kiss on her head, inhaling the fragrance of her hair.

"Neither could I ... neither could any of us."

He turns away, taking his time to circumnavigate the nursery, taking time to share a word or joke with each of the children. This room is the treasury of all his hopes and dreams. I curtsey as he leaves, respect fermenting reluctantly in my heart.

For the next three days, I spend every waking hour in the nursery until, almost dropping for want of sleep, the king orders me to rest. I retire gratefully to a small chamber close to the queen's and, without removing my clothes, I curl upon a small truckle bed and fall instantly asleep.

In my dream, I am given the task of forbidding the ravens to settle on the battlements. I have a yellow cloth in my hand and each time they fly too close to the castle, I run at them, waving my flag, and shout at them to go away. They drift up in a great black cloud, their caws akin to laughter, but they do not go far. I know they will be back. I can barely stand, can wave my arms no longer, I need to rest. And then one bird, larger than the rest, defies my efforts and settles on the wall. He cocks his head and fixes me with his bright eye.

"Fool," he says. "You cannot beat me." At his voice, his companions cackle, their laughter high and shrill ... like a woman's scream.

I spring up in bed, flinging off the blanket. Someone is screaming. I throw open the door and rush into the queen's chamber. Her face is white, her mouth wide open, her anguished cries, making me wince.

"Your Grace? What is the matter?" Then I see the nursery maid; she hovers by the door, tears streaking her grey face.

I shake my head from side to side. I do not want to hear it. She wipes her nose with her cuff.

"It is the baby." Her mouth goes a funny shape, she swings her head slowly from side to side. There is no need for her to say more.

I am frozen to the spot, unable to move, unable to imagine the horrid grief the queen suffers. Tears clog my eyes, pressure builds in my nose, and my throat closes with pain. No child should have to die; no parent should have to suffer this.

The queen stands unmoving in the centre of the room; no one dares approach her. Everyone is stock still, entranced by the spectacle of her grief. Forcing myself into action, I move forward and place a hand on her arm. It restores her to life; painful, unbearable life. For one short moment, she locks her wild eye on mine before thrusting me away.

Released from paralysis, she runs from the chamber, her footsteps fading as she speeds along the passages that lead to the nursery. The other women and I exchange glances, unsure if we should follow, uncertain how far we can intervene in her pain. They all look to me, electing me as their leader, but I am ill equipped to deal with this. I cannot begin to imagine what she must be feeling; if my own son were to die ...

I shake my head, dispelling the thought.

"I will fetch her mother; she will know what to do."

With a whisk of my skirts, I hurry in the queen's wake, taking the quickest route to the apartments of Jacquetta. Her mother will know; mothers always do.

February 1473

I miss Harry. My bed seems vast and cold without the familiar body slumbering beside me, the touch of his hand on my hip. I never recognised how much his loving meant; never realised I would ever come to miss the indignity of our coupling.

It is not only when night falls that I realise his lack; I miss his conversation at supper, our strolls about the garden at dusk. I miss his friendliness, his sincerity, his – oh, I miss everything. There is no-one to advise me now. I may be married but Stanley leads his life as a single man. I live mine as a nun.

When I am away from court, despite the new furnishings, the improvements I have introduced to the solar and the gardens, I feel like a visitor in his home. He is a busy man, always away on the king's business or in attendance on the king. As a result, when the queen requests me to return early to my duties, I am relieved to go.

She favours me, sometimes even before her close relatives, who continue to dominate the royal palace and secure for themselves the best, most prestigious appointments. Some of them are shameless in their efforts to attract the king's favour. My motives are little different. I put myself in the way of the king and queen for the sole purpose of securing Henry a safe passage back to England, but I hope my intentions are less transparent.

Compared to the restraint of King Henry's court, Edward's is brash and strident, given over to pleasure. The older families, the Talbots, and the Vaughns, look down their noses at the thrusting new members at court. The displeasure on Cecily Neville's face is eloquent, as if there is a nasty smell somewhere in the room.

This evening is no different. There are those members of the gathering who revel in the celebration, and those who clearly wish they were somewhere else. As soon as she can, the queen excuses herself, pleading a headache. The king looks up, blows her a kiss before turning back to his favourites. The last thing we hear as the doors close behind us is the laughter of Jane Shore, his favourite mistress. My back is stiff with indignation as I follow the queen to her apartment. If the king put more energy into the government of his country, and spent less time investigating the bottom of his wine cup and the intrigues beneath his mistress's petticoats, the country would be a better place.

The next day, we are confined to the castle by a heavy fall of snow. The king, obviously suffering from the excesses of the night before, slouches on his throne. His golden face is puffy and shadowed, his outbursts of temper frequent.

Beside him, Hastings has his head close to the king's latest fancy, Mistress Shore, who seems to be suffering no such ill effects. Jane is undoubtedly a pretty woman celebrated for her great wit. Her laughter can often be heard rising above that of the king's, and it is not a musical gentle sound like that of

Elizabeth, but a great belly laugh – a guffaw more suited to a hostelry.

The queen suffers her quietly, hoping against hope she will fast go the way of the king's other mistresses, smuggled away to the country to give birth to a royal bastard. He usually tires of them in a few months, but so far, Jane Shore is tenacious and the king remains besotted. I have witnessed the queen's jealousy, seen her hastily dry her eyes and don a serene smile for the sake of those watching. I am not sure I could be as controlled.

My relationship with Elizabeth perplexes me. The disdain I felt toward her when I first came to court has diminished. By living so close and witnessing her most intimate moments, I have come to know the woman beneath. Against my will, I discover similarities between us, and this endears her to me. She tries to hide her insecurities, her need to bind her husband to her but I witness it all. She has my pity and, although it hurts me to admit it, sometimes my admiration.

For all her proud, haughty manner, she is a woman like me, fighting for her place, battling to maintain her dignity, but it wins her few friends. Apart from her mother and sisters, she is quite isolated. Even I, whom she has welcomed into the bosom of her family and trusted to enter the royal nursery, am not a real friend. Pity is not liking, it is quite divorced from love, and it is not friendship that keeps me here. Every moment in her company I am aware of an ulterior motive, driving the relationship forward.

A great shout of laughter goes up; the crowd about the king explodes into applause. I look up to see a game of ninepins in progress – the king is smiling again, so it is safe to assume he is winning.

Towering above everyone else, his face is flushed, his mouth open in triumph, one arm flung casually about the plump shoulders of Jane Shore. He shouts loudly and provokingly to his opponents.

"You cannot have mastery over your king! None of you can match me!"

I shake my head in amazement and catch the eye of Jacquetta Woodville, who sits nearby. She smiles knowingly and leans back to speak to the queen who has a kerchief held to her mouth. Elizabeth closes her eyes, shakes her head.

Jacquetta sits back, looks closely at her daughter's face. Noting the triumphant joy in her eyes, I read her lips.

"You are pregnant again."

The knowledge sinks like a stone. Another child –and so soon! This will be ... I count rapidly in my head ... eight children. Elizabeth has, or will have, eight children, six of them royal, while I am blessed with only one, and he is far away.

I hate myself for the stab of unChristian envy. I bite my lip, clench my fists in my skirts until the moment passes and I can breathe again. Rising from my seat, I move to the queen's side.

"Your Grace, you look a little pale. Would you like to retire? I am sure your mother will be happy to oversee your women for the rest of the evening."

She lowers the kerchief and sighs with relief.

"Yes, Lady Margaret, thank you. That is very kind."

Once in her apartments, it does not take long for her to confess her condition to me.

"I feel as sick as a dog," she says as I help her take off her shoes and settle on the bed. "I have only felt like this four times in my life before. I will lay money on the fact I am carrying a boy."

The envy bites deeper. If her premonition is correct, my son will be thrust a little further into obscurity. Why, oh, why must this Yorkist queen be so fruitful?

"You have barely had time to recover from last time – it is very soon ..."

"Queens do not have the luxury of waiting. I must bring forth a child a year for as long as I can. The king will only be happy if I fill the royal nursery to the rafters. It is taxing, but I will do my duty – besides, I will never turn Edward from my chamber ..."

She does not need to express her fear of the king growing too fond of Jane Shore. I tuck a blanket beneath her chin.

"I shall make up an infusion of ginger, Your Grace, that should settle your stomach ... and," I pause at the door. "May I offer you my good wishes on your forthcoming confinement?"

She turns her face toward me, holds out her hand and I return to the bed and take it. Her long, slim fingers clasp mine.

"I am so glad to have you as my friend, Lady Margaret, so very grateful."

I drop to my knees and leave a Judas kiss on her knuckle.

"I am glad to be of service, Your Grace."

<u>May 1473</u>

The king has been closeted with his advisors all day and the queen is growing restless. She throws down her needlework.

"Oh, what can be keeping them? They have been in conference all day, and now it is almost time to retire. He has had no supper, you may be sure."

I look up with a ready reply, but Elizabeth Tilney forestalls me.

"Refreshments were taken into them some time ago. I saw a troop of servers leaving when I was returning from the gardens."

"Well, at least he shall not starve."

The queen sighs, shifts her position in her chair.

"Are you quite comfortable, Your Grace? Shall I fetch you another cushion?"

She looks up, smiles quickly.

"No, no, Lady Margaret. I am just restless … and very bored."

I put down my work and snap my fingers to gain the minstrel's attention.

"Play a merrier tune, the queen needs cheering."

Immediately, he pauses in the quiet lullaby he was playing and begins a lighter yet louder melody. The mood in the room instantly lifts.

The queen's sister, Anne, Lady Bouchier, rises from her chair. "Bess, why don't we dance? We don't need men, we can partner each other."

"I am queasy." The queen runs a hand across the globe of her belly. "But, please, you ladies go ahead. It will amuse me to watch you."

To oblige them, I take a turn or two, but I am not a dancer. I am never sure what step comes next, always afraid I will stumble and spoil it for everyone. With relief when my turn is done, I take my place close to the queen again. She leans toward me, waves a kerchief in the direction of the women.

"I am not familiar yet with the steps of this dance. I will have to learn it before Mistress Shore; I will not have her outshine me on the dance floor as well as in the king's bed."

I feel her fear. She is not so much jealous of the king as of her proper place being usurped.

"Your Grace, the king will never tire of you. Perhaps you should be glad of some respite from his attention, given your condition."

"I would be, were it with anyone but her. There is something about her I cannot like. I do not know how Edward can trust her for she is as free with her favours as a street harlot. I have even seen her smiling and winking her eyes at my son, Thomas, and he is not yet eighteen."

"I am surprised she dares risk the king's anger.

I am sure he will soon tire of her, and she will be gone from court, forgotten in a moment whereas nobody is ever likely to forget you, Your Grace."

"I am queen." She speaks the words as if to remind herself of it, her eyes flashing around the hall to ensure there are none to gainsay it.

"And a much beloved one, too."

We exchange smiles. I let my pity show and hope she mistakes it for love. In truth, I do not dislike her as I thought I would. I can sense her vulnerability, her lack of ease and her pretended arrogance, and I cannot help but offer what comfort I can. Elizabeth and me are akin, one to the other, and women in our position are never safe from a fall.

There are those who hate her. She may be queen, but no women, not even queens, are safe. She can never overlook the danger of her position – there are the rigours of childbirth, pestilence, and there is always the chance of a vindictive dagger concealed behind a smiling face.

I summon a boy to bring us refreshment, raise my cup to toast her health and continued happiness. I should drink to the health of her sons, but my Judas heart is too loyal to my own blood for that. Were it not for her boys, then Henry ...

I thrust the thought away, take her empty cup and place it on a tray. As I do so, a door opens and the king enters. He is alone, and I notice straight away that his usually laughing face is dark with worry. The queen struggles from her chair.

"Edward, where have you been? You've been gone all day!"

The women drift away, taking their places in the shadows at the periphery of the room. I make myself busy plumping the cushions on the window seat and arranging the queen's books on her favourite reading table, pausing to run my finger across the fine tooled covers. All the while, I keep one ear tuned to their conversation. I hear a word, a phrase here and there, and the name 'Oxford' crops up again and again. It is clear the earl must be up to his tricks again.

John de Vere is the only Lancastrian leader to persist in actively tormenting the Yorkist king. Early in Edward's reign, he was pardoned but he defected with Warwick in '71, finally fleeing the country after the battle at Barnet. Now, despite his actions having exposed his impoverished wife to the displeasure of the king, Oxford is not content to live in exile. He continues harassing the western coast, even when the king accuses him of piracy and puts a price on his head. I wonder what new mischief John de Vere is brewing now.

The king takes Elizabeth's arm and guides her into her chamber, their voices rising and falling, their words indistinguishable. I hurry after them, my petticoats rustling, and reach out to draw the heavy doors closed. As I do so, I hear the king cry, "If he sets one foot in my kingdom, I will have his head!"

It is much later when the queen calls for my company. I slip into a loose gown and hurry to her chamber. She is seated on the edge of her bed, her hair flowing, her face pale.

"I feel queasy," she says.

A glance around the room informs me that the king is absent. I procure her a cup of ginger and lemon to settle her stomach. She lies back on the pillows.

"The king and his men will ride away in an hour or so."

"Why? Where are they going?"

"John de Vere launched an attack on St Osyth; he was driven off by the locals but the king is riding to defending the shore."

She winces and rubs her hand over her belly, kicks off the blanket and shows me her swollen ankles.

"Let me rub them, Your Grace." I take her hot feet in my cool hands and begin to gently rub as if I can dispel the poisons that have gathered there.

"Ahh, that is nice." She lays her head down again.

"The capital is on high alert. All night, preparations have been taking place, and men are in position upon the city walls. Edward assures me we are safe."

"Of course, we are, Your Grace."

My soothing words are at odds with the pictures in my head. I imagine soldiers watching long into the night, or marching with their king, ready to protect the capital should they be required. Across the country, veterans are cleaning their old weapons, ready to defend us with their lives. De Vere's insurrection will be short-lived for the king, and his most trusted lords, including my own husband, are riding to defend the shores.

Shrewsbury - June 1473

For a while, it seems as if the old uncertain days might return, but as the weeks pass without Oxford being apprehended, the king orders a siege to be laid upon St Micheal's Mount where de Vere has taken hold. He returns to London, and with his presence and a return to normality, the sense of immediate threat lessens. Although the situation is unresolved, life goes on as before. Soon, the additional guards, and the watchers at the castle gate become commonplace, and we forget it has ever been any different. It is strange how one becomes accustomed even to uncertainty.

We visit the young prince at Ludlow, and once the king and queen are satisfied that he is comfortable and well looked after, with several physicians in case of illness, the king sets off on a progress of Coventry, Kenilworth and Leicester. The queen remains behind, reluctant to leave little Edward alone in the draughty castle.

"He is too small," she weeps, "too vulnerable," and her tears bring memories of my own parting with Henry. My throat closes in empathy.

To appease her fears, she prevaricates; deferring her departure from the area and announcing that her household will lodge with the Dominican friars at the abbey in Shrewsbury, some thirty miles north of Ludlow. She looks around at the pretty spot, overlooking the River Severn.

"Here, I am far enough away to appease the king yet close enough should Edward need me. It is only for a little while. If I leave him by small degrees, it will not be such a wrench."

Yet, despite her proximity, the queen continues to mourn the separation from her son. We ladies do all we can for her comfort, but it is as if she relishes the pain. Even I, who can understand her suffering better than anyone, grow impatient with her. I cannot show it. I have to hide all sign of my disdain at her behaviour. Never once in the years I have been separated from Henry have I allowed myself to wallow in grief.

With the men away, the younger ladies no longer compete for the attention of the eligible bachelors and our days pass more peaceably than before. The pile of baby linen on the table grows as we pass our time stitching earnestly for the forthcoming addition to the royal nursery.

But pregnancy is hard, even on queens, and she grows tetchy when I make myself absent, even if it is only to pray.

"Why are you always in the chapel, Margaret? Are you a great sinner that you must constantly ask for absolution? I sent a girl in search of you ages ago."

"I pray for peace in England, Your Grace, and for an easy birthing when your time comes ... and I pray for my son."

She stares at me for a long moment before turning her head away.

"You must miss him."

"Yes." I bite my lip. "My son and I were forced to part far too soon. He was just a babe in arms; not even properly weaned. One does not grow accustomed to that, Your Grace. It is as if his walking-strings are stretched tight – so tight that it pains me still, even though he is almost a man now."

"He writes to you, though? I have often seen you with a message clasped to your heart. I assumed they were from him."

"The letters cannot come often enough, not for me."

"Perhaps he could come home ... were he to make certain promises, it might be possible. I shall speak to the king."

I will never trust Edward of York. Since the day my son landed in Brittany, he has tried to lure him to England with false promises, offering bribes for the return of Henry's person. I have little doubt that while Edward is in power, should Henry ever set foot on England's shore he would not remain free for long. Exile in Brittany is preferable to the inside of an English gaol, but I cannot voice that opinion here.

"Oh, Your Grace, that is my dearest wish. I long to have him in my home, help him find a good woman to take to wife, see his children, share his happiness."

I turn away. I have revealed too much, even surprising myself as to how deeply I desire those simple things. I wipe a tear from my eye and smile sheepishly. How easily I am cheated into honesty.

The queen sighs and turns the conversation back to herself.

"I will be glad when this child is born. He kicks relentlessly, and I have another six weeks to bear it."

"Perhaps a walk in the garden will quieten him. You should take the opportunity before your confinement begins. I always found Henry seemed more peaceful when I was active. At – at Lamphey I walked quite far and even attended to the garden for the first six months ... until I was forced to leave."

"Leave?"

She falls silent while I try to formulate the story in my head.

"Edmund was injured during a skirmish. I rode out to tend him ..."

She is quiet for a long moment, her thoughts far away.

"What was he like, your first husband, Edmund Tudor? One hears such tales of him."

I curl my fingers into a fist.

"A good man, despite the gossip. He was loyal to his king, strong principled, kind to me, and eager for the birth of his child. Fate was cruel to take him from us."

I realise I have spoken too sharply, but she lets it pass.

"Yet ... he got you with child when you were but half grown. That must have been hard ..."

Heat rushes to my head, my cheeks begin to burn. Her sympathy comes too late. Edmund was slain by the henchmen of her husband. I can only be honest.

"I did not find it so, Your Grace. Not after the first few times ... as I said, he was a good man, a good husband. I was content to do my duty."

"We must all do that." She stares pensively into the fire.

"Yes, we must, no matter how discomforting it may be."

She stretches, places both hands on her belly. I can see the movement of the child through the thin stuff of her gown.

"If only it wasn't so damnably hot."

"The weeks will pass quickly. Once the child is here, your confinement will be as nothing."

In a few days, the queen will take to her apartments. The rooms will be sealed, no male visitors admitted, not even the king. For the sake of the child, she will be allowed no stimulation – all will be tranquil, all will be calm. She will not be permitted to lay her eye on anything violent, anything cruel, even the tapestries in her chamber will show floral scenes of peace. It was very different for me.

I wonder how the turmoil I suffered prior to Henry's birth affected him. The wild ride to Carmarthen, my overriding grief at Edmund's death, the wilder journey to Pembroke, the discomforts of the cramped quarters provided for us. It should never have been so. He should have been brought forth with honour in a palace, not torn from my body in a frigid, damp fortress. There was no velvet-draped crib awaiting Henry – he made do with a rough wooden cot hammered together by the castle carpenters. He is my only child, the culmination of all my passion ... he deserved more, so much more.

By August, the wet summer gives way to extreme temperatures, and the queen's apartments become stifling. Even though sleep is impossible, I am relieved I do not have to attend her at night.

The room I have been allocated is small. I do not share the old belief that night air is harmful – if that were the case, we would all have perished long ago. I throw open the windows and sleep beneath just one thin sheet. It is pleasant to wake in the morning to the scents of summer, and hear birdsong float in through the open casement.

In the morning, after I have seen to my toilette and visited the chapel, I report to the queen. She is tetchy today, and before noon has reduced her sister to tears and threatened to send half her ladies back to London.

To distract her, I show her the tiny cap I have fashioned for the new prince; an elaborate embroidered scrap of silk dressed with swansdown. She takes it, runs a long fingertip over the feathery surface and holds it to her cheek, testing the softness and inhaling the scent of lavender.

"How lovely, Lady Margaret. I pray even more earnestly for a son now, so that he shall wear it."

Her mother turns from the window to cast her critical eye over it.

"Very fine," she says. "I never realised you were so skilled. You always seem to have your nose in a book."

I smile my bland smile.

"Books are invaluable for learning, but I have other pleasures too. I like to garden, and as you know, have some proficiency in herb lore – embroidery is not my first love but my mother was keen to ensure I was endowed with all the skills necessary for a woman of my station. She was keen to secure me a good husband."

"How is your mother? I heard she was ailing."

"Her letters speak of some improvement. I think she will be up and about again by now."

Jacquetta bows her head stiffly.

"You must send her my regards."

"I will indeed ..."

A sound from the queen cuts my words short. Jacquetta and me both turn toward her. She is bent forward, a hand to her side, her lips parted, a sheen of sweat on her high clear forehead.

"Your Grace ..." I hurry to her side, supporting her elbow, helping her to sit again.

"I am all right. I got up too quickly, that is all, I think."

"I will fetch something to ease you ..." I am about to the leave the room when she clutches my arm.

"No, please, Margaret, you stay. Send someone else, the pain is beginning again. I think it is the child ..."

After three hours of watching her struggle, I begin to think it is easier to labour oneself than to witness suffering in another. The royal physician has been sent for, but the labour appears to be swift and sharp. There is nothing more I can do to ease her, but she seems to think I have some magic, some supernatural skill to erase the pain. She clings to my arm, begging me to help her, swearing her child will die if I refuse.

My belly dips; I am in a cleft stick. Should I administer pain relief or not? If she loses this child, blame may be laid upon me, and if I refuse to dose her, she will berate me for insolence when she recovers. Desperately, I face her mother.

"Did she suffer like this in her previous confinements? Is there something wrong?"

I have overseen few pregnancies, and have never claimed expertise. Her mother snorts, flicks her eyes heavenward. She takes my arm, leads me away, out of earshot of the queen.

"My daughter is not as stout of heart as she would have you believe. She makes a song and dance of every birthing – in a day, she will have forgotten it. Let us just bring this child forth safely. Leave her to the midwives, I say."

But the queen will not hear of my leaving. She refuses to release my hand. I sit beside her while she all but breaks my fingers. While the midwife presses her knees apart, I keep my eyes upon her face, from which all beauty has fled.

She is pale, a sheen of sweat covering her body, her hair darkened and damp, and there is blood on her lip where she has bitten it in her travail. With my free hand, I take a sponge and try to cool her brow, murmuring comfort.

"The head is crowning," the midwife announces. "You can push now, Your Grace. When the next pain comes, push with all your strength."

Elizabeth raises her knees to her chest, grits her teeth and bears down with a great scream of determination. I watch in wonder at the animalistic nature of birth as our usually serene queen grimaces like a monkey, baring her teeth in her effort to rid herself of her burden.

A minute of straining, yet still it is not over. When the pain lessens, she flops back on the pillows. I dribble water between her lips, stroke her hair from her face.

"You are doing well, Your Grace, your son will soon be here."

It has been hours now and her strength is failing. She pushes the cup away, spilling liquid on the bed, grabs her knees and begins to push again.

"It's now or never, my lady..." The midwife, with a look of helplessness, reaches forward, places her fingers about the child's head. The queen screams again, bares her teeth, strains with all her might and, with a gush of water, the head is born.

"Don't push for a minute, just pant, if you can, Your Grace, while I deal with this cord."

The queen glares at me with wild eyes as she puffs and pants. Later, when she recalls it, she will resent me for witnessing her indignity.

The midwife straightens up with a groan, a hand to her back.

"Very well, Madam, you can go again."

The queen raises her knees, blows out her cheeks and strains; I cannot help but look toward her nethers to see the bulging, bloodied head of the infant as it thrusts into the world. The child falls onto the sheet, floppy and wet, like something washed in from the ocean. While the queen falls backwards onto the bed, everyone fusses around the infant. The midwife rubs it vigorously with a towel. Then I hear the sound of flesh on flesh, a hiccup and a lusty cry.

I grab the queen's hand, excited beyond measure, despite myself.

"The child lives, Your Grace, and oh ... oh, it is a boy, just as you said it would be!"

Laughing and crying, I take the child from the midwife, place my lips upon his damp hair, and pass the prince into his mother's arms. As I relinquish him into her care, pain stirs deep in my heart.

Windsor - Autumn 1475

The letter I hold in my hand fills me with terror. While I have been here, ingratiating myself with the king and queen, my son has been in peril. How could I not have sensed it? With shaking hands, I cast my eyes over Henry's quickly scrawled message.

Do not worry, mother, should a rumour reach you of my capture by the emissaries sent by Edward. When Duke Francis assured me that it was safe for me to leave exile and be joined in matrimony with the Princess Elizabeth, some strange precognition warned me against it. Although I had little option but to go with them, I could hear your words of warning, and those of Jasper too. I sensed it was a trap, and knew that if I set foot on the ship I would be in Edward's hands, and that he would show me no mercy.

As we neared St Malo, I feigned sickness, obliging my escort to allow me some respite. Fortunately, in the meantime, Duke Francis remembered his oath to keep me safe and reconsidered his dubious dealings with England. He sent M. Pierre Landais to intercept us and stop the ship from embarking. He escorted me to the sanctuary of a nearby church where I was 'nursed back to health.' The ambassadors, irate that we proved so elusive, tried to lure me from sanctuary but Landais refused, and the people of the town came out in force, protecting me from English ire. I am in their debt. I have no doubt King Edward's fury will be great, and I hope it does not reflect on you. I am watched now, every waking hour, and I cannot allow myself to trust anyone. But the main thing is, I am safe, Mother, and you need not fear ...

I need have no fear? Henry and Jasper are now at the chateau l'Hermine, virtual prisoners, valuable pawns in the politics of kings. They are hounded by Edward's thugs, at the mercy of spies and scoundrels. Yet he tells me to have no fear. Oh Henry, you have no idea what it means to be a mother, when every moment is an anxious one.

I haunt the palace chapel, beseeching God and all his saints to keep them both safe; to calm the rocky ocean that is Edward's reign and bring us all safely to shore.

Windsor - October 1476

The royal children are practising a song to amuse the king. Their voices are strident rather than melodic, but the queen seems satisfied. To her, as with any mother, each one is an angel and they are certainly angelic in appearance.

Little Richard, whose birth I oversaw three years ago, is as plump and pink as the cherubs in the cathedral, but when it comes to behaviour, the likeness is less apparent. He is naughty, spending every waking moment in search of mischief, and if he does not go looking for it, then it seems to come to him. And, of course, being the only boy in the company of girls, he can do no wrong. He is pampered, spoiled and made over-much of, and I am as guilty of this as any one.

After his birth, the queen returned straight to the king's bed and as a result, there is a new baby already in the royal cradle. The latest child is a girl they named Anne. She is pink and perfect, and very content, but since those days at Shrewsbury, when I helped Elizabeth latch him to her breast, Richard has held a special place in my heart.

Of course, he comes nowhere close to the love I have for Henry, but although I grumble when he misbehaves, I am never really too busy to tell him a story or play 'peepo' from behind my psalter. Sometimes, I forget that my friendship with the king's family is supposed to be feigned, and have to remind myself that these people stand between me and my heart's desire.

The song dwindles to a tuneless end and the queen sits up and claps delightedly.

"Oh, Lady Margaret, wasn't that fine? The king will be delighted."

Young Elizabeth detaches herself from the children and comes to her mother.

"I would like to sing on my own, I am too old to sing with the children."

The queen's laughter tinkles.

"You are seven years old, Bess. There will be time for you to grow up, but it is not yet."

Bess proves her mother's words by lowering her chin to her chest and pouting. The queen and I exchange glances, trying not to laugh.

"Our prince is lucky to have a big sister to look up to," I say, trying to lift her spirits. "Such bonds are never broken. I myself came from a big family; my little brother John and ..." My words trail off as I remember my brother can never enjoy his barony because his father was attainted for fighting against the king. The damned struggle for the crown continues to stain everything, even now we are all at peace.

"Bess, go ask the nurse to fetch the children's wraps, you should all take some air before it grows dark." She rises from her seat. "There is nothing like a little fresh air to help a child sleep, Lady Margaret."

I collect a shawl and hurry downstairs ahead of the children. As I turn the corner at the bottom, I run headlong into a tall figure. Drawing hastily away, I stammer an apology and look up into the face of the king's brother.

"A thousand pardons, Lady Margaret." He bows mockingly, a smile on his face that speaks of false admiration, intrigue. He takes my hand and draws me closer, laying his lips upon it. "A happy meeting," he slurs, swamping me with the aroma of stale wine.

"My Lord of Clarence. Please forgive me, I am on an errand for the queen."

He steps aside, sweeps another bow.

"Then I shall not keep you, but I live in the hope that our next meeting will not be long away."

I do not trust George of Clarence. He smiles when there is nothing to smile about, laughs when nothing is funny. I know instinctively that his bonhomie is false, and each word he speaks is perjury.

Since he betrayed the king by siding with Warwick and fell out with Gloucester over Warwick's daughters, there are few who trust him. He is a dangerous friend. There are whispers that even now he plots against the king. The old rumour that the king is the result of Cecily Neville's illicit affair with a French archer will not die down, and we all know it is Clarence who keeps it alive.

We at court see little of his wife, Isabel, who, after giving George a daughter in '73 and a son in February last, is now soon to bring forth another child. Without her steadying influence, George grows ever more ungovernable. We all watch, and wonder at the king's patience.

The king's younger brother, Richard of Gloucester, is seldom at court. His duties keep him in the north of England, where he and Anne Neville rule in Edward's stead. The king, who sees nothing worth having north of the Humber, is happy for them to do so. The trust he places in his youngest brother, and the responsibilities entrusted to him, damage his relations with Clarence even further.

I wrap my shawl tighter about my chest, watching as George saunters away. Then I open the doors into the queen's private garden. A boy is at work, clipping the grass around the foot of the fountain. At my nod, he abandons his task and makes himself scarce. Five minutes later, when the queen and the children tumble into the open air, the garden is deserted.

The girls fan out like brightly-coloured ribbons tossed into the air. As is his habit, Richard heads straight to the fountain, climbs up to splash his fingers in the water, wetting his velvet sleeve.

"Oh, Richard, look, now you are wet. You will get cold."

As I wag his hands in the air to dry them, his fat baby laugh tugs at my heart. I haul him onto my knee and attempt to dry his fingers with my kerchief. Of all the York children, I love Richard the best. Before I let him go, I place a surreptitious kiss on the side of his head, and watch as he runs from me, his blond head nodding among the last of the marguerites.

The queen and I, with her ladies just behind, stroll amid the flowers until a messenger arrives. He catches up with us, makes his bow and offers me a package. Quickly, I scan the salutation and my heart leaps; it is from Henry. I glance at the queen, who smiles her permission for me to retire.

I do not return to my chamber but find a quiet spot in an arbour before I tear open the seal. Henry's handwriting is small and full of loops, the words close together as if he is afraid they may run away with him should he give them full rein. I bring the page close to my face as I drink in every word. He is well, he seems happy, and he sends me his love and respect.

A second letter from Jasper informs me that Henry's health is good. He is excelling in his martial training, and has recently become friends with a young woman. That news halts me in my tracks with a twinge of jealousy.

Henry is nineteen; of course, there will be women. I close my eyes, try to imagine his face, superimposing a beard on the well-remembered silken cheeks of the child I knew. I fail dreadfully, summoning a mask more suitable for the visage of a mummer. I must ask that a likeness be made of him, so that I can carry it with me always.

The letter leaves me sad. Henry's childhood has passed, I shared so little of it, and now I must remain here while his adulthood passes too. Since we were parted, my life and my happiness have been on hold, but I have always been certain of our eventual reunion.

But, as I sit here with his letter in my hand, my faith in that reunion dwindles with the dying of the day.

A footstep sounds on the path before me. I look up, leap to my feet, dabbing my eye with the corner of my glove.

"Your Grace. I am finished now."

I thrust the letters into my pocket and join her for the remainder of her walk. With every step, I can feel the edge of the parchment against my leg, the crackle of Henry's absence reminding me of who it is that keeps us apart.

That evening, word comes that Isabel Neville, lying at Tewkesbury, has borne a son whom they have named Richard. I wonder at the irony of this. Perhaps it is some joke, George and Isabel's eldest son is named Edward for the king, but everyone knows there is no love lost between George and his brother, Richard of Gloucester.

December 1476

As Christmas approaches, I prepare for another season without my son. I am to spend the holy day at court but, with the help of Reginald Bray, I ensure that my affairs at Woking and my other holdings are in order. I make provision so that they celebrate the Yule as fully as if I were present, but they have no real need of me. My husband will be, as always, at court, on hand for the king, and the queen has specifically requested that I attend her.

I have not yet decided if she shows me such favour because she values me as a person, or if she prefers to keep those she mistrusts within arm's length. I suspect the latter for, were I in her position, I would keep my enemies close, and confuse them with my kindness.

Five days before Christmas and the day is cold, a hard frost solidifying the winter mire and making the roads treacherous. I have just returned from a walk and am about to climb the hall stairs when I hear someone call my name. I turn, my face breaking into a smile when I recognise the figure dismounting from a tired horse.

Ned stands tall before me and, for the first time, I realise he is a man now. Although I should treat him as such, I am so pleased to see his familiar face that, breaking convention, I grasp both his hands and invite him straight to the apartments I share with Thomas.

He reaches out to the blazing fire before gratefully accepting the mulled wine I offer. He cups it as if it is a handful of gold. While he sips, his usual colour returns to his face, and I begin to plague him with questions. The letter he bears is from Myfanwy who, never sure where she may find me, directs all her messages to Woking.

She sends seasonal greetings and thanks for the package I sent a month or so ago. She tells me of her daughters' delight at their gifts, and thanks me for my generosity. Well aware that I could be far more generous, I frown a little.

It is my greatest regret that I cannot invite her into my household, but I know, without asking, that Thomas would never countenance it. I may be as independent as it is possible for a wife to be, but there are limits.

One day, I tell myself, I will visit her in person and we will spend a whole summer reliving the past, pretending the present has never come. But for now, I must be content with a misspelled letter, and the provincial-style kerchief she has sewn for my New Year's gift.

Her daughters must be well-grown by now, and she will soon be casting about for likely husbands for them. Under usual circumstances, it is easy to secure a decent marriage for the bastard child of an earl, but when that earl is wanted for treason and living in exile, that task becomes more difficult. I make up my mind to do what I can to help. Myfanwy was there for me when I needed her most, it is the least I can do to return the favour.

Ned sits forward in his seat, waiting for me to break from my reverie, his face earnest for news.

"Have you news from my Lord Pembroke, and Henry?"

Grateful for the chance to give full rein to the pride I have for my son, I reach for Jasper's latest letter and read it aloud. The firelight dances on Ned's face, once or twice he laughs, the sound reminding me of harsher days; days that, with the passage of time, somehow now seem rosy.

In hindsight, it is clear to see that for all the suffering and hardship of my early years, my friends made up for it. They kept me safe, kept me warm. Now, in these uncertain days, in this lonely place, unsure of whom to trust, although materially richer, I am somehow colder and almost entirely bereft of love.

The hall is set for Christmas Eve and the royal children are overflowing with excitement. Even the little ones will be allowed to attend the feast. A great Yule log burns in the hearth, the tables are laid, the gleaming plates interlaced with ropes of greenery, berries of holly and mistletoe glistening in the light of a thousand candles.

We enter the hall where I look down upon the lower tables. They are already full, a host of glowing faces cheering as we take our places on the dais. The children exclaim with delight at the festive array, even the castle dogs are wagging their tails, tongues lolling benignly.

The hall is so warm, so inviting, it reminds me of the Christmastides of my youth; those happy days at Bletsoe before I was parted from my siblings. I remember my mother smiling at the head of the table, our stepfather paying too much attention to his wine cup. We were so secure, so smug in our safe little world. None of us could ever have guessed that our king would one day be murdered, his throne passed so completely into the hands of York. Suddenly, I feel alien, an interloper at an enemy feast.

My stepfather's ghost seems to rise before me now, accusing me of dining with his foe. How can I have forsaken the cause of Lancaster when my own son is the head of that fallen house? I have forsaken his future, and taken the easy route by seeking service to the wife of a usurping king.

"Lady Margaret, are you quite well?"

I shake my head, dispelling the dismal thoughts, and find Princess Elizabeth waiting for me to move so she may take her seat beside her father.

I step back at once. "Forgive me, Your Grace. I was day dreaming."

"I know. Were you seeing demons? Our nurse says you can always tell by a person's face if they are, and you looked quite horror struck."

"No, no. I was just hoping my son is having such a good time."

"Your son; Henry, isn't it? I hope he is. Everyone should be happy at Christmas, don't you think?"

With Mary and Cecily close behind, Elizabeth takes her place beside the king, tugging at her father's sleeve for his attention.

The royal children are given too much licence. At least in public they should show deference to their parents, but King Edward openly encourages them, roaring with laughter at their misdemeanours instead of offering a reprimand.

Halfway through the first course, the king stands suddenly and demands we all drink to the health of his brother, Gloucester, whose wife has this year been brought to bed of a son, named in the king's honour.

We all raise our glasses and drink obediently, waiting for the king to raise the next toast, which we know without being told will be for the health of his other nephew, the newly-born son of George of Clarence.

As he orders his glass be refilled, the babble of voices resumes, masking the opening of the door. When a messenger stumbles forward and kneels before the high table, we are all taken by surprise.

The king's empty cup is still raised when all heads turn toward the travel-stained boy. He does not smile as he holds out the rolled parchment. Slowly, the king moistens his lips and reaches out to take it.

The king puts down his cup, breaks the seal. The court watches as Edward turns pale, an effigy of himself, the parchment in his hand trembling slightly.

He runs a hand across his face before he looks up, his eyes searching out and finding those of his mother, Cecily. When he speaks, his quiet words reach every corner of the hall.

"It is from George. His wife ... Isabel, has died ...God rest her soul."

As if in sympathy, the candles flicker at the in drawn breath of the courtiers. Isabel gave birth to her child in October last. We had all assumed she was churched, and had resumed her place in the household by now.

My thoughts turn straightway to her children, Margaret and Edward, who will now grow up without a mother; and little Richard, who will now be forced to suckle more than just nourishment from the teat of a stranger.

Isabel's mother who, since Warwick's defection, has been stripped of her vast inheritance, lands and possessions, and who has taken refuge at Beaulieu Abbey, will be further bereft, her future starker now with the loss of her daughter.

The news dampens our celebration. We continue with the meal but few of us have the appetite, and the musicians tune their instruments to a more sombre melody. There can be no more gaiety, for everyone knows full well that any sign of levity will be taken by George as disrespect. George is like a serpent beneath a rock, nobody wants to poke sticks at him; least of all the king.

A few moments ago, the company was gay. The children addressed their trenchers with glee, and spoke excitedly of the mummery to follow. Now we eat in silence.

Little Cecily puts down her spoon.

"When will the pageant begin?" she asks, her voice intrusive in the quiet solemnity of the hall.

The king does not seem to hear, his thoughts are far away, and he chews his food as if it tastes of ashes. Princess Cecily pulls impatiently at his sleeve.

"Father, Father; when are the tumblers to begin?"

Edward thumps his fist on the board and leaps to his feet, turning on his beloved child as if she has a dagger to his back.

"There will be no fucking tumblers! Not now ..."

A short shocked silence and then Cecily's face crumples, and she falls backwards into her chair. The king storms from the hall, leaving us strangled into silence.

*

"Why was Father so angry?" Cecily asks, as her nurse leads her to bed.

"Bless me, child, I don't know. I wasn't even there."

I watch them go, absentmindedly folding the strewn clothing, although it is not my place to do so. I find my hands will not be still but search for a task to distract me. Realising I should be with the queen, I turn on my heel and hurry to her apartment with Cecily's question still burning my ears.

Why was he so angry? Women die in childbed every day; there is nothing strange about it. Nothing to be so furious about.

The look on his face when he stormed from the hall made it quite clear that something about this death has unsettled him. As if he is in possession of some secret knowledge we do not share.

The queen is not in her chamber, where a few women loiter in case they should be summoned.

"Where is the queen?"

"She is with the king, Lady Margaret. They are ... having a discussion ..."

She nods pointedly toward the door. I cock my ear and, although I cannot hear their words, the tone of their voices is sharp and edged with fear. It is none of my business so I quietly withdraw.

"I will retire. Should the queen request my presence, come and inform me at once."

"I will do, Lady Margaret. I wish you good night."

Gratefully, I hurry to my chamber, the thought of my high warm bed welcome after the travails of the day. I embrace the idea of solitude and before I even reach the door have made up my mind to dismiss my women as soon as I am disrobed.

A peaceful evening with my books, some quiet prayer and contemplation is all I desire. When I enter my chamber and find my husband sprawled in my favourite chair, a cup of my best Madeira in his fist, it is no welcome surprise.

"Ah, there you are," he says, as if his presence in my private quarters is an everyday occurrence. "Bit of a shock, the king turning on little Cecily like that."

"Yes, she was quite distraught. It took a long time to get her settled."

I draw off my gloves, throw them on the table.

"Lord knows what will happen now." Thomas yawns, revealing a yellow tongue. He never does take enough rhubarb. "But you can expect Clarence to see his wife's death as a personal affront."

"There is something ... different about Clarence. As if he isn't of the same mould as his brothers ..."

"A bastard, you mean? That label is usually applied to his brother, but you would be wiser not to speak of it."

"I wasn't suggesting that. I was merely observing that he seems to feel himself to be ... lacking somehow. His behaviour is that of a man who has something to prove. The king, and even Gloucester, have no such insecurity. Clarence reminds me of a child in the nursery, jealous of his other siblings – always trying to prove he can jump higher, run faster, shoot straighter ... you know what I mean."

Thomas frowns, looks at me through his heavy eyebrows.

"You're an odd one, Margaret. I am never quite sure of your meaning."

"I speak plainly."

"Maybe, my dear, but not in any language I know."

How I long for the meaningful conversations I shared with Edmund, and Harry. Thomas is shallow, one dimensional, and sometimes I wonder how he has risen so high.

"What did you want, anyway, Thomas? I am tired and eager to retire."

"I want to know what the queen said about it. She must have spoken to the king. I will be better placed if I know his mood."

"They were still closeted when I left her apartments. She will call if she needs me."

"Hmm ..."

"What is it? What is so troubling?"

"You know Clarence is the hub of the rumours against the king? You know how he covets his power, thinks he should be on the throne in Edward's place?"

"Well, it is not something I have taken seriously ... nobody would fight for George."

Thomas leans forward, his face suddenly dark, and lowers his voice to a whisper, sending shivers through my body.

"George knows that, and so seeks other ways."

I lean closer.

"What ways? What do you mean?"

"Wait and see." Thomas places a finger alongside his nose. "Wait and see. I suspect things are about to happen, and I would advise you to watch and listen when you attend on the queen. See if she will confide in you, and then let me know."

"About what? Why are you being so mysterious?"

He stands up, tugs the bottom of his doublet.

"Because, Margaret, I value my neck, and you should value yours."

For once, Thomas is right. Things do indeed begin to happen. Within a few weeks of Isabel's death, her poor baby son, Richard, follows her to the grave.

George kicks out against it, setting up a hue and cry of conspiracy and poison. He does not stop to think what would be achieved by the murder of a sweet young woman and an innocent babe.

George has always been the thorn in Edward's flesh; the trouble maker. George is the one who whispers damaging slander against the king. If anyone should be dispensed with, it is George himself.

January – June 1477

A year has passed; a terrible year for the king, and one he clearly saw coming. Within a month of Isabel's death, George dispenses with mourning and pesters for a marriage with Mary of Burgundy. The king closes his ears to the plea, just as he pretends deafness to many other of George's requests.

Isabel's death seems to have destroyed the last vestige of reason George possessed. He speaks openly against the queen and her family, and the persistent rumour of the king's bastardy is easily traced back to him. I cannot help but admire the way proud Cecily keeps her head high as her favourite son drags her name through the mud. She quietly entreats the king to show his brother leniency, while the queen argues that a wise man would cut off the foot that plagues him.

"It is clear that Clarence was behind Oxford's rebellion; that alone is reason enough! And look at the things he accuses me of – hanging is too good for him! " The queen rages, careless of who should hear, and I think she is right. For the sake of their position, for the future security of her children, she is right to plea for the destruction of Clarence, who has always been her enemy.

The king resists. He is torn. With love in his heart for both his brother and his mother, he turns the other cheek, offers leniency in exchange for loyalty. But still, Clarence does not listen.

In May, the court is startled to learn that George, still convinced of Isabel's murder, has ordered the arrest, trial and execution of two people in his employ. Ankarette Twynyho, one of Isabel's women, is accused of having used poison against her mistress. George hangs her, and a man blamed of murdering his new born son hangs with her.

Clearly, Clarence is insane. He accuses the king of using witchcraft to rule England, of using magic against his enemies. And he declares Queen Elizabeth to be the foulest witch. Jacquetta, who well remembers the days when Warwick levelled such a crime against her, turns pale and wrings her hands but her daughter grows angry.

I am morbidly curious, and cannot help but watch the queen closely. She is shaken, consumed with hatred for her brother-in-law; and who can blame her? Filled with fear for the safety of her children, she renews her efforts to persuade the king to be rid of his brother. Yet the king bears with Clarence, patiently making excuses, assuring her that time will heal the breach. George will recover from his malady, and all will be well again.

Even her forthcoming child does not take the queen's mind from the threat posed by her brother-in-law.

"What will he accuse us of next?" she wails. I urge her to stop thinking of it for the sake of the child in her womb, but she is consumed by her hatred of George. She speaks of him day and night, constantly urging the king to act before it is too late.

On a snowy day in early spring, she gives birth to a boy, whom despite the current ill will, the king desires to name George. Elizabeth swears it is to honour our patron saint, St George, but we all suspect differently. It is the king's way of reminding the queen that George of Clarence is, despite his behaviour, the king's brother. Blood is blood, whether Clarence believes it or not.

In June, Clarence, made irate by what he sees as injustices against him, breaks into a council meeting, protesting against the king, and declaring him unfit to rule. At this outward breach of loyalty, Edward's patience wears too thin and he orders Clarence's arrest and committal to the Tower of London.

A charge is drawn up against him, accusing him of plotting to usurp the throne and do damage to the king and his family. Everyone holds their breath and waits. The sentence of death is inevitable.

January -1478

The only relief from the darkness surrounding the king and his brothers is the preparations that are under way for the wedding of my favourite royal child. At just four years old, Richard of Shrewsbury is to be joined in matrimony with the five-year-old heiress of the Norfolk estates, Anne Mowbray.

The royal tailors are summoned to measure the fast-growing boy for new clothes, and of course, his sisters must be suitably attired too.

"Will I like having a wife?" Richard asks, and everyone laughs; everyone but me, who remembers too well what it is to be a child about to be joined in marriage. Ignoring the laughter, I stroke his silken hair.

"Do not worry, Richard. Your marriage will make no difference to you just yet. You will remain here with your sisters. You will not live together until you are a man grown."

He turns his solemn eyes upon me, a tremulous smile on his lips.

"And just think," I add, with a burst of inspiration, "you will have a lovely set of new clothes, a banquet in your honour, and next week there will be a joust."

"A joust," he cries, leaping up and grabbing his wooden sword. "I wish I could fight in a joust. I will one day, won't I, Mother?"

"You will indeed, my little one," she answers, without looking up from the letter she is writing.

He accompanies his sisters back to the nursery in a happier frame of mind, and I turn my thoughts back to my needle. The last row of stitches is not as neat as those that precede it and I wonder if I should unpick them or leave it as it is. Imperfection in a piece of art is a virtue, for only God is without flaws.

Against the glorious backdrop of the royal wedding, the shadow of Clarence lingers. The hour of his death cannot be far away but the king delays, postponing the evil moment, denying all argument, even when his brother, Gloucester, travels from Yorkshire to dissuade him.

It is a long while since I have seen Anne Neville. She rides through the palace gate at her husband's side, looking about her with wide eyes. She is slight of frame, mousy in colouring, and it is easy to see she is also gentle natured, a curious partner for the battle hardened duke.

Their dress is sumptuous, their manners impeccable yet something sets them apart from us. Perhaps it is their seclusion in Yorkshire that makes them mawkish, out of step with the rest of the royal court; yet it is not that, it is more a sense of disapproval, a sense of disdain, as if they are somehow superior.

At the evening revel, Gloucester's displeasure with the queen and her family is plain to see, and the antics of the tumblers seem not to please him at all.

The duke takes no part when the men grow riotous. Both he and his wife drink sparingly, choose little from the extravagant dishes set before them. Anne eats like a little bird, tasting this, tasting that, rinsing her fingers in the bowl before partaking of her wine.

When she catches me watching, her face floods with colour, but she smiles a greeting and I decide she may not be as arrogant as she seems. No doubt she is merely missing her home and her infant son. I can understand that.

Her husband, on the other hand, offers a curt greeting and turns rudely away as if I am of no account. When I complain of it to the queen, she laughs derisively.

"Why would he show you favour when he is openly hostile to me, his queen, and all my family? I cannot bear Gloucester. He is little better than his felon of a brother."

"I wonder what he has said to the king ... about Clarence's incarceration, I mean. I can sense his anger, and there seems to be no pleasure for him at court."

The queen leans toward me, speaks into my ear.

"Everyone knows he has come here only to beg leniency for Clarence. He has no care for weddings, royal or not; but he is a fool to argue against Clarence's sentence. Has he not realised that with Clarence's demise and attainder, the entire Warwick estates will become his? Once I thought he only craved power – it is a family failing, after all; each one of them hungry for wealth and position. But perhaps I was wrong and family loyalty does have a place in his heart ..."

I raise my eyebrows. The queen could be speaking of her own family, who fight tooth and nail for the slightest preferment. Can she be so blind to their failings?

While Gloucester broods about the palace and the queen prepares for her son's wedding, I think often of Clarence who has languished so long in the Tower. How dismal his days must be; how long, tiresome and dark the nights. Pray God I am never imprisoned. If the king would treat his own blood so, how heavily his displeasure would fall upon an enemy.

Since Jasper and Henry landed in Brittany all those years ago, King Edward has done all he can to lure them into a trap. He craves the added security of having my son in his possession. He has offered rewards, tried to bribe the king of France, but each time, so far, we have evaded his attempts.

The incarceration of Clarence illustrates quite plainly that I must put aside my dreams of ever welcoming my son home while Edward of York is on the throne. Despite my longing to see him, I know it is not safe, and hope the queen has forgotten her promise to speak to the king on our behalf.

Westminster Abbey – 15th January 1478

No attempt has been made to disguise the king's greed. Such a fuss seems wasted on two children, yet for all their youth, Richard of Shrewsbury and Anne Mowbray become significant figures on their wedding day.

The sudden death of the Duke of Norfolk two years ago left Anne heiress to an immense fortune. Unable, as a female, to inherit the title of duke, Anne instead became 'Countess of Norfolk' and the ward of the king himself.

Usually, her hand would be given to the highest bidder, but King Edward desires the spoils for himself, or for his son, Richard.

A mere betrothal was not good enough. Eager to secure her monies and titles once and for all, the king insisted on a full-blown marriage ceremony, and by the look on his face, he does not seem at all perturbed by the transparency of his motives.

Everyone gathers for the royal wedding. Earls, dukes, foreign dignitaries ... all of us crammed into Westminster Abbey to celebrate the political union of two small children. Outside, the people of London line the streets, and inside, the crush is such that the people at the back surely cannot see.

I stand between Jacquetta Woodville and Cecily Neville; all three of us surreptitiously from time to time take our kerchiefs to dab our damp faces, for the heat in the crush is unbearable.

The queen looks on proudly, a slight smile on her lips, her eyes every so often filling with tears that do not fall. For hours we stand. A few places down from the queen, Princess Mary shifts restlessly from foot to foot, but Elizabeth is as straight and motionless as her mother.

For the first time, I have the leisure to observe them side by side. They are not at all alike. The queen is slim and golden haired; her daughter Elizabeth, still with the plumpness of youth, is rosier of complexion, more like her father, the king, than her mother. Yet I detect a shared determination and resilience, and a disregard for public opinion.

Little Anne Mowbray has been reminded time and time again not on any account to put her thumb in her mouth during the ceremony, but several times during the interminable marriage rite I notice it creep back. Every so often she remembers and whips it out, looking around, fearful that somebody has noticed. As time drags on, her eyes grow heavy; she shifts from foot to foot, rubs her nose and sighs heavily.

Beside her, Richard stands with one hand resting proudly on the hilt of the ceremonial sword at his hip. His eyes travel around the nave, hesitate when they meet mine. I see them crinkle into a smile, and feel as proud as if he were my own. Later, I shall delight him and his little bride with made-up tales about the triumph of their wedding day.

At long last, the ceremony draws to a close. Richard and Anne are man and wife – a union assailable only by death. All of us, even the heartiest, are weary, yet many more hours of feasting still lie ahead.

As we take our places in the hall, the chatter rises to a babble of noise. The musicians, in an attempt to be heard, play louder. I have no stomach for the rich fare but I enjoy the pageants; or at least, I enjoy the pleasure the diminutive bride and groom take in the proceedings. They lean forward, clap their hands, their faces alive with joy in the ridiculousness of the juggling tumblers.

When the dancing begins, the king and queen outshine us all, and I have to confess they are perfect in the role. Old King Henry and Margaret, as much as I loved them, never held the court in such thrall as Edward and Elizabeth do. While I admire the daintiness of their steps, I almost forget that there is more to a monarch than bonhomie and elegance. There are rules that even kings must follow; political decisions and foreign diplomacy should be first and foremost. But, as always with this king, pleasure is paramount and the banquet lasts long into the night.

Gifts are laid at the newlyweds' feet and their health is drunk, the cheers shivering the rafters of the roof. The infant bride and groom grow weary, spilling wine down their costly velvet and knuckling their eyes, made tearful by the need for sleep.

When the queen finally signals to their nurse and they are ushered to the nursery, Richard pauses at the door. He has done well today. Tentatively, I raise my hand, and flutter my fingers. Noticing my salute, he sends me a goodnight smile.

With the children out of the way, the festivities become more disorderly. The king is quite obviously in his cups, his voice rising loudly above the hubbub, his laughter shared by many, but not by all.

Gloucester, seated opposite me, watches the proceedings darkly, his wife hiding a yawn behind her hand. Everyone is tiring, our finery wilting, our carefully applied grace sagging, yet our king does not tire. He calls for more wine, raising toast after toast, drinking to everyone's health; his cheeks ruddy and his doublet open to the waist.

Jane Shore, as uproarious as her monarch, leans over him. He slides an arm about her waist as she whispers something in his ear that makes them both throw back their heads, mouths open, their shrieks reaching far across the hall.

I turn toward a sudden movement to my right and notice Gloucester whispering something furiously into his wife's ear. He rises from his seat but she grabs his sleeve, dragging him back down beside her. I watch the mummery of their silent disagreement, until, throwing off her constraining hands, Gloucester gets up and fights his way through the crowd surrounding the king's chair.

The king pushes Jane away and throws a drunken arm about his brother's shoulder, his smile of welcome fading to disappointment at Richard's whispered words. Edward shakes his head, his joy dissipating. He puts down his cup. I read his lips.

"It is too late."

Gloucester's face could be set in stone as the brothers share a long, fury-filled look. I hold my breath, wishing I were closer that I may hear their words.

What is too late? What has happened to upset Gloucester now?

In Edward's early days as king, the two brothers were united, Gloucester as loyal as a brother can be, but his dislike for the queen and her prestige-hungry family came between them. As soon as he secured Anne Neville as his wife, the pair seldom came to court, preferring their refuge in the north. Always loyal, Richard kept silent, hiding his distrust of the queen, careful to show respect when duty demanded it. The dispute with France a few years ago, and the ignoble treaty the king agreed to at Picquigny in '75, strained his loyalty even further. The breach widened, yet their love endured. On his recent return, I saw how gladly Edward received his brother, yet clearly, Gloucester is not reassured by his visit at all.

As I watch, the king's face infuses with blood, their faces contrasting sharply as Gloucester's pallor deepens. They stare at each other, Edward silently daring Richard to speak.

Gloucester's anger and disappointment is contained in his curled fists, his words clamped tight behind compressed lips. I would give up my back teeth to hear their words, and know the reason for the dispute.

As other people in the hall begin to notice the discord, the chatter lessens and all heads turn toward the dais in time to witness Gloucester shrug off the king's placating arm. Ignoring the ceremony due to the king, the duke storms from the hall. Beneath the eye of the assembly Anne also stands, makes a shaky curtsey to the royal table and patters in her husband's wake.

That night, the queen dismisses me early. In the small room adjoining her chamber, I listen to the rise and fall of her and Edward's angry voices; I would give all I have to clearly discern their words. There is something going on that I am not party too, some secret worry they share.

As I stare into the dark, trying to calculate what it might be, my eyes grow heavy and I realise it is very late. I roll onto my belly, put my head beneath the blankets and force my mind to ignore the thoughts that plague me.

I wake again at dawn, as is my unbreakable habit. Heavy-eyed, I make my way to chapel, pausing at the window to look into the courtyard below, where a cavalcade prepares to leave. Curiosity piqued, I peer closer through the gloom. Richard of Gloucester, dressed in travelling clothes, takes a lingering look at the king's apartment window before turning to help his wife into a litter. The Duke and Duchess of Gloucester are returning to the north.

"They didn't even bid goodbye to the king," the queen complains as I assist at her toilette. "But good riddance, I say. They can take their long, displeasing faces back to Yorkshire. I don't want them cluttering up our court."

Spring 1478

The English court is made up of light and darkness. Shortly after the grandiose celebration of the royal wedding, comes a scandal that reveals the house of York in a loathsome light.

In February, we learn that the king has at last carried out his threat, and George of Clarence has been put to death in his cell at the Tower. When I first hear whispered details of his end, I am dubious. I cannot comprehend that the king should stoop to so dishonourable a thing. Tales of such ignominy always pass swiftly into public knowledge, and within days, rumour is rife about the court.

Clarence, like his brother the king, was always too fond of wine. It seems that the day before he was to die he asked the king to send him a butt or two of malmsey to ease him. The king, in his kindness, complied.

The next morning, when the men arrived to carry out the sentence, they found Clarence drunk – obnoxiously so. He greeted them with curses, struggled against them when they tried to quiet him, and his feeble quest for life degenerated into a drunken brawl.

Rumour has it, that he was stabbed. He fought back until overwhelmed and finally drowned in the last dregs of the one remaining butt of malmsey wine.

A scandalous death for anyone, let alone a duke and the brother of a king.

These events leave a bad taste in the mouth. I had no love for Clarence but the king's methods were despicable. Only Elizabeth seeks to defend him. After a loathsome hour of listening to her counting off on her fingers the reasons why George is better off dead, my head is pounding.

The same morning, I encounter his mother, Cecily, on her way back from chapel. I acknowledge her presence and as we pass, she is as upright and composed as ever. Reluctant respect for her rises within me, and the smile I give her is warm with empathy.

Although the king tries to stifle the truth, the story spreads. It spills into the street and across the city; it travels overseas until every royal house, every stew in Europe knows the tale. Everyone laughs at England; everyone scorns us.

The death of Clarence leaves the court stunned. Few had cause to love him, yet all are appalled at the violence of his end. Cecily Neville leaves the court, hurt and bewildered by the whole affair. Yet life carries on. I continue to attend the queen, who chooses to pretend nothing has happened. She plans summer entertainments, the redecoration of the royal nursery, and orders a new wardrobe of clothes to be made both for herself and for her elder daughters.

Elizabeth, Mary and Cecily giggle as they stand in their shifts to be measured. Elizabeth balances on a stool while a woman measures her bust and the length of her arms. Mary pulls faces from behind the seamstress's back, making Elizabeth giggle, her body shaking with mirth. The seamstress pulls back, a measuring tape in her mouth, and waits for the joke to play out.

I am fascinated by Elizabeth. Already she is as tall as I am, although not yet as tall as her mother. There is no doubt she is going to be beautiful, and with her parentage, beauty was inevitable. Her figure is undeveloped as yet, still very much that of a child, and the ink stains on the sleeve of her otherwise pristine linen prove she is not yet out of the school room. It is scarcely credible that I was her age when I wed with Edmund.

The seamstress stands up, puffing a little at the effort, and announces that Elizabeth has grown two inches in height and an inch all round.

"You will be as fat as Dame Nell, soon," Mary laughs, and Elizabeth tosses a cushion at her sister. Dame Nell is the girls' old nurse, almost as wide as she is tall. Her continuing presence in the royal nursery is due more to the queen's loyalty than to her usefulness. She attends to light duties now, leaving the heavier work to a troop of young women who work beneath her. And with the queen producing a child a year, there is plenty of work to go around.

Mary takes her turn on the stool. The seamstress tuts over the measurements that have remained static, and Mary pouts because she won't benefit from as many new clothes as her sisters.

A summer of fun follows. Many a royal picnic is spoiled by either blustery wind or sudden showers. The sun seems to show its head the moment we retreat indoors. Summer never really takes hold and come autumn there is no need to alter how many layers we wear. Lacking the benefits of a hot summer, none of us is ready for the winter, and I predict that this year we shall all suffer more than our share of colds and chills.

March 1479

"Very well, Margaret," the queen says when I beg leave to visit our Welsh estates. "As long as you return in time for my confinement. I would like you to attend me again."

That gives me just three weeks. I wonder if it will be time enough for me to find the inner peace I seek, but I recklessly make a promise to return in plenty of time.

Taking only my favourite women, I journey into Wales. As soon as we cross the border and the soft green scenery embraces me, I realise how much I have missed it.

Memories come flooding back: riding with Edmund from Caldicot to Lamphey, our newly flourishing interest in each other making us wary and shy. I never dreamed that day that I would ever like him, let alone how much he would come to mean to me, or how short a time we would have together. I was happier then, before life really began to test me, before I had loved or lost, or suffered in any way. How silly my younger self was to think that the sadness I felt at leaving Bletsoe was the worst in the world. How much more familiar I am with sorrow now.

Today, I travel alone, my present husband preferring to remain at the side of his king. This does not displease me; I feel unencumbered and ready for a few weeks respite from court in the company of my old friend, Myfanwy.

It is a long and tedious journey with few comfortable stopping places on the way. When one of my attendants informs me we are almost there, I am filled with relief. I cannot wait to alight from this horse; my buttocks are so raw I am sure the saddle must be made of burrs.

Myfanwy comes hurrying down the steps of her house to greet me. She is no longer the lithe young woman I remember. She is beautiful still, but motherhood has thickened her waist, and the arms that welcome me are soft and motherly. I hide my shock at the difference in her, but wonder how Jasper likes the changes, for the girl he fell in love with was as slim as a reed.

"You haven't altered in the slightest," she laughs breathlessly, and I suppose, in comparison to her, I haven't. I am still small and slightly built, almost like a child beside her generous curves. Yet, in manner at least, she is still Myfanwy.

She hooks her arm through mine, and we climb the steps to the house where she has a light meal waiting. I look around at the home Jasper has provided for her; it is modest compared to my own properties, but warm and comfortably furnished. There are cushions and good quality hangings, an abandoned piece of needlework on the settle, and children's toys scattered on the floor. She has done well for a woman with no husband, and has everything she requires apart from an honest reputation.

"How is Jasper, have you heard from him?" I ask.

She pulls a face.

"He says he is well, and Henry is thriving, but they are not happy in a foreign land. I can tell from his letters that they both long to come home."

"That would not be wise. King Edward has been lenient with many of our old friends but I believe he holds a special resentment for Jasper ... and Henry is too valuable to risk ..."

"I know. I sometimes think that if Jasper had only surrendered and sworn fealty, the king might have looked kindlier upon him. They might both be home by now."

She cuts a slice of bread, places it on her plate. For a moment, I allow myself the luxury of imagining them both home, forgiven by the king, embraced at court. It is a warm, happy picture. I give myself a shake.

"There is no use in wishing for the moon. Things are as they are."

Her bosom rises and falls with the depth of her sigh.

"Life could have been so different, so ... but, you are right. Let us speak of happier things. Tell me of court; what is the queen really like? I know you cannot say much in your letters."

She offers me a pastry. I take it daintily, and break a piece off, but I do not eat it.

"She is ... not so bad, once you know her. Much of the gossip against her is false. She is just a woman, fighting for her place, afraid of being usurped in the affections of her husband, resentful of his mistresses, fond of her children, faithful to her family."

"She is a friend to you?"

"I think so ... sometimes I doubt her, but it is difficult. It is easy to find one's loyalties compromised. In this day and age, a friend is a friend only as long as it is politic to be so."

"At least you have the compensation of all the court entertainments, the latest fashions, the new dances. Look at what I am forced to wear."

She stands up, fans out her skirts, which are well made but modest, in the most provincial style. I smile politely and tell her she looks very well.

"I will send you some patterns if you like, then you can revolutionise local fashion; the women of Wales will thank you for it."

Her laugh has not altered; it bounces from the walls, and my responding smile is genuine for the first time in many a day.

"In the morning, I will show you the garden. Every time I work out there, I think of you; it is as if you are with me. 'What would Margaret do?' I ask myself, and usually the right answer pops into my head."

I reach out and clasp her hand.

"I miss you too. One day, if I am able, I will welcome you into my household. Things are so unsettled now ..."

"What is this Thomas of yours like, is he as ferocious as he sounds?"

"No, no; he pretends to be but ... he is a buffoon sometimes, unintentionally. I have to hide my disdain from him for the sake of his feelings. He is a powerful man, high in the king's favour, and as a consequence has become overly self-important. He serves the king like a lap-dog, yet I fancy his loyalty to York is not as deep as it should be."

"Why do you say that?"

I shrug and take a bite of the pastry, crumbly and sweet on my tongue. Honey trickles onto my chin and I dab at it with a napkin.

"I don't know. Just a feeling I have sometimes. Thomas and his brother are very self-serving. They are loyal to Edward because it suits them ... but this talk borders on treason; let us speak of other things. This apple chutney is delicious. We had an invasion of caterpillars at Woking a few years ago that almost wiped out our entire apple crop."

We subside into the easy pleasure of mediocre things, both of us set to enjoy a few weeks of simple pleasures. It is good to forget who I am, forget that my life has been turned upside down by war. My time with Myfanwy is a glimpse of the ordinary life enjoyed by the privileged, and for a few short weeks I plan to make the most of it.

Yet, in the morning, a messenger arrives and cuts my pleasures short.

I look up from the letter.

"I have to return to court."

Myfanwy turns from the window, her face eloquent with dismay.

"Margaret, you have gone quite pale, whatever is wrong?"

"The queen ..." My voice breaks as my throat closes, my eyes misting over, a tear dropping upon my cheek. "The queen's son, little George, has died suddenly. She is in need of comfort and bids me return as soon as I may."

Myfanwy comes close, her hand on my shoulder as she puts her cheek next to mine to read the letter.

"Poor little mite, how old was he?"

"Not yet two years ... the queen will be broken by this ... and it comes so soon after little Margaret."

So many babies are taken; Heaven must be full of motherless infants. I feel as if my heart will break for her.

"Did you not say she is about to go into confinement? Perhaps another child will help her heal, help her to forget."

I stare into space while Myfanwy's words register.

"Do you think so? Does the birth of one child mend the loss of another? All this is beyond the realm of my experience. I have just one son; I cannot even contemplate his loss without my chest tightening and a feeling of panic."

"It will not mend, no, but it must go some way toward healing."

"Or perhaps, once you realise their mortality, it just makes you value the others more. The queen will never take her children for granted as so many parents do."

"Not me," Myfanwy defends herself stoutly. "I love my girls more than myself. Should anything happen to them, I would not know how to draw my next breath. I want them to be successful, happy and healthy, but more than anything I want them to live."

I cover her hand with mine. "Then we must ensure that they do."

Our short reunion has passed too quickly. On the hasty ride back to court, I mourn the leisurely trip I took in the other direction just a few short days ago. Who knows when I might meet Myfanwy again?

Now, I must brace myself and re-enter the mourning household of the queen. It is not something I relish. Elizabeth is often difficult to comfort, reluctant to forget or forgive any wrong done to her. There is no doubt she will find someone to blame; be it God, or her enemies, or her husband for endowing their son with the name of a traitor.

When the horses draw up at the steps of the royal hall, I climb stiffly from my mount, stretch my legs, put a hand to my aching back and prepare to re-enter the fray.

I have one foot on the bottom of the queen's stairs and am about to ascend when a young girl cannons into me, almost knocking me from my feet. I grab hold of her arm, belatedly recognising one of the queen's maids of honour.

"Lady Stanley, I am so sorry, my lady, so very sorry but it is the queen. The child is coming early; her waters have broken all over the floor of the chapel."

By late afternoon, still clad in my travelling clothes, I hold the newest addition to the royal family. Elizabeth's eleventh child is a daughter, a tiny scrap of pink fragrance, born a little too soon. She lacks the ripeness of a full-term child but appears healthy enough, and when I pass her into her mother's keeping, she greedily searches for the breast. I run a finger over her soft red crown of hair, and know instinctively that she is a fighter. This child will survive.

"It happened so quickly," the queen says. "One moment I was praying, the next my petticoats were soaked. But I thank God to be spared the last few weeks of waiting. In a month, I shall be churched and back at court where I belong. I won't miss the Easter celebrations after all."

"It is fortunate that I returned in time. Had I dallied on the road, I would have missed it."

She looks up at me, presenting a very different picture to her usual perfect toilette. Her hair is dishevelled, her face covered in a sheen of sweat, and there is a streak of blood on one cheek.

While I sit at her side watching Elizabeth nurse the child, a girl brings a bowl of warm water to cleanse the queen's face.

I hold out my hand.

"Let me do it," I say, taking the soft cloth and gently wiping away the megrim of the birthing.

"Oh that is nice," she sighs. "I am so glad you have returned. Tell me, what name do you think we should choose? Edward was hoping for a boy, I know, and favours no girl's names."

"You have so many daughters you have used up most of the best ones, Your Grace. Perhaps you could name her for one of your sisters?"

"Oh yes, perhaps my youngest sister, Catherine? What do you think of that, little one?"

The child smiles with a sudden bubble of wind, and the queen laughs.

"I am not sure if that was approval or not, Your Grace."

I lean closer, the better to admire little Catherine, as she will soon be christened. As I do so, an aroma that defies description assails me. The queen lifts the child away from her body, a grimace of dismay spoiling her serenity.

"Oh lord, call the nurse, Margaret, before she covers us all in royal shit."

I hurry to the door, laughing as I go.

By the time the king comes to admire his daughter, she has been washed and freshly bound, her red face evidence of a satisfied stomach. The queen will provide her nourishment for a few days, and then she will be passed into the care of a wet nurse; a young woman from the village with a child of a similar age. It is a sought-after position and the girl is fortunate, for who of her status would not relish the opportunity to live in the royal palace and be assured of good nourishment?

The king returns just as Catherine has just been laid to sleep, bringing a gust of good humour into the room. He examines the baby again, kisses his wife on the forehead, and tells her she has done well.

"I believe you must be under some enchantment, Lizzie," he says. "Not many women birth as many infants as you have and still manage to look not a day over twenty."

"Shush, Edward. Do not speak such things, not even in jest."

The subject of witchcraft and sorcery is unwelcome in the queen's apartments since the accusations made against them by Clarence. Even the king should not speak of it.

"Here," he says, taking something from beneath his tunic. "I have a gift for you."

Elizabeth takes the package and tears away the silk wrapping to reveal a book. It is velvet bound with many pages. She opens it with a gasp as she discovers the treasure between the covers.

"My goodness, it is one of Master Caxton's! Have you been to see him, Edward?"

"I have indeed, and saw the press at work too. When you are churched, I shall take you with me, the children will enjoy it too. It is quite astonishing. He can print books in the blink of an eye. What once took months of workmanship is now produced within hours."

I suspect he exaggerates, but I crane my neck to see the wonder he describes. I have heard of Master Caxton and his magical press, but have not yet seen one of his works. I am sceptical that he can produce books of the same quality – surely, the piety of the monks must have some bearing on the result.

"Look, Lady Margaret, is this not wondrous? How did anyone ever imagine this could be done?"

Grateful to be drawn into their conversation, I take the book and gently turn the page. The ink is dark and clear, the woodcuts intricate and finely wrought. It lacks something I cannot quite determine, but I can see that this printing press is an invention that will change lives. Books will soon be available to everyone, the speed of production making them cheaper. Soon, even merchant's wives will be sporting a book beneath their arms.

I hand the book back to the queen with an appreciative smile. This is a copy of Chaucer's tales of the Pilgrims – a raucous adventure that already has her laughing. She puts a finger on the page and reads out a risqué line. Edward settles on the bed beside her, his head next to hers, joining her in merriment. They have forgotten my presence; after a moment or two of watching and waiting, I quietly slip away.

Despite myself, I am intrigued by these new printed books and order some for myself. I send some overseas to Henry, and realise that they will make ideal New Year's gifts for Myfanwy and Harry's mother too. To add a personal touch, I decide to embroider my own covers for them. I have little private leisure for needlework these days but when I am attending to the queen, we spend an hour or two instructing her daughters in needlework skills. Embroidery is a requirement for all women, even queens.

One such afternoon when a squall of rain has chased away the sun, the queen looks up from her needle.

"Lady Margaret, I spoke to the king about your son."

My heart leaps, but I do not let my excitement show.

"Indeed, Your Grace, and what did you say about him?"

"I suggested that perhaps it is time we allowed him to come home."

I have wanted to hear those words for so long, but now they have been uttered, I am engulfed by fear. I look down at my stitches, noticing that the hand that clasps the needle shakes visibly.

"And what did he say?"

She sews silently for a moment, while my anxiety increases.

"Certain conditions would have to be met, promises made, and bonds signed."

"He would need to swear fealty, you mean? That goes without saying, Your Grace. We are all loyal to King Edward."

She regards me steadily, both of us aware that Henry's existence is a continual temptation to those who still yearn to overthrow York.

"We were wondering ..." She stops mid-sentence to address her daughters. "Elizabeth, Mary, run out to the garden and see if the rain has ceased ..."

The girls gratefully put down their needles and after curtseying politely to their mother, quit the chamber. The queen turns in her seat to face me and leans forward, her hands clasped in her lap. I feel obliged to lay aside my own work and our eyes meet. I do not know what her next words will be but I suspect they will be momentous.

"The king and I were wondering about a betrothal between our daughter Elizabeth ... and your son."

My voice is stolen. Astonished, I gape and blather for a full minute before finally managing to speak.

"But I thought there was an arrangement ... a betrothal with France ..."

She waves her hand dismissively.

"That came to nothing. Edward was furious, but I suggested this match with your son; it would remove the threat he poses, and unite our houses. York and Lancaster would become one."

I look down at my red-tipped fingers, tightly entwined in my lap.

"I do not know what to say ..."

"Of course, the king will want to discuss it properly with you and your advisors. I just thought you might appreciate time to consider it before he approaches you. Margaret, just think; if it could be arranged, we would share the same grandchildren!"

A sudden image enters my mind: both of us in our dotage, she grey-haired and gracious, me wizened and wise, with a litter of small children clamouring for our attention. It is not an ill picture, but I am wary.

Elizabeth claps her hands, delight brightening her brow, and I do my best to mirror her pleasure.

Can I trust them? Is it a trick? Suppose they mean to lure Henry here, and the moment he sets foot on English soil they fall upon him, and throw him in the Tower? How would I ever live with myself?

"Thank you for forewarning me, Your Grace, I will ..."

"Forewarning? You sound like a castle about to fall under siege!"

We laugh, but my humour is false, guarded. I cannot wait to escape her presence so I may examine my feelings. Can I ignore my own warning and tell him to come home? There is no one to turn to for advice. I wish Jasper were here; if only he were not so far away.

There is my mother, of course. She will give me sound counsel, but I am not certain of her wisdom. She grows old, is ailing, and her politics waver as much as her memory. After a lifetime of living off my own wits, I am at a loss. I bite my lip, and while the queen chatters on about the assets of uniting our families, I pick up my needlework again.

By the time the king enters with my husband in tow, the chamber has grown dim. A boy comes to close the shutters and stoke the fire, light the candles. I rise to greet the king, sink low into a curtsey.

Thomas sweeps off his hat and bows over the queen's hand. As he does so, I notice he has mud on the sole of his shoe. He plays the part of a courtier well, but his heart is more suited to the stable, or the chase. His politics leave much to be desired; it is his instinct for survival that has got him this far, not intellect. Yet, I find myself in a political turmoil and Thomas, inadequate as he is, is the only ally I have.

The king and Thomas settle down among us, and soon the conversation switches from the latest dance steps and new fashioned sleeves to the situation in the north. Strife has broken out afresh between our king and the king of the Scots.

Some time ago, a treaty was drawn up between Edward and James III and, to ensure the peace lasted, a marriage was proposed between Princess Cecily and the young prince, James, with a large dowry to secure the pledge. Now, sparked by a private quarrel between the Duke of Angus and the Earl of Northumberland, strife has broken out again. The king is now preparing for a new campaign against Scotland, and Richard of Gloucester, as Lord of the North, is to command it.

Thomas is to accompany him. Before he goes, I must waste no time in speaking with him, to glean his opinion of the queen's proposal. I have little faith in his advice, but seek it I must.

The forthcoming campaign monopolises the conversation, at least where the men are concerned, and the women quickly grow bored. During the first lull in the discussion, the queen claps her hands, summons the musicians to play.

"It is hours 'til bed," she says. "Why don't we dance?"

The king, managing to disguise his impatience, obligingly leads her to the centre of the room. For a while we watch them, two beautiful people, moving in rhythm with the music.

Never in my life have I come even close to such outward perfection. They complement one another, a perfect match, a flawless union; some people are surely blessed. I try to imagine Thomas and me rising to join them. Me, as small as a ten-year-old and with no proper grasp of the steps; Thomas, as large and blundering as an ox in a parlour. No, he is better suited to the tavern, and I to the church – no wonder our marriage is not one made in Heaven.

Later, in the quiet of the chapel, I beg forgiveness for my vanity. I am grateful for my mind, my intellect, my position and, most of all, for my son. I am wicked to envy the queen her pretty face and elegant body, her status. I will do so no longer.

When I am satisfied that God has heard my repentant pleas, I rise from my knees, take up my candle and make my way back to my apartments. The door squeaks as I push it open, waking my woman who has waited up for me.

I stand quietly, listening to her chatter while she helps me from my gown and into my night shift. As she ties my hair into long thin braids, the door opens and Thomas enters.

It is rare for him to come to my private chamber, and this is the second time in as many months. I dismiss the pink-faced girl who has clearly put the wrong interpretation on his visit.

"What can I do for you, Thomas?"

I keep my voice cold and unwelcoming as he eases himself into a chair, places a hand on each knee and peers at me through the gloom.

"Has the queen spoken to you?"

"Of what? She speaks to me daily."

"Ha, you know what I mean. Has she said anything particular; anything you might want to discuss with me?"

It is clear as to what he refers but I am reluctant to be the first to speak of it.

"Tell me what you mean, and I will answer."

He rubs his nose in annoyance.

"The king suggested that ... well, it seems they are considering wedding your boy to the Princess Elizabeth. I wondered what you made of it. If you knew of it ..."

"Yes, the queen did say something about it but ... I was waiting for confirmation from the king."

"And you would agree?"

He watches me, eyes narrowed, as if I am a spider on the chamber floor and he is uncertain which way I shall run.

"I would need to learn the full terms first."

I stare unseeing into the hearth, examining my true feelings before giving voice to them. The way before me is dark. I see the hopes I have harboured for Henry piled up like gifts before me, ready for the taking ... yet something makes me hesitate. How I wish for the cool clear counsel of Harry, or Jasper.

"What would you do, Thomas? Do you think they are to be trusted? Wouldn't a sensible king take the opportunity to be rid of this rival? If he dispensed with Henry, the remnants of the Lancastrian faction would be disarmed. They would be left with no leader – the conflict over, once and for all."

He scratches his head.

"It is already over. Edward is firmly on his throne, no one can take it now – not even your son."

"I would dearly love him to come home. We have been parted for too long."

"So, when the king speaks to you, agree with his terms. It is what you both want."

"But I am afraid, Thomas, do you not understand the gravity of the risk? If they should slay him ..."

"The queen loves you, Margaret. She will not let that happen. I would wager my head on it."

"I will seek the advice of Master Bray, and send word to Jasper to glean his opinion. Do you think the king will demand an instant answer?"

Thomas does not answer right away. I speak his name impatiently. He jerks his eyes away, clears his throat in confusion. To my horror, I realise I am standing before the fire, and the outline of my legs is clearly discernible through my thin shift. I move away, my cheeks burning, and wrap myself in a mantle.

"I want to retire now," I inform him archly, and he heaves himself from the chair.

"I bid you goodnight," he says, and before he lumbers from the room, he leaves a kiss on my forehead.

*

I cannot truly believe Henry will be coming home. The discussion with the king and queen convinces me that they wish to put an end to his exile. To be welcomed back to court, Henry has only to swear fealty to the king. I even go so far as to suggest the pardon be stretched to encompass Jasper. At some stage in the future, I will also request the return of their lands and titles, but for now, I am content.

Eltham - June 1480

The queen is sickly again, and I suspect the reason. This will be her twelfth child. Since her marriage to the king barely a year has passed without her producing another. Edward, self-satisfied and growing fat with contentment, is delighted when she gives him the news. The queen may be jaded and weary, but there can never be enough royal children. Men never seem to consider the strain of regular childbirth, yet still expect their wives to be bonny and lithe, both at table, and in the marriage bed.

I begin to see the benefits of infertility. It is better to enjoy the pleasures of other people's children and not risk premature death.

In the garden, where the air is sweeter, Elizabeth suggests we seek the shade of a bower. The children are playing at some distance, every so often some dispute with their nurse floats toward us. I watch a honey bee darting in and out of the entwined honeysuckle and roses, the tiny wings a blur, the back legs covered with pollen. When he is sated, he clambers from the depths of the blossom, and hovers in mid-air, an inch from the queen's nose. She flaps at it with her hand.

"It is very hot, Margaret. I dread to think how I will manage when August arrives. I will be as fat and swollen as a toad by then."

I cannot contain my amusement at the sudden image she presents.

"I do not believe there is a woman on earth who resembles a toad less than you, Your Grace. A little extra weight is to be expected; it adds to your charm rather than detracts."

She checks her fingers for signs of swelling, flexes them, her rings winking in the sunlight.

"As long as the king sees me as you do ... but I fear he grows less enamoured."

"He will be back, Your Grace. He always is ... you cannot blame a man for his appetites."

"Oh, I can," she laughs ruefully. "Were it not for his strenuous desire, I would not be pregnant so often."

"Well, there is that, but at least you cannot be accused of not doing your duty – I have never heard of such a well-stocked royal nursery. You are a good queen, not wanting in any way."

"Despite the gossips," she spits maliciously. "I well remember how they spoke against me, accusing me of lewdness when my marriage to the king was first announced. I have proved them wrong. I hope they choke on their words."

"I believe that ill-wishing does more harm to the ill-wisher than the ill-wished. I always strive to think kindly of a person, even if it is sometimes a struggle."

Her arm flops over the side of the chair and she mops her brow with her kerchief.

"I am very hot," she repeats with a sigh. "You are right, Margaret. I do try to be gracious, but I fail miserably when it comes to Mistress Shore. I thought he would have lost interest in her by now. What is it about her? What is the attraction, do you think?"

"I do not know; I have never spoken with her. People say that for all her commonness, she is kind. I doubt she would be able to hold the king in thrall were she otherwise. Perhaps you can be glad she holds no spite against you, Your Grace. She seeks no preferment, nothing more than simple trinkets."

"She can keep her trinkets; it is his affection I deplore. When I first knew Edward, he barely realised other women existed. It is hard. I know I am losing my looks, losing his interest. I had thought he would grow out of his infatuation with her, he himself is no longer young ..."

"Now, now, Your Grace; don't be maudlin. He will be back by Christmas tide, I guarantee it."

*

A long six months follows. Most of my time is taken up with seeing to Elizabeth's comfort. The pregnancy takes its toll, but when the time comes, the child is born promptly and efficiently, as is her habit.

She names her Bridget – a tiny scrap of a thing with white-gold hair like her father. She settles in quickly, an addition to the overflowing nursery.

"I hope she is the last," Elizabeth whispers. "Although I love them all, I am tired. I need some respite."

"Then you should demand it." I frown as I tuck the covers around her. "Speak to the king; he will not want to wear you out."

Elizabeth sighs, snuggles into the pillow. "It is *her*. I cannot bear the thought of him spending all his nights with her."

"Go to sleep," I say. "I will pray little Bridget is your last, if that is your wish."

She catches my hand as I move away.

"Do that, Margaret, and may all your prayers be answered."

Fotheringhay - 1481

As the summer slips into autumn, the king turns his attention to the problems on the border. Messengers ride back and forth between the king and Gloucester who, like the king, desires a diplomatic end. Soon, however, it becomes clear the situation will not be resolved without a fight.

King Edward, feeling the need to be closer at hand, moves the court north to Fotheringhay, near Peterborough. It is a long hard ride for the queen, and we are forced to take to a litter; a mode of transport I abhor from my days in Wales.

Thomas, already ensconced in the castle for several weeks, greets me on our arrival. He gives me good welcome, grasping my shoulders and kissing me on both cheeks. I have not missed him, did not mourn his departure. Our relationship is so formal and so little do I know him that I experience no regretful pangs or fear for his safety, as I did whenever I was parted from Harry or Edmund. My marriage to Stanley is entirely different to the relationships I had with them; his loss would not be a great thing. The only thing we share is our ambition; our desire to rise as high as we can in Edward's England.

Greenwich - May 1482

The queen's screams jerk me from sleep. I leap from my bed and burst, unannounced, into her chamber. The king is there, his legs bare and hairy beneath his night shirt. He kneels before Elizabeth, shaking her by the shoulders, yelling at her to be quiet.

"Your Grace, what is the matter? What has happened?"

The king does not look up; he wraps one arm tightly about his wife and waves me away. I back out of the room. I do not know the cause of their weeping, but I am already full of grief for them. Something truly awful has happened. In a daze, I look around the antechamber, where a cluster of weeping women in sleeping robes stand, their hair in braids.

"Does anyone know what has happened? It – it is not Bridget?"

They push forward a young woman. I recognise her as one of the Lady Mary's women. Her eyes are red raw and she cuffs her nose on her sleeve. When she speaks, a drool of dribble clings to her lips.

"The Lady Mary is dead."

Horror drenches me, and my head clashes with the shock of her words. I must still be asleep and dreaming. Oh God, wake me from this nightmare!

"What? Lady Mary? No, you are wrong. She had a chill, just a little chill. I - I saw her myself!"

I push through the crowd in search of a more mature member of the household. In the next room, two physicians, close to the hearth, are shaking their heads, their faces bleak, blank flags of horror. I do not have to ask for their confirmation.

Hurrying along the passage, I hasten up the stairs to the princesses' chamber. It is empty apart from the three eldest Plantagenet sisters.

Elizabeth sits on a stool, hands clasped between her knees, her face an effigy of shock. Cecily, her face buried in the bed hanging, weeps loudly and without restraint. On the bed, beneath a white sheet drawn up to cover her face, lies her elder sister, Mary.

I stand motionless in the centre of the room, unable to believe this is not some awful dream. I cannot take my eyes from the body beneath the sheet. It is so slight, and so small.

I cannot bear to look on her, yet I have lost the power to force my eyes away. I try to swallow something hard and painful that prevents me from speaking.

Elizabeth shudders suddenly, and my instinct to protect them takes over.

"Come," I say, taking a wrap from the chair and draping it over her shoulders. "I will take you to your mother; she will have need of you."

I take Cecily's hand to lead her from the room, but as I do so, Elizabeth begins to weep at last; loud, ugly sobs that speak more of terror than of sorrow.

"Hush, Elizabeth, do not cry. Try to be brave for your mother's sake."

Releasing Cecily's hand, I grasp Elizabeth's shoulders. Her head lolls horribly, her eyes rolling.

"The wrap," she screams, tearing at her clothes. "Take it off me. I cannot bear it."

She casts the garment away, and we watch as it floats like a wraith to the hearth where it lies, forlorn among the ashes. We all stand staring at it. I look at Cecily, who is quieter now. Our eyes meet.

"The wrap belongs to Mary," she says, "but you were not to know."

Westminster - June 1482

The royal court mourns. No one dares speak louder than a whisper. There are so many subjects we cannot discuss. Bereavement has never broken the queen before; it is not the first time a child has been snatched from her. Yet Mary was almost fifteen years old, on the cusp of womanhood. She was a lady of the garter, with a position, a role at court; she will be missed, and is mourned by us all.

But life goes on. While the queen sits pale and unhappy in her apartments, the king continues with his obligations. With the queen wrapped tightly in her own sorrow, he turns at the day's end to Jane Shore for comfort. His laugh is less raucous and not as frequent, yet the silly strumpet sits on his knee, sharing bawdy jokes and feeding him sweetmeats as if the solace of food and ribaldry can compensate for the loss of a beloved child.

In June, he summons me to his presence. I approach the privy chamber, curious yet afraid. *What can he want of me?*

An usher opens the door and I slip inside, finding to my great relief that Thomas is there, and

Master Bray also. All but the king stand up when I enter and make my bow.

What has happened? What have I done? A thousand possible ways I may have offended the king teem in my mind, but then Thomas takes my arm and leads me to the table.

The king pushes a document toward me. Master Bray proceeds to read it and, as my brain makes sense of the words, I am filled with achievement. Yet, as the implications of the document become clear, doubt tinges my triumph.

The document has been drawn up in the king's presence. It states, among other less important financial details, that Henry Tudor, called Earl of Richmond, is invited to return to England to be in the grace and favour of the king's highness.

I tremble as Edward presses his ring into the wax to seal the deal. Thomas signs also and, when he beckons me forward, I make my signature with a shaky scrawl. The deed is done.

The pledge is made.

"Since they are close kin, I shall seek dispensation from the Pope, Lady Margaret, to allow Henry and Elizabeth to be wed."

I am surely dreaming; or tucked deep in my bed in one of my happy imaginings. I cannot believe it, yet it is writ large on the parchment in my hand. My son can return home – where he belongs. Our days of exile are almost done; he shall soon be restored his fortune, his properties, and his proper place at the English court. I send copious thanks to God, who has brought this to pass.

Fotheringhay - August 1482

On a hot afternoon in August, a stranger rides through the gates of Fotheringhay, and the Duke of Albany, the estranged brother of the king of Scots, takes the English court by storm. Each time he enters a room, a ripple of excitement issues from the younger, unmarried women. He regards the queen with undisguised admiration as he bends over her hand.

"My Lord Duke," she greets him with her radiant smile.

"Alexander, please, Your Grace. You may call me by my given name."

She laughs, her eyes a twinkle but I know she is laughing at him. Albany may flirt as he will, she cares only for Edward.

Later, when he encounters Jane Shore, he receives a far better reception. Poor Jane can never deny the attentions of a noble man. I watch from the corner of my eye as they dally in the shadows, and the next morning, in the garden, I see him surreptitiously place a note in her sleeve. She takes her leave of him with a blush and a quick glance about the courtyard to ensure no one is watching. Jane and Albany are playing with fire; the king's mistresses are his own, none other may sample them.

He seems quite impartial; viewing all women as fair game, whether servant or queen. The prettiest girls are reduced to giggles by his overt flirtation, but I exchange no words with him, and I notice that he seems blind to plain or elderly women; he reserves his attentions only for the fairest.

I watch this dubious duke with suspicion, suspecting he has not come to Edward's court merely to sample the women. He has an ulterior motive and I suspect it involves the current hostilities with Scotland. Rather than a whore to warm his bed, he craves instead the reinstatement of his Scottish lands, and the downfall of his brother, King James.

There seems to be a curse upon the brothers of kings. Does he not recall the fate of Clarence, and take it as a warning? I would were I him. George's attempt to oust his royal brother ended in failure and death, yet it does not occur to Albany that a similar fate might await him. Second sons are a trial; perhaps Henry should be glad he is my only son.

It is not long before I discover I was right to suspect Albany's ulterior motive. Within days, the king has formed an alliance with the duke; Edward agrees to assist Albany in his efforts to unseat his brother James from the Scottish throne and rule in his stead under the suzerainty of England. In exchange, the king demands the possession of the long disputed border town of Berwick, and other holdings.

None of us fails to recognise the similarities to Warwick's rebellion when he attempted to replace Edward with George. But the king is so eager to reinstate English dominance over the border that he does not see the irony of his new role of 'kingmaker'.

The court follows the king north, but he calls a halt at Nottingham complaining of fatigue. I watch him closely. He is unusually pale, his face no longer the exquisite visage it once was; his flesh sagging, the skin pale, a sheen of sweat on his brow.

The royal physicians examine him and dose him with some spirit-building concoction. The king rallies, but only enough to continue conducting his war from the safety of Nottingham.

The Scottish trouble is a long running dispute; it has almost become tradition for the two crowns to wrangle over the borderlands. Our armies have been harrying King James's coast for months, but now they prepare to set siege to the town of Berwick.

It is almost twenty years since Henry VI and Margaret of Anjou allowed Berwick to pass into Scottish hands, and King Edward has never forgotten it. It is a piece of England that he is determined to retrieve.

Armed to the teeth, Thomas and Gloucester ride forth to bear down upon the town with their combined armies, prepared to take back what belongs to our king. As our troops gather around the castle, armour glints in the sunshine, pikes bristle around the town walls. Yet we may be in for a long wait. The people of the town will either starve or surrender – Edward has little preference which.

To our initial joy, Lord Grey and the Earl of Crawford surrender and the town falls quickly, but the garrison holds out for Scotland, against the combined forces of the king, Gloucester, and my husband.

Long weeks pass, each side determined to sit it out, to hold on until the last man either surrenders or starves. In the end, with an irritating and time wasting delay, the army divides, leaving Thomas to continue the siege while Gloucester rides north toward Edinburgh.

We are shocked when news comes of anarchy among the Scots. It was not part of the plan, but the Earl of Angus turns upon his monarch, hangs a few of his king's favourites from Lauder Bridge, and takes King James as his prisoner.

With support for Albany waning in Scotland, Gloucester brokers a truce, securing a repayment of the monies paid as part of Cecily's dowry in the now-broken union with the Scottish prince. Leaving Albany to fight his own battles, Gloucester and his men return to court tired and frustrated. The king, however, seems content to have recouped his losses and celebrates the regaining of Berwick.

On his return, Thomas boasts of his part in the fall of Berwick Castle. In the privacy of our chambers, where there are none to gainsay his prowess, he inflates his part in it.

"You should have seen it, Margaret. My men armed to the teeth, armour polished, pennants blazing. We surrounded the castle entirely. Those inside must have been shitting their hose – I will have the king's favour now and no mistake. My achievements will surely be mentioned in parliament."

He crows of his achievements like a small boy. I hide my amusement and smile like a doting mother, telling him he has done well. He is right about one thing; Berwick is a strategic gem, and one the king is pleased to have back in his possession.

"Does the king seem well to you?" I ask, and Thomas looks up, his brow furrowed.

"I think so; I have noticed nothing amiss."

I shrug my shoulders.

"He seems a little jaded, less ebullient. I would have thought that given his recent successes he would have been more ... vigorous in his celebration."

"He feels his age perhaps, like the rest of us."

Thomas stretches his legs, a hand to his aching knees as he stands up. He tugs at the lacing on his tunic, frowns at the knot he has made, and I go forward to assist him with it.

We are standing very close, closer than we have been since we were joined. I can feel his breath on my hair and for an instant I am reminded of the intimacies I once shared with Harry and Edmund. Loneliness swamps me suddenly. I free the knotted cord but do not move away.

We both become very still.

After a moment, he places a finger beneath my chin. I try to resist as he forces me to look up at him. Our eyes meet, and my heart leaps a little, my belly swimming in a way I had quite forgotten it could – oh, but ... he is the wrong man!

As Harry's face rises before me, the brief flicker of passion withers like a flame starved of fuel.

"We are man and wife, Margaret," Thomas whispers. My throat constricts, something foreign lodged there making me choke. I step back, shaking my head to clear my head of the sudden unwarranted desire.

"Forgive me," I croak. "I am feeling quite unwell." I quit the chamber, leaving him there with his arousal unsated.

I spend a long time praying for guidance. Never before has Thomas made advances towards me, and he was quite, quite sober. I feel confused, bewildered. I had thought our relationship was clear. I have no desire to consummate our union. I like things as they are.

I have set my late husbands on pedestals far too high for the aspirations of Thomas Stanley. Yet the flutter of desire I felt when he almost kissed me has roused painful memories. I pray for a while longer, the cold of the chapel seeping through my summer clothes, quenching the heat of my desire.

I beseech God and all his saints to help me find the answer, but they do not reply. The confusion in my heart increases. For almost a week, I feel unsettled, my tranquil, pious path muddied and difficult to navigate. My mind wanders, wondering where he is, what he is doing. Each time I catch myself thinking in this ridiculous way, I reprimand myself sternly. I am determined not to fall for one passing act of affection from a man I barely like. In the end, after a week of poor sleep and difficult concentration, I seek out my priest, blindly confessing to a brief feeling of lust for my husband.

"There is no sin within marriage, my child. You are absolved."

I could accept his absolution, and go about my business, but I force myself to explain further.

"There can be no child from our union. We bear no love for one another. The desire can only have its root in lust. Lust is a sin, is it not, Father?"

"Carnal desire within marriage is ..."

He is uncertain. Unsure how to respond.

"And is my reluctance to join with him not also a sin? As his wedded wife, am I not obliged ...?"

He remains silent, scuffling in the darkness of the confessional box. He clears his throat.

"You wish to remain celibate?"

I sigh deeply, making the candles dip suddenly.

"I do, Father, with all my heart."

I do not tell him that my desire has less to do with a love of God than the love of the man who has been taken from me.

"A vow of celibacy may be the answer. If your husband gives his consent ..."

A vow of celibacy. I would be free of obligation. My desire was false, a lure set by the devil, and should I give in to it, I would swiftly come to regret it. It is not possible for a man of my husband's ilk to live up to the tenderness of Harry ... or Edmund. If I was to swear chastity, and Thomas approached me again, the sin would be his. A possible answer shines, like a far off star in a black sky.

I take a deep breath.

"Very well, Father, thank you. I will think on it."

For weeks, thoughts of Thomas are never far away. As soon as I realise I am thinking of him, I force myself to pray, to concentrate on something else. I ensure we are never alone – never close enough to feel the pull of temptation. I maintain a chilly, polite distance. If he enters a room, I leave it. If he summons me to his apartments, I plead a headache. When I wait upon the queen, he watches me in puzzlement from his place at the king's side. I can feel the tension, and hope and pray that no one else senses it.

<u>Eltham - August 1482</u>

The merriment in the king's hall has just begun. I sit with the queen and her other ladies, listening while Princess Elizabeth sings a song before the court. It is a cheeky song about the coming of summer; as the last notes fade away, the queen leans forward, claps her hands, and laughs at some remark of the king's.

Thomas has slowly edged his way through the gathering and now stands a little to my right. I am aware of him, feeling his eyes upon me. I cannot help but hold my head at what I hope is an elegant angle. I lift my chin, pull back my shoulders, and pretend to myself that I want him to move farther away, to flirt with Jane Shore as William Hastings does. But I remain where I am, sensing his closeness and trying not to relish it.

Aware all the time of his eyes upon me, I clap delightedly with the others, smile dotingly at the princess as she re-joins the other children. When someone tugs my sleeve. I turn, expecting to find Thomas but instead, I discover one of the maids of honour.

"Margery, what is it?"

She points toward the door.

"A messenger, my lady: he is asking for you."

"Oh. Excuse me."

The crowd parts to allow me passage, and I meet the envoy at the periphery of the room. As we draw closer, I notice he wears my mother's badge. Annoyed at the interruption in the entertainments, I frown a little as I take the letter, dropping a penny into the messenger's hand.

Slipping into an antechamber, I tear open the seal, my heart plummeting as I read the words, written by Edith's hand.

Oh Margaret,

After a short illness, our mother passed away this evening. She spoke of you at the end, giving you her best love; there was no time to send for you, but she asked me to ensure you received this trinket ...

Enclosed in the letter is a small, simple ring, set with an emerald stone. It is one she wore every day. My eyes mist over as I recall it winking on her finger while she bent over her needlework.

I close my eyes, reeling from the irretrievable completeness of my loss. It is so easy to imagine snuggling into her arms, inhaling her scent, reliving the comforting touch of her hand in my hair. But it is far too late, she is gone from this world, and I was not there. I would give all I have for a few more moments to tell her of my love.

My cheeks are wet. Dashing them dry with the back of my hand, I turn to rejoin the queen, and beg to be excused from the celebration. As I draw back the door curtain, I find my way barred.

"Thomas!"

The hand that clutches Edith's letter is tight against my breast. "You startled me."

"What is the matter? Why are you weeping?"

He forces me to retreat into the chamber. I open my mouth to speak, but I cannot find the words to relate what has happened. My mouth goes out of shape, and my chin wobbles. A tear drops onto my hand. He prises the parchment from my grip.

"It is my mother," I manage to wail. "It was very sudden ... I was not with her."

As the realisation of the finality of her death dawns, the utter misery of being alone in the world, never to hear her refer to me as 'little Margaret' again, my carefully guarded poise deserts me. Tears well up in my eyes, my nose tingles, and I begin to bawl like a baby.

"Hush."

He steps forward and the jewels on his tunic cut into my cheek as he cradles me close, crooning to me as if I were an infant. It is most unexpected but, weakened by grief, I give myself up to the comfort of his arms.

I wake sometime later in a tangle of sheets. As my memory returns, I turn my head as cautiously as I can.

This is Thomas's bed. He lies beside me, unclothed, his hairy arm thrown across my body, his head back, mouth open, his breath rasping in my ear.

Oh, dear God, what have I done?

As I recollect the inelegant pushing and shoving that was Thomas's love making, my cheeks grow hot with shame. My skin smarts from the roughness of his beard, my inner thighs ache from bearing his weight.

I move slightly and he snuffles, rolls over, turning his back on me, taking the sheet with him and exposing my naked state. I look down with a shudder at the marks made by his mouth on my breast, but my biggest shame lies not in his sin but the recollection of the joy I took from it.

The loathsome memory of squirming and juddering beneath him like a harlot rears like a beast in my mind.

I despise myself.

Lifting my head, I look about for my shift. Stretching out an arm, I try to hook it onto my finger. Without leaving the bed, I struggle into it, concealing my nudity, hiding my indignity from my own eyes. Thomas snores on.

I do not summon my women. I will never be able to face them again. Instead, in the antechamber, I pour water into a bowl and wash the sweat from my face, the traces of his seed from my thighs. I am struggling to lace the side of my gown when I hear his approaching footstep.

I find I cannot move. It is as if he has cast some spell upon me from which I cannot wake.

He comes close behind me and I stiffen as he slides his arms beneath mine, cupping my tiny breasts, nuzzling the side of my neck. Revulsion churns in my belly. I thrust myself away from him, taking a position near the opposite wall, as far from him as I can get.

"Thomas - I ..."

I cannot look at him, cannot bear to see his triumph, the expression of conquest on his face. Indignation begins to replace disgust.

I am not Berwick Castle; I am not his for the taking.

He slops wine into a cup and hands it to me, but with a brief shake of my head, I step past him, halting at the door. With one hand on the frame, I lower my head and speak quietly, but with finality.

"This is not going to happen again, Thomas. On that, you have my word."

He tries to speak but I do not wait to argue. Hastening from his presence, I quit the chamber, heading, incompletely attired as I am, for the sanctuary of the chapel.

Windsor - March 28th 1483

"Should we not cancel the trip, my lord?" The queen tilts her head to one side, looking plaintively at her husband.

"I will be fine, Lizzie; do not fuss so."

The king pushes her away as she tries to button his tunic, and she bites her lower lip as she watches him leave. She turns to me, her usual arrogant expression tempered with worry.

"Oh, Margaret. He was so ill again in the night, yet this morning seems quite recovered. The physicians advise rest, but I cannot force him – nobody can force him to do anything."

"Perhaps it was just a chill; sometimes, they come upon us swiftly and are gone just as fast."

I hope she does not recall that Princess Mary went to bed suffering from a mere chill. I put down my sewing and join her at the window.

Below in the courtyard, the king is surrounded by the male members of his court as they prepare for a fishing trip. It is a chilly day. I am glad to remain at Westminster where the fires are banked high.

The men hurry toward the wharf, their cloaks making a splash of colour on this dismal day. The royal barge waits at the stairs; it dips and sways as the king lowers his bulk on board and his men take their places around him. Thomas looks up briefly at the window. It is unlikely that he can see me from the distance that parts us, yet still I take an involuntarily step backwards.

The queen turns from the window and I follow her, joining the other ladies who sit in a ring about the fire. The musician picks up his harp and begins to play, his music leaping and dancing about the chamber. I bend my head over my needle, finding solace in the roses that bloom beneath my hand. I set tiny stitches close together to form one beauteous flower.

From time to time, I glance at the queen. She shows no sign of pregnancy yet, and I am beginning to suspect that she will bear no child this year. My prayers for her are working. She will welcome the respite and benefit from it.

I wonder whether she is nearing the end of her fertile years, or whether the king's ailments keep him from her bed. His sickness has not affected his doting on Jane Shore; she is ever-present at court, like a blemish on a fair face, a speck of dirt on a pristine gown. The royal court should be spotless; the likes of Jane Shore have no place within it. And then I recall that, beneath my prim ways, I am little different.

Each time I lean forward to select a new strand of silk from the table, Henry's latest letter crackles against my breast. I have read it many times. His preparations to end his exile are almost complete; soon, he will be ready to come home. I allow my mind to idle, imagining how we will spend our days, where he will choose to live, what position he will be given at court.

Sometimes, doubts beset me. I wake in the early morning and King Edward's forgiveness seems like a dream. How can such distrust, such enmity, turn to friendship? I will never forgive myself if I am leading my son into a trap.

Fear of betrayal leads to nightmares and I awaken with the sick feeling of loss, forcing me to rise earlier than ever to seek solace in the chapel.

*

The queen holds up a partlet, a small one for a child. She has sewn a ring of white roses on the black velvet.

"How lovely, Your Grace, you have such a fair touch with the needle."

"It is for Anne. She showed such admiration for the one I made for Elizabeth that I decided to make one for her. She is a vain little thing."

"She is very pretty, Your Grace; all your daughters are."

"And my sons too," she laughs, and because she is right, all the ladies join in. Edward, the Prince of Wales, is far away in Ludlow, but Richard resides with his sisters here at Westminster. Both boys are as fair as their parents. One day, they will become kings of the tiltyard and the dance floor, breaking the hearts of the court women ... as their father has done.

In the afternoon, we walk in the garden. The children, wrapped up warm against the unseasonal chill, run ahead. Their nurse-maid calls after them to come back and walk nicely, but Elizabeth stops her.

"Let them go," she says. "A little exercise now will make them less unruly when they return to the school room."

The heads of the smallest children are barely discernible above the shrubs, but the older girls, Elizabeth and Cecily, follow behind, their hands clasped decorously before them in imitation of the queen and her ladies. Eight-year-old Anne, eager to prove herself, abandons the smaller children and tries to join her elder siblings.

"They grow so fast." Elizabeth nods towards her daughters. "They are almost women."

"And very lovely women, too, Your Grace."

It still shocks me to see the two girls without their sister, Mary. It is difficult to think of her lying low in the vault while life continues as if she had never been.

There is a touch of sadness on the girls now, on the whole family; especially the queen. Sorrow sits strangely upon Princess Elizabeth's plump, pretty looks and robust health. She is a girl made for merriment, in the cast of her father. Cecily, with her mother's colouring, is slighter than Elizabeth. She is paler, less glowing and a little more serious. She is also very stubborn. What Cecily wants, Cecily usually gets, because no one has the heart to refuse her.

The queen and I, followed by a group of whispering women, walk slowly around the garden. My attempts to draw the queen from her sallow thoughts are unsuccessful, her heavy sighs competing with the brisk breeze.

Cecily approaches with a handful of primroses, which the queen accepts with a smile. She places a hand on her daughter's shoulder, and they walk on ahead, uncannily alike from behind, their gait unmistakeably the same.

Elizabeth falls into step with me, and we exchange hesitant smiles. I am not sure whether she has been told of the marriage arrangements that are underway between her and my son. I wonder what sort of daughter-in-law she will make, how she will welcome me as the mother of her husband.

She is subdued today. Usually, she has a bounce about her, reminding me of an enthusiastic pup that has been told to sit and stay.

She draws her shawl about her shoulder. "It is cold," she says. "I wish we could return to the hall."

I cast my experienced eye over her face, checking for signs of fever or the beginnings of a cold. Although she is pale, she otherwise seems well, but I have not forgotten how dismissive I was of Princess Mary's fever. I can never forgive myself for that.

When we near the far wall where the pear trees are bearing blossom, the queen halts and waits for the rest of us to catch up.

"Shall we return to the palace now? Have you had enough air for today?"

After a murmur of agreement, we follow Elizabeth and her daughters back to the hall. In the queen's chambers, the warmth of the fire brings colour to our cheeks, and I grope for a kerchief to dry my nose which has begun to run.

The queen pulls off her gloves, rubs her hands briskly together. "It is so unseasonably chilly," she complains. "Why, I have known Easters in the past that could have been mistaken for summer."

"March is an unpredictable month," I say as I signal for a girl to gather up our cloaks and take them away. "One can never be sure what it will bring. Perhaps we should all have something warm to drink?"

For the remainder of the day, we huddle about the hearth, the conversation ebbing and flowing until we lapse into our own thoughts. I reach the end of a row of stitches, break off the thread and select a new shade of silk.

The queen puts down her sewing.

"It is late. I had hoped Edward would return before nightfall."

"They will surely be back very soon now; it is too dark to fish, even with torches."

"Father will not wish to miss dinner," Cecily remarks. "I have heard it is to be eels."

We are still laughing when we hear a noise outside.

"They are back." Elizabeth hurries to the window, peering into the dark. "I can see nothing but the glare of torches."

"Thank goodness." The relief in the queen's voice is clearly discernible. "I had such a strange feeling of dread."

Elizabeth turns from the window to reclaim her seat among the circle of women about the fire. Cecily begins to relate a funny tale about a near tragedy between her pet finch and one of the kitchen cats.

I look up, ready to laugh, anticipating the twist in her tale, when the door is thrust unceremoniously open.

"Your Grace, the king has fallen ill. We have taken him to his chamber, and the physicians have been summoned."

The queen's face turns as white as her linen shift, her eyes huge dark vessels of horror. She stands slowly, gropes for my hand.

"Your Grace," I whisper, and she turns her head slowly towards me.

"Oh, Lady Margaret," she murmurs, "I fear we are in dire straits." She takes a step forward, addresses the other women. "You must pray for us, ladies. Pray with all your heart and soul. Your king has need of God's grace. Pray for us all."

She takes my arm and propels me with her, along the passage, up the stairs to Edward's private chamber.

The room is crowded and over-heated; the shutters closed tightly, the fire blazing. Amid the crush of attendants and physicians, I can just discern the high canopied bed, the bulk of the king's belly pushing up the covers.

Elizabeth gives a curt order and people part to allow her through. We halt at the bedside. Elizabeth's hand flies to her mouth, a large tear dropping from her eye.

The king's face, once so mercurial, so full of vigour is now a dirty shade of grey, like much-handled putty. There is no sign of the once golden prince, the breaker of a thousand hearts. He gasps for each breath, floundering for survival. Even as the physician steps forward with his bleeding bowl, I know his intervention will be hopeless. I have seen that look before.

The king will not live.

They come from near and far, the passages of Westminster overflow and a great crowd gathers outside the palace. Those who loved him, those who feared him, and those who merely tolerated him for the sake of peace.

I suppose, I am among the latter. He was not a good king; he was far too fond of feasting, too full of sin, too ready to let his underlings take on the responsibilities of state. Yet, I have to concede that Harry was right; Edward has proved more effective than my cousin, Henry VI.

He brought peace, and England had just begun to flourish again. What will happen now? Are we to have a child king, ruled by his elders? I am afraid not much good has ever come of that.

<u>Windsor - April 1483</u>

He lingers for three days. Unwilling to admit defeat, his physicians attempt one unlikely cure after another. In the end, William Hastings roars at them to leave the king alone, to let him die in peace, and the queen says nothing to counteract his order.

The court gathers. The girls stand weeping in the corner, while little Prince Richard is on his knees, bewildered, as if a devil is squatting on his shoulder whispering dread into his ear.

Elizabeth's fingers are entwined with the king's, her tears falling on them as thickly as her last kisses. He seems to know her, tries to speak but his tongue is thick, unmanageable, and he resorts to sign language.

At first, no one understands, but he waves a finger in the direction of Hastings, who steps forward uncertainly. Then he summons Dorset in the same manner and the two men stand awkwardly, embarrassed at the incapacity of their once-hale king. He beckons them closer, reaches for their hands, and before all the court joins them in three-way handshake.

Discord between Hastings and the queen's family has been long and vigorous. Dorset, the queen's son by her previous marriage, is Hastings' long-time rival for both the affections of the king and the attentions of Jane Shore. Now, it seems the king wishes them to swear unity, to put aside their rancour for the sake of the realm; for the sake of his son.

The two men stare at each other for a long time, grim faces recalling grimmer memories, harsh words and harsher actions, but at length Hastings tightens his grip. Dorset can only reciprocate. Their clasped hands seal the deal – the adversaries have become allies.

The king makes a sound, somewhere between strangulation and a cough, and raises a shaky finger to draw Hastings close so he may speak into his ear. The court leans forward to hear the last words of their monarch.

"My brother, Gloucester," he croaks, "is to be Lord Protector. Serve him well. Ever an honest man…"

His head lolls to one side, his hand falls onto the bed. Elizabeth snatches it up again, covers it with tears and kisses.

Their children begin to cry: beside me, I hear Thomas draw in a ragged breath, and with a calloused finger he chases moisture from his eye. The ragged sound of the king's labour slows. We wait on each breath, the gap between them increasing until it ceases altogether. Now, there is only silence, and the sound of weeping.

*

I expect the queen to dissolve into misery, but to my surprise she does just the opposite. Instead of relying on Dorset to oversee the council meeting on her behalf, she attends herself, taking little part but listening, eager to comprehend the organisation for her son's arrival in the capital.

The country is numb, reality has been suspended, and the arrangements are carried out by men who move like mummers in a play.

On the tenth day of April, the king's body travels to the chapel of St Stephens, where funeral rites will soon begin. Young Edward is proclaimed king in the capital; his coronation scheduled for the fourth of May. The cheers of the crowd are not spontaneous, but guarded, as uncertain as the hand of a boy king.

Edward and his uncle, Earl Rivers, are en route to London. The queen is determined that everything should in readiness for him and orders new clothes and new furnishings for the royal apartments. She cuts a tragic figure as dowager queen; her head remains high but her eyes swim with grief. She weeps only in private, and I offer what comfort I can.

"I wish any other than Gloucester had been named Protector," she murmurs. "That man has a deep hatred for me."

"I am sure he will do you honour as the king's mother, Your Grace."

"I am not so sure, Margaret … there are things …" She pauses, the silence stretching into minutes.

"Things?"

She stumbles, her face creasing with confusion, revealing a fleeting expression of terror before she recovers.

"There are certain stories about me that Gloucester may well believe, things about the king he must never discover. Oh, I wish he would remain in Yorkshire."

"Perhaps he will return, once he has settled the king safely on his throne."

"Oh no, he will not do that. Richard of Gloucester hates me and all my family. He will not want us to have a hand in governing the country."

"I am sure he bears no hatred for the prince," I say, forgetting the boy is now to be addressed as 'king.'

"No, not him, perhaps, but he resents our influence. He sees me as an upstart, and will do all in his power to put my family down. You watch him take away their offices and replace them with his own creatures."

"Surely, Madam, you are distraught. I warrant it is the strain of the last few weeks that makes you see demons in the dark."

I have never seen a monstrous side to Gloucester. He is more sombre than the late king, damning of sin and sinners, yet that is surely not a thing to be detested. His reputation is good, a just and able man, always a credit to his king.

"No, you are quite wrong. Me and my children are about to fall under the control of a man who is my enemy, and I will need to be strong, Margaret," she says. "Although I long to throw myself into a pit of misery, I cannot afford to do so. I must put aside grief, remain wary at all times, and express only joy in my son's accession. During these interminable days, all I have to look forward to is privacy so I may weep."

"Once the king is here, you will feel better, Madam," I say, taking a seat closer to her. "You will see."

"I am so tired. I feel I am at the end of my tether."

"Then, tomorrow I shall make you a restorative; you will soon feel better."

"You are so good, Lady Margaret."

Like the queen, I too crave a return to normality. I would like to take up the matter of Henry's return, but now is not the time.

He will miss the coronation, but I feel it is safer for him to return to England after the new king is crowned. I am more confident now, for young Edward is a far less dangerous prospect than his unpredictable father.

We will all feel better once the shock of the past few weeks has passed, and we have become accustomed to the suddenness of the king's demise. Change is always a difficult thing, but the world, and everything in it, will soon be normal again.

The queen lapses into silence. I take up my sewing and set a row of red stitches alongside the white and the green.

Westminster - May 1483

A crash wakens me. I start up in the bed. My woman, Jane, sits up beside me, sleepily knuckling her eye.

"What was that, my lady?"

"I don't know. Go and find out."

I swing my legs from the bed, throw open the shutter, and crane my neck to see if I can discover the cause of the uproar. When the chamber door is thrown furiously open, the last person I expect to see is the queen.

"Your Grace?" I flush, embarrassed by my unclothed state, but she is not inclined to be concerned about the sight of me in my shift.

"Margaret. You must move fast. There is no time to waste; just collect what you need, essentials only, and follow me."

"Follow you where, Your Grace?"

"Sanctuary."

"What?"

Still half asleep, I gape at her, wondering if I am dreaming. "Sanctuary? Why? What has happened?"

"Gloucester has happened. He has intercepted and taken possession of my son on the road to London. He has placed my brother under arrest, and now marches on London. By God, Margaret, we must hurry. He will show me no mercy should he lay hands on me."

Her panic is contagious. I can feel its breath on the back of my neck, making my skin prickle. I shudder.

"Why, Your Grace? Explain, please!"

I take hold of her arm, and force her down onto the bed, pushing my face close to hers. There is a film of sweat on her upper lip, madness in her eye. She clutches at me as she repeats her words, enunciating as if I am deaf rather than ill-informed.

"Gloucester, who hates me, has taken control of the king, and marches on London. We must get to sanctuary, to safety, before he lays hands on my other children. By God, I never did trust him, or any of them. Cecily Neville's sons are all monsters – every one, bar Edward."

She is unhinged. Briefly, she buries her face in her hands, her storm of weeping interrupted when one of her women rushes in, a coffer of jewels beneath her arm.

"We are ready, Your Grace. The servants are packing up your clothes and hangings, and will follow on after. You must come now."

The queen stands up.

"Hurry up, Margaret."

"But ..." I hesitate, trying to think clearly, trying to make sense of the gibberish she speaks. "Why do I need to come? Gloucester is not my enemy. He will not harm me."

She looks at me as if I am a snake in her path.

"Oh, you jade! Looking to yourself in my time of dire need! I thought you were on my side."

"I did not mean that, Your Grace. Listen to me. If you closet yourself away in sanctuary with all your friends about you, you will be blind to what is happening in the world. If I remain here at court, I can discover Gloucester's intentions, and keep you informed of his movements ..."

"Like a spy?"

"Yes, I suppose so. Like a spy. And I can work toward finding a way to reconcile you with the Protector."

"He will not be Protector for long. My brothers and sons will see to that. My brother Edward has control of the fleet, the treasury has been breached, and so we have funds, the makings of an army ..."

Her woman darts back into the chamber, hopping from one foot to the other.

"We must go, Your Grace."

The queen grasps my upper arms, plants a kiss on my forehead.

"God be with you, Margaret. You are a true friend."

"And may He be with you also, Your Grace."

I sink into a formal curtsey, and kiss the back of her hand. I rise just in time to see the back of her skirts as she sweeps through the door.

The queen is gone. She has fled the palace in fear of her life.

London - May 4th 1483

I watch the boy king ride into the capital. He comes by way of Barnet. The morning sun glints upon the armour of the long cavalcade of knights, the pennants snapping in the stiff breeze, the trumpets deafening.

The crowd calls a hefty welcome to the boy who sits so steely straight on his horse, but he makes no response. Gloucester shifts in his saddle, addresses the king from the corner of his mouth, and Edward obediently raises his hand, waves woodenly to the crowd who bellow in response.

Remembering to appear inconspicuous, I wave and cheer with the rest but the boy on the horse is not the Edward I knew. He seems like a stranger.

From my place on the city wall, I study the scene, examining the king, observing his relationship with his uncle. The boy looks well in body but I detect a soreness of spirit; his eyes are red-rimmed, the dark circles around them contrasting sharply against his stone white face.

Who would not be shaken? His father has recently died. The uncle he knows and loves has been thrown in gaol, replaced by an uncle he has seldom met.

His cousin, my kinsman, the Duke of Buckingham, rides proudly just behind, his Plantagenet bright hair marking his close relationship with the king. Gloucester is small and dark, in the mould of his father, the late Duke of York. He is the least comfortable member of the procession. He keeps one hand on the king's bridle and looks neither left nor right. After his coup, the seizure of power over England, I had imagined he would give some sign of joy, but his face is troubled, as if he would rather be somewhere else.

The King is taken to the Bishop of London's palace, where magnates and citizens swear their fealty to him. Soon, the palace teems with people come to pay their respects to the new king; tailors come to measure him for his coronation robes; jewellers waiting to fit his crown. While the palace is consumed by tradespeople, Richard of Gloucester remains out of sight. I imagine he concentrates on state matters.

As the queen predicted, it is not long before many of the old king's ministers are replaced with Gloucester's friends. To our relief, my husband, along with Hastings, Rotherham, Stillington and Morton remain in office. Between them, they decide that the king should follow tradition and be moved to the royal apartments at the Tower, there to await his coronation.

New coins are struck, showing the name of Edward V; it is a new era. I wonder how this reign will be remembered; a child king has never boded well for England.

When I have occasion to see my husband, I swallow my reluctance to be in his company and glean all I can of the happenings at the council. Soon, I will be able to report to the dowager queen that Gloucester's attempts to have her brother and son, along with Vaughan and Haute, accused of treason have met with resistance.

Her other brother, Edward Woodville, does not fare so well. Refusing orders to disband the royal fleet and return home, he sails indecisively just off-shore.

As soon as I have ample information, I make my first visit to the queen in sanctuary at Westminster. It comes as a shock. The accommodation is a far cry from the royal court apartments.

The queen shares one room with her children; her brother, Lionel, and her son, Tom Grey, share another. Although her coffers are full of jewels, and she is dressed in court clothes, they sit oddly with her surroundings. Tapestries adorn the damp stone walls, torn from the royal apartments on the day she fled. The light is dim, and despite the soaring temperatures outside, the air is frigid. To make things worse, the children, having no understanding of their circumstances, are bored, fractious and miserable.

In all this squalor, Elizabeth remains a queen. She orders her one servant to procure food, and complains when it is tainted or poorly cooked.

"The coronation has been moved back to the twenty-second day of June," I whisper. "Nobody knows the reason."

"I know the reason." She spits her words like venom. "He delays because he wants to lay his hands on my Richard, and once he has them both ..."

My eyes stray to where Prince Richard plays ball with Anne, who has been told to entertain him. She passes the ball sulkily back.

"You are no fun, Anne," Richard shouts. "Throw it properly."

To be incarcerated in here with six irritable children is a form of torture. I thank God and his saints I found a way to avoid accompanying her.

"And once he has them, he will seek a way to stop it altogether," the queen continues, drawing back my attention.

"He cannot do that," I hiss.

Elizabeth and Cecily, supposedly nursing Catherine and Bridget, strain their ears to hear our words. I send them a cheery smile.

"Yes. Yes, he can. Or, at least, he will try ..."

"But he will not find a way – my husband assures me the council would not tolerate it."

"Wouldn't they?"

I stare into her hollow eyes, the once radiant face now a landscape of failing hope. The candles dip and dance, the shadows deepening the lines about her eyes, enhancing her despair. She is the keeper of secrets.

The hair on my neck lifts, the sense of danger rising like a wave, drenching me with foreboding.

"Do not come here again." She scrawls a name on a piece of parchment and thrusts it into my hand. "Send to me by way of Dr Lewis; I would lay down my life on his loyalty."

Dr Lewis is my physician, who also provides his services to the queen. We grip hands, and our eyes meet. I hope they express more certainty than I feel.

Here, in the sanctuary of the church, they are as good as captives. My heart goes out to them, my determination to right the wrongs against them uppermost in my heart.

"God be with you, Margaret," she says, her eyes hollow of hope.

I nod speechlessly, suddenly acutely aware that our world, so recently stable, has been turned upside down.

We shall never right it.

I kiss her hand, and find myself suddenly swamped in her embrace. With a grim smile, I wrap my cloak about me and make my way, as quietly as I can, from the dark gloomy rooms the queen must now call home.

Creeping along close to the wall, I am a felon; the thought makes my skin quiver. Before venturing into the open, I pause beneath an arch. There is no one about so, drawing my cloak closer, I take a deep breath and prepare to leave the cover of the wall. As I do so, a figure appears from nowhere and canons into me. I glimpse dark skirts, a plain workaday coif.

"Beg pardon, my lady." The woman flees, her face averted, and I continue on my way. As I go, her voice, her accent, resonates in my ear; I recognise the sound but cannot place it.

Uncertainty and distrust leach from every conduit, every pore of Westminster Palace. My husband is close in his dealings and refuses to speak, even to me. I have no idea if he is loyal to Gloucester, or if he merely bides his time until after the coronation.

Once Edward is crowned and the uncertainty is spent, we will all breathe again. In the meantime, I have to discover what is going on, and to find out Thomas's business, I have to pry without seeming to. Careful not to raise his suspicions I ensure my voice is light, as if his answer does not matter.

None of us can know the path ahead, but I sense great events looming. Alone in my chapel, I pray that, be they good or bad, those I love may emerge unscathed.

Once the boy Edward is king, he can protect his family, the dowager queen can leave sanctuary, and things can return to normal. There will be feasting and dancing again, and Henry can come home. I pray for that; for the comfort of familiar things is the only future I can bear.

Until then, an unnamed threat hangs above our heads like a curse. Yet when the hammer of fate descends, it is so awful that all of us are taken unawares.

I sit in the solar, my eyes blind to the tapestry I pretend to work on. My head teems with ideas, with possible answers, which I dismiss as soon as they form. I have not eaten a full meal for days, the sickness to my stomach making all before me appear green and unappetising. When I hear a step on the stair, I expect to look up to find my woman bringing yet another unappealing dish to tempt me.

"Margaret."

"Thomas." My sewing falls to the floor as I leap to my feet and go to greet him. He is pale, visibly shaken. "What is the matter?"

"I – the Protector – Hastings is dead. Beheaded without trial, without warning, without shrift …"

The blood leaves my head so swiftly I fear I will fall.

"Hastings? How? Why?"

Thomas tries to conceal his trembling but he is as white as a winding sheet. I grab his hand and he winces. I look down to find us both smeared in his blood.

"You are wounded."

"There was a scuffle. I got away. Margaret, I have to tell you, I fear I am about to be arrested for treason."

"Why? What have you done? Tell me from the beginning; what has happened?"

"There was a meeting of the council. At first, it seemed like any other, but I slowly came to realise that Gloucester was uneasy, on edge. His pleasantries with Morton about the tastiness of his strawberries was stilted, like a bad mummer's play. His voice was distant, wooden, as if a curse had been laid upon him. He left us for a while, and we sat around talking, complaining of the heat. Then, when he came back – he was angry; like a beast. I have never seen him like that before. I had always thought of him as a small man ... but in his rage ...

"He began shouting about a plot against him, screaming of treachery, spies, accusing Hastings of betrayal and whoredom, of being the cause of the late king's death. We all sat agog, amazed and unable to speak, until he drew his sword and ordered that Will be taken outside and beheaded, immediately.

"It was a horrific dream. We leapt to our feet and there was a struggle; I think that is when I was injured. Gloucester was raving like a wounded bear, but there was nothing the guard could do but obey him. There was nothing any of us could do to stop him. He is Protector, after all. I have never felt so sick in all my life."

"The queen was right."

"About what?"

After a cursory glance at his wound, I tear a strip from my shift and bind it about his hand; it is just a scratch, but I would like to apply ointment and a clean bandage. There is no time. If Thomas is to escape arrest, he must leave now.

"Go to Westminster; warn the queen what has happened. Perhaps you should stay there ..."

"Sanctuary is no safeguard against York; remember Tewkesbury? No, I will take my chances. He has nothing against me. If I flee, it will make me look guilty when I am not. Margaret, I swear, I am loyal ... to whoever is crowned king."

"I know. Who else is in danger? What others were arrested?"

"Morton."

"The Bishop?"

"Yes, and John Forster too. He also accuses Jane Shore of intriguing against him."

"Jane Shore? Is she innocent?"

He laughs humourlessly.

"Of intrigue, at any rate. Her loyalty to the late king is undeniable, and I see no reason why she would not support his son. Her loyalty to Gloucester is more doubtful."

Suddenly, I recollect the shadowy female form hurrying toward Westminster sanctuary; the voice I could not place. Everything falls into place. I did not recognise Jane Shore without the splendour of her court attire, the merriment stripped from her voice, but I know without doubt it was her.

Thomas watches me, trying to read my explosive thoughts. I gather my wits, before he suspects me of intrigue too.

"This plot. What do you know of it?"

"Nothing! I swear it, Margaret."

He looks unflinchingly into my eyes, and I believe him.

"Nevertheless, you must go now, Thomas, if you value your life."

"I have done nothing wrong."

"No, but remember, my lord, neither had Hastings."

15th June 1483

The day of Jane Shore's shame is the first that I feel any liking for, or any empathy with her. The Protector, a virtuous man compared with his late brother, has a vendetta against fornication, and he punishes Jane by forcing her to make a public walk of penance.

The streets are lined with people come to witness her disgrace, but it will not be her sin that is remembered in the taverns this night. When they recall the punishment of the king's whore, men will speak only of her beauty.

The finery, donated by the late king, has been stripped away, leaving the outline of her body clearly visible through her kirtle. Yet her pride is undamaged, her loveliness undimmed, and she keeps her head high.

I see her with new eyes, discover a lurking admiration and realise there is more to Jane Shore than wantonness.

Some say she did not wait for the king to die before taking up with her lover, William Hastings. It is clear she has colluded with him since and is guilty of intrigue, but Gloucester can prove nothing. Instead, he blames her for the fall of his brother, and for leading his one-time friend into sin.

He charges her with harlotry and, yes, of that she is guilty, but surely, surely no woman on earth deserves punishment such as this.

As I witness her disgrace, I am shamed too, as if this punishment is levelled at all women. How is it that men feel the right to inflict so harsh a penalty? Were it not for male lust, there would be no whores. Jane's virtues, of which there must be many, count for nothing, yet she is not an evil woman.

During her time at court I have never heard her utter an unkind word. Her love for the king was undeniable, her attempts to heal discord at court admirable. Once, when Prince Richard fell in the gardens, I saw Jane take him upon her knee, kiss the sore place on his leg, and distract him by showing him a popinjay. That was not the act of a sinner.

No one is pure; every one of us is touched by sin. Perhaps Gloucester should take care lest his lack of charity comes back to haunt him.

Occasions such as this are usually accompanied by ribaldry; the crowd screaming insults, hurling clods of filth, in some cases punching and kicking the hapless victim. But today, the crowd stays silent as she passes. Her radiant beauty contrasts sharply with the drab streets; the mizzling rain and the bright halo of her hair cast doubt upon the depravity of which she is accused.

As she draws close to where I stand, I lower my eyes, embarrassed in case she should see me watching. I follow her bare, bloodstained feet as they move through the shite of the gutter. My silent prayer is for humanity, for all of us are sinners.

*

I return home with a heavy heart, my thoughts mired with trouble, and find Thomas pacing the floor in the parlour.

"They released you!" I cry, inexplicably pleased to see him. His spell in gaol after his arrest as a suspect in Hastings' plot against the Protector is over. I thank God he has been released so soon.

"You must be starving."

I summon a maid, sending her to fetch us a light supper, and order a bath be made ready in his chambers. We seldom eat together in the privacy of our apartments but distrust and uncertainty are so rife at the court that, tonight, we instinctively keep our own company.

From time to time during our meal, I look up and smile, but Thomas is silent, his thoughts far away. I want to ask about his involvement in the plot. I think I know his mind; I believe his loyalty is to the young king, and he shares my reservations about Gloucester's suitability as Protector, but we do not speak of it. It is safer not to.

Instead, I pour another cup of wine, remarking upon its sweetness, the tastiness of the game pie, the deliciousness of the honeyed tart. His noncommittal grunts serve as reply.

As we finish our meal, Dr Lewis arrives, and I meet him in the privacy of an antechamber. He throws back his concealing hood to reveal a care-lined face that forewarns me of heavy news.

"Gloucester went yesterday morning to see the queen. She says he entreated her to leave sanctuary, promising her safety and a prominent place at court as the king's mother. She refused, will not even consider it."

"Would you trust him, if he had thrown your brother into gaol?"

"Probably not." Dr Lewis shakes his head. "When she refused, he asked that her boy, Richard, be released into his care. He claimed the king is lonely and in need of his brother's company."

I raise my eyebrows at this. Edward and Richard, despite their brotherhood, are not well acquainted. Edward's upbringing took place on the Welsh border, and Richard was raised at Westminster – even when their father was alive, they only met on high days and holidays.

"The queen refuses to leave, and she refuses to give up her son," Dr Lewis whispers. "She accuses the

Protector of ill deeds against her. She says he bullies her. As a result, Gloucester has lost patience and has placed a ring of guards about the sanctuary. I can no longer enter unobserved."

"The queen will know to feign sickness so that you will be permitted to see her. Gloucester will not want her to die; that would look bad for him."

He shakes his sorry head, rubs his beard, which rasps beneath his fingers.

"I will be watched. I have a bad feeling," he says. "The Protector means to have his way."

Our eyes meet. His are bloodshot and tired. What can we do? What can any of us do to stop this?

I perch on the edge of the table, my thoughts scurrying in search of a path through this maze of doubt. Nothing is sure, and nobody is a certain friend. I cast my thoughts back to other times when I knew not whom to trust. Was there ever a woman as fraught with trouble as I?

The face of Anne Neville floats before me, her return to court after Tewkesbury before Gloucester first took her for his wife. She was as lost then as ever a woman has been. An idea suddenly springs into my mind, as if from nowhere.

"I have heard that the Protector's wife travelled south for the coronation. Perhaps I could pay her a visit, discover if she is party to her husband's plans."

"Oh, be careful, my lady. If you are implicated with the dowager queen ..."

"I am aware of that, Dr Lewis. The Lady Anne is a good, trusting soul. I will be quite safe. Be alert for a summons. I may be feeling unwell in a day or two and have need of you."

I order my women to make ready my finest clothes. Despite her status, Anne Neville is a modest woman; it should not be difficult to overwhelm her with grandeur. Pretending more confidence than I feel, I sweep up the stairs of Crosby Place and ask to be conducted to her apartment.

"Lady Margaret, this is a surprise," she says when I am shown into her presence. I look for deceit in the warmth of her greeting, but find none. Her parlour is littered with embroidery silks and scraps of fabric. "I do apologise, I was not expecting guests."

She begins to tidy up the table, placing colour upon colour while I look about and take a seat without invitation.

"I hope you are well." I cast my eye over her delicate features and decide she does not look hale. Always thin, she is now drawn as well, as if marriage to the Duke of Gloucester is wearing.

"I am a little tired from the journey. I do not travel well."

"And your son, he is well too, I trust?"

"Oh." Her face softens. "Yes, he is very well. I miss him when I come away; that is why we spent so much time in Yorkshire before ..."

"You have no need to tell me about missing a son, Lady Anne. I have been parted from mine for ... oh, it must be twelve years or more now. The pain of missing him still bites deep."

She looks at me, pale and calm, her eyes shining with unshed tears. I suddenly realise the futility of challenging such a pliant woman, and my body relaxes. I feel like a bully and lower my gaze to the floor. The hem of her gown is muddy, the leg of her chair has been chewed, and a bone with scraps of meat still on rests on the edge of the hearth. She follows the direction of my eye.

"Richard gave me a puppy ... to stop me from fretting. His teeth are very sharp."

I am tempted to ask if it is the puppy or her husband whose bite is sharp. But she is not worthy prey. I cluck my tongue when she shows me her wrist, which is peppered with tiny red teeth marks, and then I change the subject.

"We are all looking forward to the coronation. Such a shame it was postponed."

She giggles. "Such a funny thing. The coronation robes had been made too small, and had to be done again. Richard was quite furious, but boys are like that, are they not? They grow in fits and spurts."

"Henry was much the same," I murmur, hoping against hope her explanation is true.

"It is only a few days to wait now," she says. "Oh, look, here are our refreshments." Our conversation lapses while a girl places the platters on the table, and pours wine into two cups. "I am so sorry that the queen – the dowager queen - will miss the ceremony. If it were my son, I would not miss it for the world."

"Nor I," I say, momentarily distracted by the sudden image of Henry, splendidly arrayed at Westminster Cathedral while the crown of England is lowered onto his head.

I shake myself and smile wider to disguise the Judas words I must speak. "I fear the loss of her husband has unhinged the queen a little, and pray to God she makes a speedy recovery."

"At least she saw sense and allowed her littlest boy to join the king. My husband was relieved when she gave in."

"She released Richard? He is in the Tower with his brother?"

"Yes, did you not know? My husband managed to persuade her it was for the best. We were so relieved, it was causing such gossip. We are going to visit them later ... I have some lovely gifts for them."

My heart thumps; I can hear clearly, loud it in my ears. Both boys are in the Tower. How did this happen without my knowledge?

The queen must be out of her mind. Gloucester must have applied force, or maybe Elizabeth learned something that gave her peace of mind, made her feel safe to trust him.

I cast aside the thought of little Richard in that oppressive place, and manage to smile brightly.

"So, will you live permanently at court now that your husband is Lord Protector?"

She plucks at a loose thread on her skirt.

"Not ... I doubt I will be here all the time. Edward ... it is better for the children to live at Middleham."

"Children? I thought there was just the one son?"

She flushes, her pale face suddenly as red as her bodice.

"Richard's natural son and daughter, John and Catherine, make their home with us. They are part of the family now."

"How nice," I say, my mind reeling with the knowledge that Gloucester, who is so damning of fornication, is not innocent of the sin himself.

I am torn between my need to meet the queen again and my desire to remain outwardly impartial. If I am caught fraternising with those who make an enemy of the Protector, I could damage my status at court. I have to think of Henry. If I find favour with the Protector, there is still the chance he will allow my son to come home.

Falling foul of Gloucester could mean that I end up in need of sanctuary too. That will not do at all. I decide to make a friend of Anne Neville, to become as involved with the forthcoming coronation as I can, and to curry favour with Gloucester.

We put aside talk of politics and concentrate on smaller things. I learn that she likes to hunt on the moors around her childhood home; she has a hawk named Nemesis, and a puppy called Troy. We have just begun to share our love of flowers when a door opens. We both turn toward the sounds of footsteps when she leaps from her chair.

"Richard, my lord. Lady Margaret has called."

Gloucester moves forward with a smile of greeting, an outstretched hand.

"Lady Margaret, we are honoured."

His hand is warm. He bends over me, his lips skimming the back of my wrist. I pretend not to be flustered.

"I meant to call on Lady Anne sooner, my lord, but – I recently suffered a chill."

I will make penance for the small lie later. We settle down, resume our conversation. Gloucester perches on the arm of his wife's chair, his hand on her shoulder, one finger caressing the base of her neck. It is an unconscious act, as if touching her is part of his nature.

"The gardens at Middleham are lovely, Lady Margaret; one day you must come and visit them. They are at their best in July; the summer takes a little longer to reach us in the north."

"I would love to come. You must visit my house at Woking. It is my favourite residence."

When the maid comes back with the puppy, it gambols into the room, tracking mud on the floor and planting two large footprints on the duke's tunic. Laughing, Gloucester picks him up by the scruff of his neck and tucks him beneath his arm.

"I am going to rue the day I brought this chap into the household," he laughs, tickling the pup behind the ear.

During the afternoon, although my conversation is mainly with Anne, I watch Gloucester carefully. I am confused. It is impossible to comprehend that this mild-mannered man, so obviously in love with his plain little wife, is the same fellow who sent Hastings to his death; who is not above bullying the queen for possession of her son; and who does not even attempt to disguise his hatred for the queen's family. He is attentive and pleasant, amusing and gentle. Either he is playing a game and blatantly deceiving me, or he is not the tyrant rumour reports him to be.

I take my leave of them, more confused than I was before, and with few answers to the questions that rattle in my mind.

On the day that Richard of Gloucester dispenses with his mourning clothes and appears in public clad in purple, speculation bubbles from the bowels of the city.

There is much to do before a coronation, many details, both small and large, to attend to, but rumour has it that the business he pursues is not that of the young king.

The Protector rides through the streets, between Baynard's Castle and Crosby Place, a great train of lords in his wake. Rumour is rife in the taverns and hostelries, malicious tales of evil intent, but no one can untangle truth from lie. We have just a few days to wait until the coronation; surely, nothing can go amiss now.

I have a new crimson gown with sarcanet sleeves, a headdress in the latest style, and a lightweight summer cloak. The arrangements have been made, the royal robes are ready, the streets swept and washed, and the crown of England polished and buffed ready to grace young Edward's brow.

Soon it will be done, I tell myself, and once the new king is on the throne, all will be well and things will return to normal.

St Paul's, London - 22nd June 1483

The sun, tardy so far this year, chooses this day to raise its head. It burns down like a punishment upon the nobles, magnates and commoners summoned to St. Paul's Cross.

Dr Shaw, an obese man unsuited to so hot a morning, emerges from the church, takes his place before the cross, and clears his throat. A trickle of sweat journeys down his brow to the ridge of his nose. He wipes it away and looks with apprehension at the gathered crowd. After a glance at the sheaf of papers in his hand, he begins to speak.

His voice wavers, and then grows stronger. He glances up at us, and then away again. The people at the front begin to repeat his words dully, and as the intent behind them magnifies, murmurs of disbelief turn to outrage. The news swims swiftly through the assembly, like a flame held to the edge of a paper.

"Bastard slips shall take no root ..." he cries, his sweat running like tears. While I stand fixed to the ground like a rock, brother turns to brother, neighbour to neighbour, questioning, sceptical ... uncertain.

"What is he saying?" a woman near me asks her friend. "The prince is a bastard? The king's marriage was no marriage?"

"That's what he said."

"What's a pre-contract then? What does that mean?"

"It means he wasn't free to marry her. The Woodville woman was his whore ... for all those years ... and when I think of all her airs and graces ..."

They wander into the crowd, but still I cannot move. The significance of this moment does not immediately register in my mind. I hear a loud buzzing, like a swarm of bees. I think it is in my head.

A pre-contract? Can it be true? Elizabeth, the king's mistress, no better than Jane Shore? Those darling boys, those perfect princesses, bastards all?

I remember Elizabeth's fear, Elizabeth's white face on the day she clutched my sleeve and spoke the words. "There are things Gloucester must never discover about the king."

Instinctively, I know it is true. Poor Elizabeth is disliked by commoner and courtier alike; her virtue and grace never able to overcome the unforgivable stain of her common stock.

My feet lead me back toward the litter. I climb numbly on board and travel, without noticing, to Westminster. On the stairs, I bump into Thomas, and seeing my dazed state he turns and leads me to our apartments. The familiar rooms seem strange after the events of the morning. Nothing will be the same again. We stand, as if spell bound, not knowing what to do, what to say.

"It is not going to happen then?" His face is dark, lined, and troubled.

"It does not seem so."

We both stare at nothing; the drapes on the bed, my book of hours left open, the brightness of the page so clean, so pure against the grime of the world we live in. I am so tired; my limbs are too heavy and the air in the chamber feels like treacle.

"What will happen now?"

He runs his big hands across his face, which has the pallor of putty, and into his hair, leaving it standing upright, as if it, too, is shocked. Our eyes meet in a horrid acknowledgement of his words before he speaks them.

"Gloucester will have the crown."

I think for a moment, shaking my head to try to clear my mind and organise my thoughts.

"What of Warwick's boy? Clarence's son - what of him?"

"Well, there is an attainder on him for his father's sins. Besides, Gloucester has the support of the council – no one wants a boy king."

"Not even you."

He turns bleak, defeated eyes upon me.

"No, Margaret, not even me."

26th June 1483

I feel sick. Everyone feels sick. When the lords petition the Protector to accept the throne, he makes great protest against it. He is not born to be king, he says, he is happier in the north. Yet after just one day of dissembling, he agrees. King Edward's marriage to Elizabeth is declared invalid, their offspring bastards. The sons of York are deposed – as simple as that.

Later, when I have soaked for an hour in a hot bath, suffered warm oil to be rubbed into my skin and my hair is smoothed and braided, a knock falls on my chamber door.

I hasten into a loose robe, thinking, *surely there cannot be more bad news.*

"Dr Lewis, at this late hour? I am sorry for keeping you waiting…"

The flames from the hearth throw fleeting shadows across his face, and I cannot determine if his expression is one of fear or sorrow. His words, when they come, speak of both.

"These are terrible times, my lady, terrible times, but I fear it will get worse. The queen is tearing out her hair ..."

"I would imagine she is. I will try to see her as soon-"

He holds up his hand, rudely silencing me.

"You do not know the half of it, my lady. The queen learned this afternoon that, yesterday, on the orders of the Lord Protector, her brother Lord Rivers, and her son Richard Grey were beheaded at Pontefract Castle."

*

I borrow the clothes of one of my servants, wrap her threadbare hood about my head and sneak from the house under cover of darkness. The night hides me from unwelcome eyes, but still I keep to the deepest shadows, walking as close as I dare to the wall.

Street refuse is thick beneath my feet and beggars lurk on the blackest corners. Fear churns in my belly. I have never been abroad unaccompanied so late before.

On my arm, I carry a basket of herbs; in my belt, for the sake of security, my knife is unsheathed. I should have confided in Ned, sent him in my stead, but I know it is me Elizabeth wants to see. She will not trust a go-between, not anymore.

For weeks, the Protector's men have ringed the sanctuary, watching and reporting every visit, but now that both princes are in his hands, the queen is no longer watched so closely. I work my way around the perimeter until I reach the northwest corner of the precinct. There is just one door. I sidle toward it, looking over my shoulder for signs of pursuit. My hand creeps up the thick oak, groping for the knocker. I hang on to it before letting it fall, the resounding noise of my quest for admittance echoing along the passages.

It feels as if I wait forever for admittance. I bite my lip, sure that any moment a hand will fall upon my shoulder. Footsteps sound inside, and the grille slides back. A pair of wide blue eyes stares out, blinking into the darkness. I lift the edge of my hood and turn my face slightly into the moonlight. The door opens, and I squeeze through the small space.

Princess Elizabeth's cheeks are ghostly white and her once merry face is sullen, her eyes ringed with worry and lack of fresh air. Here in sanctuary, she is like a pearl on the murky ocean floor; as the tide of sorrow rises, her beauty remains unadmired, her potential hidden.

"Where is the queen?"

I follow the direction of her pointing finger, her footsteps pattering in my wake.

"We cannot make her stop weeping, she will not listen ... it has been days."

The gloom in the inner vault is lifted only by the light of a single torch. The royal children sit in a row on a narrow bench, where Cecily nurses baby Bridget in her lap. On the low uncurtained bed, a figure lies prostrate. I step closer and put down my basket.

"Your Grace? I came as soon as I heard."

This is not true. I detest myself for taking time to bathe, and see to my own selfish needs. I hope she never learns of it. On hearing my voice, she stirs, raising her head from the pillows to look at me.

Her face is ravaged, reddened and lined with weeping, her hair snarled and matted, as if it has not seen a comb for a month.

"Margaret..." Her voice is thick, hoarse from weeping. Our once glorious queen pulls herself up to sit hunched on the edge of the bed, staring at the floor. To keep my mouth from falling open, I clench my jaw until my teeth hurt.

"I have brought food, medicine ... chamomile ..." I rummage in the basket and turn to the princess. "Elizabeth, could you prepare your mother an infusion of chamomile?"

The princess, who has never received orders in her life, takes the package and wordlessly goes to do as she is bid.

"When did you last eat, Your Grace?"

Her eyes are hollow and her skin sallow; when she speaks, I realise that the sparkle that won her the love of the king has died during the course of these last sad weeks. The last vestige of her youth has fled. She shakes her head.

"I do not remember."

"Here. I brought you some pastries."

I hold one out to her and slowly she takes it, holding it as if she is unsure what to do with it.

"Try a bite, Your Grace. They are very tasty."

Like an ailing child, she nibbles the edge, chews as if it is made of soot. Crumbs cling to her lips but she does not lick them off. I hold out a cup of wine, but she shakes her head, and the hand holding the pastry drops to her lap.

"You heard what he did?"

"I did, yes. I – I am so ... sorry."

What a futile word 'sorry' is; if only I could think of a better one. She laughs mirthlessly.

"Why are you sorry? You had nothing to do with it. It is Gloucester who will be sorry ..."

Spitting crumbs and dribble, she speaks his name as if it is anathema. I realise that the balance of her mind is quite lost, and have no idea what to do, or how to help her.

"Elizabeth is making a tisane of chamomile," I say, for want of something better.

"Chamomile? What good will that do? It is a sword I need, an army and a strong king to lead it! Oh god, Margaret, I always feared this would happen ... I warned Edward ..."

She stops suddenly, as if afraid of saying too much. It is true then; the pre-contract, the lie they spun to the realm. Her sons have no true claim to the throne. Those poor little boys ...

I pick up a comb. "Let me brush your hair, Your Grace. You know how it soothes you."

I can feel the tension in her shoulders, the set of her head. I pick up a strand of matted hair. There are traces of silver in it now; just a few months ago, she was as fair as an angel.

It just illustrates what love and loss can do. As I tease out knots, I relate news of mutual friends, anything to keep her mind from her bereavement, and my own mind from the taunting realisation that the illegitimacy of her sons adds abounding strength to my Henry's claim to the throne.

"I curse Gloucester," she growls, as if she is endowed with the powers of witchcraft. "I curse him and all those he loves. I condemn him to pain and suffering such as he has inflicted on me, and I wish it to come upon him speedily."

Under other circumstances, I would laugh, but our gentle queen plays the part of a loathsome sorceress very well. I shudder. If I were not so reluctant to offend her, I would cross myself against evil.

The comb slides though her hair. One side is smooth now, free of tangles. I select another section and begin work on it.

"I saw your sons the other day."

She turns suddenly, grabbing my wrist, making me drop the comb.

"What did they say? Are they well? Do they forgive me for placing them in the hands of that ... beast?"

"I did not see them to speak to. They were playing on the Tower green as I passed by. They were shooting arrows, and seemed very well."

"For now." She subsides into melancholy again. "Oh, what will become of them? Why did I let this happen? Margaret, listen to me; if you ever find yourself working against your better judgement, think again. Our inner minds always warn us when we are about to err, but we seldom listen ... we seldom listen."

Elizabeth enters with a tray of steaming cups, but I barely notice her arrival. The queen's words have more than a ring of truth; I heard that inner voice before I left our apartments this evening.

Stay home, it said. *Do not meddle.* But I did not heed it. I came anyway.

I take the cup the princess offers; it is too hot, so I place it on the table and turn back to the queen's toilette.

Cecily is telling the children a story about a knight on a quest to rescue his anointed queen. The fair heads of York's children are poised for the conclusion of the tale.

What will become of them now? Royal bastards, their fortunes and future lost.

It is as if fate takes hold of me, forces me into action, and puts words into my mouth I have no wish to speak.

"Your Grace." I kneel in front of her and grasp her hands. "Gloucester has the support of the council, but there are many who resent and despise his actions. There are many who were loyal to King Edward whose true allegiance is with your son. Perhaps all is not yet lost."

She stares unseeing, unspeaking, her lack of response prompting me to continue.

"You must have patience, and put your faith in God. He will instruct us, if we only listen. I think, for the time being, we should pretend to support the Protector's claim. There may yet be ways and means for us to win back what is lost. God will show us the way ..."

"Gloucester is a monster; a usurper; the murderer of my son, and my brother. How can I feign trust in him when every fibre of my being cries out for his destruction?"

I sigh and frown into the sulky flames of the brazier, trying to fit the picture she paints to the man who entertained me so pleasantly the other afternoon. Gloucester does not have the eyes of a monster. Whichever way I look at it, I cannot make that picture fit.

"Your Grace, if I have realised one thing, it is that no human is purely evil; each of us must do as we must do, and suffer the consequences. If our own plans are to be fulfilled, then there are those who will suffer. They in turn will denounce us. If we fail in our resolve, we will be remembered as monstrous women – like Margaret of Anjou –or ... or Isabella of France. She was no she-wolf, yet that is how she is remembered. Gloucester is not a monster; he is a man of greed, a man of ambition, and he will do anything to achieve what he wants. Just as you would; just as I would."

Her eyes bore into mine. I detect a little madness, and a great determination.

"Just as we *will* do, Margaret. You and I *will* succeed in ousting Gloucester from my son's throne. If it is the last thing I do, or if I must deal with the devil to do it, Gloucester shall not keep his stolen crown."

Westminster - July 5th 1485

I have been summoned by Anne Neville to attend her later this afternoon, but first my husband and I wait upon the man who is soon to be king.

When we are shown into his presence, Gloucester is seated at a desk piled high with papers, scratching words upon a page. He stands when he sees us, wipes his ink-stained fingers on a cloth and moves toward us, hand outstretched.

He wears a short gown of crimson velvet with drip tassels and tawny sleeves. My immediate thought is how quickly and easily he put aside mourning for his beloved brother. His eyes are shadowed, but I can detect no sign of remorse for his callous actions.

"Stanley, Lady Margaret. I am glad to see you."

My husband and I make the proper response; Thomas's smile is wide and genuine, while mine is false. He ushers me to a seat and, as I take my place, a knock comes on the door and William Hussey, the lord's chief justice, enters and joins us around the table.

Gloucester wastes no time on idle talk.

"We value your support in these unhappy times, and we are pleased to reward our friends."

Thomas's chest swells in gratitude. I make a soundless mew with my lips and smile feigned affection.

"Lady Margaret, it has been brought to my notice that there is some dispute between you and the Orleans family. Some debt that is outstanding?"

"That is so, my lord."

I am wary now, uncertain of his intentions. For a moment, our eyes lock. His face closed and serious and I pray mine is the same. I must give no indication of resentment, never let him suspect my heart is with the deposed prince, and his little brother, Richard.

What are they feeling or thinking now, with no idea what is happening? Shut away from the world, deprived of their mother and family. Has this man no heart?

"I shall order it to be paid forthwith."

I had not expected that. My face relaxes into a smile as I realise he has not summoned me to inflict some sort of punishment, but to buy me as his friend.

I wonder if it is a good time to broach the subject of Henry's pardon. I open my mouth to speak but Gloucester sits down, running his hands over his face before turning to Hussey. "See that it is done," he says.

I splutter my thanks, while Thomas beams his pleasure and turns the talk to tomorrow's coronation.

For all the underlying sorrow of a population still reeling from the deposition of the boy king, Gloucester is determined it will be a splendid day. The arrangements for young Edward's crowning remain in place; the only change in the proceedings is the monarch himself.

"I have ordered extra guards to ensure security is tight. Our cousin ... ah!" He breaks off as the door opens to admit Henry Stafford, the Duke of

Buckingham. He is tall and fair in the style of the late king, an imposing figure in any company. Although wed to Elizabeth's sister, he is no friend to the Woodvilles, and has hitherto kept from court, returning only with the rise of Gloucester.

"I was just speaking of you," Gloucester says, sweeping his arm wide to invite Buckingham into the company. As the duke takes his place among us, I examine him for some family likeness, but see none.

Ignoring me, the men delve into the plans for the next day. I lower my gaze to my lap where my fingers are furiously entwined. How dare they ignore my presence and exclude me from the conversation as if I were of no account?

"Lady Margaret." Gloucester breaks the conversation. "This is dull talk. I believe you have an engagement with my wife this afternoon. She could talk of nothing else over breakfast. Would you like to leave us?"

After a startled pause, I rise to my feet and curtsey in a middling way, since until tomorrow he is my equal, not my king.

"You are very kind, my lord. I thank you."

Thomas accompanies me to the door and kisses my hand before we part, pleasure at the events of the morning kindling in his eye.

As I walk swiftly through the palace, my mind is teeming; gratitude and resentment battling for supremacy.

*

Anne stands at the window. She turns when I am announced and hurries forward to meet me in the centre of the room.

"I hope you did not think my invitation was a summons," she says apologetically, gripping my hands tightly. "I meant it as a request from a friend."

"Of course." My smile for Gloucester's wife is genuine. She has done nothing yet to earn my distrust.

"Come, let us sit down." She leads me to the window, where she has spent the morning with her needle. She moves a piece of half-stitched linen. "So much has happened since I saw you last, Lady Margaret. I hardly know what to say."

"So I would imagine. It is a surprising turn of events."

"You cannot be more astonished than I. It is not something I ever looked for, I was quite happy ..."

"You told me so before. Is your son coming for the ceremony? I suppose there will not be time."

"No. Everything happened so fast. Those poor little boys must be so ... confused. Their lives turned upside down."

I clutch my fingers tightly, and keep my lips sealed. I can never give voice to all that I would like to say.

"Did you visit them since ... the news ..."

"We went a few days ago, but ... things did not go well. They are resentful, believing it was Richard's plan all along. I swear to you, Margaret, it was not. They were sulky and quite rude, I fear. The elder boy, Edward, complained he felt unwell, and little Richard is bored. He complained of missing his mother, and asked to go home."

My heart squirms as I imagine his sorrow. My poor little lord. There is no one to comfort him there.

"Hopefully, they will be back in their mother's care soon."

Anne's eyes are bloodshot, swimming with tears, her thin throat working with emotion.

"Richard says not. He says they cannot be released into her care until she leaves sanctuary and swears fealty to him as king."

The sun will rise in the west before that day comes. I sigh and murmur platitudes, watching as she pours us both a cup of wine.

"I must get used to waiting for the servants to do this sort of thing for me," she sighs. "I have ever been one to look to myself, ever since George imprisoned me in that cookhouse."

I splutter into my cup, cough a little and dab my lips with a kerchief.

"I had always supposed that to be false rumour, Lady Anne. You mean it was true?"

"Oh yes. He – he did not want to share my father's wealth with Richard, and when he discovered we wanted to wed, he took me there under false pretences and ordered me not to leave. He – he was not … very nice. He threatened all sorts of dire retribution on my mother and Isabel if I disobeyed."

She plucks her skirt with long thin fingers, biting her lip as her mind returns to those dark days. Anne has lived as rough a life as I; worse in fact. At least I am strong and, as far as I am able, have taken control of my future. All her life, Anne has been buffeted by the men who had jurisdiction over her. First married to Edward of Lancaster at her father's whim; then widowed and passed into the charge of her brother-in-law; then held hostage in a bake house. Now, just when she has achieved all her desires and borne a son to a loving husband, her life is turned upside down again.

I believe Anne when she claims she has never craved power or riches, and I know without doubt she does not look to be queen but, as usual, she will do as she is told. The strain on her face prompts me to search for words to make her feel better. I adopt a cheery smile.

"Sometimes, when it seems our path is littered with troubles, those troubles become joy."

I think of my unlooked-for marriage to Edmund, and the unexpected happiness that followed. Even his death, that broke my heart, was tempered by the birth of Henry. "When life looks bleak, there is always light behind the next cloud."

"Oh, I do hope so, Lady Margaret. Your words give me comfort. I was wondering if you would be so kind as to bear my train tomorrow, and serve me at the banquet. I am anxious about the trials of the day, and it will be reassuring to have a friend close at hand. You can intervene if it looks as if I am about to do something wrong."

This time, my smile is genuine.

"I shall be honoured, Your Grace. And remember, you will be queen. Queens can do no wrong."

Westminster - 6th July 1483

Anne is trembling. Her fear is tangible through the velvet and ermine train that I clasp between my fingers. As testament to their humility, the king and queen walk barefoot on a crimson carpet, but that is where the self-effacement ends.

No expense has been spared for this coronation; even the royal dogs have new jewelled collars. The streets of London have been decked with cloth of gold, and the white boar flies high above our heads. Some say that the joy of the crowd has been purchased, and if that is the case, then they do well, for their cries of *God Save the King* are deafening. The fickle hearts of commoners pay no heed to the fallen who paved Gloucester's way to his stolen crown.

The sun glints across the sea of gold, red and blue; it dances on the bristling maces, mitres and crosiers. I have seen formality before, but none such as this. This day takes ceremony to the extreme and no one wants to miss it. Every notable in the country is here; some come with gladness, relieved that the problem of a boy king has been avoided. Some come with trepidation, suspicious of the new king but anxious to ingratiate themselves with him.

Gossips whisper of how the dowager queen screamed with fury when she learned of the honour bestowed upon me, and although I keep my chin high, my thoughts do stray to her.

How must she feel today? Gloucester's crown seals the fall of her son, severing her elite path, spelling the demise of her power. Now and forever, she will be just Elizabeth Grey, the mistress of the late king. How capricious is fortune, how she must curse it. To think I envied her once.

The procession passes slowly through the crowded street, a vast serpent of power crawling ever closer to the cathedral. From a balcony above the street, young girls cast flower petals into the air and they rain down upon us like jewels in a shower of white and red. I can see little from my place of honour behind the queen, but somewhere up ahead, Thomas, bearing the Constable's mace, takes precedence over every duke and earl present. He will gloat of his triumph later. He has high hopes for Gloucester's reign, swears we will rise high beneath him.

Anne stumbles, dragging my thoughts back to the present. We pause momentarily while she steadies herself. I ensure her train is straight and follow as she moves on again. The head of the cavalcade is ascending the steps to the church. I wonder if Elizabeth and her daughters can see us. They cannot fail to hear the clarion of trumpets, the traitorous pleasure of the crowd.

At the west door, we pause again. Anne turns to me, her face tight with tension.

"Oh, Lady Margaret, I feel I will be sick."

"No, you won't, Your Grace. You must not even think of it."

A piece of rose petal flutters down and sticks to her chin. I reach forward and remove it, show her it on the tip of my finger.

"Thank you," she says. "Are my cheeks as red as they feel?"

Embarrassed at so much attention, her cheeks are scarlet, a sheen of sweat on her nose. Her lips are pale; her eyes red; poor Anne is not the stuff queens are made of.

I feel a sudden empathy with her. If I were in her place, I would not look the part either; few women possess the natural poise of Elizabeth Woodville. I have heard that it was wet on the day of her coronation, yet she shone like a diamond through the drops of rain. Anne is so homely, even the sunshine cannot make her fair.

"You are glowing, Your Grace, and quite beautiful," I lie. She blushes all the deeper and flaps her hand at me.

"I fear you exaggerate, Lady Margaret. If beauty were wealth, I would surely be a beggar."

"Come, they are waiting for you."

She grimaces before turning around to face the coming ordeal. As I pick up the end of her heavy train again, the doors open wide and a fanfare of music greets us as we enter the nave.

As Anne takes her place beside the king, I have the leisure to observe him for the first time this day. Beside Buckingham and the Duke of Norfolk, he seems small; his face is pinched and pensive. For a moment, I am reminded of a boy in his big brother's clothes, ill-at-ease, uncomfortable, as if his sumptuous velvet robes are lined with thorns. The look he gives Anne when she takes her place beside him is one of compassion, as if he understands her anxiety and shares it.

The great golden shrine of Westminster Abbey endures, as we must endure the interminable ceremony. Richard of Gloucester takes his place in a line of monarchs stretching endlessly into the past. When the time comes, Richard and Anne's upper clothes are removed, and Thomas Bourchier, the Archbishop of Canterbury, anoints them both with holy oil.

I wonder it does not burn him.

The ceremony over, the company retires to Westminster Hall, where the king and queen retire from the company for a while. I help her from the heavy robe and escort her to a withdrawing room before returning to the throng.

A babble of voices greets me as people cram into a hall hung for a banquet. Everywhere I look, I see cloth of gold and crimson; candles and torches blaze, and there are garlands of flowers, petals strewn on pristine table cloths.

A great cry goes up, and squeals of delighted terror from the women, as the Duke of Norfolk rides a gold-trapped charger into the hall. A shiver of delight spreads across the company as he halts at the dais, the great hooves striking sparks from the floor. In a bellowing voice, he orders the spectators to quit the palace to allow the feasting to begin.

They slowly leave, craning their necks for one last look at the grandeur of the royal palace. As the crowd thins and Norfolk nudges his horse away, I realise my hands are covering my mouth. I drop them to my sides, regain my composure and take my seat.

When the king and queen re-join us, the company stands as one, raising their voices in welcome. Then, one by one, we take turns to swear fealty. When it is my turn to leave my kiss upon the royal ring, I summon my composure, forcing serenity into my movement.

As I rise from my knees, the king catches my eye. "We are pleased to have you here, Lady Margaret," he says, his voice low but resonant with meaning.

He gives a smile, fleeting, like an arrow in flight, and then it is gone. As I return to my seat, careful not to turn my back on them, his face becomes sombre again.

The feast begins. King Richard sits at the centre of the table, two squires prone at his feet. He is served by Norfolk and Surrey, while Lord Audeley carves his meat. The king's closest friends, Percy, and Lovell, offer him morsels from dishes of silver and gold. It must seem strange to them to pay homage to a boyhood friend, to show dutiful obedience to one with whom they once tumbled in play.

A procession of young men ushers in bowls of food and jugs of wine. Beside me, the king's sister, the Duchess of Suffolk, shakes out a napkin.

As server to the queen, I take my place at her shoulder and, as the cloth of estate is raised over her, I can see from the set of her head and the tension in her shoulders that she longs for an end to it all.

She nibbles at each dish set before her, drinks sparingly of the wine. She has just raised a cup to her lips when the door is thrown open with a bang and a fanfare of trumpets. She jumps visibly, as if expecting an attack, and I hurry forward to dab the splash of wine from her gown. She smiles nervously.

"Thank you, Margaret. I am such a fool to be so startled."

"The hall is more like a stable today, Your Grace," I murmur as Sir Robert Dymmock, the King's Champion spurs his red-and-white trapped steed to the foot of the dais. Sir Robert, clad in white armour, sits tall in the saddle to deliver his challenge.

The company respond with a shattering cry. "King Richard! King Richard!"

Anne winces, cowering a little from the din, but manages to maintain her smile. I mouth the words along with the rest, but emit no sound.

Elizabeth, in the squalor of her chosen retreat, must surely hear it. She will picture me here, cheering for the usurper. I am torn between pity for her and compassion for this new queen, who I doubt has the heart to bear it.

As I watch the champion drink from the golden chalice, I send up a silent prayer for them both. Having drunk his fill, Sir Robert casts the dregs of his wine cup onto the floor, bows to the king and queen, and kicks his horse into retreat, leaving the hall ringing with cheers.

I look about at the ruddy faces, the loyal subjects of King Richard the Third. How fickle they are. I once saw many of these people swear allegiance to King Henry, and later, I witnessed their pledges of obedience to the usurping Edward of York. Now, despite Gloucester's offences, they turn their coats again to become loyal subjects to another son of York.

As I watch them, I wonder if all men are inconstant, if all loyalty is transient. I must remember always to be wary, to place my trust in no-one.

A few days later, the king and queen leave for a royal progress. Pleading a slight malady, I remain behind, and at the first opportunity make my way by stealth to the sanctuary at St Peter's.

"I heard you were there," she says, "carrying the baggage's train, serving her at the banquet – how could you do that?"

I should defend Anne; she is not a baggage, just a woman caught up in a male game, as we all are, but defending Anne to Elizabeth would be like waving a stick at a serpent. I opt instead for appeasement.

"I did as I was told, as I always have. Serving her does not dent my allegiance to you."

"You no longer address me as is my right. It used to be 'Your Grace this – Your Grace that.' What happened to your subservience?"

I sigh and look across at the children, who are gathered in the light of the one small window as if hungry for freedom and air.

"I am sure there are more important things to be discussed. Have you forgotten our plan? Do you have any news to share with me?"

"So you can take it all to him? To your friend, the usurper?"

I keep my eyes lowered, my temper tightly bound.

"I would not do that. Anyway, the k-- they are on progress until the end of the summer."

She makes no apology for her accusation.

"Did you hear that my brother has taken two ships of the line and a small fortune in gold and joined your son in Brittany?"

"No, I have had no word from Henry for some time."

I begin to consider what this could mean, but Elizabeth interrupts me again, drawing me along another train of thought.

"And what of my sons? Have you news of them? Are they safe? Lord, what must they make of all this?"

"Everyone is safe in the Tower, Madam, from outside forces at least."

I do not miss her smug smile at my absentminded use of the title 'Madam.'

"We have to get them out; get them to safety overseas."

"But how is that possible? How can we gain access to the Tower? It will do no good asking permission to visit. We cannot come and go from the Tower as we please."

I make a mental list of those with the authority to enter the Tower. As each name appears in my mind, writ clear in large black letters, I strike them through with my imaginary pen. I trust none of them.

"What about Buckingham? He is your kin is he not?"

"And in Gloucester's pocket!"

"Perhaps those pockets are not as snug or as deep as we think. I have resources; we could bribe him."

"Elizabeth, we must be cautious. We cannot run at this like a bull at a gate. Buckingham is as rich as you and I. It would need something more, some carrot he cannot refuse ..."

"Like what? An offer of power perhaps, when we succeed in restoring my son to his throne?"

Elizabeth leans forward and grabs my hand, her former hostility abandoned. "We can offer him the Protectorship, or something equally lucrative."

"He is already Lord High Constable – there is nothing higher. Oh, there must be a way. I need to think ..."

I put my face in my hands to shut out the oppression of these gloomy chambers. What would tempt a man like Buckingham?

"We need a man of stealth, of iron will – someone we can trust."

"We can trust no one."

The light is failing and her eyes shine in the glow of the candle.

"If only Morton were still at large. He was invaluable before; everyone trusts a man of God. If only our previous strategy had not failed."

I prick my ears. This is the first mention she has made of her involvement in the plot that spelled the end of William Hastings.

"You worked with them? You and Morton were in league with Hastings ... and Jane Shore?"

She shrugs.

"For the good it did any of us. Look at us now. Hastings is dead, Morton under lock and key in Brecknock, the Shore Whore humiliated and languishing in Ludgate gaol; and me ... Margaret, just look at me ..."

She breaks off, plunges her face into her hands. I watch helplessly as her back heaves. God forfend that I should ever fall so low.

"Where is Buckingham now?"

She raises her head, wiping away tears with the back of her hand.

"I do not know."

"I wonder if he rode north with the king, or if he is planning to return to his estates in Wales ..."

She sniffs inelegantly.

"And if he has?"

"Then, perchance, I might be riding that way too and meet him on the road."

Bridgenorth - August 1483

The day is hot, the dust of the road stifling. I long to order the steward to stop at the next inn, but if my plan to intercept Buckingham is to succeed, then I must bear the discomfort with as much grace as possible.

I have sent most of the household ahead, and follow on with a small company of guards, my steward, and Master Bray for company. It has been necessary to take him into my confidence and he rides at my side like a spider fearful of being stepped upon. He constantly turns in the saddle to peer over his shoulder, or cranes his neck to view the road ahead.

"Master Bray," I whisper when I can bear it no longer, "your lack of ease will give the game away."

He puts a finger beneath his collar and tugs at it, revealing the sheen of sweat on his neck.

"I beg pardon, Madam. I am ill-suited to intrigue."

"Oh, it isn't intrigue, Master Bray. I merely wish to pass the time of day with the duke without the eyes of court upon us."

"Yes, my lady," he says, quite unconvinced.

An hour later, one of our outriders comes cantering along the road toward us. He pulls his horse to a halt.

"A large party is coming in the opposite direction, my lady. There will not be room for both to pass."

"There is an inn ahead, I believe," Master Bray interjects.

"Ah, most excellent. We will stop there and give the other party room to pass."

As the rider canters away to announce our impending arrival at the inn, I lean toward Bray and speak into his ear.

"Ride ahead, Master Bray. If it is the Duke of Buckingham who approaches, pray bid him stop so I may greet him."

Bray pushes back his cap to scratch his damp forehead.

"And if he declines?"

"Then he declines. I can do no more."

In truth, I am not as calm as I pretend. My heart is hammering, my palms sticky on the reins. As best he can, Master Bray bows his head and urges his horse forward. I keep my eye on the road, looking neither left nor right until we call a halt at the small inn nestled by the side of the road.

The proprietor, ingratiating and squat, emerges from the gloomy interior.

"We are honoured, my lady, by such great company. I will order my best wine brought from the cellar."

I incline my head but do not reply. Such people are beneath my notice. I allow a groom to help me dismount, and follow my woman Jane, beneath the low lintel. I blink into the darkness, squinting around the room, and find it empty apart from a drunkard asleep in one corner. Despite the heat of the day, it is chilly inside, making me shudder. Jane steps forward to ease a wrap about my shoulders.

"Thank you." I smile and take a seat at a rough table, where a platter of griddle cakes and a jug of wine have been placed. Clearly, the inn is unaccustomed to people of rank calling in for refreshment.

A few moments later, Bray appears, hot from the road. He takes off his cap and I beckon him close so he may speak unheard.

"The duke will be delighted to break his journey for so great a lady," he murmurs.

I wait in trepidation, wishing I were elsewhere; back at court with Anne, or safe in sanctuary with Elizabeth.

I have received several reports of Buckingham's displeasure with the new king, small indications of dissatisfaction, disagreement over policies and royal appointments. But how am I to sway his loyalty, push him into rebellion? I cannot speak plainly, but neither can I leave him in any doubt as to my intention. It is a narrow path I walk, as uncertain as a dagger's edge.

The courtyard bustles with those of my party whom I have instructed to wait outside. When Buckingham's company clatters into the yard, the innkeeper cannot believe his luck. He throws down the grubby cloth with which he was polishing cups, and loosens his filthy apron.

"Gripes," I hear him say, "we've had no travellers in for a week, and now two noble parties grace us on the same blimmin' afternoon."

Buckingham stoops beneath the door, blocking out the light, and spies me at the scarred table. He strides forward and makes a sweeping bow, his fair hair the brightest thing in the room.

"Lady Margaret, what a surprise."

"My lord. When they told me your train approached, I could not let you pass without a greeting."

He signals to the squirming proprietor to bring another cup.

"Is the wine good?" he says, pouring himself a generous measure.

"Well." I look with some dismay into my cup. "It is wet, my lord."

He shouts with laughter and slaps his knee.

"That is good enough for me," he cries, and tilts back his head to drain it in one draught. I have never before been acclaimed for my wit.

"How is Thomas, is he not with you?"

"No, I ride alone, on a visit to my ... sister. Where are you travelling?"

"To my estates at Brecnock. I have neglected my own affairs since in attendance upon the king."

I smile with what I hope is warmth.

"I must congratulate you on your new appointments. You are a powerful man now - deservedly so."

He leans back in his chair and regards me down the length of his nose.

"Thank you. What are your plans now, Lady Margaret? Have you been invited to attend the queen? I know she speaks well of you."

"Yes, but she hopes to travel north shortly. I will remain in London and attend her when she returns. I wonder ..." I break off; look at my clasped hands, hesitating. It is unfortunate that I am not the sort of woman to turn prettily pink at will.

He leans closer. "What is it that you wonder, Lady Margaret?"

"I – I ... since you are so close to the king, I wondered whether you would speak to him on my behalf."

"Of course ... what is the matter you wish to raise?"

"Well, before the late king grew sick, negotiations were in hand for the pardon and return of my son. I would be so glad were King Richard to honour his brother's promise."

He blows out his cheeks, pouring himself a second cup of wine. When the jug hovers above my own, I cover it with my hand and shake my head.

"No, thank you. I do not think I could bear another."

"You have a delicate palate, Madam; I fear mine has been jaded by many years of abuse."

I make a sympathetic noise as he relaxes into his seat. He takes a long draught and pulls a face as the acrid taste bites his tongue.

"I will see what I can do for you, Lady Margaret. I have never met your son, but I've heard no ill of him. If he swears fealty to Richard, I see no reason to deny him the chance to make recompense."

Recompense for what? I want to scream. For being born? But I maintain my serenity and lean forward, my hands clasped with gratitude.

"I am in your debt, my lord."

While he continues to talk of trivial things, I search for a way to bring Morton into the conversation. I wish I could dispense with stealth and speak plainly. At length, he stands up.

"I must be on my way, or I will be on the road all night."

I allow him to take my hand. I have to speak now. I must say something or it will be too late and all this will have been for nothing.

"You are hoping to reach Brecknock this evening?"

"I was, but the day is waning."

"I believe Bishop Morton is ... enjoying your hospitality."

He picks up his riding gloves and begins to pull; them on.

"He is, yes." His look is piercing; I can feel the blood rushing to my face as my heartbeat increases.

"Would you tell him we met on the road, and give him my best regards?"

"I can see no harm in that."

"Oh no, my lord, no harm intended."

I have not spoken plainly. He is not subtle enough to have gleaned meaning from my pathetic hints. He bows, spins on his heel and exits the inn, calling for his groom.

I can do no more. I can only pray Morton can persuade him to our cause. Tension leaches from my body and my head is suddenly light. I fall into the chair, fumble for my cup and take a large swig of wine. As it hits the back of my throat, I splutter and cough, spitting it down my front.

"Christ and his saints, that is foul!" I cry, as Jane hurries from the shadows to mop my stained bodice.

*

The king's men are very much in evidence. On my return to London, my train is forced more than once to make way. The populace seems edgy; nobody looks the other in the eye. It is a little over a month since the coronation and the king remains on his progress north, yet the city boils with unease and distrust. Can our plans have been discovered when they have barely been formed?

My interview with Buckingham has probably gained little. I rebuke myself for not making my intentions clearer. My oblique message to Morton will never be passed on. I am a fool. Elizabeth will berate me when she learns how I wasted the opportunity to win the duke's support.

When I dismount and hurry to our apartment, all I can think of is divesting myself of these travel-blemished clothes and ordering a hot bath. As I climb the stairs, I draw off my gloves and flex my fingers that are tight and aching from gripping the reins.

"My lady, welcome back." My women swarm around me, following me to my chamber where they help me into a loose robe.

A pile of letters waits on the table. Taking a cup of wine, I sit and sift through them while a troop of chamberers brings pails of hot water. There is nothing but bills and receipts so I get up and pace about the room, pausing to trail my finger across my embroidery, left abandoned when I embarked upon my travels.

"Madam, Master Bray wishes to see you." I had not noticed the girl approach me.

"Very well, show him in."

I tighten my robe, ensuring I am decent. Master Bray has seen me without my head covered before. He comes in, and I can tell instantly that he has news of import.

"My lady ..."

"What? What is it?"

He clears his throat, assuming a pained expression.

"It seems that in our absence, an attempt was made to free the Lords Bastard from the Tower."

"What? Are you sure? Who was behind it? The attempt was foiled?"

"It was, my lady. It seems the king got wind of it and sent orders for the Tower to be secured. Those who were apprehended now face the penalty for treason."

"Who was behind it? Do you have names?"

"Erm, some middling folk, Madam: a groom of the stirrup, a pardoner, a sergeant, a wardrobe of the Tower ... Apparently they set fires, several of them, to draw the Tower watch into the city and leave the princes unguarded and the way clear for their abductors."

Poor Bray; he is uncertain if this act should be applauded or abhorred.

"How close did they come?"

"Not close at all, Madam, but now the princes – the Lords Bastard - have been given new, more secure quarters. Madam, I feel I should add that rumour places Sir John Cheney at the head of the conspiracy."

"Cheney?" I stare at him as my mind struggles to discover the root of this plot that has ruined everything. Cheney was Edward IV's bodyguard, his master of horse. I recently watched him swear fealty to Richard ... a little while before I did so myself. He loved the old king and would be loyal to his sons, to his family. Realisation dawns.

"Elizabeth! How could she? She has jeopardised everything by moving too soon!"

Bray struggles to keep up as I pace the floor of the chamber, fury raging in my heart. How could she do this? She has ruined her son's chances of reinstatement. With the boys now under tight guard, there is not a chance of us laying hands on them ... not unless Buckingham can be persuaded to our cause. And I have surely failed in that.

A few days later, news comes that the princes' servants have been dismissed from the Tower. Swiftly on the heels of this information comes Dr Lewis. He arrives in a flurry of summer rain, shaking drops from his cloak all over the polished floor.

"My lady," he says. "I hope you are well."

"In body, if not in spirit," I reply tersely, and he looks up at me, his brow quirked with questions.

"The queen sends her blessings."

For a moment, I think he means Anne, but I quickly right myself.

"How is she after this recent set-back?"

It is difficult to speak without speaking, to infer much while stating little.

"She is ... distraught and repentant, and requests your advice, your wisdom. She swears she will heed whatever you think best."

Cynicism is close to sin, yet I cannot help it. Elizabeth will never listen; she is rash and acts on the dictates of her heart, not her head.

"Then I urge her to show caution. She must not act again without the sanction of everyone involved. Tell her that. I will try to discover the location of her sons, but I think she should seek peace with the king. It will be easier to take action as a free woman. If she swears allegiance to Gloucester, he will be merciful – he is not unjust."

There is that conundrum again. The king is just, the king is forgiving – why then, can we not trust him?

"Can you not tell her that yourself?"

"No. I cannot visit sanctuary too often without raising suspicion. Since the failed plot to free the boys, the king's spies will be alert for dissent. I do not want my name linked with hers; but fear not, my husband is a close confidant of the king. I can learn much from him. Tell her not to lose heart."

September 1483

September blows in wet and chilly, bringing a sodden end to a pretty summer. There is nothing to do but read or sew or pray, and in these strange, uncertain days, I pray a lot.

Thomas is with the king, leaving me free to work with the queen toward our goal. I dare not visit her and I am afraid to write; all communication between us is passed verbally. This is a most unsatisfactory arrangement. I cannot see her eyes, cannot judge what she may be thinking, or predetermine her next move.

A week ago, a letter arrived by stealth from Morton assuring me that Buckingham is hooked, recruited to our side by promises of direct power over the boy king if he aids in his restoration. Since then, I have been beset with terror that his allegiance to our cause may be a trick; perhaps he is luring us into treason so that, at the last minute, he can reveal all to the king.

I do not trust him. I do not trust anyone. I am isolated by the intrigue, afraid to speak for the fear I will reveal my own treachery.

I sit down to write to Henry, hoping he will read the message hidden among my cheery enquiries after his health. I dare not speak plainly.

When the letter is finished, I will take the risk of fully informing my trusted messenger so that he may ensure it is delivered to its intended mark. When the letter is signed and sealed, I fetch a bag of coin from the locked coffer in my chamber and summon Ned. He has never yet ridden overseas on my business, but he is trustworthy. He would lay down his life in my service.

He arrives, slightly damp from the afternoon rain.

"You wanted to see me, my lady?"

"Yes." I smile widely and beckon him into the room. He hesitates, gestures to the door.

"There is someone here to see you; I should come back later."

"Who is it?"

"Your physician. Dr Lewis I think his name is."

"Dr Lewis." My heart flips alarmingly. "Yes, yes, come back in an hour, Ned; that will give us more time. I had better see what my physician wants."

Dr Lewis always has the appearance of someone in a hurry. He closes the door behind him, and almost scurries to the hearth where I stand. He bows and gives me greeting while I wait impatiently for his news.

"You have word from the queen?"

"I do, my lady, and the bishop too. All is in readiness. Buckingham has rallied his men, your son and his followers are alert in Brittany. In October, they will make their move."

My body suddenly feels more alive, as if the blood surges just beneath my skin; my heart races. I clench my fists. The time is soon. Henry will come home. With Elizabeth's son on the throne and Henry wed to her daughter, he will be brother-in-law to the king, his lands and titles reinstated. It is good enough. I will be content with that.

"God will aid us. He will not fail us, for our cause, the cause of King Edward, is just."

He bows in acknowledgement and takes his leave. We cannot fail, not now. Francis of Brittany has pledged us ten thousand crowns, and five thousand mercenaries and ships. With that, together with the large portion of the treasury provided by Edward Woodville, we are more than well equipped. Soon, at last, my son will be home. There is no need to send the letter now; by the time it reaches Brittany, he will be here with me.

The next few weeks drag by. On the 18th of October, we have arranged for a rebellion in Kent. Our hope is that this will distract Richard from the heart of the matter. For, at the same time, Buckingham will rise in the west and my son, arriving from Brittany, will join him. Everything is arranged in fine detail.

We keep our heads down, pretending loyalty to King Richard. I make a great show of riding about the country visiting friends; being conspicuous in London; writing to the queen at Middleham and pretending to be anxious for her return. My life is now entirely comprised of deceit.

October 1483

"My lady!" Ned bursts into the chamber unannounced but I do not reprimand him. I know his news is pressing.

"What is it? What has happened?"

My women sit watching open-mouthed at the intrusion and my unwarranted response to Ned's yell. Taking him by the upper arm, I propel him from the room into a small antechamber. He is breathing hard, as if he has been running.

"I saw Dr Lewis. He is in a proper state, my lady. The men of Kent, they have risen too soon."

With a hand to his chest, he coughs. For once, I do not even think of his health.

"Oh, my God ... what else do you know?"

"They marched on London, but Norfolk intercepted them. They are under interrogation. If they talk, my lady, the whole scheme will fall apart."

"Henry. I must get word to my son."

"How, my lady? They've already sailed!"

We stare at each other. We are helpless; there is nothing I can do. Henry will be sailing into a trap.

"Ned." I grab his sleeve. "Ride for the coast. The port of Plymouth. Get a message to the ship. Warn Henry not to land."

I spin round and dash into the other room, into my chamber, fumbling for the key to my coffer. Ned follows. I thrust a bag of coin into his hands. He looks at me, fear and excitement fighting for dominance.

"You can do this, Ned. I trust you above any other."

He bows fleetingly, turns on his heel and runs from the room. I move in a waking nightmare into the other chamber. Jane and Elizabeth look up from their sewing.

"Is everything all right, my lady?"

No, I think. *No, everything is not all right.*

I keep to my rooms, applying myself to sewing and praying; reading, although I do not see the page. Instead of admiring the bright illuminations or absorbing the philosophies of the text, my mind writhes with conflicting thoughts. I even pray that Thomas will return home; at least he would have reliable news.

London is alive with rumour. While violence breaks out to the south, King Richard sends his men to hunt down the perpetrators. He names Morton and Dorset as traitors, offers a thousand pounds for Buckingham's capture, and the king, beset on every side by treason, names him 'the most untrue creature living.'

I can discover no firm news. Some say that Buckingham has been taken and that his plot against King Richard is the talk of the taverns. And then a message from one of my own arrives, confirming his capture, King Richard has him under interrogation at Salisbury.

Please God, I pray, *please do not let him speak against us. Let him remain true to our cause, even in death.*

There is not a hope that Buckingham will live. We have all seen King Richard's retribution against his betrayers. The treachery of Buckingham - his cousin, his erstwhile friend and ally - will be on a par with that of Hastings. None of us expect leniency now, and we are all aware that, if our involvement in the plot is discovered, we will swiftly follow him to the scaffold.

I sit and sew, outwardly calm, inwardly tempestuous.

November 1483

As soon as the doctor enters I sense something is wrong. His eyes are wide, and sore as if he has been weeping. I jerk my head to tell my women to leave me and draw him close to the hearth.

"What is it?" I whisper, somehow afraid, unwilling to hear his answer.

"Have you heard any news, my lady?"

"No, nothing solid, not for a week or so. Why? Has something else gone wrong?"

"I fear so, my lady. Dreadfully wrong."

He swallows and shakes his head, his jowls vibrating, and his eyes sorrowful.

"I had it from a reliable source that Buckingham is claiming the boys are dead."

For a moment, time seems frozen. My mind turns blank and a loud ringing begins in my ears, making it difficult to think.

"Boys?" I repeat dumbly.

"The princes, my lady. He says they were murdered on the order of the king."

"NO!" I stand up, pace away, turn at the wall and hurry back again. "This cannot be true. Gloucester would never stoop to that; he is a godly man. If he cannot stomach lechery, he would never countenance murder."

Dr Lewis splutters, unable to form an answer, and I plunge on without listening. "And what would it serve him? He has the crown; the world accepts the boys as bastards. To have them kil-" I cannot say the word. "-would only serve to stir up hate against him. Gloucester may be many things, but he is no fool."

"I hope you are right, my lady. I – perhaps he feels that in view of the latest uprisings, he would be better placed without them."

I steeple my hands over my nose, fixing my eyes upon his.

"In my experience, Gloucester has only ever acted violently in rage ... he cannot feel anger toward little boys."

"I wonder ... should the queen be told?"

Elizabeth.

This news will finish her. She has lost too much to bear this so swiftly on the heels of our recent failure. If they are dead, it will take away her fight, her reason for living.

Panic rises in my throat; I will drown in it if I cannot scream. I take a deep breath and blow out slowly, puffing out my cheeks, forcing my mind to the matter in hand.

"Say nothing yet. Let me discover the truth of it first. It may only be a rumour. I hope to God it is."

When he is gone, I push away the thought of little Richard lying murdered in the Tower, and apply my mind stringently to practicalities. I cannot afford to break now.

I must act, but how, I cannot imagine. If only Thomas would come home. I sit by the fire, staring into the flames, wishing with all my heart that I had remained loyal. If my part in this catastrophe remains undiscovered, I swear I will never plot against the king again.

Perhaps I was rash. Gloucester is not so bad. I do not believe he would harm his nephews; he loved his brother too well. Perhaps he would be a good king if we only gave him a chance.

I look up from the hearth as a girl enters and hands me a letter which, by its seal, hails from my husband. With my mind still on my troubles, I break the seal. The words plunge me straight back into a violent hatred for the king.

I am sorry to inform you, Margaret, that your brother, John Welles, has been arrested in the company of other conspirators. The king regrets that he has no option but to imprison him, and remove his titles and lands for perpetuity.

Surely, it can get no worse than this. My brother attainted? He will curse me, for it was I who led him into this tangled mess. Because of me and my determination to fight injustice, his own children will never see their rightful inheritance, or their rightful position at court. Misery heaps upon misery.

Failed. I have failed in all my attempts. I should have listened to Harry; did he not always warn me not to meddle? Oh Harry, how I wish you were here.

The letter drifts from my fingers and falls upon the cold ashes scattered around the hearth. I am alone and beaten. I cannot imagine I will ever hold my head high again. With my face in my hands and tears on my cheeks, I beseech God to vent justice upon King Richard and all his heirs.

It is dark when something wakes me. I part the bed curtains and peer into the shadowy chamber. I shiver as memories of the previous day bring dread rushing back. Somebody is standing before the hearth, his bulk outlined by the dying embers, his sword hilt glinting.

"Thomas?"

I slide from the bed, take two steps toward him and then stop. If it were Harry, I would run to him, leap into his arms, sure of my welcome, safe in the sanctuary of his care. But it is not Harry, he is dead. My husband is now Thomas Stanley, and I can tell by the set of his shoulders that he is displeased. I decide to pretend I have not noticed.

"I was not expecting you," I say, as if nothing has happened since our last meeting. Groping for my wrap, I slide it about my shoulders and move closer to the fire.

"I have been sent by the king."

"Do you have news? London is beset with rumour and one cannot tell truth from lie."

He shifts from one leg to the other, his sword clanking at his hip.

"Can you ever?"

"Can I ever what?"

"Tell truth from lie."

I hesitate, give a shaky half laugh, and then decide that sobriety is more in order.

"What do you mean?"

He thrusts his face close to mine.

"Buckingham is dead. He has been deep in deceit for some time, spreading lies about the king. He was content at first, glad of the favours provided by Richard ... until someone whispered sedition into his ear and turned his head with promises of something more."

"Why are you telling me? I had nothing to do with it."

"There you go again. More lies."

I open my mouth to contradict him but he holds up his hands, continues with his tirade. "I know you are involved, Margaret. It has your mark all over it. We know your son came this close," he holds his finger and thumb an inch apart, "to landing on our shores. He could not have done that without assistance, without money. How did you think to get away with it, and why? The king and I have lately been discussing your son's pardon, his return and reinstatement, but he will not get it now. No, your meddling has ensured that his exile will be permanent."

A sob escapes me. He is right. I am a fool. I should have been patient.

I fumble for a kerchief and dab my eyes.

"That's it; cry as much as you want. You will not soften me with your hollow tears."

I make no reply but perch on the edge of a chair, attempting to stop unstoppable misery.

"Your friend Morton has fled the country and is, no doubt cosied up with your son, plotting more trouble. They have hung you out to dry, and 'hung' may yet be the right word for it. The king knows all about you, Margaret."

I stare at him, blinking my sore eyes, my throat choked with fear. I am going to be imprisoned, or worse. Oh God, give me the strength to bear it if I have to die for this.

"Will he send me to the scaffold?"

Stanley regards me for a long time. With each passing second, my agony increases. At last, he speaks, giving vent to his fury, his face softening into contempt.

"Probably; I do not know. He wants to see you. I am to escort you to him in the morning. If I were you, Margaret, I would devise a convincing plea for mercy."

Woking and Westminster - November 1483

I cannot sleep. My mind writhes with half-formed remedies, ill-considered answers. I hear every creak and groan of the palace, each toll of the bell, each fart and whimper Jane makes as she tosses on her truckle bed. I have been a fool. I have been arrogant. I have been proud. By the time the prime bell rings, I am already on my knees, praying frantically for Heavenly assistance.

If ever I needed God's favour, it is now. I remain there for a long time, seeking peace in the quiet piety of the chapel, yet never quite finding it. Mice scratch in the wainscot, like the worry in my mind, nibbling at my sanity, destroying my rationality with sharp yellow teeth.

"Come on; you cannot hide in here all day. We have a long ride ahead of us."

Thomas's voice echoes around the nave, tolling out my end and spelling doom. I hastily finish my prayer, make genuflection before the rood, and follow him back to the hall.

I climb onto my horse, shivering in the frigid morning. He rides ahead, and I keep my gaze fastened to the rump of his chestnut steed. My fingers soon become frozen, the cold seeping into my joints, my knuckles groaning and stiff.

How did I ever come to this? My dreams for my son have ended in attainder. He has no hope now of ever regaining what was stolen from him; no hope of ever returning from exile.

I might die tomorrow and never look upon the man my son has become. I berate myself for relying on others, for placing my trust in the weak, and, most of all, for underestimating the reach of King Richard's spies.

Thomas's angry back leads me along a path I have no wish to travel. As the spires of the capital come into view and the stench of the city reaches us, my heart plummets, my belly rolling with rebellion. I have never thought myself a coward before, but now I know myself to be craven.

Had we been victorious, I would be riding into the city to a clarion of trumpets, waving banners and cheering crowds. As a traitor, I am shunted in via the backdoor, a felon's noose turning slowly in the forefront of my mind. Dabbling in treason is only for heroes, or fools.

*

The king appears little different to when I saw him last: a little paler, perhaps, a little more shadowed about the eyes. I had expected rage, even vindictiveness, but he greets me with politely, and with much sorrow, making me ashamed.

He gestures to a chair and I move toward it with shaking knees. Thomas stands behind me, his hand on my shoulder as if he fears I will flee. Richard rests his elbows on the table, presses the tips of his fingers together, and regards me gravely. One of his hounds cleans himself near the hearth, his disgusting slobbery sounds making a mockery of our solemnity.

"I would like you to explain why, Lady Margaret."

I am trapped like a bee in the web of his mournful eyes. I flounder there, drowning, trying to remember the reasons why I betrayed an anointed king. I cannot find my voice. He fills the silence.

"We had thought you our friend. My wife, the queen, was pleased to have you in her service. Tell me, was your early show of welcome just that? Merely a show?"

"No. I – I ... Your Grace, I cannot explain my reasons. Perhaps my allegiance to the quee – the dowager queen, Elizabeth Grey – conflicted my loyalty to you."

"So you were persuaded ... Are you always so easily swayed?"

"No. I was confused, Your Grace. I have always craved the return of my son. The late king made promises ... I simply wanted justice for Henry."

Our eyes clash. I am determined not to look away. He wanted the truth; I might as well give it to him. I will probably die soon, anyway.

"We would have welcomed him home."

His words are like a smack on the face. His expression does not alter; he maintains a blank, sorry demeanour. I cannot let myself believe him. It is easy to say that now; although ... Thomas also claims the matter was in hand.

"I beg pardon, Your Grace. I see I was misled."

"You must have all been so sure of victory. You, your son, your brother, the Woodvilles, Morton ... and Buckingham. Yet where has it got you? Attainted for treason. Imprisonment ... Death."

I cannot help it. When he speaks the word, I flinch, my hands trembling, my chin juddering. I should be defiant. I should shout at him, tell him plainly that I am glad I worked against him, and would do so again.

He is a usurper, a bully ... and worse. But I lack the courage of my conviction and lapse into guilty tears.

Thomas clears his throat.

"There is something else, Your Grace; something Margaret says she was told; a rumour that perhaps forced her to act against her better judgement."

I frown into my lap, unsure whether Thomas speaks in my defence or not.

King Richard sighs, his breath ruffling the papers before him on the desk; papers that might be my death warrant.

"Is that true, Lady Margaret? You heard the rumour also?"

He continues to regard me while I search for the best answer. Suddenly, I realise what a fool I was to believe the tale Buckingham spread.

"I – I - Yes, Your Grace, but I give the rumours no credit; not now."

"You do not believe them? Then why act against me?"

I flounder beneath his steely honesty. Not sure of the truth myself, now that it is done and we have failed, I cannot imagine why I ever thought this man could be thwarted.

"I do not know."

He leans back in his chair with a humourless laugh. "You do not know? You organise a wide-scale uprising involving half the men of my court; you send money abroad; you fraternize with traitors to the crown – yet you do not know why?"

He leans forward, so close I can see the hairs growing on his upper lip. "I say you do know. I say you are a liar and a traitor, and should suffer a traitor's punishment."

A cry escapes me. The pressure of Thomas's fingers increases on my shoulder. My hand creeps up to find his and remains there, squeezing, seeking his strength. Momentarily, my mind clarifies. If I am to die, I am determined to do it well.

"I would like to know if Prince Edward and Richard are safe, Your Grace."

He laughs humourlessly.

"They are secure, Lady Margaret. Since the failed attempt to free them in July, they have been moved to a place of greater safety."

Relief floods through me, but I will not allow myself to unbend. Drawing all my strength, I release Thomas's hand and keep my back stiff, my face expressionless. I cannot let Gloucester see my terror.

"I am glad to hear that."

While he takes up his quill and scratches some words on a document, I keep my eyes on my fingers wrestling in my lap. Somewhere nearby, a door opens, followed by running footsteps, and farther away, another door slams. Thomas drums his fingers on my shoulder as the moments drag slowly by. At last, the king looks up from his parchment.

"You will, of course, realise that I cannot allow you to go unpunished."

My mouth forms the words but no sound comes as he passes the document into my hands. I look down, the words he has written dancing and leaping until I blink to bring order to my vision.

Forasmuch as Margaret, Countess of Richmond, Mother to the king's great rebel and traitor, Henry, Earl of Richmond, hath of late conspired, confederated, and committed high treason against our sovereign lord the king, Richard the third, in diverse and sundry ways, and in especial in sending messages, writings and tokens to the said Henry ...

My eyes skim across the page where my name is writ large, condemned as a traitor of the commonest degree, my disgrace made solid in law, the impact of my actions made real. I am a traitor. I deserve a traitor's death. I continue to read, absorbing his pleasure in my punishment, but as his looped script nears the end of the page, my breath stalls. I travel back, read the passage again.

Remembering the good and faithful service that Thomas, Lord Stanley, hath done, and intends to do to our said Sovereign lord, and for the good love and trust that the king hath in him, and for his sake, remit and will forbear the great punishment of attainder of the said countess ...

My hand flies to my throat and my eyes begin to sting. Blinking rapidly, overwhelmed with relief, I gape at the king.

"You intend to show me mercy, Your Grace?"

He regards me dispassionately, replacing his quill in the ink pot.

"It is a virtue, I am told."

I do not deserve this. If our roles were reversed, I do not think I would be so generous. All at once, I have no care for the lands and goods that he orders confiscated. I have no care for the taint that will forever rest upon the name of Beaufort.

I am not to die.

This man, whom I have sinned against, commutes the sentence of death to one of life imprisonment. And life is suddenly very, very sweet.

Lathom - December 1483

December is cold, but my heart is colder. Early in the month, King Richard orders the execution of the conspirators in the October plot; a plot that was mostly of my making.

When word comes of the deaths of George Brown, William Clifford, William Knight, Richard Cruse, William Frost, Richard Potter, Richard Fischer, John Boutayne, Roger Kelsale, and William Strode, the names become branded on my heart. Long hours spent in the chapel praying for their souls do nothing to alleviate my sense of culpability.

I can never make penance enough.

I look about my comfortable room, the pretty view across the garden. It is a gentle punishment indeed, although I can never leave. My household has been disbanded, and I am served by strangers now. My day is divided between prayer, sewing, and walking but my world is small. The perimeter garden wall is the extent of my prison.

In a week's time, it will be Christmas, and while the royal court spends it in extravagant celebration, I will be here in isolation. I have never before seen my path ahead so clearly. This week and the years that will follow stretch before me, a yawning chasm of boredom and discontentment.

It is only the third time I have seen Thomas since I was brought here. He clumps up the stairs and bursts into my chamber without preamble. Ordinarily I would let my irritation show but I am learning that solitude turns even his limited company into a boon.

I put down my sewing and turn meek eyes upon him, touched in spite of myself that he has come.

"How are you, Margaret?" He lowers himself into a chair. "Keeping out of trouble, I hope."

"Of course. I am hardly able to do otherwise."

He glares at me from beneath his brows.

"And if you were able?"

"I have told you before; I will obey you as my husband. I am grateful for your intervention with the king."

"See that you do."

He gets up and pours wine, brings me a cup.

"I suppose you will be attending the Christmas court?"

Thomas yawns without hiding it.

"Yes, I will." He looks about the room, the cosy fire, the scattering of cushions, and my sewing on the table at my knee. "And you will be here."

"As I am every day. I already feel I have been in this house forever."

"Hmm. Perhaps, sometime in the future, we can persuade the king to let you move from house to house, if I promise to guard you well."

Such a small concession now seems like a gift. The freedom to move from here to Woking, to the Stanley estates in Lancashire, will be as wings to a snail.

"Oh, Thomas, if you only could!"

When he takes his leave of me, he draws a small package from his tunic.

"Open it on Christmas morning," he says, "and not a day sooner."

I place the package on a small table beside my bed. Every day upon waking, my eyes fall upon it, and a shrim of excitement runs through me. It cannot be a gift of great value, probably some token of his growing affection but I am cast so low that just the knowledge that someone thinks of me is now precious.

Christmas morning dawns bright. Still unused to waking alone, I sit up in bed and take up the package. I clutch it to my breast for a while, closing my eyes, imagining the glories it might contain. To prolong the pleasure, I slip on a wrap and go to the window, throwing open the shutters to allow the wintry sunshine to stream into the chamber.

At last, I draw in my breath and tear the outer wrapping from the package. It contains a letter. My heart begins to thump, loud and slow.

Henry! It is from Henry. Had I imagined for one moment that it contained news from my son, I would have ignored Thomas's order and opened it right away. My former reluctance forgotten, I break the seal and unfold the parchment with fumbling fingers.

My eyes absorb the beloved script.

My dear lady mother, he writes

I have heard of your current straits and will do all I can to bring your suffering to an end. In the mean time I hope this finds you well, in body if not in spirit. As another Christmas season comes upon us, I find myself regretting those we have missed together.

On Christmas morning, I am determined to pledge myself before God to Elizabeth of York. This, I trust, will bring hope to those who still hold a desire to put an end to Gloucester's usurpation, and bring justice once more to England.

I look up from my letter, close my eyes and give thanks to God who has, after all, not deserted me, or my cause.

Outside, the church bells begin to peal. It is a bright blue morning, spelling joy on this day of days. I fall to my knees and beseech the Lord for his continuing favour.

March 1484

Even the advent of spring cannot leaven the interminable days of solitude. I am bored with sewing, I have read all my books four or five times, and the garden is too wet to work. All I have is prayer, and I am sure God grows tired of my repetitive pleas.

The mirror shows me a face that is pale and peaked, but I lack the vigour to dose myself. My still-room lies neglected; the stitches on the chair covers I have been working are irregular and ugly. In my plainest gown, I wait at the window watching the rain. Even the sound of a horse arriving fails to spark my interest; it is probably a delivery of grain, or a man come to mend the broken casement. When the door opens and Thomas enters, I am taken by surprise.

I leap up, wipe my tears on the back of my hand and flap at my drab skirts.

"Thomas, I had not expected …"

He comes toward me, kisses my brow.

"You look dreadful, Margaret. If you do not keep yourself tidy, I will not want to ride all this way to see you."

My ire piqued, I frown but the expression dissolves as his last words distract me.

"Why do you come?"

"I told the king I would keep an eye on you."

"Are your servants not doing a good enough job? I can barely shit without someone making note of it."

I had intended my vulgarity to offend him, but instead he throws back his head in a burst of laughter. I watch with displeasure as he wipes his eyes.

"Ah, Margaret, let us not fight. Come down off your high horse and admit you are glad to see me."

"I have no other company. I would be glad to see the devil."

"Well, maybe I should go. Perhaps you do not want to hear the news I bring."

"What news? Is it Henry? Have you heard something from overseas?"

"No. He may be my stepson but he is not likely to write to me of his news. No, it is Dame Grey ..."

"The queen? Is she ill?"

He holds up his hand, silencing me.

"Just listen and I will tell you. And she is not the queen; she is merely Dame Elizabeth Grey. You would do well to remember that."

I swallow, nodding my head like a naughty child.

"She has relented at last and come to an agreement with the king to release her daughters into his custody."

"What? Are you certain?"

"Of course I am certain. I would not bring you rumours."

"But – but how can she trust him? The last time I spoke to her, she blamed him for the death of her sons."

"But the boys still live; perhaps he has provided evidence of that. I do not know the details. I just know they are leaving sanctuary."

"Elizabeth too?"

"So I believe, to some secret house with someone Richard trusts to keep a wary eye on her. The girls will be a welcome addition to Queen Anne's household, the elder ones at least. They are beauties ..."

"I cannot understand ... why would she surrender to him now? What has changed?"

"Nothing I know of. Now, I have in my saddle bag a choice bottle of Rhenish I bought from London. Would you care to share it with me?"

I have little taste for wine, but can hardly refuse. I nod my head absentmindedly while I contemplate possible reasons for Elizabeth's change of heart.

Thomas goes on to tell me that Richard swore an oath before the lords spiritual and temporal promising that if Elizabeth and her daughters left sanctuary, he would stand surety for their lives. He swore not to imprison them but to ensure the girls were married to gentlemen born.

"He has also promised them seven hundred marks a year."

"And Elizabeth agreed? She must have something up her sleeve."

Thomas shrugs.

"Maybe so, but she will be watched. Richard has set John Nesfield to keep an eye on her, so at the least hint of treason, he will fall on her like a cat on a mouse."

After three glasses of wine, Thomas unfastens his tunic and loosens his collar.

"You must be lonely, Margaret. How do you stand it?"

I look about my enclosure - the books, the sewing, all of which now bore me to tears.

"I do not know. I never thought I would miss the idle chatter of my women but I would give all I possess to have Jane or Elizabeth back in my service. The women you have set to serve me are ill-bred and uneducated. I am starved of intelligent conversation."

"And all you have is me." He reaches out to touch my shoulder and I feel the heat of his hand burn through my clothes. I join him in laughter at his self-effacing comment.

"You are most welcome, my lord. You have proved yourself a good husband, a good man. I owe you my life, and I thank you for it."

"Well, I cannot return that compliment I fear. You have been nothing but trouble."

"Nothing but trouble? Surely some good has come of it?"

"Hush." He places his finger on my lips. "I was teasing. Do you not understand what teasing is?"

My mind rushes back to the nursery, where I was the butt of my brother Oliver's taunting. My eyes fill with unexpected tears. I try to look away, lower my eyes, but his finger moves beneath my chin and he forces me to look at him.

"I am not teasing now," he says.

My loneliness rushes in; I can feel it all round me. When he leaves, my solitary existence will continue. I crave the touch of another human being, even if it is only Thomas. I forget my former pledge to deny him my body and do not move away as his lips press against mine.

Thomas's love making is as wild and rough as his unskilled courtship. Tomorrow, I will regret it, I will hate myself, but for now, it is an escape from the confines of my gaol.

His touch frees my mind from care. When he finally rolls away from me, I snuggle to his side and watch him drift off to sleep. Perhaps, the last sound he is conscious of is my whispering voice speculating on how grand it might be to be the step-father of a king.

Late March 1484

Thomas stays for a week or more. We spend our days riding in the park, walking in the garden, and sometimes, when the April showers come rushing in, we retire to our shadowy chamber where I set the inner Margaret free.

It is Thomas's joke that another Margaret lurks deep within me, a persona brought into being only by his kisses. I let him think it, and if he wishes to label our relationship as love, then I let him do that also. For me, Thomas is my lifeline.

I know that he will soon leave again, and I will be plunged once more into isolation. While he lords it at court, I will be here, held captive behind invisible bars, with silken cushions that are stuffed with barbs.

He leaves tomorrow to re-join the king, who is holding court at Nottingham. Thomas says the queen has left the north and is with her husband.

"She sends you her good wishes," he says, and I widen my eyes, astounded and touched that she should do so after my betrayal.

"Is she well?" I ask him. "I thought, when I was with her, that I detected a sallowness that spoke of ailment."

"She is one of those pallid creatures, I think," he replies, lifting my hair from my shoulder so that he may kiss my neck. I close my eyes as my innards shift at his caress. I am a fool and a wanton to be so easily distracted. I pull away.

"I have a headache."

"But I will be gone tomorrow," he complains, sounding like a small boy refused an outing. "Will you not miss me just a little?"

He takes me in his arms, and I crane my neck to look up at him.

"That letter you gave me, Thomas. How did you come by it?"

"Letter?" He nuzzles my neck again, his left hand creeping to my breast.

"From Henry. Will there – can you bring me more?"

"I might." He pulls back, looks teasingly into my eyes. "If the tithe is paid."

My arms slide up around his neck, my body limply compliant in his arms.

April 1484

I knew I would be lonely when Thomas left, but I had not expected to be assailed by such misery as this. He said he would return by summer's end, or as soon as his duties at court allowed. That is a long time away.

The early spring days drip like cold honey, the sweetness replaced by bitterness. When his letters come, I snatch them up as eagerly as I once did Henry's; I tear them open and drink in his words, my mind racing across the page without fully comprehending the contents. I stop, falter, a hand to my throat as I absorb the news.

Oh no! Poor Anne; poor, poor Anne. She now lives through my worst nightmare; the thing every mother fears has happened. How she must berate herself for leaving him behind.

Her son, Edward, the Prince of Wales and King Richard's only heir has died at the age of just ten years while both his parents were away at Nottingham. I close my eyes and send up a hasty prayer before sitting down to write to her.

I can only hope that Princess Elizabeth offers her what comfort she can ... unless, of course, she finds ways to exacerbate her suffering. If she is indeed her mother's daughter, then Elizabeth will not forgive, or forget, easily. Poor, poor Anne.

I am halfway through my condolence before I pause. Looking down at the page, I realise she will think my words false. She will not believe my pity is genuine. I gain too much from it.

The death of her son, and the disappearance of Elizabeth's boys, leaves the path open for mine. Henry is a direct threat to her husband. They know he waits overseas, ready to come and claim what is theirs. I put down the pen and instead of writing to her, I pray for Henry.

Summer 1484

A horrible season, with few visits from Thomas to leaven my ennui. With little else to do, my mind returns constantly to matters at court. It is like a never-ending game of hoodman blind. I can imagine the key players but cannot see them, cannot quite grasp their next move. Something tells me it will not be long before trouble begins brew.

Early in the summer, my ageing chaplain falls sick and another is appointed. I resign myself to admitting a new member to my restricted household. I am so starved of company that when he arrives, I watch from the window as he dismounts. He fumbles with the harness, detaching a pack from the saddle, and turns toward the hall. I cannot see his features, for although the day is bright, a cloak swaddles him from head to toe. I take my place at the hearth and wait for him to be shown into my presence.

The door opens slowly and the figure ambles toward me. There is something ... familiar ...

"Dr Lewis? What are you doing here? I thought you were overseas!"

"I am, Lady Margaret, to all intents and purposes. I have news for you."

I look around the chamber to ensure we are alone.

"You are taking an enormous risk. I hope your news is good; I am in need of cheer." I hold out my hand for a letter, but he shakes his head.

"I have nothing writ down; it is all here."

He taps a fingertip against his temple. I grasp my hands together tightly and hold my breath as I wait for him to speak.

"The queen has not forgotten us. Preparations are underway across the channel; your son is ready to move, as soon as the time is right."

"Move? He still plans to invade? To contest the throne? Is he properly prepared?"

I am sure that without my advice he will have overlooked some vital detail. Dr Lewis smiles slowly and nods his head.

"I think it is safe to say so. My lord Jasper is at his side. I am sent to tell you and the queen to be on your guard for news."

If Henry fails this time, my life will be forfeit. The thought fills me with fear, but I have always said I would lay down my life for my son.

Now I am in possession of the facts, I cannot keep still. Time must pass more quickly, for if I am incarcerated here much longer, I will surely go mad. I walk in the garden as if marching to battle, my pace too quick for the girl who watches me. She pants along in my wake, and I take satisfaction from knowing that I tire my gaoler.

Life is a round of prayer and reading; I eat, I sleep, I pray, I walk and then I eat again. Thomas comes at the end of the month and we sit until late in the golden sunshine of the dying day before retiring for the night.

"How are Princess Elizabeth and her sisters settling at court?"

Thomas stretches out his legs to balance his feet on a stool.

"I would not say they settle. They are flighty, like butterflies, teasing all the young men and antagonising the women with their beauty."

I can imagine them. So recently released from the dark recesses of Westminster, their freedom would rush to their heads. I can almost hear the squeals of their laughter. I wonder how their bright splash of youthful joy grates upon the sorrowing queen.

"I imagine court is sombre while the king and queen mourn the loss of their son."

"The king will not have it so. He was mad with grief for a while, but now he plans a lavish Christmas, inviting all and sundry to the feast."

"All but me. I will remain here."

I cannot help the wistfulness that creeps into my voice.

"That is no one's fault but your own. It is too soon to seek the king's leniency. We must wait and let the punishment run a while longer."

"But you will speak for me when the time is right."

"I will. Now, come and sit here and tell me what you do all day."

"Nothing!" I cry, getting up and doing as I am told. "There is nothing to do. I am out of my mind with boredom."

He hands me a cup and I drink, although I am not thirsty.

"Well, see you keep out of trouble, or nothing I can do will save you."

I do not reply, the guilty secret of Dr Lewis's stealthy visit like a bell in my mind.

"Margaret. You are not embroiled in any ..."

"No. Nothing. I am sure there is nothing to be embroiled in at all."

I am a bad liar; I can feel my cheeks beginning to burn. He puts his hand on my chin, turns my face up to his.

"Why do I not believe you?"

"Because you are a disbelieving bully," I retort, summoning as much indignation as I can.

"Hmm. I had hoped I could trust you, but I see I cannot."

"What do you mean?"

He stands up, catching hold of my upper arm.

"Come to bed. It will be harder for you to lie when I have divested you of your shift."

As he hauls me off to the bedchamber, I sputter with indignation, determined to deny him. He picks me up and tosses me onto the mattress, and I scramble up the bed, taking refuge among the pillows. He loosens his belt and I cannot take my eye from the gleaming buckle.

"I had a visit from my brother, William." His words draw my eyes to his.

"Did you? And how - how is he?"

"Very well. Up to his neck in treason, by all accounts."

"Treason? You mean he hatches a plot?"

My evasion is as clear as a crystal glass.

"As you very well know. He urges me to join you."

My heart beat increases, and my palms are damp with sweat. Can I trust him? It could be a trap. My husband is a loyal man. Had his brother really revealed the details of a plot against the king, Thomas would betray him. I have no doubt about that.

"What is the plot?" I ask in a small voice.

"You mean you know nothing about the fact that your son and his uncle Jasper have raised an army and are preparing to sail?"

"No." I do not want to lie to him. I wish I could explain, persuade him of the validity of my son's claim. He pulls his shirt over his head and discards it on the floor.

"My brother has sworn his support, and so have many other powerful men. William is trying to tempt me; persuading me of the many virtues of being stepfather to the king of England."

I let my breath go suddenly, unaware I had been holding it.

"And what was your reply?"

"No, of course. What would you expect it to be?"

He leans toward me, pulls off my cap and begins to play with my hair. He reeks of wine and wood smoke, and there is a gleam in his eye that I have not seen before. It is not lust, it is not humour. As his fingers creep up and gently squeeze my throat, I realise his expression is one of greed.

<u>March 1485</u>

I swear I will go mad. Each moment is a year, each month a decade, each year a lifetime. When I count back the days, I can scarce believe it has not yet been sixteen months. Sometimes, it seems as if I was born here and have never set foot outside the gates of Lathom. My previous life feels like a dream. The child who rode to Wales, birthed a son, and wed four husbands, danced at court and served two queens, has almost ceased to exist. She has become nothing more than a story I read a long time ago.

I am Margaret the forgotten.
Margaret the restless.
Margaret the very ill used.

Thomas refuses to enlighten me as to his intentions. He refuses to commit to Henry's cause, yet his failure to reveal our plot to King Richard speaks loudly of wavering loyalty.

If there were a risk-free way to tempt him to our side, I would do it. If only I could confide in him how deeply I am involved in the invasion plan, but I am too afraid. The jeopardy is too great, and I am not ignorant of the fact that this will be our final attempt. Should Henry fail in his mission, Richard will show no mercy. Already stripped of my assets, I will, without doubt, face death and dishonour.

On the day that Thomas rides back to court, I stand lonely on the tower and watch him go. A short while before, the sun was bright, the birds singing in the trees. Yet, as his figure shrinks toward the horizon, the sky turns black like an ominous foretelling of doom. I rub my arms, shivering in the sudden chill.

It is eerie, the tower isolated, as if all else has been obliterated and I am all alone beneath the vast and empty sky. The silence stretches on. I cling to the parapet wall, my courage dwindling, my heart pounding. It seems a long time later that the darkness begins to lighten, the birds stir in the trees again.

It must be an eclipse. I have read of such things; they are believed to be things of evil portent. Before turning to fumble my way back to the hall, I cross myself, and send up a prayer for all mankind.

Thomas's departure leaves me more unsettled than ever. I am afraid that his affection for his king may out measure his loyalty to me. For a few days, I can dwell upon nothing else.

One moment, I see Henry high upon a dais, the crown of England gleaming on his brow; the next, I see him cast low in a vault, torn and bleeding, soon to be nothing but dust. I swat the thought away as if it were a wasp. Henry must succeed in this. Everything depends upon it.

I am in the garden when I hear a horse cantering into the stable yard. I cock my head, listening for voices. It is not Thomas, I am sure of that. His habit is to leap off his horse in the bailey and loudly call my name as he makes his way straight up the steps to the hall. It must be a message; perhaps he writes to tell me that his arrival will be delayed. From the length of time the messenger takes to reach me, I can tell it is not urgent.

"My lady?"

I look up to see Thomas's squire making his way toward me through the garden. The beds are mostly empty now, the cold spring making the new shoots tardy. He bows, holding out a letter, and I recognise my husband's seal. With a quavering heart, I remove the black ribbon and break the wax.

I regret to inform you of the death of Queen Anne. The news came a few days ago; she died at the time of the eclipse.

Thomas's typically blunt announcement takes my breath away. *Had she even been ill?* I had heard of her extreme sorrow, her passive grief, but ... no rumour of imminent death had reached me.

I look up from the letter, sorrow for Anne obliterating every other thought. I cast my mind back to the day the sun turned dark and remember my certainty that it was an ill omen. Yet my fear was for my son and his cause; I had not thought its darkness might fall upon another.

I move slowly along the path, frightening a robin foraging for worms beneath a hedge. He flies up, startling me, showing a flash of red breast before diving into the covert. Poor Anne; she is with her son now. Her suffering is over. Mine goes on.

Thomas's letter informs me that his return to Lathom will be delayed for a few weeks more, since the king is beset with trouble. As I read, the significance of his words increases and I fear the king has had wind of the plot and refuses to let Thomas out of his sight. I sit down at once to write a carefully veiled letter, asking after his health and that of his brother, William.

June 1485

It has been a long three months. Thomas dismounts and walks wearily toward me, his face grim. I wait with my hands clasped before me, unwilling to let him sense how much I have missed him.

"Are you well, my lord?" I ask when he is within speaking distance.

"Sick at heart, but well enough in body. I will tell you of it inside."

As we climb the steps to the hall, his hand is heavy on my shoulder. Dismissing the servants, I pour him a cup of wine and put it in his hand. His dour looks make me nervous, fearful that he is regretting his decision to change his allegiance and support my cause.

"So, your decision is made?" I ask uncertainly.

He sighs. "I think so. I asked for leave of absence, pleading fatigue. I told him I would be better placed here to raise my men when the time comes."

"Does he suspect anything?"

"I hope to God not, because he insisted on George taking my place as surety against my return."

My eyes widen at this. George is Thomas's best-loved son; his heir.

"Then he does suspect you; what will happen to your son when your allegiance changes to Henry?"

He tilts back his head, blinks at the ceiling.

"I do not know. I can only cling to the knowledge of his former leniency. He is not a vindictive man. I do not think – I hope he would not wreak vengeance on a man for the sin of his father."

"I hope so too, but ...." I do not finish my sentence. It is not for me to point out that Richard's possible retribution against George rests entirely on the success of my son. Should George be harmed, then our own punishment will follow soon after.

My heart is bleak. Such a short while ago I was triumphant at having secured my husband's support. Now, it looks as though he might be sacrificing his son for the sake of mine. Life is harsh, our actions affect others. No decision, no act, is without its consequences. I add George to the list of people I must pray for.

"Is there other news? I am so cut off from everything here."

He looks at me, his brow furrowed as he contemplates any court rumour he may have forgotten to impart.

"You know about the scandal with young Elizabeth, I suppose?"

"Some of it, yes. My chaplain told me of the king's public denial of the rumours of a marriage between him and his niece. But what do you think? Is there any truth behind it?"

He shrugs, shaking his head.

"Not as far as I know. The king is too busy trying to hang on to his crown to be swayed by pretty girls, although ... if he was wise ..."

"It would be a political triumph, putting an end to Henry's plans and salving the indignation of those who are loyal to Edward and all his offspring. It would pacify the dowager queen too – but the scandal would be too great. I cannot see him seriously contemplating it."

Thomas yawns, stretching his arms above his head.

"I believe he hopes for a union with Portugal. Anyway, he has scotched the rumour of an alliance between him and Elizabeth; she is still available for your son."

"And you are happy to give your support to Henry now? I will ensure you are well rewarded once he is king."

He squirms irritably in his seat.

"It is the lack of certainty I deplore. If the invasion fails, Margaret, we will be ruined. You will face execution and I probably will as well. I plan to exercise caution. I will know how to act when the time comes."

I stand up, displeasure seething in my belly, and sneer at him down my nose.

"It is your risk to take, Thomas, but if you fail us and my son wins his throne, you may well live to regret it."

I am so irritated, I go to my chamber and bolt the door, barring him from my company but I pass a restless, lonely night fraught with nightmares.

August 1485

"Thomas! Thomas!" I hurry through the house, through the garden and into the meadow where he is practising with his bow. He looks up at my call and I flutter the letter in the air, moving quickly through the long grass, disturbing small flying insects in my haste.

"He has landed, he is here." I place a hand to my ribs, breathing hard from the exertion. "My son is home."

Thomas takes the letter and quickly scans it.

"At Milford Haven. Then I must expect a summons from the king."

"You can delay, Thomas. Plead illness, plead a broken limb – anything, but do not ride with the king."

It is like a nightmare return to the days when Harry pledged himself to Edward of York; an allegiance that ended disastrously for both of us.

"Come, I had best take to my bed. When the summons comes, I can better plead a fever from there."

He picks up his bow, slings the quiver across his back, and takes my hand. His pace back to the house is so rapid that I am forced to hop and skip beside him to keep up.

In our chamber, he pulls off his clothes, scattering them on the floor before climbing naked into bed.

"Now," he says. "To make it look authentic, clutter the table with bottles and potions, and put on some other garb; something more workaday. When the messenger comes, have him shown in here; that way he will take a convincing picture of ill health back to the king."

"I could dose you with something to make you truly sick, Thomas, to make it easier for you to feign a malady."

Missing the teasing note in my voice, he frowns.

"I do not think that will be necessary. Go, do as I say."

At first, as I hasten to the still-room, my step is light. My son is on English soil for the first time in fourteen years. I can almost reach out and touch him. If I were to mount a horse and ride it hard, I would be with him by daybreak. Yet, as I gather a few bottles and begin to fill a basket, I remember that nothing is certain. There is so much that could go wrong; our very existence hangs in the balance.

Henry could lose the battle. He could be killed and once my part in it is discovered, I will face death too, as will all my friends and family who are in this with us.

I bundle the remedies into the basket and hurry back to Thomas, who lies disconsolately on the pillow. His face is tight and white when he looks at me.

"Before God, Margaret, if this goes awry ..."

There is no need for him to finish. We both know the enormity of the task ahead.

How must Henry feel? Is he thinking of me now, or of the crown that dangles just a little way from his reach? Is he sure of victory, or fearful of defeat?

I close my eyes and try to picture him, leading his men across the land of his birth toward some unknown battlefield where destiny awaits him, be it sword or sceptre.

When the king's messenger arrives, I summon him to the sick room. He enters reluctantly, fearful of infection, and takes a position as near the door as is polite. The king's letter orders Thomas to rally his men and go at once to the muster. He reminds him, that his son George is eager for his father's presence. I see Thomas bite his lip, then, remembering his feigned sickness, he coughs pathetically.

"My husband is sick with fever," I say, brushing imagined sweat from my brow with the back of my hand. "He will ride to join the king as soon as it has broken and he can sit a horse."

The fellow looks doubtful. I take a step closer to him and place my hand on his sleeve.

"I hope the contagion doesn't spread," I say, with a pained expression. "I have nursed him night and day." I cough twice before turning my head away, and he stammers a farewell before fleeing our presence.

His footsteps are still clattering on the stair when Thomas throws back the covers and takes hold of me, leaving a smacking kiss on my cheek.

"Margaret, you are a liar and a devil, and I could almost love you for it."

As I help Thomas dress, I batter him with a list of instructions he can never hope to follow. He is to muster troops as he has been instructed, but he is not to join with King Richard, but with Henry. At the back of my mind is the knowledge that Thomas's eldest son is hostage to his behaviour. Should King Richard learn of Thomas's intended betrayal, George Stanley will be dead before dawn.

As he approaches his horse, I hear a sound behind me and turn to find Ned, armed and ready to ride.

"What are you doing?"

I take hold of his arm and try to push him back toward the house, but he shrugs my hand away.

"I am riding with your husband, my lady. You cannot expect me to stay behind like a woman when Henry's future is at stake."

"But your chest ... your lungs. Ned, you may not survive."

"Then my life will have been well spent. You cannot stop me, my lady. I will find a way to go whether you give me your blessing or not."

Ned has changed. He is a man grown, albeit a weak one. How can he hope to withstand the rigours of battle? I want to order my men to lay hands upon him, to lock him up in one of the dungeons until it is safe to let him out. But I cannot do that, and nothing I say will deter him.

Unable to speak, I make do with squeezing his arm, and watch through a veil of tears as he mounts his horse and moves into rank behind Thomas.

They ride away.

My life moves in circles. I have been here before, suffered this gnawing dread as fate draws back its lips to bare sharp yellow teeth.

Another husband; another battle. This time, I pray to God he comes home unscathed. I want to order my horse made ready and follow after, be part of the action I have planned and dreamed of for so long. But I can only wait here.

While Thomas and Henry, Ned and Jasper risk their lives in battle, I must face my woman's fight. As soon as the dust on the road dissipates, I hasten to the chapel to once again attempt to strike a desperate deal with God.

If He will just grant me this one thing, I will ask nothing more. From the day my son is crowned, I will put aside my scheming ways and live a spotless life. I will be kind and charitable. I will be a creature of God. I swear it.

22nd August 1485

It is almost midnight. I have been in the chapel all day. My knees are aching, the skin roughened with kneeling. I have been praying for so long that when I rise, I cling to the altar, stumble and almost fall.

I limp through the darkened passages back to my chamber, back to a frugal supper, for I have sworn that until my son is king, I shall live as a nun. I discover a certain peace in giving myself up to God's mercy. The words of my prayers are the only nourishment I allow, the muted humidity of the chapel the only air I breathe.

The last word I had from the outside world was from Thomas two days ago, telling me of his meeting with Henry at Athelstone. His words are brief, but encouraging.

Henry understands that my son is hostage to my allegiance to Richard, and makes no demands on me. I will do all I can.

What will Thomas do? The royal army is far larger than ours. Richard is a seasoned warrior, renowned for his prowess in battle. The odds are not in our favour but God is on our side. He will not let the victory go to Richard; surely he will guide Thomas, help him make the right decision to fight for my boy and me. If George is the sacrifice we must make, well, Thomas has other sons.

The message bearer assured me he would ride back as soon as the battle was won ... or lost. I had hoped to know by now.

In the solitude of my chamber, I pull apart a piece of bread, push it between unwilling lips and dispatch it to a reluctant stomach. Everything I eat is tainted by my fear; everything tastes of dirt, or failure.

I push the plate away and get up, begin to pace the room, wringing my hands. Every so often, a wail of anguish rises from somewhere deep within me, resonating in the loneliness of the chamber.

I would know it if Henry were dead. I would feel it. If his heart were to cease, then surely mine would too. Oh, I must hear something soon. I *must* hear something soon.

I keep vigil throughout the night, refusing to go to bed, or even to rest by the fireside. I am cold, still standing at the window, my eyes raw with exhaustion, when the early bird begins to sing in the dark.

Dawn arrives, dragging behind it a tardy pink sky, a dreary welcome to the new day. As the dusk lightens, I hear a cry, and the sounds of a hard-ridden horse careering into the bailey.

How many times have I hastened down the stairs, eager for news? How many times has my future depended on an exhausted despatch bearer? Never before have the contents of a letter meant so much. There can be only one answer.

There *must* be only one answer.

The boy stumbles from his horse, hanging onto the stirrup leather. There is blood spattered on his face and foam from his exhausted mount smeared across his coat. His eyes are hollowed by the horrors he has witnessed but they tell me nothing.

I dare not hope.

My heart hammers and vomit swirls in my empty stomach.

I snatch the parchment, turn my back and walk away from him as I break the seal. The words blur and swim beneath the emotion that gathers in my eyes.

This day, (Thomas writes) *as the sun reached its zenith, I placed the crown of England on the head of your son. We are victorious.*

I crush the parchment to my chest, and throw back my head. *Oh, blesséd God. Blesséd, blesséd God.*

Turning on my heel, I hurry in search of the steward.

"Order my horse made ready."

His wet mouth falls open in surprise.

"But, my lady ..."

Turning the full measure of my loathing upon my gaoler, I almost spit the words that free me from his keeping.

"Do as you are told. King Richard is dead, and his punishment of me no longer stands. My son, the king, has redeemed me."

With no further argument, he bows his head and scrambles to do my bidding.

An hour later, I am galloping toward Leicester. Outpacing my retainers, I show my horse no mercy. My heartbeat echoes the pounding of the hooves beneath me, assuming the sound of my son's name.

Henry, Henry, Henry!

On the road, I pass the dregs of Gloucester's vanquished army; ragged, bloodstained nobodies, blocking my path.

"Get out of my way!" I yell as I thunder past them, my cloak billowing behind.

"My lady! Wait for us!" The calls of my companions sound faintly in my ears, but I have been kept from Henry's side for too long. The years I spent quietly campaigning for his return, and later for his crown, have come to fruition. I am not prepared to wait any longer. I will be part of his victory, part of his triumph, and part of his future.

I have earned it.

Changing horses at every inn, ignoring pain, ignoring fatigue, I ride relentlessly on. Just outside Macclesfield, I call a halt at a small priory, where I pray, eat sparingly, and toss restlessly on a narrow bed before rising at dawn to continue my journey.

While my body demands respite from the road, my mind craves the journey's end. By night fall, I will be with Henry.

The stench of the tanners wafting from the riverside informs me that I approach the gates of Leicester. Despite the momentous events that have taken place nearby, despite the presence of the new king, life in the town goes on. I urge my tired mount through the market place, becoming caught up in a flock of sheep. I use my whip to force my way through, the idiotic sound of their protests loud in my ears.

My horse treads carefully through litter and dung toward the castle. Wounded men line my route. I turn my face from their suffering, but every so often, a woman in a dark habit hurries past with jugs of water, or baskets of bandages. I make a note to reimburse them for their trouble. As the king's mother, it will be my duty to show charity to the unfortunate, to fund hospitals and seats of learning throughout my son's realm.

I haul on the head of my flagging horse and urge him on. Just a little farther. I clatter over the bridge, through the gate, and into a castle yard seething with men.

Few pay me any attention. My clothes are mired from the road, my face coated with dust; they mistake me for a woman of no account.

I slide from the saddle, drop the reins, and abandon my horse as I climb the steps to the hall. I pass a company of laughing young retainers, duck through a low door and halt as the darkness of the interior blinds me. My eyes quickly adjust and my feet move toward indistinct voices, my steps loud on the stone floor. Pushing aside a curtain, I enter a small ante-chamber.

The blood-stained standard of Cadwalader leans drunkenly against the wall. Beneath it, a group of men stand at a table, their backs toward me. I recognise my husband, his brother Will, and Jasper. Beside them is another figure; a tall man with bright golden hair.

I stand for a long moment, just watching, drinking him in, their words lost to me. Then, Thomas looks over his shoulder, his eyes opening in surprise.

"Margaret?"

All heads turn toward me. Thomas hurries forward, but I push him aside, my eyes locked on the man with the bright hair. His head turns, eyes wide and unsure as we regard each other for a long, long time. How I have missed him! I watch, my heart leaping and dancing, as his body relaxes. His eyes are warm as his mouth stretches slowly upward.

He gropes behind him, fumbling for something on the table. Then he stands proudly and places a circlet of gold upon his brow. My eyes mist, my throat closes.

Oh, my son. My king ...

Later, in the chamber hastily provided for me, I cannot sleep. My mind will not relinquish the events of the day; the long harrowing ride, the joyous reunion, and the riotous evening of celebration.

My son, the king. My son, Henry; home at last, never to leave these shores again. Exile is a horrible thing. Life has been hard, but now ...

Change is imminent. There is no one now to tell me what to do, where to go, what to wear, whom to befriend. The word 'friend' shines in my mind, hanging in the air in large golden letters, reminding me that there is one thing I have overlooked.

Rising from bed, I hasten to the table. I pick up my pen, writing quickly, without thought to grammar or spelling. Who can judge me now?

Myfanwy, my Dear Friend,
My son is victorious and Henry is now king. Jasper is safe and the whole of England celebrates.
You must ride to London for the coronation, for fortune now shines upon us, and you will find a glad welcome at my son's court.

Throughout all the changes and insecurities of my life, Henry remains my one constant; he is the world and I the benign and loving sun that warms him. He is now no longer merely the king of my heart, but the king of all England.

And I have placed him there.

I tap the pen against my teeth, hesitate, and then, with a satisfied scrawl, I make my mark at the bottom of the letter.

Margaret R. The King's Mother.

A review is the best way to let an author know you have enjoyed their books.

Author's note

Margaret Beaufort became one of the most powerful women in Medieval England. During this time, as mother to King Henry VII, she was consulted on many matters pertaining to his rule and treated with the utmost deference. Yet it was not always so; the wealth, status and bearing of her latter years is a direct contrast to the uncertainties of her youth and childhood.

Margaret, heiress to the Beaufort fortune, is believed to have been born and raised at Bletsoe castle. Her first marriage to John de la Pole took place when Margaret was six and John was eight, the union an attempt by the disgraced Duke of Suffolk to use Margaret's close proximity to the throne to bolster his rapidly declining position as the most powerful man in England. When Suffolk, his political career in ruins, was seized and beheaded, Margaret's marriage to John was annulled. Those are the bare bones of her history and we do not know for certain whether Margaret and John ever met. In *The Beaufort Bride,* I have embellished the known facts and used her first marriage to shape her character. With Margaret back on the marriage market, her mother sought another suitably beneficial match. Very little is known about Margaret Beauchamp, and her depiction in this novel is for dramatic purposes. She was successful in securing beneficial marriages for all her children, but that was the medieval way. In reality, she may have been a very caring mother. Nonetheless, she married the twelve-year-old Margaret to a powerful, rich man who was twice her daughter's age. Margaret's marriage to Edmund Tudor is more documented than her first, but we still have only bare facts. We know nothing of her thoughts or feelings; we can only guess at those.

Edmund Tudor was half-brother to Henry VI, a favourite of the king and endowed with lands and titles to befit his station. As Earl of Richmond, he was a good match for Margaret, and the difference in their ages was not particularly remarkable for the era in which they lived. What was remarkable was the immediate consummation of the marriage. Most child brides were given time to mature before being taken into their husbands' beds, and history has condemned Edmund Tudor for ensuring possession of Margaret's lands and estates by getting her with child when she was just twelve years old.

Margaret and Edmund made their home at Caldicot Castle and at Lamphey Bishop's Palace in South Wales, where Edmund fulfilled his duty as peacekeeper for the king. After a skirmish and siege, Tudor died in Carmarthen Castle before Margaret had time to give birth. Vulnerable and alone, she turned for protection to Edmund's brother, Jasper, at his fortress at Pembroke Castle, where she gave birth to a son, whom she named Henry Tudor. Underdeveloped and possibly ill attended, Margaret's body was so damaged by the birth that she was never able to conceive again.

Margaret's third marriage to Henry Stafford, a younger son of the Duke of Buckingham, provided a stable and beneficial match. The marriage seems to have been a happy one, the couple spending much of their time together, with Stafford going some way toward filling the empty shoes of Henry's father. Although Henry was left in the care of his Uncle Jasper at Pembroke, Margaret and Stafford sent gifts and letters and paid regular visits. However, as the battle for the throne warmed up and York defeated Lancaster, Edward IV took the throne, precipitating a change in circumstances for both Margaret and her son.

Henry was a lucrative opportunity, and he was given into the custody of William Herbert, to be raised at Raglan Castle in Wales. Contrary to depictions elsewhere in historical fiction, it was quite normal for sons to be raised in the household of a knight. Under any other circumstances, Margaret would have been delighted at his appointment to the household of William Herbert, who was one of Edward IV's most trusted friends. Of course, in the circumstances after the death of Edward of Lancaster, which saw Henry become the Lancastrian heir, Margaret must have had concerns. Still, we can only speculate.

Henry was treated well; clothed and educated as befitted his status as Earl of Richmond. Although his estates were given to the king's brother, George, Duke of Clarence, Henry continued to be addressed as 'Richmond'. This suggests that the king perhaps intended to reinstate Henry in the future. Herbert's desire for a marriage between Henry and his daughter, Maud, reinforces this belief. Yet Henry lived in tumultuous times and was destined for an unstable childhood.

After Warwick's defection and defeat at Barnet in 1471, the Yorkist king took measures to secure his hold on the throne. The deposed and mentally unstable Henry VI was reported to have suddenly died of 'melancholy,' but it is now historically accepted that he was put to death for the security of the realm. With the death of the old king, and his heir, Edward of Lancaster, killed at Tewkesbury the same year, Lancastrian hopes rested solely upon the narrow shoulders of Henry Tudor. Jasper Tudor, realising his nephew's vulnerability, arranged to have the boy shipped to safety in France, where, to Margaret's sorrow, he remained for fourteen years.

The House of York was securely in control of the realm and Henry Tudor's claim seemed feeble indeed. Edward IV soon had two male heirs to add to his bevy of daughters, and the future of the House of York seemed set. Fate, however, once more took a sharp turn.

Edward IV, rather like his grandson, Henry VIII, enjoyed an excessive lifestyle; eating too much, drinking too much, and allowing his government of the country to slip. He grew corpulent and over-indulgent, and in 1483, Edward IV collapsed during a fishing trip and died shortly afterwards. The instant the news of his death was made known, trouble broke out again, this time with the dowager queen, Elizabeth Woodville, pitting her will against that of Edward IV's youngest brother, Richard of Gloucester.

Initially supportive of his nephew, Gloucester began making arrangements for Edward V's coronation, but then he made a sudden U-turn. Edward's heirs were deposed, Gloucester was crowned Richard III in Edward V's stead, and England was once more plunged into instability. There has been much violent debate over the reasons behind Gloucester's actions. It could have been a lustful desire for a crown that was not his, or it could have been a genuine concern for the future of England. Before this, Gloucester had been a loyal subject to his brother. Indeed, in his short reign, he showed signs of proving to be a just king. Yet he lacked support, and England was once more rife with intrigue.

Margaret, now married to her fourth husband, Thomas Stanley, moved stealthily into action. There is little evidence that she was overly fond of the dowager queen, but at this point Margaret united with Elizabeth Woodville and began to work against King Richard. The two women agreed that, on his future ascension to the throne, Henry Tudor should take Elizabeth's daughter, the heir of York, as his wife and queen. This agreement united Lancaster with the previous adherents of York, who now opposed Gloucester.

Henry, still in exile, continued to receive the support of his mother. Margaret played a very dangerous game, sending money and letters to keep Henry informed of the events at the English court. After an abortive attempt at invasion, their plotting came to fruition with his victory at the Battle of Bosworth in 1485. After a delay, while Henry established himself as king in his own right, his marriage to Elizabeth went ahead, uniting the Houses of York and Lancaster and putting an end to the family feud we now know as The Wars of the Roses.

It may have been the fact that Henry was her only son that prompted such devotion in Margaret, or perhaps it was her nature, but she never gave up her dream of seeing her son inherit the crown of England. Her years of unwavering devotion to her son's cause finally received their reward, and she revelled in his success.

***

The Beaufort Woman is *Book Two* of *The Beaufort Chronicle available in paperback, kindle and audiobook*

The King's Mother is *Book Three of The Beaufort Chronicle* and available on Kindle and in paperback and audiobook.

Book Three: *The King's Mother* tracks her path to become the most powerful woman in England and valued advisor to her son, the king.

Other books by Judith Arnopp

The Beaufort Bride: Book one of The Beaufort Chronicle
The King's Mother: Book three of The Beaufort Chronicle
Sisters of Arden: on the Pilgrimage of Grace
The Heretic Wind: the story of Mary Tudor, Queen of England

A Song of Sixpence: the story of Elizabeth of York and Perkin Warbeck
The Winchester Goose: at the court of Henry VIII
The Kiss of the Concubine: a story of Anne Boleyn
Intractable Heart: the story of Katheryn Parr
The Forest Dwellers: and the killing of William Rufus
The Song of Heledd
Peaceweaver: the story of Eadgyth Aelfgarsdottir

All books available on Amazon Kindle or paperback and some titles as audiobooks.

author.to/juditharnoppbooks

www.juditharnopp.com

Printed in Great Britain
by Amazon